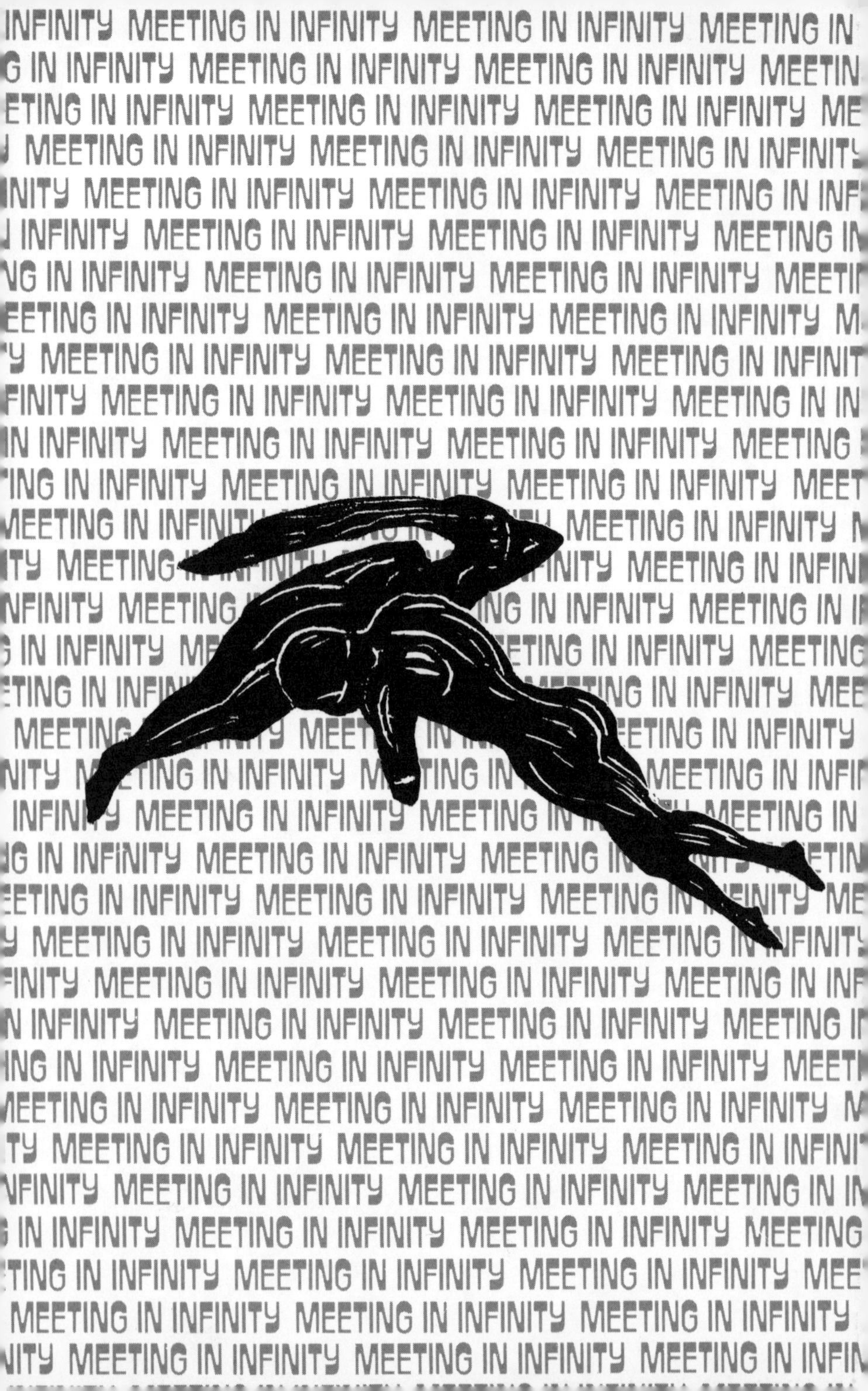
MEETING IN INFINITY

allegories & extrapolations by

JOHN KESSEL

with photomontage interiors by

J. K. POTTER

arkham house publishers, inc.

Library of Congress Cataloging-in-Publication Data
Kessel, John.
  Meeting in infinity : allegories & extrapolations / by John Kessel
; with photomontage interiors by J. K. Potter.—1st ed.
    p.   cm.
  ISBN 0-87054-164-1 (acid-free)
  1. Fantastic fiction, American. I. Title.
PS3561.E6675M4 1992
813'.54—dc20   91-45949

Printed in the United States of America
Book design by JATworks, Ltd.
First Edition

58,704

FOR JIM KELLY
best writer, best friend

ACKNOWLEDGMENTS

I'd like to thank the many people who helped me with these stories in one way or another, not the least of whom was Tim Roth, responsible for "Not Responsible!" Editors Gardner Dozois, Ed Ferman, Shawna McCarthy, Sheila Williams, Michael Bishop, Anne Jordan, and Jim Turner. Friends and critics Lucius Shepard, Mark Van Name, and Bruce Sterling, excellent writers all. And Sue Hall, for her patience and prose sense.

I must especially thank ace story doctor Jim Kelly, who's seen all of these in chrysalis stage, for his advice, friendship, strong shoulders, and way too many of the jokes in "Faustfeathers." Without him, Harpo would be speechless.

Some of these stories were hammered into shape at Ed Bryant's Milfords, Tom Maddox's Evergreen, the Sycamore Hill Writers' Workshops (the guilty will admit their culpability), and during classes I've taught at North Carolina State University. Those who can, do. Those who teach, steal from their students.

contents

MY MOTHER'S FATHER WAS A RETIRED STONEMASON FROM SICILY named Vincent Giorlandino. He lived in a nice house on Elmwood Avenue in Buffalo, and every other Sunday our family would drive into the city to have dinner there. For us kids this was not the most exciting way to spend a Sunday afternoon. We were not allowed to play around in the living room, which was kept by our grandmother as a sort of museum of overstuffed furniture and delicate glass objects. I remember a ceramic bust of a noble-looking man in a funny hat that sat on the mantelpiece; years later my father revealed to me that it was a bust of Benito Mussolini. We were not allowed to watch television until the adults did later in the evening, and when they did they only wanted to watch Ed Sullivan. The only good outcome of this as far as I am concerned is that because of my grandparents' habit I saw the Beatles in their first U.S. performance. Until dinner the adults would sit around in the kitchen in the winter or in the tiny backyard in the summer and talk about things that were deadly boring for a boy like me. Half the time, when my father was not participating in the conversation, they would speak Italian, of which I knew about four words.

Under such circumstances I cast about desperately for something to do. Mostly I would bring books or comics to read. One

September Sunday in 1963 (a couple of months before President Kennedy was assassinated), when I had forgotten to bring something to read that would keep me occupied through the endless afternoon, I walked down the street to see whether I could buy a comic book. Cosentino's Delicatessen had a magazine rack, and on that rack I found my first science-fiction magazine, the October 1963 *Fantasy and Science Fiction*. Although I had been reading science fiction for years, exhausting the children's section of the public libraries of three suburbs, I had never heard of SF magazines. I bought the *F&SF* and read it. Next month the cover story was Roger Zelazny's "A Rose for Ecclesiastes." After that I was hooked, and although I still relied on the library for books, I began subscribing to *F&SF* and *Analog*.

As I look back on them, those Sundays seem to me a paradigm of my boyhood. If you could have read my mind then, you would have heard me screaming, "Get me out of here!" I won't go any further into the circumstances that drove me to want to escape. In most ways they were the unexceptional frustrations, the feeling of being trapped, that, sadly, so many children feel. My answer then was books, specifically science-fiction books. My favorite novel for years was L. Sprague de Camp and Fletcher Pratt's *The Incomplete Enchanter*. It wasn't until years later, long after I'd written an ironic replay of the situation of that novel in "Another Orphan," that I realized that the Harold Shea stories are about a person, frustrated with his life in the real world, who literally escapes into books.

For me, and I think for a lot of us who turned to SF at an early age, this use of stories as escape was fundamental. I used to be very sensitive about being accused of being an escapist. J. R. R. Tolkien offers a defense of kids like me by distinguishing between the escape of the prisoner and the flight of the deserter. It is a point well-taken. The problem, as I see it, is that those of us who begin our habit of escape because in some ways we are imprisoned, run the risk, after our circumstances have changed, of having developed a habit of desertion. It is liberating to contemplate freeing ourselves from limitations, even those, like our mortality, that we know we are unlikely ever to escape. When this natural desire, however, becomes escape as an alternative to working to change those limitations that can be changed, or learning to accept those that can't, then escape becomes another prison.

At age twelve I didn't have much power to change my life. My first attempt to affect that world I couldn't change was to write my own stories. As early as grade school I was writing stories and collecting them into a handwritten and illustrated magazine. Later I got a typewriter and produced a typed version. Shortly after that fall of 1963 I submitted my first story to *F&SF*, and was thrilled to receive a rejection slip printed on the back of a full-color cover of the magazine.

Here I am, thirty years later, still writing SF. I'd like to think there is more to it now than sheer escapism. Yet if I don't want to admit to escapism as my continuing motive, then why am I doing this? If you don't want to accept that as your reason for reading, then what better reason is there?

∞   ∞   ∞

In summer school after tenth grade, I took geometry. I would get up early in the morning and ride the bus to West Seneca High School. Outside the classroom the sun shone on green grass, kids playing baseball, cumulus clouds, blooming flowers, and poplars rustled by cool western New York breezes.

Inside the classroom, Mr. Miller taught us that parallel lines meet in infinity. This did not make a whole lot of sense to me. On the one hand he was telling us that the lines did meet, but on the other that they never met. Which was it? Was this just some linguistic foolery, or did it mean something?

In Mr. Miller's class we went on to other theorems, and the question was never answered. But the paradox still nagged at me. It's the kind of abstract conundrum, with seemingly no connection to the real world, that caught at my imagination then and still does today. In the afternoons, I rode the bus home and read science fiction. I didn't see any connection then, but it occurs to me now that, in addition to the desire to flee, the other reason I was hooked on science fiction is that in SF, as in geometry, things that never come together in reality meet in infinity.

Science fiction naturally seems to go to extremes, fusing together things that don't belong together. This is the source both of its strength and of its habitual weaknesses. It is why even a well-written SF book may be accused of bad taste. A person who is afraid of bad taste is not likely ever to get hooked on SF. Mainstream fiction, at least the overwhelmingly realistic mainstream fiction of my youth, struggles to maintain a proper sense of proportion, based on the assumptions that man is the measure of all things and that present circumstances are sensible, the result of understandable logical processes, somehow more natural than alternatives. SF violates these assumptions, often to its peril as fiction. Lots of absurd things happen in the infinity of SF. People sometimes are so small that they seem insignificant. The background overwhelms the characters; in classic SF the author is not interested in the characters as people so much as examples or exemplars or observers of the fantastic developments occurring around them.

SF has, in this way, an affinity with allegory. I used to think, after experiencing traditional examples like Bunyan's *Pilgrim's Progress* or Nathaniel Hawthorne's "The Celestial Railroad," that I hated allegory, but now I realize that it is one of the things that most interests me in fiction. The allegory must be clever and point in more than one direction. In places it must at least run the risk of acting against itself. Within the allegorical framework the writer has set up, the characters must be treated with as much respect as can be mustered. Given these provisos, allegory can seem like naturalistic fiction, yet still give something extra. I love those moments in stories, and have striven to create them, where a scene that seems to be conceived and operating wholly in the realm of conventional realism suddenly reveals an allegorical level of meaning. The reader falls through the surface of the story, with a kind of sickening lurch, into a realm of bizarre secondary meanings, meanings much larger than the drama he has been following so intently up until then.

Among my allegorical stories here are "Not Responsible!" "Buddha Nostril Bird," and "The Lecturer." Even those stories not so explicitly allegorical, like "Another Orphan," gain strength, it seems to me, where some other meaning works through them. With some of these stories, as I wrote I did not even know I was writing allegory. I don't always have control over these secondary meanings, nor do I think it is desirable to have total control over them. To have total control in an allegory is to create a moralizing schematic rather than a story. The thing that made me think that I didn't like allegory when I was younger is this "wiring diagram" quality I found in Bunyan or Hawthorne. These may not be exactly the kind of wiring-diagram stories people have in mind when they use the term in SF, but I think it's true for the *Analog* story and the *Faerie Queene* that in both cases the characters and storyline are dominated by some abstract idea. I think John W. Campbell must have, at some level, been aware of the allegorical implications of SF when he renamed his magazine *Analog*.

But when the analogy isn't so schematic, then the story gets interesting. When we are definitely aware that the white whale represents something other than just a marine mammal—although it is also a marine mammal and in the context of the story does nothing that a marine mammal might not do—yet when we cannot precisely pin down exactly what this whale represents, then we are in waters I have found myself wanting to sail. The writer is taking big risks, and no matter that the picture seems a little distorted, the chance exists for wondrous rewards. We are in that place where the perspective lines converge and the infinite meets the real, the logically impossible becomes the inevitable.

This is not territory comfortable to all readers. Like the abstract world of geometry, it can seem inhuman and inhumane, not to say gauche and malproportioned. As critic William Harrison Ainsworth wrote about *Moby Dick* in 1853, such fiction can read like "hyperbolic slang, maudlin sentimentalism, and tragicomic bubble and squeak . . . remote, too frequently, from good taste, good manners, and good sense." It's a charge that much SF has had to labor under. But I believe that the rewards of the voyage are worth a little bad taste.

∞   ∞   ∞

So at twelve I pursued meetings in infinity both for escape, and for their ability to inspire the proverbial sense of wonder. It only occurred to me later that the flip side of wonder is laughter. In putting these stories together for this collection I've come to recognize that, even in the most serious of them, I am writing comedy. Though I have always liked comedy, my family and everyone else back in 1963 always took me for the most serious of boys, and I never thought I could be intentionally funny. Reading these stories over again, I see that one of my characteristic and most ingrained traits is a sense of irony, paradox, and the absurd humor that arises from them.

Doctor Faustus meets the Marx Brothers. Raymond Chandler meets Philip Marlowe. A commodities broker meets *Moby Dick*. Pizarro meets aliens from outer space. Allen Bloom meets Flash Gordon. The 1954 *Car and Driver* meets Horatio Alger. Mrs. Shummel and Sandy Ellison meet their deepest fantasies.

These juxtapositions are all basically unnatural. Yet even when I treat such meetings with high seriousness, even when my aim is to evoke tragedy, at the heart of the story is potential comedy. I suppose this should not come as a surprise to me; looked at from the proper viewpoint, all tragedy could be farce. And that a tragedy's fundamental base is comic does not in the end negate the tragedy. Oedipus may not laugh at the absurd series of coincidences that leads to his destruction, but the gods, when not weeping, chuckle.

"Man is a very clever animal that behaves like an idiot." This observation was made, not by Woody Allen, but by Albert Schweitzer. The attraction of geometry may be its clean precision, but the house I live in, the trees in my yard, the hands that type these words, are not composed of sections of circles. Science fiction is about ideas, but people aren't ideas. A fiction that tells us so often that we are the apex of evolution needs to be reminded now and then that, for creatures that aspire to the stars, we fart an awful lot. So I try to let the people who inhabit my stories be more than geometrical figures. I want the stuff of life. Without the objects, tastes, smells, sights, and sounds of ordinary physical reality, for me the abstractions of SF become hollow, booming with Significance but no humanity.

It's a funny and scary world, where a retired stonemason, a decent and ordinary man, would make a hero of Benito Mussolini. There I sat in that stuffy living room watching "The Ed Sullivan Show." Through my head ran a thousand fantasies. Kennedy's assassination and the Beatles waited a few months in the future. Outside the house full of immigrants was an industrial city beginning to undergo a slide into a postindustrial age. It was all there in that house on Elmwood Avenue: politics, technology, social change, ethnic collision, art, limitation, and desire. Escape, wonder, comedy. If I can get a little of this into a story I feel like I've gotten it right.

My answer now to "Get me out of here!"—a phrase that still rings in my mind more often than I'd like to admit—is to try to engage the world more directly than I had the power to do in 1963. The way I engage is, half the time, through my writing. The other half is my teaching. I suppose there's a third half, my personal life, which makes one too many halves, a result Mr. Miller might not approve but that seems not only possible but appropriate to those of us absurd folk meeting here in infinity.

∞   ∞   ∞

J. K.

Raleigh, North Carolina
19 May 1991

MEETING IN INFINITY MEETING IN INFINITY

MEETING IN INFINITY MEETING IN INFINITY MEETING IN INFINITY MEETING
TING IN INFINITY MEETING IN INFINITY MEETING IN INFINITY MEE
MEETING IN INFINITY MEETING IN INFINITY MEETING IN INFINITY
NITY MEETING IN INFINITY MEETING IN INFINITY MEETING IN INFI
INFINITY MEETING IN INFINITY MEETING IN INFINITY MEETING IN
G IN INFINITY MEETING IN INFINITY MEETING IN INFINITY MEETIN
ETING IN INFINITY MEETING IN INFINITY MEETING IN INFINITY ME
MEETING IN INFINITY MEETING IN INFINITY MEETING IN INFINITY
INITY ME ING IN INF
N INFINITY MEETING II
NG IN INFINITY MEETING IN INFINITY MEETING IN INFINITY MEET
EETING IN INFINITY MEETING IN INFINITY MEETING IN INFINITY M
Y MEETING IN INFINITY MEETING IN INFINITY MEETING IN INFINI
FINITY MEETING IN INFINITY MEETING IN INFINITY MEETING IN IN
IN INFINITY MEETING IN INFINITY MEETING IN INFINITY MEETING

the pure product

I ARRIVED IN KANSAS CITY AT ONE O'CLOCK ON THE AFTERNOON OF THE thirteenth of August. A Tuesday. I was driving the beige 1983 Chevrolet Citation that I had stolen two days earlier in Pocatello, Idaho. The Kansas plates on the car I'd taken from a different car in a parking lot in Salt Lake City. Salt Lake City was founded by the Mormons, whose god tells them that in the future Jesus Christ will come again.

I drove through Kansas City with the windows open and the sun beating down through the windshield. The car had no air conditioning, and my shirt was stuck to my back from seven hours behind the wheel. Finally I found a hardware store, "Hector's" on Wornall. I pulled into the lot. The Citation's engine dieseled after I turned off the ignition; I pumped the accelerator once and it coughed and died. The heat was like syrup. The sun drove shadows deep into corners, left them flattened at the feet of the people on the sidewalk. It made the plate glass of the store window into a dark negative of the positive print that was Wornall Road. August.

The man behind the counter in the hardware store I took to be Hector himself. He looked like Hector, slain in vengeance beneath the walls of paintbrushes—the kind of semifriendly, publicly optimistic man who would tell you about his crazy wife and his tenpenny nails. I bought a gallon of kerosene and a plastic paint funnel, put them into the trunk of the Citation, then walked down the block to the Mark Twain Bank. Mark Twain died at the age of seventy-five with a heart full of bitter accusations against the Calvinist god and no hope for the future of humanity. Inside the bank I went to one of the desks, at which sat a Nice Young Lady. I asked about starting a business checking account. She gave me a form to fill out, then sent me to the office of Mr. Graves.

Mr. Graves wielded a formidable handshake. "What can I do for you, Mr. . . . ?"

"Tillotsen, Gerald Tillotsen," I said. Gerald Tillotsen, of Tacoma, Washington, died of diphtheria at the age of four weeks— on September 24, 1938. I have a copy of his birth certificate.

"I'm new to Kansas City. I'd like to open a business account here, and perhaps take out a loan. I trust this is a reputable bank? What's your exposure in Brazil?" I looked around the office as if Graves were hiding a woman behind the hatstand, then flashed him my most ingratiating smile.

Mr. Graves did his best. He tried smiling back, then looked as if he had decided to ignore my little joke. "We're very sound, Mr. Tillotsen."

I continued smiling.

"What kind of business do you own?"

"I'm in insurance. Mutual Assurance of Hartford. Our regional office is in Oklahoma City, and I'm setting up an agency here, at 103rd and State Line." Just off the interstate.

He examined the form. His absorption was too tempting.

"Maybe I can fix you up with a policy? You look like dead meat."

Graves's head snapped up, his mouth half-open. He closed it and watched me guardedly. The dullness of it all! How I tire. He was like some cow, like most of the rest of you in this silly age, unwilling to break the rules in order to take offense. "Did he really say that?" he was thinking. "Was that his idea of a joke? He looks normal enough." I did look normal, exactly like an insurance agent. I was the right kind of person, and I could do anything. If at times I grate, if at times I fall a little short of or go a little beyond convention, there is not one of you who can call me to account.

Graves was coming around. All business.

"Ah—yes, Mr. Tillotsen. If you'll wait a moment, I'm sure we can take care of this checking account. As for the loan—"

"Forget it."

That should have stopped him. He should have asked after my credentials, he should have done a dozen things. He looked at me, and I stared calmly back at him. And I knew that, looking into my honest blue eyes, he could not think of a thing.

"I'll just start the checking account with this money order," I said, reaching into my pocket. "That will be acceptable, won't it?"

"It will be fine," he said. He took the form and the order over to one of the secretaries while I sat at the desk. I lit a cigar and blew some smoke rings. I'd purchased the money order the day before in a post office in Denver. Thirty dollars. I didn't intend to use the account very long. Graves returned with my sample checks, shook hands earnestly, and wished me a good day. Have a *good* day, he said. I *will*, I said.

Outside, the heat was still stifling. I took off my sports coat. I was sweating so much I had to check my hair in the sideview mirror of my car. I walked down the street to a liquor store and bought a bottle of chardonnay and a bottle of Chivas Regal. I got some paper cups from a nearby grocery. One final errand, then I could relax for a few hours.

In the shopping center that I had told Graves would be the location for my nonexistent insurance office, I had noticed a sporting goods store. It was about three o'clock when I parked in the lot and ambled into the shop. I looked at various golf clubs: irons, woods, even one set with fiberglass shafts. Finally I selected a set of eight Spalding irons with matching woods, a large bag, and several boxes of Top-Flites. The salesman, who had been occupied with another customer at the rear of the store, hustled up, his eyes full of commission money. I gave him little time to think. The total cost was $612.32. I paid with a check drawn on my new account, cordially thanked the man, and had him carry all the equipment out to the trunk of the car.

I drove to a park near the bank; Loose Park, they called it. I felt loose. Cut loose, drifting free, like one of the kites people were flying that had broken its string and was ascending into the sun. Beneath the trees it was still hot, though the sunlight was reduced to a shuffling of light and shadow on the brown grass. Kids ran, jumped, swung on playground equipment. I uncorked my bottle of wine, filled one of the paper cups, and lay down beneath a tree, enjoying the children, watching young men and women walking along the footpaths.

A girl approached. She didn't look any older than seventeen.

Short, slender, with clean blonde hair cut to her shoulders. Her shorts were very tight. I watched her unabashedly; she saw me watching and left the path to come over to me. She stopped a few feet away, hands on her hips. "What are you looking at?" she asked.

"Your legs," I said. "Would you like some wine?"

"No thanks. My mother told me never to accept wine from strangers." She looked right through me.

"I take what I can get from strangers," I said. "Because I'm a stranger, too."

I guess she liked that. She was different. She sat down and we chatted for a while. There was something wrong about her imitation of a seventeen-year-old; I began to wonder whether hookers worked the park. She crossed her legs and her shorts got tighter. "Where are you from?" she asked.

"San Francisco. But I've just moved here to stay. I have a part interest in the sporting goods store at the Eastridge Plaza."

"You live near here?"

"On West Eighty-ninth." I had driven down Eighty-ninth on my way to the bank.

"I live on Eighty-ninth! We're neighbors."

It was exactly what one of my own might have said to test me. I took a drink of wine and changed the subject. "Would you like to visit San Francisco someday?"

She brushed her hair back behind one ear. She pursed her lips, showing off her fine cheekbones. "Have you got something going?" she asked, in queerly accented English.

"Excuse me?"

"I said, have you got something going," she repeated, still with the accent—the accent of my own time.

I took another sip. "A bottle of wine," I replied in good midwestern 1980s.

She wasn't having any of it. "No artwork, please. I don't like artwork."

I had to laugh: my life was devoted to artwork. I had not met anyone real in a long time. At the beginning I hadn't wanted to, and in the ensuing years I had given up expecting it. If there's anything more boring than you people it's us people. But that was an old attitude. When she came to me in K.C. I was lonely and she was something new.

"Okay," I said. "It's not much, but you can come for the ride.

Do you want to?"

She smiled and said yes.

As we walked to my car, she brushed her hip against my leg. I switched the bottle to my left hand and put my arm around her shoulders in a fatherly way. We got into the front seat, beneath the trees on a street at the edge of the park. It was quiet. I reached over, grabbed her hair at the nape of her neck, and jerked her face toward me, covering her little mouth with mine. Surprise: she threw her arms around my neck and slid across the seat into my lap. We did not talk. I yanked at the shorts; she thrust her hand into my pants. St. Augustine asked the Lord for chastity, but not right away.

At the end she slipped off me, calmly buttoned her blouse, brushed her hair back from her forehead. "How about a push?" she asked. She had a nail file out and was filing her index fingernail to a point.

I shook my head and looked at her. She resembled my grandmother. I had never run into my grandmother, but she had a hellish reputation. "No thanks. What's your name?"

"Call me Ruth." She scratched the inside of her left elbow with her nail. She leaned back in her seat, sighed deeply. Her eyes became a very bright, very hard blue.

While she was aloft I got out, opened the trunk, emptied the rest of the chardonnay into the gutter, and used the funnel to fill the bottle with kerosene. I plugged it with a kerosene-soaked rag. Afternoon was sliding into evening as I started the car and cruised down one of the residential streets. The houses were like those of any city or town of that era of the Midwest USA: white frame, forty or fifty years old, with large porches and small front yards. Dying elms hung over the street. Shadows stretched across the sidewalks. Ruth's nose wrinkled; she turned her face lazily toward me, saw the kerosene bottle, and smiled.

Ahead on the left-hand sidewalk I saw a man walking leisurely. He was an average sort of man, middle-aged, probably just returning from work, enjoying the quiet pause dusk was bringing to the hot day. It might have been Hector; it might have been Graves. It might have been any one of you. I punched the cigarette lighter, readied the bottle in my right hand, steering with my leg as the car moved slowly forward.

"Let me help," Ruth said. She reached out and steadied the wheel with her slender fingertips. The lighter popped out. I touched it to the rag; it smoldered and caught. Greasy smoke stung my eyes. By now the man had noticed us. I hung my arm, holding the bottle, out the window. As we passed him, I tossed the bottle at the sidewalk like a newsboy tossing a rolled-up newspaper. The rag flamed brighter as it whipped through the air; the bottle landed at his feet and exploded, dousing him with burning kerosene. I floored the accelerator; the motor coughed, then roared, the tires and Ruth both squealing in delight. I could see the flaming man in the rear-view mirror as we sped away.

∞   ∞   ∞

On the Great American Plains, the summer nights are not silent. The fields sing the summer songs of insects—not individual sounds, but a high-pitched drone of locusts, crickets, cicadas, small chirping things for which I have no names. You drive along the super-highway and that sound blends with the sound of wind rushing through your opened windows, hiding the thrum of the automobile, conveying the impression of incredible velocity. Wheels vibrate, tires beat against the pavement, the steering wheel shudders, alive in your hands, droning insects alive in your ears. Reflecting posts at the roadside leap from the darkness with metronomic regularity, glowing amber in the headlights, only to vanish abruptly into the ready night when you pass. You lose track of time, how long you have been on the road, where you are going. The fields scream in your ears like a thousand lost, mechanical souls, and you press your foot to the accelerator, hurrying away.

When we left Kansas City that evening we were indeed hurrying. Our direction was in one sense precise: Interstate 70, more or less due east, through Missouri in a dream. They might remember me in Kansas City, at the same time wondering who and why. Mr. Graves scans the morning paper over his grapefruit: MAN BURNED BY GASOLINE BOMB. The clerk wonders why he ever accepted an unverified counter check, without a name or address printed on it, for six hundred dollars. The check bounces. They discover it was a bottle of chardonnay. The story is pieced together. They would eventually figure out how—I wouldn't lie to myself about that (I never lie to myself)—but the why would always escape them. Organized crime, they would say. A plot that misfired.

Of course, they still might have caught me. The car became more of a liability the longer I held on to it. But Ruth, humming to herself, did not seem to care, and neither did I. You have to improvise those things; that's what gives them whatever interest they have.

Just shy of Columbia, Missouri, Ruth stopped humming and asked me, "Do you know why Helen Keller can't have any children?"

"No."

"Because she's dead."

I rolled up the window so I could hear her better. "That's pretty funny," I said.

"Yes. I overheard it in a restaurant." After a minute she asked, "Who's Helen Keller?"

"A dead woman." An insect splattered itself against the windshield. The lights of the oncoming cars glinted against the smear it left.

"She must be famous," said Ruth. "I like famous people. Have you met any? Was that man you burned famous?"

"Probably not. I don't care about famous people anymore." The last time I had anything to do, even peripherally, with anyone famous was when I changed the direction of the tape over the lock in the Watergate so Frank Wills would see it. Ruth did not look like the kind who would know about that. "I was there for the Kennedy assassination," I said, "but I had nothing to do with it."

"Who was Kennedy?"

That made me smile. "How long have you been here?" I pointed at her tiny purse. "That's all you've got with you?"

She slid across the seat and leaned her head against my shoulder. "I don't need anything else."

"No clothes?"

"I left them in Kansas City. We can get more."

"Sure," I said.

She opened the purse and took out a plastic Bayer aspirin case. From it she selected two blue-and-yellow caps. She shoved her palm up under my nose. "Serometh?"

"No thanks."

She put one of the caps back into the box and popped the other under her nose. She sighed and snuggled tighter against me. We had reached Columbia and I was hungry. When I pulled in at a McDonald's she ran across the lot into the shopping mall before I could stop her. I was a little nervous about the car and sat watching it as I ate (Big Mac, small Dr. Pepper). She did not come back. I crossed the lot to the mall, found a drugstore, and bought some cigars.

When I strolled back to the car she was waiting for me, hopping from one foot to another and tugging at the door handle. Serometh makes you impatient. She was wearing a pair of shiny black pants, pink- and white-checked sneakers, and a hot pink blouse. "'s go!" she hissed.

I moved even slower. She looked like she was about to wet herself, biting her soft lower lip with a line of perfect white teeth. I dawdled over my keys. A security guard and a young man in a shirt and tie hurried out of the mall entrance and scanned the lot. "Nice outfit," I said. "Must have cost you something."

She looked over her shoulder, saw the security guard, who saw her. "Hey!" he called, running toward us. I slid into the car, opened the passenger door. Ruth had snapped open her purse and pulled out a small gun. I grabbed her arm and yanked her into the car; she squawked and her shot went wide. The guard fell down anyway, scared shitless. For the second time that day I tested the Citation's acceleration; Ruth's door slammed shut and we were gone.

"You scut," she said as we hit the entrance ramp of the interstate. "You're a scut-pumping Conservative. You made me miss." But she was smiling, running her hand up the inside of my thigh. I could tell she hadn't ever had so much fun in the twentieth century.

For some reason I was shaking. "Give me one of those serometh," I said.

∞ ∞ ∞

Around midnight we stopped in St. Louis at a Holiday Inn. We registered as Mr. and Mrs. Gerald Bruno (an old acquaintance) and paid in advance. No one remarked on the apparent difference in our ages. So discreet. I bought a copy of the *Post-Dispatch*, and we went to the room. Ruth flopped down on the bed, looking bored, but thanks to her gunplay I had a few more things to take care of. I poured myself a glass of Chivas, went into the bathroom, removed the toupee and flushed it down the toilet, showered, put a new blade in my old razor, and shaved the rest of the hair from my head. The Lex Luthor look. I cut my scalp. That got me laughing, and I could not stop. Ruth peeked through the doorway to find me dabbing the crown of my head with a bloody kleenex.

"You're a wreck," she said.

I almost fell off the toilet laughing. She was absolutely right. Between giggles I managed to say, "You must not stay anywhere too long, if you're as careless as you were tonight."

She shrugged. "I bet I've been at it longer than you." She stripped and got into the shower. I got into bed.

The room enfolded me in its gold-carpet green-bedspread mediocrity. Sometimes it's hard to remember that things were ever different. In 1596 I rode to court with Essex; I slept in a chamber of supreme garishness (gilt escutcheons in the corners of the ceiling, pink cupids romping on the walls), in a bed warmed by any of the trollops of the city I might want. And there in the Holiday Inn I sat with my drink, in my pastel blue pajama bottoms, reading a late-twentieth-century newspaper, smoking a cigar. An earthquake in Peru estimated to have killed eight thousand in Lima alone. Nope. A steelworker in Gary, Indiana, discovered to be the murderer of six prepubescent children, bodies found buried in his basement. Perhaps. The president refuses to enforce the ruling of his Supreme Court because it "subverts the will of the American people." Probably not.

We are everywhere. But not everywhere.

Ruth came out of the bathroom, saw me, did a double take. "You look—perfect!" she said. She slid in the bed beside me, naked, and sniffed at my glass of Chivas. Her lip curled. She looked over my shoulder at the paper. "You can understand that stuff?"

"Don't kid me. Reading is a survival skill. You couldn't last here without it."

"Wrong."

I drained the scotch. Took a puff on the cigar. Dropped the paper to the floor beside the bed. I looked her over. Even relaxed, the muscles in her arms and along the tops of her thighs were well-defined.

"You even smell like one of them," she said.

"How did you get the clothes past their store security? They have those beeper tags clipped to them."

"Easy. I tried on the shoes and walked out when they weren't looking. In the second store I took the pants into a dressing room, cut the alarm tag out of the waistband, and put them on. I held the alarm tag that was clipped to the blouse in my armpit and walked out of that store, too. I put the blouse on in the mall women's room."

"If you can't read, how did you know which was the women's room?"

"There's a picture on the door."

I felt tired and old. Ruth moved close. She rubbed her foot up my leg, drawing the pajama leg up with it. Her thigh slid across my groin. I started to get hard. "Cut it out," I said. She licked my nipple.

I could not stand it. I got off the bed. "I don't like you."

She looked at me with true innocence. "I don't like you, either."

Although he was repulsed by the human body, Jonathan Swift was passionately in love with a woman named Esther Johnson. "What you did at the mall was stupid," I said. "You would have killed that guard."

"Which would have made us even for the day."

"Kansas City was different."

"We should ask the cops there what they think."

"You don't understand. That had some grace to it. But what you did was inelegant. Worst of all it was not gratuitous. You stole those clothes for yourself, and I hate that." I was shaking.

"Who made all these laws?"

"I did."

She looked at me with amazement. "You're not just a Conservative. You've gone native!"

I wanted her so much I ached. "No I haven't," I said, but even to me my voice sounded frightened.

Ruth got out of the bed. She glided over, reached one hand around to the small of my back, pulled herself close. She looked up at me with a face that held nothing but avidity. "You can do whatever you want," she whispered. With a feeling that I was losing everything, I kissed her. You don't need to know what happened then.

I woke when she displaced herself: there was a sound like the sweep of an arm across fabric, a stirring of air to fill the place where she had been. I looked around the still brightly lit room. It was not yet morning. The chain was across the door; her clothes lay on the dresser. She had left the aspirin box beside my bottle of scotch.

She was gone. Good, I thought, now I can go on. But I found that I couldn't sleep, could not keep from thinking. Ruth must be very good at that, or perhaps her thought is a different kind of thought from mine. I got out of the bed, resolved to try again but still fearing the inevitable. I filled the tub with hot water. I got in, breathing heavily. I took the blade from my razor. Holding my arm just beneath the surface of the water, hesitating only a moment, I cut deeply one, two, three times along the veins in my left wrist. The shock was still there, as great as ever. With blood streaming from me I cut the right wrist. Quickly, smoothly. My heart beat fast and light, the blood flowed frighteningly; already the water was stained. I felt faint—yes—it was going to work this time, yes. My vision began to fade—but in the last moments before consciousness fell away I saw, with sick despair, the futile wounds closing themselves once again, as they had so many times before. For in the future the practice of medicine may progress to the point where men need have little fear of death.

∞   ∞   ∞

The dawn's rosy fingers found me still unconscious. I came to myself about eleven, my head throbbing, so weak I could hardly rise from the cold bloody water. There were no scars. I stumbled into the other room and washed down one of Ruth's megamphetamines with two fingers of scotch. I felt better immediately. It's funny how that works sometimes, isn't it? The maid knocked as I was cleaning the bathroom. I shouted for her to come back later, finished as quickly as possible, and left the motel immediately. I ate shredded wheat with milk and strawberries for breakfast. I was full of ideas. A phone book gave me the location of a likely country club.

The Oak Hill Country Club of Florissant, Missouri, is not a spectacularly wealthy institution, or at least it does not give that impression. I'll bet you that the membership is not as purely white as the stucco clubhouse. That was all right with me. I parked the Citation in the mostly empty parking lot, hauled my new equipment from the trunk, and set off for the locker room, trying hard to look like a dentist. I successfully ran the gauntlet of the pro shop, where the proprietor was telling a bored caddy why the Cardinals would fade in the stretch. I could hear running water from the showers as I shuffled into the locker room and slung the bag into a corner. Someone was singing the "Ode to Joy," abominably.

I began to rifle through the lockers, hoping to find an open one with someone's clothes in it. I would take the keys from my benefactor's pocket and proceed along my merry way. Ruth would have accused me of self-interest; there was a moment in which I accused myself. Such hesitation is the seed of failure: as I paused before a locker containing a likely set of clothes, another golfer entered the room along with the locker-room attendant. I immediately began undressing, lowering my head so that the locker door hid my face. The golfer was soon gone, but the attendant sat down and began to leaf through a worn copy of *Penthouse*. I could come up with no better plan than to strip and enter the showers. Amphetamine daze. Perhaps the kid would develop a hard-on and go to the john to take care of it.

There was only one other man in the shower, the symphonic soloist, a somewhat portly gentleman who mercifully shut up as soon as I entered. He worked hard at ignoring me. I ignored him in return: *alle Menschen werden Brüder.* I waited a long five minutes after he left; two more men came into the showers, and I walked out with what composure I could muster. The locker-room boy was stacking towels on a table. I fished a five from my jacket in the locker and walked up behind him. Casually I took a towel.

"Son, get me a pack of Marlboros, will you?"

He took the money and left.

In the second locker I found a pair of pants that contained the keys to some sort of Audi. I was not choosy. Dressed in record time, I left the new clubs beside the rifled locker. My note read, "The pure products of America go crazy." There were three eligible cars in the lot, two 4000s and a Fox. The key would not open the door of the Fox. I was jumpy, but almost home free, coming around the front of a big Chrysler. . . .

"Hey!"

My knee gave way and I ran into the fender of the car. The keys slipped out of my hand and skittered across the hood to the ground, jingling. Grimacing, I hopped toward them, plucked them up, glancing over my shoulder at my pursuer as I stooped. It was the locker-room attendant.

"Your cigarettes." He looked at me the way a sixteen-year-old looks at his father; that is, with bored skepticism. All our gods in the end become pitiful. It was time for me to be abruptly courteous. As it was, he would remember me too well.

"Thanks," I said. I limped over, put the pack into my shirt pocket. He started to go, but I couldn't help myself. "What about my change?"

Oh, such an insolent silence! I wonder what you told them when they asked you about me, boy. He handed over the money. I tipped him a quarter, gave him a piece of Mr. Graves's professional smile. He studied me. I turned and inserted the key into the lock of the Audi. A fifty percent chance. Had I been the praying kind I might have prayed to one of those pitiful gods. The key turned without resistance; the door opened. The kid slouched back toward the clubhouse, pissed at me and his lackey's job. Or per-

tance to go into fourth, but I didn't care. The encounter with Milo had gone exactly as such things should go, and was especially pleasing because it had been totally unplanned. An accident—no order, one would guess—but exactly as if I had laid it all out beforehand. I came into Detroit late at night via Route 12, which eventually turned into Michigan Avenue. The air was hot and sticky. I remember driving past the Cadillac plant; multitudes of red, yellow, and green lights glinting off dull masonry and the smell of auto exhaust along the city streets. I found the sort of neighborhood I wanted not far from Tiger Stadium: pawnshops, an all-night deli, laundromats, dimly lit bars with red Stroh's signs in the windows. Men on street corners walked casually from noplace to noplace.

I parked on a side street just around the corner from a 7-Eleven. I left the motor running. In the store I dawdled over a magazine rack until at last I heard the racing of an engine and saw the Audi flash by the window. I bought a copy of *Time* and caught a downtown bus at the corner. At the Greyhound station I purchased a ticket for the next bus to Toronto and sat reading my magazine until departure time.

We got onto the bus. Across the river we stopped at customs and got off again. "Name?" they asked me.

"Gerald Spotsworth."

"Place of birth?"

"Calgary." I gave them my credentials. The passport photo showed me with hair. They looked me over. They let me go.

I work in the library of the University of Toronto. I am well-read, a student of history, a solid Canadian citizen. There I lead a sedentary life. The subways are clean, the people are friendly, the restaurants are excellent. The sky is blue. The cat is on the mat.

We got back on the bus. There were few other passengers, and most of them were soon asleep; the only light in the darkened interior was that which shone above my head. I was very tired, but I did not want to sleep. Then I remembered that I had Ruth's pills in my jacket pocket. I smiled, thinking of the customs people. All that was left in the box were a couple of tiny pink tabs. I did not know what they were, but I broke one down the middle with my fingernail and took it anyway. It perked me up immediately. Everything I could see seemed sharply defined. The dark green plastic of the seats. The rubber mat in the aisle. My fingernails. All details were separate and distinct, all interdependent. I must have been focused on the threads in the weave of my pants leg for ten minutes when I was surprised by someone sitting down next to me. It was Ruth. "You're back!" I exclaimed.

"We're all back," she said. I looked around and it was true: on the opposite side of the aisle, two seats ahead, Milo sat watching me over his shoulder, a trickle of blood running down his forehead. One corner of his mouth pulled tighter in a rueful smile. Mr. Graves came back from the front seat and shook my hand. I saw the fat singer from the country club, still naked. The locker-room boy. A flickering light from the back of the bus: when I turned around there stood the burning man, his eye sockets two dark hollows behind the wavering flames. The shopping-mall guard. Hector from the hardware store. They all looked at me.

"What are you doing here?" I asked Ruth.

"We couldn't let you go on thinking like you do. You act like I'm some monster. I'm just a person."

"A rather nice-looking young lady," Graves added.

"People are monsters," I said.

"Like you, huh?" Ruth said. "But they can be saints, too."

That made me laugh. "Don't feed me platitudes. You can't even read."

"You make such a big deal out of reading. Yeah, well, times change. I get along fine, don't I?"

The mall guard broke in. "Actually, miss, the reason we caught on to you is that someone saw you walk into the men's room." He looked embarrassed.

"But you didn't catch me, did you?" Ruth snapped back. She turned to me. "You're afraid of change. No wonder you live back here."

"This is all in my imagination," I said. "It's because of your drugs."

"It is all in your imagination," the burning man repeated. His voice was a whisper. "What you see in the future is what you are able to see. You have no faith in God or your fellowman."

"He's right," said Ruth.

"Bull. Psychobabble."

"Speaking of babble," Milo said, "I figured out where you got that goo-goo-goo stuff. Talk—"

"Never mind that," Ruth broke in. "Here's the truth. The future is just a place. The people there are just people. They live differently. So what? People make what they want of the world. You can't escape human failings by running into the past." She rested her hand on my leg. "I'll tell you what you'll find when you get to Toronto," she said. "Another city full of human beings."

This was crazy. I knew it was crazy, I knew it was all unreal, but somehow I was getting more and more afraid. "So the future is just the present writ large," I said bitterly. "More bull."

"You tell her, pal," the locker-room boy said.

Hector, who had been listening quietly, broke in. "For a man from the future, you talk a lot like a native."

"You're the king of bullshit, man," Milo said. " 'Some people devote themselves to artwork'! Jesus!"

I felt dizzy. "Scut down, Milo. That means 'Fuck you too.' " I shook my head to try to make them go away. That was a mistake: the bus began to pitch like a sailboat. I grabbed for Ruth's arm but missed. "Who's driving this thing?" I asked, trying to get out of the seat.

"Don't worry," said Graves. "He knows what he's doing."

"He's brain-dead," Milo said.

"You couldn't do any better," said Ruth, pulling me back down.

"No one is driving," said the burning man.

"We'll crash!" I was so dizzy now that I could hardly keep fro m being sick. I closed my eyes and swallowed. That seemed to help. A long time passed; eventually I must have fallen asleep.

When I woke it was late morning and we were entering the city, cruising down Eglinton Avenue. The bus had a driver after all—a slender black man with neatly trimmed sideburns who wore his uniform hat at a rakish angle. A sign above the windshield said, YOUR DRIVER—SAFE, COURTEOUS, and below that, on the slide-in nameplate, WILBERT CAUL. I felt like I was coming out of a nightmare. I felt happy. I stretched some of the knots out of my back. A young soldier seated across the aisle from me looked my way; I smiled, and he returned it briefly.

"You were mumbling to yourself in your sleep last night," he said.

"Sorry. Sometimes I have bad dreams."

"It's okay. I do too, sometimes." He had a round open face, an apologetic grin. He was twenty, maybe. Who knew where his dreams came from? We chatted until the bus reached the station; he shook my hand and said he was pleased to meet me. He called me "sir."

I was not due back at the library until Monday, so I walked

over to Yonge Street. The stores were busy, the tourists were out in droves, the adult theaters were doing a brisk business. Policemen in sharply creased trousers, white gloves, sauntered along among the pedestrians. It was a bright, cloudless day, but the breeze coming up the street from the lake was cool. I stood on the sidewalk outside one of the strip joints and watched the videotaped come-on over the closed circuit. The Princess Laya. Sondra Nieve, the Human Operator. Technology replaces the traditional barker, but the bodies are more or less the same. The persistence of your faith in sex and machines is evidence of your capacity to hope.

Francis Bacon, in his masterwork *The New Atlantis*, foresaw the utopian world that would arise through the application of experimental science to social problems. Bacon, however, could not solve the problems of his own time and was eventually accused of accepting bribes, fined £40,000, and imprisoned in the Tower of London. He made no appeal to God, but instead applied himself to the development of the virtues of patience and acceptance. Eventually he was freed. Soon after, on a freezing day in late March, we were driving near Highgate when I suggested to him that cold might delay the process of decay. He was excited by the idea. On impulse he stopped the carriage, purchased a hen, wrung its neck, and stuffed it with snow. He eagerly looked forward to the results of his experiment. Unfortunately, in haggling with the street vendor he had exposed himself thoroughly to the cold and was seized by a chill that rapidly led to pneumonia, of which he died on April 9, 1626.

There's no way to predict these things.

When the videotape started repeating itself I got bored, crossed the street, and lost myself in the crowd.

MEETING IN INFINITY MEETING IN INFINITY MEETING IN INFINITY MEETING
TING IN INFINITY MEETING IN INFINITY MEETING IN INFINITY ME
MEETING IN INFINITY MEETING IN INFINITY MEETING IN INFINITY
ITY MEETING IN INFINITY MEETING IN INFINITY MEETING IN INF
INFINITY MEETING IN INFINITY MEETING IN INFINITY MEETING IN
G IN INFINITY FINITY MEETII
ETING IN INF IN INFINITY M
J MEETING IN INFINITY MEETING IN INFINITY MEETING IN INFINIT
INITY MEETI MEETING IN INI
N INFINITY ITY MEETING I
NG IN INFINITY MEETING IN INFINITY MEETING IN INFINITY MEET
EETING IN INFINITY MEETING IN INFINITY MEETING IN INFINITY M
Y MEETING IN INFINITY MEETING IN INFINITY MEETING IN INFINI
FINITY MEETING IN INFINITY MEETING IN INFINITY MEETING IN IN
IN INFINITY MEETING IN INFINITY MEETING IN INFINITY MEETING

mrs. shummel
exits a winner

THE BINGO HALL AT THE PFC WOODROW TRUESMITH VFW POST WAS
filling when Martha Shummel and her friend Betty Alcyk arrived. To the right of the platform where the machine sat
waiting, in the gloom that would be dispelled once the caller
stepped up to begin the game, hung the flag of Florida. To
the left hung the tattered flag of the United States that Pete Cullum
had brought back from Saigon. They said that the brown stain that
ran up the right edge was from the mortal wound of one of the
heroes who died in the Tet Offensive, but although Martha did not
question the story she always wondered how that could have happened unless he had wrapped himself in it. The rows of wooden
tables with TRUESMITH stenciled on their centers were already half
covered with mosaics of bingo boards; people leaned back in the
folding chairs and filled the hall with cigarette smoke and the buzz
of conversation.

Martha did not like arriving so late. She liked to be early enough
to get her favorite seat, set her boards neatly in order, and sit back
and watch the people come in. She would chat with her neighbors
about children and politics and the weather while the feeling of excitement grew. Once a month or so she worked in the kitchen, and
sometimes on the other nights she brought in her special pineapple
cake. It was like being in a club. You got together as friends, forgot

how bad your digestion was or how hard it was to pay the bills or how long it had been since your kids had called. You took a little chance. Maybe when you left you still had to go back through streets where punks sold drugs on the corners, to a stuffy room in a retirement home, but for a couple of hours you could put that away and have some fun.

But Betty had not been ready when Martha came by. So instead of getting there early they got stuck in line behind Sarah Kinsella, the human cable-news network. With Sarah you could hardly get a word in edgewise, despite the fact that she had emphysema and her voice sounded like it was coming at you through an aqualung. She told them about the UFO landing port beneath Apalachee Bay, about the Cuban spies pawing through her trash cans, and about how well her grandson Hugh was doing at the University of Florida —starting linebacker on the football team, treasurer of his fraternity, and he was making straight A's. Martha and Betty listened patiently even though they had heard it all before. Finally they got to the front of the line. Sarah bought five boards and headed past the table, down an aisle. The two women sighed in relief.

"He makes straight A's," Betty muttered.

"Yes," said Martha. "But his B's are a little crooked." They both laughed until their eyes were damp.

Ed Kelly, who sold the boards, smiled at them. "Come on, girls. Settle down. You're gonna wet those cute pants."

"Don't be fresh," Martha said. "Six." She handed over twelve dollars.

Betty bought three boards and they went their separate ways. Betty's eyesight was failing, so she insisted on sitting close to the front where she could peer up at the number board. But Martha's eyes were fine—she could handle the twelve game panels on her six boards without trouble—and the people who sat in front were too eager for her. They made her mad when they shouted "Bingo!" so loud, as if someone was trying to cheat them. Her own spot was over against the windows on the side, with her back to one of the mock Greek pillars. When she got to her place a young man was already sitting there. Martha began to put down her purse and boards. She started to say, "Son, this is my spot—" but then the boy looked up at her.

His tousled hair, in dazzling contrast to the narrow face beneath it, shone downy white. He had the darkest of brown eyes. His expression was one of dazed accusation, as if he had just awoken

from being beaten senseless to find Martha gazing at him. His bruised eyes reminded her of David's. She stood there, holding the straps of her purse, neither setting it down nor picking it up.

Finally she managed to speak. "This is my spot," she said. "Please go someplace else."

The boy sighed. Instead of getting up he pulled a card and a stylus from the gym bag beside him. It was a magic slate, a film of plastic laid over a black background. Martha's children had played with such slates. On the slate, before he pulled up the plastic sheet to erase them, she read the words, CHARITY NEVER FAILETH. The boy cleared the old message and wrote, then held the slate up for Martha to see: FUCK OFF BITCH.

Martha felt her heart skip a beat, then race. Were people watching? Just when she decided to call one of the men, the boy pulled up the plastic sheet and the neatly printed block letters vanished.

He looked at her, then silently slid his slate and his single bingo board to the opposite side of the table. He walked around and sat, facing her, with his back to the front of the room and the bingo machine. He straightened his board in front of himself. Martha hesitated, then sat down. She spread out her boards, got the plastic box of chips and magnetic wand from her purse. She covered the free square of each panel with one of the metal-rimmed red chips. When she looked up again the boy was staring at her.

Martha wondered if she had seen him in the neighborhood. He was probably one of those boys who could get your prescriptions filled cheap. The intensity of his stare made her nervous, and for a moment she wished she'd sat someplace else. But she'd be damned if she'd let some punk push her around, let alone a mute, retarded one. If you did that then pretty soon you were at their mercy. She'd seen it happen.

The boy sat back in the wooden folding chair, somehow managing to look innocent and alert at the same time. Martha had at first thought his hair was bleached, but now she decided it was naturally white. His face was cool as the moon on a hot night. Watching him, Martha felt her heart still sprinting, and she could not draw her breath. She did her best not to let on. It was like the beginning of one of her dizzy spells.

Trying hard not to be aware of the boy, she looked around the hall. From the kitchen at the back came the smells of pizza and hot dogs. Men and women returned from the bar carrying beer in plastic cups and slices of pizza on paper plates with the grease already soaking through. The light was dying outside the rows of windows, and the gabble of voices competed with the whir of the ceiling fans.

Martha could spot dozens of people she knew from the Paradise Beach condos, and those she did not know by name she recognized as regulars at the Private Truesmith. They were of every color, Italians, Germans, Poles, blacks, Cubans, Vietnamese, and Anglos, ex–New Yorkers and ex-Chicagoans and native Southerners, the newly wed and the nearly dead, Republicans, Democrats, Libertarians, and even Hyman Spivek, who preached a loudmouthed brand of Communism, men turned milk white by leukemia and women turned to brown leather by the sun, Baptists, Jews, Episcopalians, Catholics, and Seventh-Day Adventists, some with money to burn and others without two dimes to rub together, tolerable people like Betty, and fools like Sarah. Most were senior citizens managing to scrape along on pensions and savings, talking trash and hoping to win the $250 coverall so they could enjoy themselves a little more before the last trip to the hospital. As decent a crowd of people, Martha supposed, as you could scrape together in all the panhandle of Florida.

All of which made the sudden appearance of this mute boy even more puzzling: he couldn't be any more than fifteen and he acted more like he'd grown up on Mars than in America. He was a total stranger.

Her heartbeat seemed to be slowing. It was almost time to begin. Tony Schuster passed by them up the aisle, joking with the women on his way to the platform. He fired up the bingo machine: the board lit up, the numbered balls rattled into the transparent box and began to dance around like popcorn on the jet of air. "First game," he announced through the P.A., "regular bingo on your cards, inside corners, outside corners, horizontal, vertical, diagonal rows. Ready for your first number?" The machine made a noise like a man with his larynx cut out taking breath, and sucked up a ball. "I-18," Schuster called.

Martha covered the number on two of her boards. One of them was an inside corner. "G-52." She had two of those, too, but they were on different panels from the first number. "G-47." Nothing. "I-29." Three covers. She looked up. Ed Kelly, now patrolling the aisles, was glancing over the boy's shoulder: on his top panel the boy had covered the four inside corners. He seemed oblivious. "Bingo!" Kelly called out, just as Schuster was about to announce the next number. The crowd groaned; Martha sighed.

"I-18, I-29, G-52, G-47," Kelly read aloud.

"We have a bingo," Schuster called. The room was filled with the clicking of chips being wiped from several hundred boards, a field full of locusts singing. Martha ran her wand over her boards and pulled up her own chips while Kelly counted twenty dollars out to the silent boy. "Speak up next time, kid," Kelly said good-naturedly.

"He's deaf and dumb," Martha said.

"Can't be deaf, Martha—he's got his back to the machine. Whyn't you help him out?"

Martha just stared at Kelly, and he went away. Schuster began the second game, a series beginning with a fifteen-dollar regular bingo and ending in an eighty-dollar coverall. Martha tried to ignore the boy and the injustice of his playing only one board yet winning. She managed to get four in the "O" column before someone across the room yelled "Bingo!" She sighed again. In the follow-up, the inner square, she had gotten nowhere when a black woman in the front bingoed. While the attendant called out the numbers for Schuster to check, Martha glanced over at the boy's card. The inner square on one panel was completely covered.

Martha thought about pointing it out to him, but held back. He turned his face up to her. He smiled. She ducked her head to look at her own boards.

The kid was lucky but didn't even know it. Luck was like that. Who could say how the numbers would come: Martha only knew that they did not come for her often enough to make up for her losses. Only the night before she had blown twenty dollars when the Red Sox lost the series to the Mets. She had never seen as clear a case of bad luck as had cost the Sox the series. Martha had been a Red Sox fan since she was a girl. She had met her husband Sam at Fenway Park on June 18, 1938, Sox over the Yankees 6–2.

Sam was lucky about the Sox—he had won more than his share of bets on them over the years, which was no easy job—but not so lucky when the cancer ate him up at fifty-five. He had collected baseball cards. For fifteen years after his death Martha kept them, even though they didn't mean anything to her. Sometimes she would take the cards out of their plastic envelopes and look at them, remember how Sam would worry over them and rearrange their vacations so they could go to swap meets where he might pick up a 1950 Vern Stephens or Walt Dropo. He had cared for those cards more than for her. She would sigh in resignation. Staring at some corny action photo or head-and-shoulders shot of a bullet-headed ballplayer wearing an old-fashioned uniform, it would become all she could do to keep from crying. She would slide the card back into its envelope, stick the envelope in among the others, shove the collection back on its shelf in the closet. She would poke at her eyes with the wrist of her sweater and make a cup of coffee. It would almost be time for "The Young and the Restless."

Of their three kids, Robert, the eldest, was a CPA in Portland, and Gloria bought clothes for Macy's in New York. Their youngest, David, her favorite, a beautiful boy—in some ways as beautiful a boy as this punk who insulted her in the Truesmith—had died at the age of fifteen, in 1961. David had snuck off to Cape Cod one weekend with his friends. He did not have her permission, would never have gotten it if he had asked. Despite the fact that he had been a very good swimmer, he had drowned off the beach at Hyannis.

After that her life started to go to pieces. Sam and she had moved to Florida in 1970, and a year later he was dead, too. His pension had seemed to shrink as time went by. Last year she had sold the baseball cards to raise some cash.

"B-9." She placed her chips, glanced up from her board and saw the boy covering the number on his own, completing the outer square, covering the complete panel as well. He made no attempt to draw the attention of one of the men. Schuster called three more numbers. The kid had all of those numbers too, on the lower panel of his board. With the fourth number came simultaneous shouts of "Bingo!" from three spots around the hall. The crowd groaned. The boy just sat there. He didn't yell, he didn't sigh, he didn't even seem to realize that he had won, did not seem even to hear the babble of disappointed voices filling the room.

Martha felt herself getting mad. They ought not to allow such a fool into the place. She supposed she could call out for him, but that would only tie her to him, and he had insulted her. If he won, she couldn't. The men finished checking the winners' boards and divided up the money.

"Now, for the eighty-dollar coverall," Schuster announced. "I-22." Martha was so distracted staring at the boy's board, completely covered with red chips, that she forgot to check her own boards. "O-74."

"Bingo!" a man shouted.

The boy tilted his board, and all the chips slid off onto the table. The kid was trying to get to her. He had to have been cheating.

That was why he had not called out—he knew that when the attendant came to check his board, they would find that he had not really won. She decided to keep an eye on him through the next game.

Schuster called five numbers. The boy had four of them, a clear winning diagonal that shot across the board like an arrow into Martha's heart. He remained mute as a snake, and somebody else won two numbers later. He had both of those numbers, too.

She sat there and, with an anxiety that grew like a tumor, watched him win the next five games in a row, none of which he called out. The room faded into the background until all there was was the boy's bingo board. Schuster would call a number, and it was as if he were reading them off the kid's battered pasteboard. Still the boy said nothing. He let other people take $150 that could have been his.

Martha had trouble breathing. She needed some air. But more than air, more than life itself, she needed that board.

∞   ∞   ∞

By the time of the break after the tenth game, Martha's anxiety had been transformed from anger to fear. The boy had won every game and called out none. There was no way one card could win game after game unless the numbers on it changed, but as close as she watched Martha could not see them change. At the end of the last coverall, when two women, one of them Betty Alcyk, shouted bingo, the boy looked up at Martha. Placidly, he pointed to the cards in front of her. She had not covered half of her own numbers. The boy wrote on his slate: DON'T YOU WANT TO WIN?

"Shut up!" she said, loud enough so that the people at the next table looked over at them.

He ripped off the old words and printed something new. He held up the slate and the bingo board simultaneously, scattering colored chips across the table. One of them rolled off into her lap. YOU WANT IT?

Martha bit her lip. She feared a trick. She nodded furtively.

He wrote: COME OUTSIDE.

The boy got up quickly and went out the double doors at the side of the auditorium without looking back at her. After a minute Martha followed. She tried to look as if she was going outside for a breath of air, and in truth the weight of the evening and her losses seemed to have lodged in her chest like a stone.

Outside, in the parking lot, a few men and women were talking

and smoking. Paula Lorenzetti waved to her as she came out, but
Martha acted as if she did not see her. She spotted the boy standing
by the street under one of the lights. At first that reassured her, but
then she realized it was only because he needed the light to use his
slate.

When she got to him he held the bingo board out toward her.
She took it. It seemed perfectly normal. A Capitol: dog-eared
pasteboard, two game grids printed green and black on white, a little picture of the dome of the Congress in each of the free squares.
In the corner someone had written, in childish handwriting, "Pas-
sions Rule!"

"How much?" she asked.

He wrote on the slate: YOUR VOICE.

"What?"

YOU WILL GIVE UP YOUR VOICE.

Martha felt flushed. She could see everything so clearly it almost hurt. Her senses seemed as sharp as if she were twenty again;
her eyes picked out every hair on the boy's arm, she smelled the
aroma of food from the hall and garbage from the alley. Across the
city somewhere a truck was climbing up the gears away from a
stoplight.

"You're kidding."

NO.

"How will you take my voice?"

I DON'T TAKE—YOU GIVE.

"How can I give you my voice?"

SAY YES.

What did she have to lose? There was no way he could steal a
person's voice. Besides, you had to take a chance in your life. "All
right," she said.

"Good-bye," said the boy: softly, almost a whisper.

He lifted his chin and turned. Something in the way he did this
so reminded her of the insolence with which David used to defy her
that she felt it like a blow—it *was* David, or some ghost come to
torment her with his silence and insult—and she almost cried out
for him to wait, to please, please speak to her. She hesitated, and in
a moment he was down an alley and around the corner. She held
the board in her damp hand. She moved, sweating, back toward
the hall. She felt light, as if at any moment her step might push her
away from the earth and she would float into the night.

She remembered making the long drive with Sam down to the
hospital, fighting the traffic on the Sagamore Bridge. Sam had

urged her not to go; it was no thing for a woman to have to do, but she had insisted in a voice that even Sam could hear that she was going. The emergency room was hot and smelled of Lysol. The staff had wheeled David from a bay in emergency to a side corridor, left him on the gurney against the wall with a sheet over him like a used tray from room service. For the first time in her life she had the feeling that her body was not her: she was merely living in it, peering out through the eyes, running her arms and legs like a man running a backhoe. There was David, pale, calm. His hair, long on the sides and in back so he could comb it into the silly D.A. that they had fought over, was still damp but not wet, beginning to stand away from his head. She touched his face, and it was cool as a satin sofa pillow. Sam had to pull her away, trying to talk to her. It was a day before she spoke to him, and then it was only to tell him to be quiet.

"Martha!"

It was Paula, come across the lot to speak to her. "What are you doing? Who was that boy?" She looked at the card in Martha's hand, looked away.

It took a moment for Martha to come back to reality. This would be the test. "Some punk kid," she said. "Hot night."

"It's that ozone layer. Messing up the air."

"It's always hot in October." Her voice flowed as easily as water.

"Not like this," said Paula.

"I like your blouse."

"This? It's cheap. If you don't like the pattern, all you got to do is wash it."

Martha laughed. They went back into the hall. Most of the people were already seated. Martha hurried to her place. She put her other boards aside and set the new one directly in front of her. Magenta chips for the center squares. Mel Shiffman, balding, athletic, wearing his teasing grin, took over the platform to announce the rest of the games.

"Settle down, settle down," he said, like a homeroom teacher coming into class just after the bell. "Eleventh game, on your reg'lar boards, straight bingo. First number: under the O, 65."

The room was dead silent. Martha had that number, on the lower playing card—bottom right corner.

"B-14." Upper left corner.

"N-33." Middle top.

"N-42." No cover. Martha began to worry.

"O-72." Upper right. One more for the outer corners: B-1. B-1, she thought.

"B-1."

It was a flood of light, a joy that filled her, as if the number machine, the voice of Mel Shiffman, the world itself, were under her control. "Bingo!" she shouted. The voices of the people buzzed in her ears. Ed Kelly came by and checked off her numbers. "We have a bingo," Mel announced.

Kelly paid out twenty dollars to her. The bills were crisp and dry as dead leaves. "Inner or outer square," Shiffman called. The people settled down. "Next number: I-25." Both panels on Martha's board had that number. Shiffman called three more. Each number was on her board. All her senses were heightened: the board before her stood out with the three dimensionality of a child's View-Master picture; its colors were distinct and pure. In the air she could pick out the mingled smells of pizza and cigarette smoke and a wisp of bus exhaust that trailed through the window. She heard the gasps and mutterings of the restless crowd, could almost identify the individual voices of her friends as they hovered above their bingo boards, wishing, hoping, to win. Except Martha knew that they wouldn't: *she* would. As if ordered by God, the numbers fell to her, one by one, and the inner square was covered. "Bingo!" she shouted again.

She heard the groan of the crowd more clearly, an explosive sigh heavy with frustration, and immediately after, the voices: "Twice in a row." "She's lucky tonight." "I never win." "N-32; that's all I needed!" "She always wins." The last was Betty's voice, from twenty feet away as clear as if she were whispering in Martha's ear.

Kelly came by and paid out the forty dollars. Forty dollars would keep her for a week. She could buy a new dress, get the toilet fixed, buy a pound of sirloin. "Looks like your night," Kelly said. "Or maybe it's just this table."

"I never won like this before," she said.

"Don't act too guilty," Kelly said, and winked at her.

She started to protest, but he was gone. There was something wrong with her hearing. She heard too well. The next game began. Martha tried to concentrate. She could feel the tension, and every sigh she heard as a number was called that was on her board and not on that of the sigher was like a needle in her chest. When the last number came, the one that both completed the outer square on her upper game panel and covered the entire panel, it was a moment before she could muster the breath to shout, "Bingo!"

The groan that came was full of barely repressed jealousy. Despair. Even hatred. It boomed hollowly in Martha's altered hearing. She looked up and saw envious faces turned to her. Across the room she saw Betty's peevish squint. The crowd buzzed. Kelly read the numbers off her board. Someone shushed someone else. Shiffman announced that this was indeed, miraculously, a valid bingo. Kelly paid out the combined prize of $120, an amount that would see some of these people through a month. She smiled sickly up at him. He counted out the bills without comment.

It was all she could do to cover the free squares for the next game. Shiffman, so nervous now that his smile had faded for the first time in Martha's memory, began. The first four numbers he called, like a dream turning into a nightmare, ran a diagonal winner across Martha's board. When she stammered out "bingo," it was with half the force that she had managed before.

The cries of dismay were crushing. The hall seemed filled with envious voices. A worm of pain moved in her chest. She tried not to take the money, but Kelly insisted. Each bill as it was counted out was like a blow, and when he was at last done she could not find breath to thank him.

When, in the next game, she saw that she had won again, she realized that she could not stand it. She didn't even put chips on the squares, until at last another woman in the room shouted "Bingo!" The woman's triumphant screech was greeted by cheers.

Martha tried to leave, but her legs were too weak. She sat through the last games, watching her card, silent, as the pain climbed from her chest to her throat. Had she been able to face her neighbors, she could have taken every dollar. At last it was over. She gathered up her chips and markers and stumbled toward the door. Friends tried to talk to her. Betty Alcyk called her name. But the memory of Betty's voice among the others silenced her. She couldn't talk to Betty. Their friendship had been only a pact of losers, unable to stand the strain of one of them winning.

But there was worse. If someone else had had the magic card, even if that person was the dearest one in the world to Martha—Betty—Sam, her lost husband—even her beautiful lost son, David—would her own voice have held that same hatred?

The people filed out. Their voices rang in her head. She had nothing to say to them.

THE LIGHTS OF THE CAR DAVIN WAS TAILING SUDDENLY SWERVED right and dropped out of sight; it had run off the road and down the embankment. Davin jerked his Chevy to a stop on the shoulder. A splintered gap in the white wooden retaining fence showed in his headlights, and beyond them the lights of Los Angeles lay spread across the valley.

He slid down the slope, kicking up dust and catching his jacket on the brush. The 1928 Chrysler lay overturned at the bottom, its lights still on. He smelled gasoline. The driver had been thrown from the wreck but was already trying to get up; he crouched a few yards away, touching a hand to his head. Davin got his arm around the man's shoulders and helped him stand.

"You all right?" he asked.

"Sure I'm all right." The man's voice was thick with booze. "I always take this shortcut."

Davin smiled. "Me, I couldn't take the wear and tear."

"You get used to it."

The man was able to walk, and together they managed to get back to Davin's car. They climbed in and Davin started down the mountain again.

"The cops will spot that break in the fence within a couple of hours," he said. "You want to see a doctor?"

"No. Just take me home. 2950 Leeward. I'll call the police from there."

Davin kept his eyes on the road; the Chevy needed its brakes tightened. His passenger seemed to sober remarkably quickly. He sat straighter in the seat and brushed his hair back with his hands like a college kid before a date. Maybe the fact that he'd almost killed himself had actually made an impression on him. "I'm lucky you happened along," the man said. "What's your name?"

"Michael Davin."

"Irish?" There was a casual contempt in his voice.

"On my father's side."

"My father was a swine. Mother was Irish. Not Catholic, though." The contempt flashed again.

"Maybe you ought to go a little easier," Davin said.

The man tensed as if about to take a poke at Davin, then relaxed. He seemed completely sober now. "Perhaps you're right."

Davin recognized the accent: British, faded from long residence in the U.S. The wife hadn't told him that. They rode in silence until they hit the outskirts of the city. Town, really. Despite what the Chamber of Commerce and the Planning Commission and the Police Department could do about it, the neighborhoods still had some of the sleepy feel of Hutchinson, Kansas. Davin sometimes felt right at home helping a businessman keep track of his partner— they would do that in Kansas, too; that would just be good town sense. And that reminded him that no matter how sick he got of L.A., he couldn't stand to go back to the Midwest.

Davin knew that the address the man gave him was not his home. It was a Spanish-style bungalow court apartment in a middle-class neighborhood; Davin had begun trailing him at his real home on West Twelfth Street earlier that day. He pulled over. The man hesitated before getting out.

"I'm sorry about that remark. The Irish, I mean. My grandmother was a terrible snob."

"Don't worry about it. You better have someone take a look at that bump on your head."

"I'll have my wife look at it." The man stood holding the door open, leaning in. His features were thrown into relief by the streetlight ahead of them. "Thank you," he said. "You might have saved my life."

Davin suddenly felt dizzy. He seemed to be outside himself, floating two feet above his own shoulder, listening to himself talk and think.

"All in a day's work," I said, and watched as he turned and strode up the walk to the door of bungalow number seven. He let himself in with his own key. An attractive young woman—his mistress—embraced him on the doorstep. They call L.A. the City of the Angels, but a private dick knows better.

∞   ∞   ∞

It had started very quietly the day before, Friday. Before the knock on his door, there had been no dizziness, no feeling of doing things he did not want to say or do. Davin had been sitting in his office in the late afternoon, legs up on the scarred desk top and tie loosened against the stifling heat. Dust motes swirled in the sunlight slicing through the window over his shoulder. In the harsh light, the cheap sofa against the wall seemed to be radiating dust into the room. The blinds cut the light into parallel lances that slashed across the room like the tines of a fork.

It was the second week of the heat wave. The days seemed endless, and thinking was more effort than his mind wanted to make. He remembered waking one morning that week and imagining himself back in Wichita on one of those days that dawn warm and moist in early August and you know that by three o'clock there'll be reports of at least four old people dropping dead in airless apartments. That was how hot it had been in L.A.—for two solid weeks.

He had the bottle of bootleg gin out, and the glass beside it was half-empty. Then the knock sounded on the door.

Davin drained the glass and stashed the bottle in the bottom desk drawer. "Come in," he said. "It's not locked."

A young woman entered.

Davin was tugging his tie straight when he realized the woman wasn't young after all. She sat in the chair opposite him and crossed her legs coquettishly, but worn hands and the tired line of her jaw gave her away. She wore a cloche hat and sunglasses—probably to mask crow's-feet—and a white silk dress cut just above the knee. The hair curling out from under the hat was bleached blonde. Davin guessed she was a woman who had become used to men's attention at an early age. "Mr. Davin?"

"That's right. How may I help you, ma'am?"

She fluttered for about five seconds, then answered in a voice so alluring it made him shiver. He wanted to close his eyes and simply listen to her voice.

"I need to speak to you about my husband. I'm terribly worried about him. He's been behaving in a way I can only describe as destructive. He's threatening our marriage, and I'm afraid that he may eventually hurt himself."

"What would you like me to do, Mrs. . . ."

"Chandler. Mrs. Raymond Chandler." She smiled, and more lines showed around her mouth. "You may call me Cecily."

"Keeping people's husbands from hurting themselves is not normally in my line of business, Mrs. Chandler."

"That's not exactly what I want you to do." She hesitated. "I want you to follow him and find out where he's going. Sometimes he disappears and I don't know where he is."

So far it was something short of self-destruction. "How often does this happen, and how long is he gone?"

Cecily Chandler bit her lip. "It's been more and more frequent. Two or three times a month—in addition to the times he comes home late. Sometimes he's gone for days."

Davin reacted to her story as if she had handed him a script and told him to start reading.

I could have told her the problem was probably blonde. "Where does he work?" I asked.

"The South Basin Oil Company. The office is on South Olive Street. He's the vice president."

I told myself to bump the fee to twenty-five a day. "Okay," I said. "I'll keep tabs on your husband for a week, Mrs. Chandler, but I'll be blunt with you. It's a common thing in this town for husbands to stray. There's too much bad money and too many eager starlets out for a percentage. One way or the other, no matter what I find out, you're going to have to work this problem out with him yourself."

The woman smiled. "You don't need to treat me like an ingenue, Mr. Davin. . . ."

McKinley had been president when she was an ingenue.

"Wives stray, too," she continued, her voice like sunlight on silk. "I won't be surprised if you come to me with that kind of news. I only want Raymond to be happy."

Sure, I thought. Me too. Then I thought about my bank account. This smelled like divorce, but a couple of hundred dollars would go a long way toward perfuming my outlook on life. We talked terms, and I asked a few more questions.

Somewhere in the middle of this conversation the script got

lost, and bemused, Davin fell back into his own person.

"How long have you been married?"

"Five years."

"What kind of car does your husband drive?"

"He has two. A Hupmobile for business and a Chrysler roadster for his own."

"Do you have a picture of him?"

Cecily Chandler opened her tiny purse and pulled out a two-by-three Kodak. It showed a dark-haired man with a strong chin, lips slightly pursed, penetrating dark eyes. A good-looking man in his thirties—at least fifteen years younger than the woman in Davin's office.

∞   ∞   ∞

Davin sat in his car outside the Leeward bungalow and waited. He had driven off after he'd let Chandler out, cruised around the neighborhood for five minutes, and come back to park down the street, in the dark between two streetlights, where he could watch the door to number seven and not be spotted easily.

It seemed that he spent a great deal of time watching things— people's houses, men at Santa Anita, an orange grove so far out Whittier Boulevard you couldn't smell City Hall, people's cars, waitresses in restaurants, the light fixture over his bed, young men and women in Arroyo Seco Park—and almost as much time making sure he wasn't spotted. That was how you found out things. You watched and waited and sometimes they came to you. Davin wondered what the hell had gotten into him when the Chandler woman walked into his office. He had felt ready to judge Chandler and his wife and anyone else who might drop by as if he were the pope and they were there for the weekend discount on absolutions. He was no smart mouth. He'd always been the type of man who got inconspicuous when the trouble started. Maybe all the watching was getting to him.

It hadn't taken long after Cecily Chandler hired him for Davin to find out about the mistress in number seven. He had followed Chandler after he left work at the Bank of Italy building Friday afternoon. The woman had met him at a restaurant not far away, and they had gone right to her bungalow.

So it was a simple case of infidelity, as he had known the minute the wife had talked about her husband's disappearances. Davin hated the smell of marriages gone bad. He should tell her and let the lawyers sort it out. That was the logical next step. But something kept Davin from writing it off at that. First, Chandler's wife had clearly known he was seeing some other woman before she came to see Davin. She had not hired him for that information.

A Ford with the top down and a couple of sailors in it drove by slowly, and Davin slid lower as the headlights flashed over the front seat of his car. The sailors seemed to be looking for an address. Maybe Chandler's girlfriend—M. Peterson, according to the name on her mailbox—took in boarders.

Second, there was the question of why Chandler had married a woman old enough to be his mother. Money was the usual answer. But South Basin was one of the strongest companies to come out of the Signal Hill strikes, and a vice president had to have a lot of scratch in his own name. He could have married Cecily for love. But there was another possibility: Cecily Chandler had something she could use against her husband, and that was how they had gotten married. And that was why he wasn't faithful, and that led to the third thing that kept Davin from ending his investigation.

Chandler *was* acting as if he wanted to kill himself. Davin had started following him again Saturday morning, had stuck with Chandler as he opened the day with lunch at a cheap restaurant and went home to Cecily in the afternoon. Davin ate a sandwich in his car. He picked up Chandler again as he headed to an airfield with another man of about his age and watched as they went for an airplane ride. Someone in the family had to have money.

Davin had loitered around the hangar until they returned. A kid working on the oil pan of a Pierce-Arrow told him that Chandler and his friend, Philleo, came out to go flying every month or so. When the plane landed the pilot jumped out, cussing Chandler, and stalked toward the office; Philleo was helping Chandler walk and Chandler was laughing. A mechanic asked what was going on, and the pilot told him loudly that Chandler had unbuckled himself when they were doing a series of barrel rolls and stood up in his seat.

Chandler got a bottle of gin out of the backseat of his roadster. Philleo tried to stop him, but soon they'd driven up into the hills to a roadhouse outside the city limits. When Chandler left in his white Chrysler, Davin had followed him down the winding road until he'd run through the fence.

The Ford with the sailors in it passed him going the other way, now. Other than that there was little traffic. Chandler was sure to stay put for the night. Davin thought about getting something to eat. He thought about going to sleep in a real bed. He was stiff from all the time he had spent sitting in his car. The heat made his shirt stick to his back. Worst of all, this line of work got you in the kidneys. He tried to remember why he'd gotten into it.

After the war, joining the Pinkertons had seemed like a good idea, putting down strikers during the Red Scare. L.A. had to keep its good business reputation and Davin had done his part, until one night when he caught a union organizer in a railyard and realized that he liked using a club on an unconscious man. If one of the other cops had not pulled Davin off he would have beaten the man to death. He'd woken up feeling great the next day and only began to tremble when he remembered why he felt so good. It scared him. He didn't want to kill anybody, but after that night he realized that he could do it easily, and enjoy it. So he quit the Pinkertons, but he couldn't quite quit the work. He was his own agent now. He sat and watched and waited for that violence to happen again. In the meantime he stirred up other people's dirt at twenty bucks a day.

Well, he had enough dirt for two days' work. As he was about to start the car, he noticed a flare of light in the rearview mirror as someone lit a cigarette in a parked car on the other side of the street.

Davin got out, crossed the street, and walked down the sidewalk toward the car. A woman sat inside, leaning sideways against the door, smoking. She was watching the apartments where Chandler had met his girlfriend. She glanced at Davin as he approached but made no effort to hide. As he came abreast of the car he pulled out a cigarette and fumbled in his jacket as if searching for a match.

"Say, miss, do you have a light?"

She looked up at him and without a word handed him a book of matches. He lit up.

"Thanks." Her hair looked black in the faint light of the street. It was cut very short; her lips were full and her nose straight.

"Are you waiting for someone?" Davin asked.

"Not you."

Davin took a guess. "Chandler's not going to be out again tonight, you know."

Bull's-eye. The girl looked from the bungalow toward him. She ground out her cigarette. "I don't know what you're talking about."

"Chandler and the Peterson woman are having a party. We

weren't invited. Maybe we ought to get a cup of coffee and figure out why."

The girl reached for the ignition, and Davin put a hand through the window to stop her. She tensed, then relaxed.

"All right," she said. "Get in."

She drove to an all-night diner on Wilshire. In the bright light Davin saw that she was small and very tired. Slender, well-dressed, she did not look like a woman who was used to following married men around. Davin wondered if he looked like the kind of man who was.

"My name is Michael Davin, Miss . . .?"

"Estelle Lloyd." She seemed worried.

"Miss Lloyd. I have some business with Mr. Chandler, and that makes me want to know why you're watching him."

"Cissy hired you."

Davin was surprised. "Who's Cissy?"

"Cissy is his wife. I know she wants to know what he's been doing. He's killing himself."

"What difference should that make to you?"

Estelle looked at him steadily for a few seconds. She was something short of thirty, but she was no kid.

"I love him too," she said.

∞   ∞   ∞

Estelle's father, Warren Lloyd, was a philosophy professor, and her uncle Ralph was a partner of Joseph Dabney, founder of the South Basin Oil Company. She told Davin that when she was just a girl her father and mother had been friends with Julian and Cissy Pascal, and that the two families had helped out a young man from England named Raymond Chandler when he arrived in California before the war.

Estelle had a crush on him from the time she reached her teens, and he in turn treated her like his favorite girl. It was all very romantic, the kind of play where men and women pretended there was no such thing as sex. When Chandler went away to the war, Estelle worried and prayed, and when he came back she had not been the only one to expect a romance to develop. One did: between Chandler and Cissy Pascal, eighteen years his senior.

Cissy filed for divorce. Estelle was confused and hurt, and Chandler would have nothing to do with her. The minute she had become old enough for real love, he had abandoned her.

Chandler's mother did not like Cissy, and so Raymond did not marry her right away. Instead he took an apartment for Cissy at Hermosa Beach and another for his mother in Redondo Beach. Estelle's uncle had helped Chandler get a job in the oil business, and despite the scandal he rose rapidly in the company. Estelle kept her opinions to herself, but although she dated some nice young men, she was never serious. Davin wanted to like her. Looking into her open face, he wasn't sure he could keep himself from doing so.

"So why are you waiting around outside his girlfriend's apartment?"

Estelle looked at him speculatively. "Did Cissy hire you to watch him, or do you just like peeking in bedroom windows?"

He did like her. "Touché. I won't ask any more rude questions."

"I'll tell you anyway. I just don't want to see him hurt himself. I know there's no chance for me anymore—I knew it a long time ago." She hesitated, and when she spoke there was a trace of scorn in her voice. "There's something wrong with Raymond anyway. He's not made Cissy happy, and he would be making me miserable too if I were in her place."

"What do you think the problem is?"

She smiled sadly. "I don't think he likes women. He idealizes them, chases them, gets disgusted because they let themselves be caught—and calls it love."

"Now you sound bitter."

"I'm not, really. He's a good man at heart."

Davin finished his coffee. Everyone was worried about Chandler. "It's late," he said. "It's time for you to take me back."

It was no cooler in the street than it had been in the diner. Davin lit a cigarette while Estelle drove, and when she spoke the strange mood of the last two days was on him again.

Hesitantly, softly, in a voice that promised more warmth than the California night, she said to me, "You don't have to stay there watching all night. I have an apartment at the Bryson."

It was the last thing I expected. Her eyes flitted over me as if she were measuring me for a suit. I could smell her faint perfume.

"No thanks," I said. I felt dizzy with the sweet scent of her. Ten minutes before I had liked her. It was tough enough to keep clean in this town; I'd expected better of this one.

She let me off in the deserted street and drove away. I stood on the sidewalk watching the retreating lights of her car, inhaling deeply the scent of bougainvillea and night-blooming jasmine like overripe dreams, trying to figure out who was pulling Estelle's strings.

A light was on in the Peterson bungalow. The curtains were partly drawn, and the eucalyptus outside the window obscured his view. The night had cooled, and a breeze rustled the trees as it wafted heavy sweet air from the courtyard garden. A few clouds slid north toward the hills where Chandler's roadster lay at the bottom of an embankment; the high full moon turned Leeward Avenue silver and black. Davin wondered at his own prudishness. He had not been propositioned so readily in a long time and had not turned down an offer like that in a longer one. As he reached his car he noticed a Ford with its top down parked in front of him. The sailors had found their address.

Something kept him from leaving. Instead he circled around the back of the bungalows until he reached number seven. The rear windows were unlit. Remembering Estelle's taunt, he crept to the side and peeked in the lighted window. Through the gap in the curtains he could see a woman curled in the corner of a sofa beside a chintzy table lamp. She wore scarlet lounging pajamas. Her hair curled around her cheeks in a blonde bob; her lips were a bright red Cupid's bow, and she was painting her toenails fastidiously in the same color. Davin could not tell if there was anyone else in the room, but the woman did not act like she expected to be interrupted. Sometimes that was the best time to interrupt.

He walked around to the front and rang the bell. The scent of jasmine was even stronger. The door opened a crack, fastened by a chain, and the red lips spoke to him.

"Do you know what time it is? Who are you?"

"My name is Michael Davin. You're awake. I'd like to talk to you."

"We're talking."

"Pardon me. I thought we were playing peekaboo with a door between us."

The red lips smiled. Her eyes—startling blue—didn't.

"All right, Davin. Come in and be a tough guy in the light where I can get a look at you." She unchained the door. That meant Chandler was gone. "Don't get me wrong. I'm not in the habit of letting strange men in to see me in the middle of the night."

"Sure." She led him into the small living room. The pajamas were silk, with the name "May" stitched in gold over her left breast, and had probably cost more than the chair she offered Davin.

He sat on the sofa next to her instead. She ignored him and returned to painting her nails. The room was furnished with cheap imitations of expensive furniture: the curtains that looked like plush velvet the color of dark blood were too readily disturbed by the slight breeze through the window to be the real thing. The Spanish-style carpet was more Tijuana than Barcelona. May Peterson held her chin high to show off a fine profile and the clear white skin of her shoulders, but the blonde hair had once been brown. The figure, however, was genuine.

"You like this color?" she asked him.

"It's very nice."

She looked at him. "You're really here to talk? So talk."

May's boldness attracted him. It was not just brass; she acted as if she knew what she was doing and had nothing to hide. As if she knew exactly who she was at every moment.

"Where's Chandler?" he asked her.

She did not flinch; her eyes were steady on his. "Gone. Sometimes he doesn't stay all night. You should try his wife."

"Maybe I should. Apparently he doesn't anymore."

"That's not my fault."

"Didn't say it was. But I bet you make it easier for him to forget where he lives."

May dipped the brush in the polish and finished off a perfect baby toe.

"You don't know Ray very well if you think I had to seduce him. Sure, he likes to think it was out of his control—lotsa men do. But before me he was all over half the girls in the office."

"You work in his office?"

"Six months in accounting. He hired me himself. Maybe he didn't think he hired me because I got a nice figure, but I knew pretty quick that was in the back of his mind." She smiled. "Pretty soon it was in front."

If May was worried about what Davin was after, who he was or why he was asking questions, she did not show it. That didn't make sense. Maybe she was setting him up for some fall, or maybe he was in detectives' paradise, where all the questions had answers and all the women wanted to go to bed.

May removed the cotton balls from between her toes and closed the bottle of polish. "There," she said, leaning toward me. "Doesn't that look fine?"

Beneath the smell of the nail polish I smelled her musky perfume. It seemed to be my night for propositions; I felt unclean. I needed to plunge into cold salt water to peel away the smell of my own flesh and hers. The world revolves by people rutting away like apes in the zoo, but I had enough self-respect to keep away from the cage. As much as I wanted to sometimes, I couldn't let myself be drawn down into the mire; I had to keep free because I had a job to do.

Wait a minute, Davin thought. Even if May knew he was a detective, she had to realize that bedding him wouldn't protect Chandler. So why be a monk? Cold salt water? Rutting in the zoo?

I didn't move an eyelash. The pajamas fit her like rainwater. Lloyd's of London probably carried the insurance on her perfect breasts. The nipples were beautifully erect. I stood up.

"All right, May, pack it up for the night; I'm not in the market. Tell your friend Raymond that he's going to find himself in trouble if he keeps playing hookey. And you can bring your sailor pals back into the slip as soon as I leave."

"Sailor pals? What are you talking about?"

"Don't forget your manners, now. You're the hostess."

She looked at me as if I'd turned to white marble by an Italian master. Davin, rampant.

"Look, I'm not stupid," she said. "I figure you must be working for his wife. Big deal."

I looked down into her very blue eyes: maybe she was just a girl who worked in an office after all, one who got involved with the boss and didn't want any trouble. Maybe she was okay. But a voice whispered to me to see her the way she was—that a woman who looked like May, who said the things she said, was a whore.

"Sure, you're not stupid, May. But some people take marriage seriously. Good night."

She stayed on the sofa, watching him; as soon as he closed the door behind him, he felt lost. He had just exited on some line about the sanctity of marriage. He'd pulled away from her as if she had leprosy, as if she had tempted him to jump off a cliff. He wasn't a kid, and this wasn't some Boy Scout story. He was talking like a smart aleck and acting like an undergraduate at a Baptist college.

He fumbled in his pocket for his cigarettes. The moon was gone, and morning would not be long in coming. For all that, the city was still as hot as May's red nail polish; the heat wave would not let up.

He started up the walk toward the street, and a blow like someone dropping a cinder block on the back of his head knocked him
senseless.

∞   ∞   ∞

The jasmine smelled good, but lying under a bush in a flower bed
dimmed your appreciation. Davin rolled over and looked for the
back of his skull. It was not in plain sight. He got to his knees, then
stood. He didn't know how long he'd been out. It was still dark, but
the eastern sky was smoked glass turning to mother-of-pearl. The
door to May Peterson's bungalow was ajar, and her light was still
on. Head throbbing, Davin pushed the door open and stepped in.

The lounging pajamas were torn open, and she lay on the floor
with one leg partway under the sofa and the other twisted awkwardly at the knee. Her neck had not gone purple from the bruises
yet. All in all, she had died without putting up much of a struggle.
The shade of the table lamp was awry, but the bottle of nail polish
was just where she'd left it. Someone had taken the trouble to pull
the phony curtains completely closed.

Davin knelt over her and brushed her hair back from her forehead. Her hair was soft and thick and still fragrant. A deep cut on
her scalp left the back of her head dark and wet with blood. The
very blue eyes were open and staring as if she were trying to com-
prehend what had happened to her.

Davin shuddered. Light was beginning to seep in through the
curtains. The small kitchen was in immaculate order, the two-
burner gas stove spotless in the dim morning light. In the back
room the bedclothes of a large bed were disordered, and a cut-glass
decanter of scotch stood on the dressing table with its stopper and
two glasses beside it. Davin felt a hundred years old. He rubbed the
swelling at the back of his head where he'd been slugged—the pain
shot through his temples—and left May Peterson's apartment.

At the diner where he and Estelle had coffee he found a pay
phone. He fumbled to find the number in his wallet—whoever had
hit him hadn't bothered to rob him—and dialed the Chandler
home. A sleepy woman answered the phone.

"Mrs. Chandler?"

"Yes?"

"This is Michael Davin. Is your husband at home?"

A pause. He could see her debating whether to try to save her
pride. "No," she said. "I haven't seen him since he went out with
Milton Philleo yesterday afternoon."

"Okay. Listen to me carefully. Your husband is in serious trouble, and he needs your help. The police are going to try to connect him with a murder. I don't think he had anything to do with it. Tell them the truth about him, but don't tell them about me."

"Have you found out what Raymond has been involved in?"

Davin hesitated.

"Mr. Davin—I'm paying you for information. Don't leave me in the dark." The voice that had been so thrillingly sexy two days before was that of a worried old woman.

The light in the telephone booth seemed cruelly harsh; the air in the cramped space smelled of stale cigarette smoke. Behind the counter of the diner a waitress in white was refilling a stainless-steel coffee urn.

"The less you know right now the easier it will go when the police call you," Davin said. There was no immediate answer. He felt sorry for her, and he thought about that hurt look in Estelle's eyes. "It's pretty much what I told you I suspected in my office."

"Oh."

Davin shook his head to dispel his weariness. "There's one more thing. Do you know of anyone who has it in for your husband? Anyone who'd like to see him in trouble?"

"John Abrams." She sounded certain.

"Who is he?"

"He works for South Basin, in the Signal Hill field. He and Raymond have never gotten along. He resents Raymond's ability."

"Do you know where he lives?"

"In Santa Monica. If you'll wait a minute I can see whether Raymond has his address in his book."

"Don't bother. Remember now—when the police call, say nothing about me. Your husband is not involved in this."

Davin hung up and opened the door of the booth, but did not get up immediately. It was full day outside; the waitress was drawing coffee for herself and the dayside short-order cook. Davin wanted some. He decided against it but made himself eat two eggs over easy, with toast, then headed home for a couple of hours sleep. He wished he were as certain that Chandler hadn't killed May as he'd told Cissy.

∞   ∞   ∞

The sun shining in his eyes woke Davin the next day; the sun never came in through his bedroom window that early. The sheets, sticky with sweat, were twisted around his legs. The air was stifling and his mouth felt like a dustpan. He fumbled for the clock on the bedside table and saw it was already one-thirty. The phone rang.

"Is this Mr. Michael Davin?"

"What is it, Mrs. Chandler?"

"The police just left here a few minutes ago. I have to thank you for warning me. They told me about May Peterson."

She stopped as if she were waiting for some response. He was still half-asleep, and the back of his head was suing for divorce. After a moment she went on.

"I didn't tell them anything, as you suggested, but in the course of their questions they told me the neighbor who found Miss Peterson's body saw a man leave her apartment in the early morning. Was it Raymond? Do you know?"

"It was me," Davin said wearily. "Have you heard anything from him?"

"No."

"Then why don't you let me do the investigating, Cissy—Mrs. Chandler."

There was an offended silence, then the phone clicked. Davin let the dial tone mock him for a moment before he hung up. He ought not to have been so blunt, but what did the woman expect? He wondered if Cissy had had any doubts before divorcing Pascal for Chandler. Pascal was a concert cellist, Estelle told him. Older than Cissy. She had married for love that time. Davin imagined her a woman who had always been beautiful, bright, the center of attention. He supposed it was hard for such a woman to grow old: she would become reclusive, self-doubting, alternating between attempts to be youthful and knowledge that she wasn't anymore. He wondered what Chandler thought about her.

The speculations tasted worse than his cotton mouth. Men and women—over and over again Davin's job rubbed his nose in cases of them fouling each other up. Maybe beating up union men for a living was cleaner work, after all. He pulled himself out of bed and into the bathroom. He felt hung over but without the compensation of having been drunk the night before.

A shower helped and a shave made him look almost alert. Measuring his square jaw and pug nose in the mirror, he tried to imagine what had gotten those women so hot last night. What had moved May to let him into her apartment so easily? Maybe that had only been a pleasant fantasy; fantasies sometimes were called upon to serve for a sex life, as both Cissy Chandler and Davin knew. His revulsion toward both May and Estelle had been a less pleasant fantasy.

The memory of May Peterson's dead, bemused stare—that was neither pleasant nor fantasy.

While he dressed he turned on the radio and heard a report about the brutal murder that had taken place on Leeward Avenue the previous night. The weather forecast was for a high of one hundred that afternoon. Davin pawed through the drawer in the table beside his bed until he found a black notebook and his Harold Lloyd glasses. He sat down and called the Santa Monica operator. There was a John Abrams on Harvard Street.

It was a white frame house that might have been shipped in from Des Moines. The wide porch was shaded by a slanting roof. Carefully tended poinsettias fronted the porch, and a lawn only slightly better kept than the Wilshire Country Club sloped down to a sidewalk so white that the reflected sunlight hurt Davin's eyes. The leaded glass window in the front door was cut in a large oval with prisms in the corners. Davin pressed the button and heard a bell ring inside.

The man who came to the door was large; his face was broad, with the high cheekbones and big nose of an Indian. He wore khaki pants with suspenders and a good dress shirt, collarless, the top buttons undone.

"Are you Mr. John Abrams? You work for the Dabney Oil Syndicate?"

The blunt face stayed blunt. "Yes."

Davin held out his hand. "My name is Albert Parker, Mr. Abrams. I'm with Mutual Assurance of Hartford. We're running an investigation on another employee of South Basin and would like to ask you a few questions. Anything you say will be held strictly confidential, of course."

"Who are you investigating?"

"A Mr. Raymond Chandler."

Abrams's eyebrows flicked a fraction of an inch. "Come in," he said. He led Davin into the living room. They sat down, Davin got out his notebook, and Abrams looked him over—the kind of look that was supposed to make employees stiffen and try to look dependable.

Abrams leaned forward. "Is this about any litigation he's started lately? I wouldn't want to talk about anything that's in court."

"No. This is entirely a matter between Mutual and Mr. Chandler. We are seeking information about his character. In your opinion, is Mr. Chandler a reliable man?"

"I don't consider him reliable," Abrams said, watching for Davin's reaction. Davin gave him nothing. "We've got a hundred wells out on Signal Hill, and I'm the field manager," Abrams continued. "I like working for Mr. Dabney. He's a good man." He paused, and the silence stretched.

"Look, I don't know who told you to talk to me, but I'll tell you right now I don't like Chandler. He's a martinet and a hypocrite; he'll flatter Mr. Dabney on Tuesday morning and cuss him out for not backing one of his lawsuits on Tuesday afternoon. He runs that office like his little harem. If you'd watch him for a week you'd know."

"Yes."

Abrams got up and began pacing. "I've got no stomach for talking about a man behind his back," he said. "But Chandler is hurting the company and Mr. Dabney. He's dragged us into lawsuits just to prove how tough he is; he had us in court last year on a personal injury suit that the insurance company was ready to settle on, and then after he won—he did win—he turned around and canceled the policy. That soured a lot of people on South Basin Oil.

"The only reason he was hired was because he had an in with Ralph Lloyd. He started in accounting. So he sucks up to Bartlett, the auditor, and gets the reputation for being some kind of fair-haired college boy. A year later Bartlett gets arrested for embezzling thirty thousand dollars. Tried and convicted.

"Now it gets real interesting. Instead of promoting Chandler, Dabney goes out and hires a man named John Ballantine from a private accounting firm. This suits Chandler just fine because Ballantine's from Scotland and Chandler impresses the hell out of him with his British upper-crust manners. Ballantine makes Chandler his assistant. A year later Ballantine drops dead in the office. Chandler helps the coroner, and the coroner decides it was a heart attack. Mr. Dabney gives up and makes Chandler the new auditor, and within another year he's office manager and vice president. Very neat, huh?"

Abrams had worked himself into a lather. Davin could have let him run on with just a few more neutral questions, but instead, as if someone else had taken over and was using his body like a ventriloquist's dummy, he said,

"You really hate him, don't you?"

Abrams froze. After a moment his big shoulders relaxed and his voice was back under control. "You've got to admit the story smells like a day-old mackerel."

"To hear you tell it."

"You don't have to believe me. Ask anyone on Olive Street. Check it with the coroner or the cops."

"If the cops thought there was anything to it, I wouldn't have to check with them. Chandler would be spending his weekends in the exercise yard instead of with those girls you tell me about."

Abrams's brow furrowed. He looked like a theologian trying to fathom Aimee Semple McPherson. "Cops aren't always too smart," he said.

"A startling revelation." I was getting to like Abrams. He reduced the moral complexities of this case. He reminded me of a hand grenade ready to explode, and I was going to throw my body at him to save Raymond Chandler. "Mostly they aren't smart when somebody pays them not to be," I said. "Does the vice president of an oil company have that kind of money?"

"Don't overestimate a cop's integrity."

"Who, me? I'm just an insurance investigator. You're the one who knows what it costs to bribe cops."

The big shoulders were getting tense again, but the voice was under control. "Look, I didn't start this talk about bribes. You asked me my opinion. I gave it. Let's leave it at that."

He was right; I should have left it at that. Instead I pushed on like a fighter who knows the fix is in and it's only a matter of time before the other guy takes a dive.

"So Chandler killed Ballantine?" I said. "What about May Peterson?"

"Peterson? Never heard of her. What kind of insurance man are you, anyway?"

"I'm investigating an accident. Maybe you were out a little late last night?"

Abrams took a step toward me. "Let's see your credentials, pal."

I got up. "You wouldn't hit a man with glasses on, Abrams. Let me turn my back."

"Get the hell out of here."

A woman wearing a gardening apron and gloves came into the room. The house, which had seemed so cool when I had entered, *felt like an inferno. I slid the notebook into my pocket and left. The porch swing hung steady as a candle flame in a tomb; the sun on the sidewalk woke my headache. Abrams stood in the doorway watching as I walked down to the car. When I reached it he went back inside.*

Davin shuddered, loosened his tie, leaned against the car. He squinted and focused on the street to keep the fear down: he was a sick man. He'd totally lost control of himself in Abrams's house. He wondered if that was what it felt like to go crazy—to do and say things as if you were watching yourself in a movie. He lifted his hand, looked at the backs of his knuckles. He touched his thumb to each of his fingertips. His hand did exactly what he told it to. He seemed able to do whatever he wanted; he could call Cissy Chandler and tell her to sweat out her marriage by herself. He could drive home and sleep for twelve hours and wake up alone and free. What was to stop him?

Davin was about to get into the car when he noticed a piece of wire lying on the pavement below his running board. The freshly clipped end glinted in the sunlight. He bent over and tried to pick it up: it was attached to something beneath the car. Getting down on one knee, he saw the trailing wires where someone had cut each of his brake cables.

∞   ∞   ∞

He rode the interurban east on Santa Monica Boulevard. Along the way he enjoyed what little breeze the streetcar's passage gave to the hot syrupy air. He got off at Cahuenga and walked north toward his office on Ivar and Hollywood Boulevard, trying to piece together what had happened.

Abrams could have told his wife to take her pruning shears and cut the cables as soon as he recognized Davin on the porch. Abrams would have recognized him only if he was the one who had slugged Davin and gone on to murder May Peterson. He might have done it out of some misplaced desire to get back at Chandler.

But there was a problem with this theory. Why would Abrams proceed to slander Chandler so badly? It would look better if he hid any hostility.

When Davin considered the picture of a middle-aged woman in gardening gloves crawling under a car on a residential street in broad daylight to cut brake cables, the whole cardhouse collapsed. It couldn't be done, and not only that—Abrams simply had no reason to try such a stupid thing.

Then there was the question of why Davin had been slugged in the first place. Something about that had bothered him all day, and now he knew what it was: whoever killed May had no reason to knock out Davin. Davin had been on his way out, and sapping him only meant he would be around to find her dead. It didn't make any sense.

Near the corner of Cahuenga and the boulevard he spotted a penny lying on the sidewalk. The bright copper shone in the late afternoon sun like a chip of heaven dropped at his feet. Normally he would have stopped to pick it up; one of the habits bred of a boyhood spent in a small town where a penny meant your pick of the best candies on display in Sudlow's Dry Goods. Instead he crossed the street.

But his mind, bemused by the puzzles of the cut brake cables and the senseless blow on the head, got stuck on this new mystery. If he'd paused to pick up the penny, he would have been a little later getting to the office. The whole sequence of events afterward would be subtly different; it was as if stopping or not stopping marked a fork in the chain of happenings that made his life.

The strange frame of mind refused to leave him. Normally he would have stopped, so by not stopping he had set himself down a track of possibilities he would not normally have followed. Why hadn't he stopped? What had pushed him down this particular path? The incident expanded frighteningly in his mind until it swept away all other thoughts. Something had hold of him. It was just like the conversation with Abrams where he'd gone for the jugular —something was changing every decision he made, no matter how minor. With a conviction that chilled him on this hottest of days, he knew that he was being manipulated and that there was nothing he could do about it. He wondered how long it had been happening without his knowing it. He should have picked up that penny.

After a moment the conviction went away. He was tired and he needed a drink. He could talk himself into all kinds of doubts if he let himself. He ought to take a good punch at the next passerby just to prove he could do whatever he wanted.

He didn't punch anybody.

Davin took the elevator up seven floors to his office. Quintanella and Sanderson from homicide were in the waiting room.

"You don't keep your door locked," Sanderson said.

"I can't afford to turn away business."

Sanderson mashed his cigarette out in the standing ashtray and got up from the sofa. "Let's have a talk," he said.

Davin led them into the inner room. "What brings you two out to see me on a Sunday?"

"A dead woman," Quintanella said. His face, pocked with acne scars, was stiff as a pine board.

Davin lit a cigarette, shook out the wooden match, broke it in half, and dropped the pieces into an ashtray. They pinged as they hit the glass. The afternoon sun was shooting into the room at the same angle it had taken when Cissy Chandler had come into his office.

I'd had about enough of them already.

"That's too bad," I said. "It's a rough business you're in. You going to try to solve this one?"

Sanderson belched. "We are," he said. "And you're gonna help us. You're gonna start by telling us where Raymond Chandler is."

"Don't know the man. Sure you've got the right Davin? There's a couple in the book."

"Will you tell this guy to cut the crap, Dutch?" Quintanella said to Sanderson. "He makes me sick."

"I didn't think they ran to delicate stomachs down at homicide," I said. "You have to swallow so many lies and keep your mouth shut."

"Tell him to shut up, Dutch."

"Calm down, Davin," Sanderson said.

"You tell me to talk, he tells me to shut up. Every time you guys get a burr in your paws, you make guys like me pull it out for you."

"We can do this downtown," Sanderson said. "It's a lot hotter there."

"You got a subpoena in that ugly suit?" The words were rolling out now, and I was riding them. "If you don't, save the back room and the hose for some poor greaser. You want any answers from me, you've got to tell me what's going on. I'm not going to get bruised telling you things you've got no business knowing."

Quintanella mopped his brow. "C'mon, Dutch, let's take him in."

"Shut up, Tony." Sanderson looked pained. "Don't try to kid us, Davin. We got a call from Mrs. Chandler this afternoon telling us she hired you last week. She said you knew about the murder of this tramp last night."

Tramp. The word momentarily shook Davin out of it. That was what Cissy would say, and guys like Sanderson would figure that was the only kind of woman who got murdered.

"Cissy Chandler's not the most reliable source," Davin said.

"That's why we came to you. The neighbor lady at the Rosinante Apartments said she saw a man hanging around there last night. You fit the description. So why don't you tell us what's going on. Or should we let Tony take care of it?"

Davin watched them watch him. Quintanella was on the sofa near the door, flexing his hands. This case was getting beyond Davin fast. He had no reason to protect Chandler when for all he knew the man had killed May.

"Jesus," Davin said. "You're crazy if you think I need this kind of heat. I'm not in this business to draw fire. I'll talk." He loosened his collar. "Will you let me get a drink out of the desk? No guns, just a little gin."

Sanderson came over behind the desk; Quintanella tensed. "You let me get it," Sanderson said. "Which drawer?"

"Bottom right."

Do it. Do it now. Davin felt what was coming and tried to resist, but it was like his blood talking to him, like the night in the freight yard with the club in his hand. Like walking past the penny.

When Sanderson opened the drawer and reached for the bottle, I punched him in the side of the throat. He fell back, hitting the corner of the desk, and Quintanella, fumbling for his gun, leapt toward me. I slipped around the other side of the desk and out the door before the big man could get the heater out. I was down the stairs and out the rear exit before they hit the lobby; I zigzagged half a block between the buildings that backed the alley, crossed the street, and slipped into the service entrance of an apartment building on the opposite side of Ivar. I had just thrown away my investigator's license. I caught my breath and wondered what the hell I was going to do next.

∞   ∞   ∞

Davin called Estelle from the lobby of the Bryson, and she told him to come up. Although it was only early evening, she was in her robe. Her dark hair shone; her face was calm, with a trace of insouciance. She looked like Louise Brooks.

"I've got some trouble," Davin said. "Can I stay here for a while?"

"Yes."

She offered him coffee. They sat facing each other in the small living room. The two windows that fronted the street were open, and a hot, humid wind waved the curtains like a tired maid shaking out bedsheets. The air smelled of coming rain. Maybe the heat wave would be broken. Davin told her about his talk with Abrams.

"You don't believe those things he said." There was an urgency in Estelle's voice that Davin supposed came from her love for Chandler. He realized that he didn't want her to care about Chandler.

"Did they happen?"

"Bartlett was convicted of embezzling. Ballantine died of a heart attack. Raymond had nothing to do with either of those things."

"He was just lucky."

Estelle exhaled cigarette smoke sharply. "I wouldn't use that word."

"I'm not trying to be sarcastic," Davin said. He hadn't had to try at all lately. "But you have to admit that it all has worked out nicely for him. He meets the right people, makes the right impression, and events break just the way you'd expect them to break if he was in the business of planning embezzlements and heart attacks. I can't blame a guy like Abrams for taking it the wrong way."

"Things don't always work out for Raymond. I know him better than you do. Look at his marriage."

"Okay, let's. Why did he marry her?"

Her brow knit. "He loves her, I guess."

"Why did he wait until his mother died?"

"She didn't approve."

"I'm not surprised. Age difference. But he was pretty old to still be listening to Mom."

Estelle took a last pull on her cigarette, then snuffed it out. Her dark eyes watched him. "I don't know. I don't know if I care anymore."

Davin wanted not to care about the whole case. But he had been hired to watch a man and he had lost that man. In the process a woman had been killed, and he couldn't bring himself to think she deserved it. *It was a matter of professional ethics.*

Ethics? Jesus. He wasn't some white knight on a horse. The idea of ethics in his business was ludicrous; it made him mad that such an idea had worked its way into his head. Only a schoolboy would expect ethics from a private eye. Only a schoolboy would avoid May Peterson because she had slept with Chandler. Only a schoolboy would have turned Estelle down the previous night.

"I was surprised you asked me here last night," he said.

"That sounds sarcastic, too."

"Not necessarily."

The wind had strengthened, and it was blissfully cool. With a sound of distant thunder, the rain started. Estelle got up to close the windows. She drew her robe tighter about her as she stood in the breeze; Davin watched her slender shoulders and hips as she pulled the windows shut. When she came back she folded her legs up under her on the sofa. The line of her neck and shoulders against the darkness of the next room was as pure as the sweep of a child's sparkler through a Fourth of July night. She spoke somberly.

"I used to be a good girl. Being in love with a married man made me think that over. I'm not a good or bad girl anymore; I'm not any kind of girl." She paused. "You don't look to me like you're really the kind of man you're supposed to be."

Davin felt free of compulsion for the first time in the last three days.

"I'm not," he said. "I feel like I've been playing some kind of game—or dreaming someone else's dream. I feel like I'm just waking."

Estelle watched him.

"I'd like to stay with you tonight," Davin said.

She smiled. "Not a very romantic pickup line. Raymond would do it funnier, or more poetic."

"He would?"

"Certainly. He's very poetic. He even wrote poetry—still does, as far as I know. You don't know that?"

"I haven't been on this case very long. Is it any good?"

"When I was nineteen I loved it. Now I think it'd be too sentimental for me."

"That's too bad."

Estelle came to Davin, sat on the arm of his chair, kissed him. She pulled away, a little out of breath.

"No, it isn't," she said.

∞   ∞   ∞

All during their lovemaking he felt something trying to make him pull away, like a voice whispering over and over, *get up and leave. Go now. She will push you, absorb you. Doesn't she smell bad? She's an animal.*

It wasn't conscience. It was something outside him, alien, the same thing that had pulled him away from May Peterson. But

Davin had finally picked up that penny, and he felt better, as he lay on the border of sleep, than he had in as long as he could remember. Being with Estelle was the first really good thing that he had done on his own since Friday afternoon. He felt that they were breaking a pattern merely by lying together, tired, limbs entwined. Estelle's breathing was regular, and Davin, listening to the rain, fell asleep.

Davin dreamt there had been a shipwreck and that he and the other passengers were floundering among the debris, trying to keep afloat. There was no sound. He knew the others in the water: Estelle was there, and Cissy, and Abrams and May Peterson and some others he could not make out—and Chandler. Chandler could not swim, and he clutched at them, one after the other, as if they were pieces of wreckage that he could climb up on in order to keep afloat. They might have made it themselves, but they were all being shoved beneath the waves by the desperate man, and they would drown trying to save him. But Chandler never would drown, and would never understand the people dying around him. He could not even see them. He fumbled for Davin's head, his fingers in Davin's eyes, and Davin found he did not have the strength to shove him away. Davin coughed and sputtered and struggled toward the surface. Fighting against him in the salt sea, Davin saw that for Chandler, he was little more than a broken spar, an inanimate thing to be used without compunction because it was never alive. Drowning, Davin saw that Chandler had forced him under without even realizing what he had done.

He woke. It was still dark. Estelle still slept; some noise from the other room had stirred him. The rain had stopped, and streetlights threw a pale wedge of light against the ceiling. Through the doorway, Davin saw something move. Two men slipped quietly into the room.

In the faint light Davin saw that they wore sailors' uniforms and that the smaller of the two had a sap in his hand. Davin snatched the bedside clock and threw it at him.

The man ducked and it glanced off his shoulder. Davin leapt out of the bed, dragging the bedclothes after him. He heard Estelle gasp behind him as he hit the smaller sailor full in the chest. They slammed into the wall, and the man hit his head against the doorjamb. He slumped to the floor. Davin struggled to his feet, still tangled in the sheets, and turned to see that the big man had Estelle by the arm, a hand the size of a baseball mitt smothering her cries. He dragged her out of bed.

"Quiet now, buddy," the big sailor said in a soft voice. "Else I wring the little girl's neck."

The man on the floor moaned.

"What's the deal?" Davin asked. Estelle's frightened eyes glinted in the dark.

"No deal. We just got some business to take care of."

Davin stood there naked, helpless. He was no Houdini. All he had to keep them alive was words.

"You killed May Peterson," he said. "Why?"

"We had to. To get at that bastard Chandler. He makes a good impression. We wanna see what kind of impression he makes on the cops."

Davin shifted his feet and stepped on something hard. The sap.

"What have you got against him?"

The big man seemed content to stand there all night with his arm around Estelle. He gasped, almost a chuckle. "Personal injury is what. Ten thousand bucks he cheated us outta. We hadda accident with one of his oil trucks. We had it as good as won until he made 'em go to court."

The man at Davin's feet rolled over, started to get up. "Be quiet, Lou," he said.

"What difference's it make," the big sailor said. "They're dead already."

"Be quiet and let's do it. There's other people in this place."

Davin's thoughts raced. "It makes no sense to kill us. I'm no friend of Chandler's. I've been tailing him."

"You was there last night," the small sailor said, poking around the floor in the dark for the sap. "That's good enough. We've got to get rid of you."

"Who says?"

Neither one answered.

"What the hell are you looking for?" Davin asked.

"You'll know soon enough," the short one said.

"Damn, you guys are stupid. This doesn't make any sense. How do you expect to get away with this?"

Big Lou jerked back on his arm and Estelle struggled. "It was you two that got caught in the bed together, right? Like a coupla animals? You don't deserve to live." He spoke with wounded innocence, as if he had explained everything. As if, Davin realized, he was hearing the same voice that had whispered to him. Davin trembled, furious, holding himself back, feeling himself ready to fight and afraid of what might happen if he did. Don't move, he thought.

Move.

The runt was still obsessed with finding his weapon, shuffling through the sheets on the floor, picking up Estelle's discarded camisole with two fingers as if it were a dead carp.

"Let me help," I said; I snatched the sap from beneath my foot and laid him out with a blow across the temple. He hit the floor like the loser in a prelim. At the same time I heard Lou yell. Estelle had bitten his hand. Lou threw her aside, shook the pain away, and catlike, quickly for such a big man, moved toward me.

Lou wasn't too big. Tunney could have taken him in twelve. I tried to dance out of his way, but he cut me off and worked me toward the corner of the room. I swung the sap at his head; Lou caught the blow on his forearm, and I tried to knee him in the groin. He danced back a half-step. I stumbled forward. As I tried to get up I got hit in the ear with a fist that felt like a bowling ball. Just to show there were no hard feelings, Lou kicked me in the ribs.

"Stop!" Estelle yelled. "I've got a gun."

Lou turned slowly. Estelle was kneeling on the bed, shaking. She had a small automatic pointed at him.

Lou charged her. Two shots, painfully loud in the small room, sounded before he got there. He knocked the gun away, grabbed Estelle's head in one hand, and smashed it against the brass bedstead once, twice, and she was still. I was on him by then. Oh, yes, I was real quick. Lou shook me off his back and onto the floor, grunting now with the effort and the realization that he was shot.

He shook his head as if dazed and stumbled toward me again. When he hit me, I stood and heaved him over my shoulder. There was a crash and a rush of air into the room: Lou had gone through the window. Six stories to the street.

Davin shuddered with rage—not at what Lou had done, but at himself. The other sailor was still out. Estelle lay half off the bed, her head hanging, mouth open. Her straight, short hair brushed the floor. Davin lifted her onto the bed. He listened for her heartbeat and heard nothing. He touched her throat and felt no pulse. He lay his cheek against her lips and felt no wisp of breath.

A great anger, an anger close to despair, built in him. He knew who had killed Estelle, and why, and it was not the sailors.

No one had yet responded to the shots or the dead man in the street. Davin pulled on his clothes and left.

∞　∞　∞

Davin didn't know how much time he would have. He burned with rage and impatience—and fear. He shouldn't have moved. He was not a hero. Somebody had made him. Somebody had made him walk by that penny on the sidewalk, too, and as damp night gave way to dawn his confusion gave way to cold certainty: Chandler was his man. And, Davin realized, laughing aloud, he was Chandler's.

He took the streetcar downtown, past the construction site of the new civic center. He got off at Seventh and Hill and walked a block to South Olive. He was hungry but would not eat; he wondered if it was Chandler who decided whether he should become hungry. He watched the office workers come in for the beginning of the new week and wondered who was trapped in Chandler's web and who wasn't. In the men's room of the Bank of Italy building he washed the crusted trickle of blood from his ear, combed his hair, straightened his clothes.

Nothing that had happened in the last three days had made sense. Cissy hiring Davin, Chandler running off the road, Davin getting knocked out at May's apartment, the sailors killing May and then Estelle, the cutting of Davin's brake cables, Sanderson and Quintanella letting him get away so easily—and the crazy way things fit together, coincidence straight out of a bad novel. All of these things ought not to have happened in any sensible world. The only way they could have was if he were being pulled from his own life into a nightmare. Chandler's nightmare.

Somehow, probably without his even knowing it, whatever Chandler wanted to happen, happened. Lives got jerked into new patterns, and a gin-soaked businessman's fantasies came true. Maybe it went back to Bartlett's embezzlement and Ballantine's heart attack; maybe it went back to Chandler's childhood. Whatever, the things that had been happening to Cissy and May and Estelle and even Big Lou and his partner—even the things Davin could not imagine any man consciously wanting to come true—were all what Chandler wanted to happen. Estelle was dead. There was no place in Chandler's world for women who liked sex and weren't afraid to go out and get it. There was no place in Chandler's world for the ordinary kind of private detective Davin was. He had to find Chandler before the next disaster occurred.

He waited until he saw Philleo show up for work at South Basin Oil and followed him up to the fourth floor. Most of the staff was there already and talking about May Peterson. They stared at Davin as if he were an apparition—he felt like one—and Philleo turned to face him.

"May I help you?"

"Let's talk in your office, Mr. Philleo."

The man motioned toward the corner room. They shut the door. Davin refused to sit down.

"Where's Raymond Chandler?" he asked.

"I talked to the police yesterday. You're no policeman."

"That's right. Where is he?"

"I have no idea," Philleo said. "And I'm not going—"

The phone rang. Philleo looked irritated, then picked it up. "Yes?" he said. There was a silence, and Philleo looked as if he had swallowed a stone. "Put him on."

Davin smiled grimly: yet another improbable coincidence. He had known the moment the phone rang who was calling. Philleo listened; he looked distressed. After a moment Davin took the receiver from his unresisting hand.

The man on the phone spoke in a voice choked with emotion and slurred by alcohol, with a trace of a British accent.

"—swear to God I'll do it this time, Milt, I can't bear to think what a rat I am and what I'm doing to Cissy—"

"Where are you?" Davin said softly.

"Milt?"

"This isn't Milt. This is Michael Davin. I'm the man who helped you the other night when you ran off the road. Where are you?"

There was a pause, and Chandler's voice came back, more sober. "I want to talk to Milt."

"He doesn't want to talk to you anymore, Raymond. He's sick of you. He wants me to help you out instead."

Another silence.

"Well, you can tell that bastard that I'm in the Mayfair Hotel and if he wants to help me he can identify my body when they pull it off the sidewalk because I'm going to do it this time."

"No you won't. I'll be there in ten minutes." Davin gave the phone back to Philleo, who looked ashen. "He says he's going to kill himself."

"He's threatened before. I could tell you stories—"

"Just talk to him."

Davin ignored the elevator and ran down to the lobby, flagged a cab that took him speeding down Seventh Street. He didn't know what he was going to do when he got there, but he knew he had to reach Chandler. The ride seemed maddeningly slow. He peered out the window at the buildings and pedestrians, the sunlight flashing on storefronts and streetcars, searching for a sign that something had changed. Nothing happened. When Chandler died, would any of them who were controlled by him feel the difference? Would Davin collapse in the backseat of the taxi like a discarded puppet, leaving the driver with a ticking meter and a comatose man to pay the fare? Or would Chandler's death instead set Davin free? If Davin could only be sure of that, he would kill Chandler himself.

Maybe he would kill him anyway. He needed to stay mad to keep from thinking about whether he could have saved Estelle. If Davin had walked out of her apartment instead of asking to stay, if she had kicked him out, then she would probably still be alive. She'd be a good girl, and he'd be a strong man. If May had slammed the door in his face—

They reached the Mayfair, and Davin threw a couple of dollars at the driver. The desk clerk had a Mr. Chandler in room 712.

The door was not locked. The room stank of tobacco smoke and sweat and booze. Chandler had to have his own private bootlegger to stay drunk so consistently. The man was sitting in the opened window wearing rumpled trousers, shoes without socks, and a sleeveless T-shirt. An almost-empty bottle stood on the sill in the crook of his knee. The phone lay on its side on the bedside table with the receiver dangling and a voice sounding tinnily from it. A book was opened facedown on the bed, which looked as if it hadn't been made up in a couple of days. Beside the book lay a pulp magazine. *Black Mask*. Above a lurid picture of a man pointing a gun at another man, who held a blonde in front of him as a shield, was the slogan, "Smashing Detective Stories."

Chandler did not notice him enter. Davin crossed to the phone, stood it up, and quietly hung up the receiver. The silencing of the voice seemed to rouse Chandler. He lifted his head.

"Who are you?"

Davin's weariness suddenly caught up with him, and he sat down on the edge of the bed. Even up to that moment he had felt some sympathy for Chandler, but seeing the man, and remembering Estelle's startled dead face, he now knew only disgust. Everyone who loved this man defended him, and he remained oblivious to it all, self-pitying and innocent when he ought to feel guilty.

"You're the guy—" Chandler started.

"I'm the guy who pulled you out of the wreck. I'm the private eye hired by Cissy to keep you from hurting yourself. She didn't say anything about keeping you from hurting anyone else, and I was too stupid to catch on. Before Friday I had a life of my own, but now I'm the man you want me to be. I get beat up for twenty bucks a day and say please and thank-you. I'm a regular guy and a strange one. I talk sex with the ladies and never follow through. I crack wise to the cops. I'm the best man in your world and good enough for any world. I go down these mean streets and don't get tarnished, and I'm not afraid. I'm the hero."

"What are you talking about?"

"You're mystified, huh? Before Friday I could touch a woman and not have to worry about her getting killed for it. Now I'm busy taking care of a sleazy momma's boy."

Chandler pointed a shaking finger at him. "Don't you mock me," he said. "I know what I've done. I know—"

Davin was raging inside. "What have you done?" he said grimly. "You sound like you've got a big conscience. So tell me."

Chandler's weeping had turned into anger. "I've betrayed my wife. I'm not surprised she put you onto me—I would have told her to do that myself. I've . . ." his voice became choked, ". . . I've consorted with women who aren't any good. Women with death in their eyes who reek of cheap perfume."

"Are you serious?" Davin wanted to laugh. "Where do you get all this malarkey? May and Estelle are dead. Really dead—not perfume dead."

Chandler jerked as if he had touched a live wire. He knocked his bottle out the window, and seconds later came the crash. His expression turned sour. "I'm not surprised about May. She led a fast life." He paused, and his voice became philosophical. "Even Estelle —it doesn't surprise me. I finally figured out that she wasn't the innocent she pretended to be."

Davin's rage grew. He got up from the bed; the book beside him fell off. He could see the cover: *The Great Gatsby*.

"May and Estelle were killed by those sailors you fought in the insurance suit. They said they were out to get revenge against you."

Chandler was shook again. "That makes no sense," he said. "May and Estelle had nothing to do with that. Anyone out to get me should come for me. There must have been some other reason."

Davin grabbed Chandler by the arm. He wanted to push him out the window; it would be easy, easier than the night in the rail-yard. Nobody would know: Philleo would talk and the cops would call it suicide. It was a perfect setup. For the first time, Chandler looked him in the eye. Davin saw desperation there and something more: Chandler seemed to know what he was thinking, was grant-ing him permission, making an appeal. He didn't try to escape. Davin fought the desire to give the one quick shove that would end it; the frustrated need, the rage of the years of keeping himself sane, pushed him toward it. The whole struggle was the matter of an in-stant. He pulled Chandler into the room.

"Quit the suicide act. What have you been doing since you left May?"

If Chandler had felt anything of the communication that had passed between them, he did not show it. "I couldn't stay with her; when I first met her I thought she was innocent, defenseless, but I learned the kind she was quick. I couldn't go home and face Cissy. I came here." He looked toward the window. "If I had any guts it wouldn't be an act."

"Those sailors had no reason to kill except you. They did it in the stupidest way possible. Not for revenge. Just so things could work out the way you want them to."

Chandler pushed by him and went into the bathroom; Davin heard the sound of running water. He was getting ready to shave. He seemed to be sobering fast.

"You're crazy," Chandler called out. "The way I wanted? Look, I feel like the bastard I am, but what did I have to do with any of this? Am I supposed to stop defending the company when we're in the right? I've got to try to do the right thing, don't I?"

Davin said nothing. After a few minutes, Chandler came out of the bathroom. Hair combed, freshly shaven, he seemed already to be on the way to becoming an executive again. The news of the deaths, the moment on the windowsill, had knocked the booze out of him; knocked the guilt down in him, too. He picked up his shirt and began buttoning it.

Davin felt he was going to be sick.

"You know, that credo you spouted—you were just joking, I realize—but there's something to it," Chandler said. " 'Down these mean streets.' I'd like to believe in that. I'd like to be able to live up to that code—if we could only get all the other bastards to."

Davin rushed into the bathroom and threw up into the toilet. Chandler stuck his head into the room. "Are you all right?"

Davin gasped for breath. He wet a towel and rubbed his face.

Chandler had his tie knotted and put on the jacket of his rumpled summer suit. "You should take better care of yourself," he said. "You look awful. What's your name?"

"Michael Davin."

"Irish, huh?"

"On my father's side."

"I'll bet being a private investigator is interesting work. There's a kind of honor to it. You ought to write up your experiences someday."

Estelle was dead, lying upside down with her hair brushing the dusty floor. Her mouth was open. "Most of them I'd rather forget," Davin said.

Chandler took the copy of *Black Mask* from the bed. Davin felt hollow, but the way Chandler held the magazine, so reverently, sparked his anger again.

"You actually read that junk?"

The man ignored him. He bent over, a little unsteadiness the only evidence of his bender and the fact he'd been ready to launch himself out the window half an hour earlier. He picked up the copy of *Gatsby*.

"I've always wanted to be a writer," he said. "I used to write essays—even some poetry."

"Estelle told me that."

Chandler looked only momentarily uncomfortable. He motioned with the book in his hand. "So you don't like detective stories. Have you tried Fitzgerald?"

"No."

"Best damn writer in America. Best damn book. About a man chasing his dream."

"Does he catch it?"

Sadly, Chandler replied, "No, he doesn't."

"He ought to quit dreaming, then."

Chandler put his hand on Davin's shoulder. "We can't do that. We've got nothing else."

Davin wanted to tell him what a load of crap that was, but Chandler had turned his back and walked out of the room.

IN INFINITY MEETING IN INFINITY MEETING IN INFINITY MEETIN
TING IN INFINITY MEETING IN INFINITY MEETING IN INFINITY ME
MEETING IN INFINITY MEETING IN INFINITY MEETING IN INFINITY
NITY MEETING IN INFINITY MEETING IN INFINITY MEETING IN INFI
INFINITY MEETING IN INFINITY MEETING IN INFINITY MEETING IN
G IN INFINITY MEETING IN INFINITY MEETING IN INFINITY MEETIN
ETING IN INFINITY MEETING IN INFINITY MEETING IN INFINITY M
J MEETING IN INFINITY MEETING IN INFINITY MEETING IN INFINIT
INITY MEETING the lecturer J MEETING IN IN
N INFINITY MEE FINITY MEETING
NG IN INFINITY MEETING IN INFINITY MEETING IN INFINITY MEET
EETING IN INFINITY MEETING IN INFINITY MEETING IN INFINITY N
TY MEETING IN INFINITY MEETING IN INFINITY MEETING IN INFINI
FINITY MEETING IN INFINITY MEETING IN INFINITY MEETING IN I
IN INFINITY MEETING IN INFINITY MEETING IN INFINITY MEETING

HAD, OF COURSE, HEARD ABOUT THE LECTURER BEFORE I ACCEPTED the position at the university. Stories of him had reached the West Coast, but his was not the kind of notoriety that makes any deep impression. The university, though large and reasonably well-known, was not first-rate, and the Lecturer's existence was less remarked upon than the record of the school's football team. None of this mattered to me. I could scarcely care less about unique features of the campus; all I knew was that no one had worked harder than I had to earn a degree, and no one deserved a tenure-track position more. When I received the job offer I felt a triumph that did not lessen my bitterness. When I told my friends, they did not talk about the Lecturer, but about how severe the winters in the Northeast were.

The move exhausted both of us; Jane and I worked very hard trying to make something of the small house we were able to rent on an assistant professor's salary. Money was tight for some time, and Jane was unable to find work. Yet it seemed we were quite happy at first. We spent our evenings reading or listening to music, we took turns cooking, we took walks on the Saturdays of that In-dian summer through the wooded lanes outside the town. When the possibility of a job at the university gallery fell through, Jane concentrated on her painting, ran off some flyers, and started teaching a class in oils out of our home.

Each morning I would rise early and walk up to the campus, which was only five blocks from our house. The department was located in a building on the far side of the quadrangle, and so I would have to walk past the Lecturer where he stood on the truncated Greek pillar at the top of the slope in front of the library. The first few times I strolled by self-consciously, trying to act as if I were accustomed to him; I kept my eyes on the buildings ahead and gripped the handle of my briefcase tighter. I did not hear what he was saying. A few days later I was comfortable enough with the new surroundings to stop for some minutes and listen. It was soon after classes had started and the campus bustled with students: a few sprawled on the grass of the quadrangle, and a nervous freshman here and there had also stopped to listen. Other students threw their Frisbees past him.

"The first notable feature of contemporary architecture is its concern with a greater and more profound reality than that encompassed by the psyche of one individual," he was saying. "The proper focus of architecture, the modernist tells us, is on the space outside the individual and the clash of impersonal forces within that outer space. There is no place in architecture for the kind of philosophy that sees reality as determined by individual perception."

He looked exactly like a stocky middle-aged man. His legs were short and strong, and he had the neck of a pit bulldog. He was not going to fat. His complexion was florid, his hair bright red, thinning on top, and a bushy mustache dominated his face. I was later told that during the sixties he had worn his hair long with a red bandanna tied around his head, and I came across an old yearbook photograph of him, taken in the 1890s, that showed him with full beard, neatly trimmed, and flowing academic robes. My first September at the university he wore a wool suit despite the high heat of the waning summer, and he was to wear that same suit through the year, adding a scarf and heavy overcoat as winter approached.

He spoke vigorously. Gestures of his right arm would punctuate his rhetoric; spreading his fingers, he would slice home a point with a sweep of his extended hand. His voice was strong, if rather high-pitched. His tone was dogmatic. There could be no doubt, it told us, that the things he said were the absolute truth.

Architecture is not one of my interests, and I soon moved on to my office. I had had to listen to too much of such academic sausage-grinding in my graduate career. Now that I had moved on, I worked hard at teaching, rewriting my dissertation for publication and being agreeable to all factions in my new department. Yet he bothered me, perhaps especially because he seemed to bother no one else; I could not keep myself from occasionally thinking about the man on the pedestal. The responses of my colleagues to my questions were not illuminating. Once at lunch I managed to turn the conversation around to the Lecturer.

"Why do they keep him around?" I asked.

"Nobody's keeping him," said Duthie, whose specialty was the Restoration. "He's free to do whatever he likes. You might as well ask why they keep the weather."

Judy Boisner, who wore bright scarves and a grin, said, "It's a tradition. Like the exam policy and the Chancellor's Oak."

I nodded at both of them. I was not skeptical.

"Nobody knows," old Dr. White said, not lifting his eyes from his corned beef on rye. "I wondered once. I was convinced there was a good reason. It doesn't matter."

"I see," I said.

Killworthy, sitting next to me, said nothing. Later, as we walked back to our offices, shoulders hunched and hands holding lapels closed against a cold breeze, he told me the real reason was political.

"The Lecturer has nothing to do with the university." His voice was bright with eagerness to initiate me. "It's all a matter of creating the proper impression on those whose decisions can really make a difference to the people who want to continue in positions of comfortable security—and influence—in this circus. Ask yourself: who stands to gain the most from such a creature as the Lecturer?"

I opened the door for him, and we shook ourselves in the warmth of the hallway. We retreated to our separate offices. I had no idea what Killworthy was talking about. I doubted that he did himself.

Our small house smelled of the oils with which Jane and her few students cluttered the spare bedroom. The artistic crowd—or more accurately, the crowd of artistic dilettantes—Jane was keeping company with did not appeal to me. I began to spend more time on campus reading, grading papers, sitting in my office staring out the window at the treetops, gazing absently down at the footpaths crisscrossing the quad.

In November I assigned the students in my composition class a paper on the Lecturer. A five-hundred-word description. Many of the male students wrote papers that began like this:

> Throughout history there has been many types of institutions of higher learning from the Middle Ages until now. Many of these presented the university professor as the originator of information it was useful for the students to have. Here at State is the home of the famous Lecturer that is reknown not only for his superior brain and his intellectual lectures, but also the ability of anyone that touches his shoe before a date to have sexual "relations" that very night.

Few of the women mentioned shoes or sex. During conferences that week I made some inquiries and discovered that "rubbing the Lecturer" for luck was authentic campus folklore. For sure, Chuck Bennetti, a freshman, told me.

The unspoken truth was that the Lecturer was unconscionably boring, and the students realized it, and the only notice they took of him—such as that surrounding the sex-charm stories—was the result of their boredom. Before homecoming, students from arch-rival Syracuse would paint the Lecturer orange, but it aroused little indignation on campus and it did not slow him down. His methods for dealing with hecklers were antiquated.

"According to Faraday's Law, the line integral of the electric field around a closed path is equal to the time rate of change of the flux of the magnetic field calculated over the open surface bounded by the path of integration. . . ."

"Shut up, shut up! I don't want to hear it!" a young man walking across the quad would shout, while his companions burst into laughter.

The Lecturer would ignore him. "If the surface of integration is fixed in space. . . ."

"You mean lost in space, airhead!" one of the others would shout.

The Lecturer then might actually look at them, and smile. Not a smile of superior knowledge, or tolerance, or contempt. Not a smile older than the university, than any university. "No applause," he might say then. "Just throw money."

"I'm in pain," the first student would say. "I'm laughing so hard, Grandpa."

"So stop laughing and listen, Bub. You might learn something. If the surface of integration is. . . ."

"SHUT UP!"

He would stop. "Student here wants to speak. What do you want to tell us, student?"

"Screw you."

"That's all?"

"Screw you! Asshole! Screw you!"

"Thanks very much," the Lecturer would say. "If the surface of integration is fixed. . . ."

I saw one such encounter late in the semester, a day when I was preoccupied with late papers and my first committee assignment. It made me unaccountably melancholy. On impulse I walked up to his pedestal.

It was around six, dark already. The campus was virtually empty of students, and the regular staff had all gone home. No one paid any attention after the hecklers moved away. The Lecturer glanced down at me without pausing in his delineation of the ideals of Jeffersonian democracy. I reached out and touched his left shoe. The leather was dull from generations of furtive contacts; I wondered that it had not been worn away entirely. Perhaps these were not the same shoes that he had worn fifty years before. But to begin to consider the source of his clothing was to open the first Chinese box in an infinite series of boxes, with little assurance of an answer in the opening and less that one would ever be able to stop.

I had a slight smudge of dirt on my fingertips. Nothing more. Feeling foolish, I returned to my office and a stack of ungraded papers.

The first flakes of the winter storm that had been predicted for that evening—the first of the season—had begun falling outside my window when a knock caused me to look up from the paper on which I was working. Stacey Branham, a student in my Postwar American Fiction class, stood uncertainly in the doorway.

It was quite late for an office visit. "Yes, Stacey," I said. "What's up?"

She shifted from foot to foot. "Can I talk to you about my term paper?"

"Sure."

She came in, closing the door behind her. I put the papers aside. She sat on the edge of the chair beside my desk and told me she was having trouble coming up with things to say. I had never noticed this problem as she dealt deftly with the boys who talked to her before and after class: she was a tall, slender blonde with intelligent gray eyes. I had more than once watched her cross her legs in the first row of seats in the Walton Annex. Lecture Hall B.

It soon became clear that she had not come to talk about her term paper, and that she had not happened by in the early evening, when the humanities building was deserted, by accident. She put her purse on the floor beside her, drew her chair closer, and as she leaned forward to ask an earnest question about Flannery O'Connor, rested her finely manicured hand on my leg.

"Stacey," I said. "You're not really interested in Flannery O'Connor, are you?"

"Yes, I am. 'Everything That Rises Must Converge' is my favorite story."

"Well." I was very nervous. "It's a masterpiece of irony."

"That's what I'm having trouble with." She smiled; I drew a deep breath. She smelled of Chanel.

I wheeled my chair back suddenly. "Why don't you come back, then . . . when you've worked out your ideas more completely."

She looked puzzled, a little frightened. "I didn't mean to—"

"No problem. I'll see you in class Friday, right?"

She took her purse and left, drawing her wool coat tighter around her hips as she swirled out the door.

I sat there for some time, closed my eyes, breathed slowly. My mind was without thought. I looked down at my hands resting on the desk; they shook ever so slightly, and I realized that I was terrified. There was a smudge of dirt on the first two fingers of my right hand.

By the time I left the building, a couple of inches of snow had accumulated. Instead of crossing the quad I went down the access road behind the building so that I could avoid him. It was one of those crisp, cold nights on which sound carries for great distances. I could faintly hear his voice despite the still-falling snow. My vision seemed exceptionally clear: I could see every swirling flake in the pools of light beneath the streetlights. I felt my warm breath on my face, the moisture freezing in my mustache; I saw the condensation in the air. My footsteps made no sound on the sidewalk.

Jane had already eaten, and I could hear her in the studio with one of her students, Marsha, when I reached home. I didn't go up to say hello; instead I fixed my own supper from the lukewarm Stroganoff on the stove and the day-old salad in the refrigerator. I watched part of one of the Shakespeare plays—*A Midsummer Night's Dream*—on PBS and went to bed before it was over. Marsha hadn't left yet. I got into bed and turned off the light, but could not get to sleep. Papers remained to be graded, Stacey Branham remained to be faced, the man remained speaking on the quadrangle as snow caught and melted in his hair. I could hear the low voices of Jane and Marsha but could not make out more than a few words of Jane's instructions on how to use the palette knife.

I got up and washed the dirt from my fingers.

When Jane came to bed I was still not asleep. The clock radio read 12:17.

"I'm sorry I woke you," she said quietly.

"That's okay. It's late."

"Marsha stayed to talk and have some wine."

I turned from her, adjusted my arm beneath my pillow. After a moment I felt her touch my back.

"What's the matter?" she asked.

"Nothing," I answered quickly, then said, more slowly, "I don't know."

"You want me to stop this class."

I still did not turn to her. "No. It's important that you teach."

She moved close, slipped her arm under mine and held me. We lay silent for a while. Her breath was warm against my back. She moved her leg over my hip; I rolled onto my back and she slid on top of me.

We made love with an intensity we hadn't had in a very long time. Jane wanted, needed me: the shock of that burned each moment into my senses. I realized that I needed her as much, if not more, and wondered that we had been living together for the last three months—and before that, back in California—so unaware of each other that we might only have been sharing an office. These truths came to me without thought, showed themselves in a carnality that was frightening in directness and austerity. Jane rocked over me with her eyes closed, the lines at their corners drawn so tight she looked to be in pain. I ran my hands over her hips and waist; her skin was feverish. The muscles of my belly were tight, my back arched. I cried and held Jane to me as if to make up for years of indifference in those few moments, as if we were doing penance for a multitude of casual sins, as if I might never have her again. She touched my face.

Jane fell asleep as if she had been poisoned. I lay awake while my sweat slowly dried; I shivered in the cold bedroom, wondering what had happened. Where were we? How had we gotten there?

The Lecturer. Like the body of a drowned man surfacing in a lake days after the storm that drew him under, he rose to trouble my circling thoughts. He came to the center, and he did not go away.

He did not go away. I tried to concentrate on the sound of Jane's slow breathing, the ticking of the furnace, the soft flip as the clock counted out each minute, the wind outside. I could not keep him out. I slipped quietly out of bed, pulled on clothes, and left Jane asleep. Unable to find my gloves, I threw on my coat and headed up to the campus, hands jammed into my pockets. It was bitterly cold. I walked briskly, but my feet were soon freezing.

I could hear his voice before I could see him. He was speaking as strongly, gesturing as fervently, as he did when there were people up and around to hear him. Instead he faced an unbroken sweep of snow that ran two hundred yards, from the library, over footpaths, beneath lampposts and trees, to the administration building at the other end of the quadrangle. As I approached, he turned to me and I could make out what he was saying.

"Descartes's second objection to placing faith in the reality of sensory experience amounts to this: however good our empirical evidence may be for the proposition that, for instance, we see a man, another feeling being, in front of us, such evidence is never good enough that reason is forced to accept it. The creature we see might be a diabolically ingenious conjuring trick by the malignant demon. And this possibility of error will apply to any empirical proposition; to be true it must be certified in a way stronger than any amount of empirical evidence could ever provide."

I stopped directly in front of him, in a snowdrift halfway to my knees. I looked up at him; he looked down at me. He kept talking.

"I want to speak to you," I said.

"Descartes found his solution in mathematics—"

"Please listen to me," I said.

"I'm doing the talking; you listen. You might learn something.

In mathematics, some propositions we know to be intuitively true—"

"What are you doing? How did you come to be here?"

He then smiled that vacant smile. He sighed, and his breath fogged the air. "Student here has something to say. Speak up, student."

"That legend about you. Does what happened to me mean that it's true?"

"Accept as true only what can clearly and distinctly be perceived as being so."

My face burned. "What's that supposed to mean?" I said angrily. "The words you say don't mean anything. Things happen anyway."

"Analyze any problem into its simplest possible elements." The snow had gathered so thickly on his head that the strong light from the lamps behind him gave him a glittering halo. He ought to have caught pneumonia.

"Damn you! Give me a straight answer!"

"I don't give answers. I give lectures."

He towered over me, so obtuse he might have been made of stone. Suddenly I could not stand it. I leapt forward and grabbed his leg with both of my hands. He was taken by surprise, I think; this had to have happened to him before, but perhaps he did not expect violence from someone asking the bitter questions that only a man who didn't have any answers—a faculty member—would ask. I tugged furiously; I screamed at him, not knowing what or why I screamed. He slipped momentarily, regained his balance and beat me on the head and shoulders with his fists. My rage grew and gave me a blind strength. I braced my leg against the pedestal and jerked harder, and this time when he lost his footing he came tumbling down on top of me. We sprawled in the snow. Once I had him off I lost my purpose. He struggled out of my grasp and got to his feet. He was breathing hard. He was just another man, like me; he might have been Duthie, he might have been Killworthy.

"Excuse me," he said, and climbed back onto the pedestal.

That was fifteen years ago. He's still out there. He's still talking.

MEETING IN INFINITY MEETING IN INFINITY

hearts do not in eyes shine

CONNIE FOUND HARRY IN THE BAR AT MARIO'S. AS SOON AS SHE walked in, he finished his drink and stood up.

"You came," he said, fumbling in his jacket pocket. "I have something for you." He found a small envelope in an inside pocket and handed it to her; it felt like a card. "Don't open it now," he said. "Wait until later."

Connie felt strangely calm. "Okay. Let's eat."

She let him do most of the talking; he seemed to have marshalled his arguments. "I know this must seem like a crazy idea. I think I'm half-crazy to suggest it, but people do it all the time and I couldn't let you go without trying something."

"You're not letting me go. You let me go a long time ago."

He pulled at his lower lip and sat silent. "You're right. I don't deny it."

"You can't."

"Please. I know I've made mistakes; we've both made mistakes. But think about the way we felt about each other when we first met. The emotions then were real. You can't ignore that. That's why I'm here asking this, even though I know I don't deserve to. In the last month or two, I've gone crazy thinking about the good times we spent together."

Connie tried to stay calm, to think rationally. "Harry, why do we have to go through this? It's too hard. I remember other times. We wouldn't be separated otherwise."

"No. I think you're wrong there. We made mistakes and did things to hurt each other, but I've thought about it a lot—I've hardly thought about anything else—and I know, I *know* we are basically compatible. I knew that the first time I saw you. The things that pushed us apart are only things that happened to us— they aren't who we are. Who we are doesn't change. That's the whole point of getting erased. We stay the same people, but we get rid of the bad things that happened and get another chance to build our marriage again. Please, Connie. You know this is the truth."

She didn't know anything. She sipped her wine, sat back and watched him. Harry seemed uncomfortable under her gaze. He closed his eyes, breathed deeply, opened them again. That was always the sign of his exasperation with her, when he couldn't get her to believe what he wanted, when the words failed him. The words had not failed him yet. He must have thought them up a long time before he had the nerve to call her. Maybe the letter from her lawyer had jolted him. Maybe the erasure clinic had given him the arguments he was using on her. That was something she would never have suspected of Harry in the early days; she would have taken him at his face value.

Connie must have smiled at her own cynicism: he looked at her angrily and said, "Don't laugh at me, Connie."

"I'm sorry."

"That's okay. Just don't laugh."

There wasn't much trust left in her, and suddenly she realized that she did not like it. What had he done to her that she had come to be so suspicious, that the honesty of her emotions had been leached away until she responded to him as if he were a pitchman for a sex show? Maybe his exasperation—if it was exasperation, and not just fear or confusion—had a reason.

"I don't know, Harry. I'm afraid. You've hurt me too much, and I can never forget the things you've done."

He leaned forward. "That's right," he said quietly. "But they can make us forget. You don't have to give up anything. You just have to be willing to take a chance."

She played with the card he had given her, turned it over, ran her index finger along the edge of the smooth rectangle of cream-colored paper. "I don't know."

The silence stretched. Harry looked hurt. "Look, Connie,

maybe this was a bad idea. Don't make me feel any more a fool than I am."

"I'm not making you a fool." God. The last thing she wanted was to feel sorry for him.

"I'm sorry I tried to make you do something you didn't want to do. Can you blame me for trying?" He looked at her levelly. This was not going the way it ought to have gone. They ought not to let men like Harry live to reach twenty-one. They ought to test them when they hit puberty, and if the test showed a person who didn't know the difference between the truth and a lie, they could castrate him. While they were at it they could get rid of the ones with Harry's green eyes and Harry's voice.

She held up the card and stood to leave. "Can I open this now?"

He smiled a little sadly. "It doesn't say 'I love you.'"

Connie slid a fingernail under the flap and opened the envelope. The front of the card was blank, and inside was written, "No matter what you decide, I will never lie to you again."

She put the card back in the envelope, put the envelope into her purse. At his station, the maitre d' had already cleared their table on his service screen and was watching them impatiently. Connie looked at him, looked at Harry, and sat down again.

∞   ∞   ∞

She told Harry she would call him later and returned to the office without having made up her mind. She spent that afternoon trading foreign currencies, with Fox, her computer trading model, hooked into her left ear and the newsline on the window. She stayed in front of the terminal without a break until the session ended, then retreated to her office to take client calls until most of the staff had left for the day. The lowering clouds that threatened Connie and the other bicyclists riding home suggested that perhaps the streetcar would have been a better idea that morning. But the rain held off until after she got home. She lived in a large old house in a neighborhood that had declined to a near-slum in the third quarter of the century only to be refurbished in the eighties before its second genteel slide after the turn of the century. Harry and Connie had moved into the white frame monstrosity a year before they contracted. Seven years later he had moved out, and it had taken her months to feel comfortable again there after a period of rattling around its twelve rooms like the drunkard in the random-walk theorem.

That night a relapse threatened. In the mail printout she found a brochure for an erasure company, New Life Choices, Inc. She did not recognize the name. Harry had to have sent it; she threw it into the wastebasket without reading it. She skipped supper, fixed several stiff drinks, and tried to forget about erasure. She walked through the house listening to the spring drizzle and breathing deep the humid air that blew through opened windows. She picked up her clothes from about the bedroom, did the laundry, had a couple more drinks, smoked a joint, tried to read a book. She sat by the phone for twenty minutes, then dialed Harry's number quickly to tell him to forget it. The face of a middle-aged woman came onto the screen and told her curtly she had the wrong number. She hesitated, then searched the wastebasket for the brochure.

FREEDOM IS A STATE OF MIND

THE IMMORTAL BARD, WILLIAM SHAKESPEARE (1564–1616) ASKED,

> Can you cure a troubled mind,
> Plunge a deep sorrow out of the memory
> Erase the troubles written on a brain
> And with a sweet potion
> Clean all the pain and sadness
> From a heavy heart?

—AT NEW LIFE CHOICES, WE CAN.

The next page told Connie:

We see the world through dark glass. By selective forgetting, we can take off the dark glasses that superimpose the fearful past on the present, and begin to know that love is forever present. The Jacobovsky Process is used to selectively edit the memory. Forgiveness then becomes a process of letting go of whatever we thought others may have done to us, or whatever we may think we have done to others. Our safety and security are the simple words, "I don't remember."

Harry had been bright and moody and could make her laugh whenever he wanted. Connie remembered quite well. She had loved to watch him fix things. He had beautiful hands, strong and skilled. His hands knew just how much force to give, could feel out the source of a problem without his having to think about it. Normally he was a talkative man, but when he was in his attic workroom he became a quiet one, concentrating on the task before him, devoted only to finding the solution to the problem; patient, intuitive. His eyes would sober, without the anger they would show during his depressions, and he would look at the machine as if somehow, if he waited in the right way, it might speak to him—and he would not be surprised when it did.

Harry had that look for her, at first. She felt that, when she spoke to him, he listened with all his substance. It made her want to say only true things—not to be silly or lie. He would laugh at her when she got so serious.

"You act like I might go away," he would tell her. "I won't go away."

Harry worked for Triangle Data Services. Connie had met him when he came in to replace their old computer trading link with the new Triangle system. He seemed unaware of the class difference between a workman like himself and someone like Connie, with a couple of degrees in economics and a triple-A credit rating. He did not seem self-conscious hanging around their terminals watching, asking an occasional question. Strangely, the changeover was made without disrupting their work, and when, on his way out of the building on his last day there, Harry stopped by to ask Connie out for dinner, she had surprised herself by saying yes.

The rain increased from a drizzle to a downpour, and Connie went through the house again, closing windows against the storm. She turned out all the lights and went to bed.

Harry had lied to her more than once. They'd lived together so naturally in that first year that it amazed her she'd been able to live alone for so long. It was an open marriage, with disclosure, ten years and an option, with penalties for a breach on either side. Three years into it Connie realized that Harry saw other women without telling her. At first she said nothing, out of love or perhaps fear that facing it would make the truth of his betrayal undeniable. Why should he keep his lovers a secret when she had agreed to accept anything he told her? She did not see herself as the jealous spouse, but keeping her knowledge to herself only made her anger grow. When at last she confronted him, Harry was unsurprised that she knew. He would have felt ashamed to tell her of those affairs, even though it was okay to have them, he said. He still loved her, he said. It had nothing to do with her, he said.

Though it took her years more to realize it, it *had* nothing to do with her. It was not her fault, and whether or not it was Harry's was beyond her. She tried not to care. She just wanted to be done with trying to understand him when he did not understand her, done with his talk that never went anywhere and his silence that left her out, done with the fighting, his sudden joys and kindnesses, his silly jokes, his casual cruelty, his quiet eyes and calm hands, his lies, the pain of watching him and knowing that she loved and hated him. She might have done better. But it was not her fault.

Why did that sound too easy?

The rain beat heavily on the roof now, punctuated by lightning that brought the darkened room into momentary sharp relief, like sudden memories. Connie realized that the windows in the workroom were probably open. She got her robe and went up the narrow stairs.

The lamp over Harry's workbench did not come on when she flipped the switch. The curtains of the west window snapped with the force of the wind, and the rain blew well into the middle of the cluttered room. Like a person walking a tightrope, Connie stepped carefully between the broken machines with their spoor of dismantled parts. It was all that Harry had left when she'd kicked him out, and she had threatened more than once to throw all his toys away if he did not move them. Her feet were cold. The window was stuck; the counterweights in the frame scraped and the pulleys squeaked as she leaned heavily on it. The window went down crookedly, one side fighting the other. She beat on the top with her fist, growing angrier as it inched its stubborn way down. The wind whistled as the gap closed, she became soaked with the rain, and the shadowed forms of Harry's machines watched impassively as she struggled. There was still a gap when she gave up, two inches at one end and one at the other, uneven, hopelessly jammed, the wind louder as it shot through the narrow slit, the curtains flapping fitfully. She sat on the floor crying. It was Harry's damned window, and she couldn't close it for him.

∞   ∞   ∞

She found herself in the lobby of New Life Choices on a day she and Harry picked for the erasing. Connie would have been more comfortable with the dignified conservatism of Associated or Stratford: the walls of the New Life lobby were knotty pine hung with Miró prints; the receptionist had his irises silvered in the latest nihilist style. Some people might have liked it.

She and Harry sat quietly until one of the "counselors" came to greet them.

"Harry." He shook hands. "Good to see you again. I see you've persuaded her." He turned to Connie. "You've made the right decision, Constance. I'm John Holland. Call me John."

He insisted on shaking her hand as well, holding on a moment as if to reassure her. It was all she could do to keep him from putting his arm across her shoulder as he led them to his office.

Behind his desk he was more businesslike. "First of all, are you taking advantage of the special this week?"

Harry looked pained, glanced briefly at Connie, then took the coupon from his pocket. "No jokes about paying in advance, John. Let's get on with it."

"We have to do this by the book, Harry. It's not so unpleasant as all that, is it? You two are about to get a second chance, thanks to the service we're offering. People throughout history have longed for that chance. They've gone to their graves dreaming of it. They've killed each other and themselves because they couldn't get it. Now you can have it; think how blessed you are."

He drew two contracts from a desk drawer. "I myself have had numerous traumas erased," he continued. "So completely that the only way I know about them is that I kept records. My mother's death. The time I struck out with the bases loaded in the college world series. My baptism. I can talk frankly about these things now, without a trace of guilt or anger, because for me those events no longer exist. The people who hurt me no longer exist. Fifty years ago a psychiatrist might treat you for a decade trying to convince you that the past is over and can't hurt you. By this afternoon the past that hangs over both of you like a cloud—I can see it there now, and it's keeping you apart—will be gone. All that will be left will be the love you still feel for each other."

Connie wondered whether she could get them to erase this meeting for no extra charge. Harry looked as if he wanted to die. Connie could almost believe Holland was taking some perverse pleasure in Harry's discomfort. Or perhaps this was part of the treatment: make the patient realize the significance of the step he was taking, magnify the pain of the events he wants to have erased so that he will leap at the opportunity to have them expunged. If so, then Holland ought to be able to afford a better suit.

Holland placed one contract before each of them, and they talked for a while about what memories they wanted to have erased, and longer about exactly what they wanted to remember of their time together. Though there might be a few "echo losses," as

he called them, he assured Connie that anything she wanted to keep
would be preserved, and she would lose nothing vital to her job.
She would remember the difference between short covering and
profit-taking. If she was a champion skiier, then she would remain
one.

They signed the contracts. Harry took her hand, and they were
led to the preparation rooms for memory pretesting. His palm was
sweaty. In another room they were greeted by attendants whom
Holland briefed, though they had all the relevant facts in their computer. Harry embraced her, and they were taken to separate rooms.

Once alone Connie began to panic. They gave her an injection.
The machine they hooked her up to smelled of the hundreds of
others who had come before her to have their pasts negated. The
headset that let them map her cortex was cold and hard. The tech-
nicians did not know her; they did not care who she was, and it
would not matter to them if by mistake they wiped out her personality entirely. Harry had no right to do this to her. She couldn't remember anything about him that would make her want to go back.
She started to speak, she started to sit up and take the headset off.
Or did she just think that? Harry had no right to take away her
memories. She felt sleepy; the room did not look so threatening.
The clean smell of disinfectant reminded her of the hospital emergency room where she'd taken Harry after he'd cut his hand so
badly carrying a video display across the workroom. That was a
piece of junk. It was still up there. He simply had no right.

∞   ∞   ∞

Connie got a call at work the next day. She asked Mary to keep an
eye on forex trading and went to her office to use the viewphone.

"Constance, this is Harry," the man on the screen said, as if she
could not see him. When she didn't answer immediately, he added,
"Harry Gray."

Her pulse quickened. "Don't worry, Harry. I remember you."

He closed his eyes for a beat, opened them again. His hair was
light brown, worn longer than the general style. He seemed to be
trying to smile, but uncertain how she would take it. They stared at
each other, uncomfortable.

"Long time no see," Harry said.

She laughed. He looked so timid, yet aware of the absurdity.

"I feel funny talking to you," he said. "I feel like I'm imposing
where I don't know what to say. Maybe we ought to wait awhile."

"No," she said suddenly, surprising herself. "I think we need to get to know each other. Why don't we meet for lunch? Do you know where Mario's is on Twelfth Street?"

He looked momentarily dazed, and then the smile came. "It's one of my favorites."

She liked his voice, his tentativeness. "Mine too," she said. She realized then that her memories of Mario's were spotty. She could remember the maitre d's name, and that the veal was the best thing on the menu, but she could not recall many specific visits to the restaurant.

The maitre d' knew them both: he gave them a secluded table. The conversation started tentatively. Connie hesitated to ask Harry if he remembered anything, while at the same time she was probing her own memory. In some ways it seemed that nothing had changed —she remembered their meeting, the first time they had made love, his favorite color, their honeymoon on *Orbital 6*, saving up to buy the house, his tinkering in the attic. But then there were curious half-memories of things she had done herself that did not seem complete, undoubtedly because Harry had been involved in some way. Holland had told her, in the posttesting, that she might lose memory of persons and things she strongly associated with Harry. And then there were whole periods from the last year or two that were fuzzy or blank. It was as if Harry had faded from her life a couple of years ago. Now here he was, back.

Connie wasn't sure she wanted to speculate about the hole in her memory of their marriage. But listening to Harry's self-deprecating little jokes, his warm voice, she could not help but realize that she had had some reason to have this man erased from her memory. She wondered what that reason was. Harry told her about his recent work at Triangle; she told him about commission trading in the foreign exchange markets. He seemed legitimately interested. His attention to her seemed complete.

They sat at the table long after the meal, ordered wine and talked. Harry's eyes were shy, and kind. He put his hand out to touch hers. They leaned forward in the light of the candle wrapped in plastic netting at the center of their table. He offered her some Lift; she declined, and he added a few drops to his own glass. Connie did not approve, but he did not seem to lose interest and his eyes remained bright and alert. She tried to remember the last time they'd slept together.

When they were about to leave he offered to take her home. She thought that meant he had his own car, but all he meant was that he'd ride the streetcar back with her. She wasn't sure she wanted to go that fast, knowing he would want to spend the night. Connie hesitated while the waiter took her credit card. Harry said nothing. Looking into her purse to avoid his expectant gaze, she found a small card tucked into one of the pockets. She pulled it out far enough to read, in Harry's handwriting: "No matter what you decide, I will never lie to you again." She slid it back into her purse. "Okay," she said. "It's a cool evening. It'll be a nice ride."

∞   ∞   ∞

Connie was in love again. Soon he moved in with her; in the evenings he took to tinkering with his machines in the workroom. Connie found herself with new energy in her job. She had her mind right on the edge of trading, was able to get in and out of market positions before others in the electronic network even knew they had been established or were crumbling. She began trading for her own account in spare moments and made a killing when the Philippines exploded its first nuclear device and the yen dropped the limit. Harry and Connie talked about how to spend the windfall. They decided on an orbital vacation on *Habitat 3.*

In the weeks before they left, some things about Harry began to pluck at the edges of Connie's contentment. At times he seemed too desperately happy. He would take her hands in his and tell her how much he loved her, and the next day would return late from work Lifted out of sight. He would never criticize her and he always seemed more than contented, but sometimes she wondered if Harry was actually seeing her, or only some projection of his own desire. When he became aware of her moments of silence in the midst of their new happiness, he begged her not to dwell on the past. How could she dwell on a past she couldn't remember?

On a hot July day one of Harry's friends came by in a company electric van and took them to the tube station where they boarded the magnetic train for the Cape. They spent three days in the hotel on the beach, swimming and sailing and eating seafood, a luxury they seldom saw in the Midwest. After that they took the shuttle up to the resort. They went to the free-fall ballet and did some dancing of their own. They spent hours in the transparent centrifugal pool, watching the universe wheel in lazy circles below them as they swam low-G arabesques in the water. Beneath the observation dome Connie got a very nice tan despite the ultraviolet screen that protected them from the hard sunlight of the vacuum. They ate in the many restaurants and watched the intricate exchange of partners that took place in the bar every night. Few of the guests were paired as strongly as Connie and Harry, and soon the propositions ended.

Making love in free-fall was familiar, but one of those experiences of which her memory would yield no details. Somehow this comforted her. She knew the reason for this was the forgotten knowledge that Harry had been her only partner.

At the end of the first week, Connie met a woman in the lounge who was vaguely familiar. She wore the uniform of one of the staff. "Hello! I saw Harry this afternoon in the sauna. He told me you were back again."

Connie could not place her. The name "Alice" presented itself to her, unbidden. "Alice. How are you?"

Alice smiled. "Oh, I can see you must have been Lifted pretty high last night. A little hung over?"

"Not really. It's been a long time since I've seen you."

Alice would not accept that. She probed until Connie admitted she'd been erased. "Erased! How interesting! I wonder why Harry didn't tell me."

Given Alice's apparent nose for news it was not something Connie would have told her either. "Maybe it just didn't occur to him."

"But I asked him all about you. We rehashed old times. You look like you're doing better on the sunburn front now. Harry said you'd learned your lesson after that horrible burn you picked up last time."

Connie remembered the sunburn. But as Alice rambled on, the thought nagged at her.

"Harry talked with you about my sunburn? From the last trip?"

"Just in passing. He said you'd vowed never to let anything so dumb put you in the hospital again."

"You talked about our last trip?"

Alice looked puzzled. "Dear heart, you must be a little strung out. You sure you didn't do a little too much last night?"

Alice kept the puzzled expression as Connie made her excuses and left. She found Harry in their suite, adjusting his jewelry in the mirror. "Hi," he said. "Am I late? I was just about to come down to the lounge."

She watched his eyes in the mirror. "I ran into Alice," she said. His glance caught hers, then shifted away. He brushed his hair back from his earring. "I saw her today, too. I'm surprised we didn't run into her sooner; you know how nosey she is. She just lives to know what's going on among the guests."

"I didn't remember her."

"Oh." He turned from the mirror. "You must have associated her more with me than I connected her with you, so the erasing wiped her out of your memory. John told me this might happen."

"You and John are pretty friendly."

He embraced her, ran his hand lightly down her spine. "What's the matter?" he asked.

He sounded perfectly sincere. He did not seem to be afraid to look at her. She ought to let it go at that. But it bothered her that something had happened then between them, something bad, that she couldn't recall. She remembered the card she still carried in her purse. "I will never lie to you again" meant that, although she could not remember it, he had lied to her before.

"Alice said you talked about my sunburn."

"She brought it up, yes. So what?"

"You remembered?"

"Yes, I did, vaguely. What's wrong with that?"

"I could hardly bring it back. How come you remember things that I don't?"

"I didn't remember any more than you. When she brought it up, it was all I could do to figure out what she was talking about."

"But you acted as if you knew."

"I must be a better actor than I imagine, then." He laughed; he moved away. "Connie, I just didn't want to admit that I'd been erased. You must have felt the same way when she started in on you. She's a gossip. She acted as if we were old friends, so I pretended to remember all the stuff she was talking about. I was embarrassed." He sat down on the edge of the bed and played with his wedding ring, turning it around his finger. "Why are you so suspicious?"

Connie watched him sitting there, and shuddered. *He had not been erased.*

She felt drugged, unable to grasp so huge a betrayal. She stared at him. She felt sick. She rushed into the bathroom and closed the door. She sat on the edge of the tub and put her head in her hands, attempting to slow her breathing.

Harry didn't come to the door. He didn't ask her what was wrong, he didn't plead. Stand and fight, her mind screamed, but as the minutes passed with still no response from him she began to have second thoughts. She couldn't know what he thought; she only had herself. The truth was that she *was* suspicious. The whole point of erasure was to give yourself a second chance. Maybe she had no reason to jump to such a drastic conclusion from such slim evidence.

The pastel floor tile gave no reassurance. Her shock faded. Harry could not be such a monster. He could not have coldly tricked her into giving herself away; he was not so clever or heartless or selfish as to steal a second chance for himself without paying in equal coin. The card in her purse was—had to be—a voucher of his love for her, not a warning of his unreliability.

She opened the door. Still sitting on the bed, he looked up expectantly. "Are you all right?" he asked.

"Yes." She felt like a ventriloquist speaking through a dummy.

"You have to believe me. I didn't know you'd take it this way. I lied to her; I didn't lie to you."

She sat beside him.

"Sometimes I wonder about the things we erased, too," he said.

She held him tightly and rested her head, eyes closed, on his shoulder.

"Go ahead," Harry said. "Sleep with Alice. I don't care."

A laugh forced itself to her lips. Tears stood in her eyes. "Let's forget it," she said.

∞   ∞   ∞

Connie told Harry she was concerned about being away from the markets for so long. He suggested she arrange a private com-link through the resort over which she could transact her business as well as she might at home. She told him she wouldn't feel comfortable; a link could easily be tapped, and moreover her clients would have trouble reaching her. So they cut the vacation short.

At home they settled into a routine that left them less time with each other. Connie took on several new accounts that kept her busy in the office after the trading session ended each day, and she began working on a new economic model she wanted to merge into Fox. Harry had risen among the ranks of troubleshooters and was being sent out-of-town frequently to train people in other cities. When home, he spent more time in his workroom. On the surface everything was all right.

The one area of their lives that improved was sex. Harry seemed to want her more as the weeks went by, and Connie found herself trembling at his touch. She told herself she did not like being attacked with such energy; it was almost as if she were an object to him in those moments of frenzy, but his attention would be focused on her. He asked her continually what she wanted. He would be by turns rough and extraordinarily tender, as if she were as evanescent as snow in late spring, fallen way past its time, beautiful, transitory. She could ask him to do anything, and he would do it. His warm breath on her shoulder was like the light, mysterious breath of a cat. She could no more read his thoughts than she could a cat's, yet she suspected something of the same feral blankness behind the eyes that gleamed in the darkness of their bedroom.

She responded with the same passion, surrendering thought in the night as she could less and less give it up during the day. The further she drifted from him, the more pleasure she took in their lovemaking. *I'll never lie to you again.* She had thrown away the card the day they returned to earth. But it would not go away, and eventually she took an afternoon off and went to the office of New Life Choices.

Holland was busy and would be all afternoon, they told her, but she insisted on waiting. Ten minutes later he came out to the lobby and escorted her to his office.

"How can I help you, Constance."

"I want to see your copies of the contracts."

He got them. She examined Harry's. Everything was in order. She compared the signature with one she had from their marriage license; it was the same. The terms of Harry's contract were identical to hers. Holland watched her silently.

"Something bothering you?" he asked when she put the papers down.

"Did you know Harry before we came here to be erased?"

"Not well. We met at a party a couple of months earlier. Had a few drinks. He was pretty broken up about your separation."

"You didn't talk business then?"

Holland seemed calm. "I suggested he get erased. It's my business, and he seemed a good prospect. It was a surprise to me later when he told me he was asking you to do it, too."

Harry had asked *her* to get erased. For the first time Connie understood that it had not been her idea. Why had they erased that from her memory? "That's all there was to it? And you erased him when you did me?"

Holland frowned. "I know you don't like me," he said. "That's too bad. But you're not the first person to come in here accusing us of fraud. They come in and tell me we didn't really erase them, that they can remember everything they paid to have wiped out. Or that we erased too much. Or that their personality's changed. Or that they can't do their jobs. You name it.

"You think I erased you and not Harry? How long do you think we could stay in business, if that's true? There are laws. There are ethics of the business."

Connie almost laughed. "Ethics."

Holland did not get indignant. "Believe it or not. We did the job we were paid to do."

"That's an equivocation."

"We erased Harry Gray. You're married to him. Why don't you ask him?"

"Suppose he changed his mind on the couch, at the last minute."

"I'm not lying to you."

"That's what Harry says."

"So you did ask him?"

Connie didn't say anything. Holland was not the lightweight she had taken him for, or maybe he had practiced this conversation. Some palm readers, they said, even believed the predictions they made.

"Look," Holland said. "You're smart. I'll tell you something I've found out that I don't like to admit. We can erase the memories— 'Pluck from the memory a rooted sorrow.' That's no problem. I used to think that we could 'minister to a mind diseased.' I'm not so sure anymore. The thing that makes a troubled memory is whatever happens to you. But people aren't as innocent as I used to think. They aren't just victims. Lots of things that 'just happened to them' they worked long and hard to get themselves into."

Connie stood. "Don't preach to me."

"We can't change the person. If you don't trust Harry, it's likely you didn't trust him before you were erased. Erasure doesn't change who you are. No matter what we advertise."

"It didn't change Harry."

" 'Therein the patient must minister to himself.' I'd like to take you out for a drink, Connie, but if you're going to keep this up you might as well just talk to our lawyers."

"I bet they're good ones. Do they quote Shakespeare, too?"

Holland gestured at the door. "Too bad," he said. "We might have had things to talk about."

∞   ∞   ∞

It had been like a suicide pact. They had agreed to kill their memories together. But if Harry had not gone through with it while Connie did, then he had murdered her.

She had lunch with her lawyer, Barbara Curran. The weather had turned cold that morning and the first real autumn storm threatened, so they met at the seafood bar below Center City. Connie told Barbara about her suspicions and the visit to New Life. Barbara told her that no erasure company had ever been proved to have defaulted on a contract, a record of which the industry was so protective that the American Erasure Association had established a huge legal defense fund. Several suits were nonetheless pending. Barbara suggested that Connie probably should have gone through with the divorce she had planned, instead of deciding to get erased. Divorce. Connie felt as if someone had slapped her. Seeing how upset she was, after a little hesitation Barbara gave her a brief history of the breakup as Connie had told it to her a year earlier.

Harry was waiting in her office when Connie returned to the brokerage that afternoon. The other dealers were trying not to look curious.

"Harry. What brings you here?" She hung up her coat, trying to avoid his stare.

"I ran into John Holland today."

"Yes?"

"Why are you going around behind my back like this, Connie? If you've got some problem with the way things are going, why don't you tell me?"

She sat down behind her desk. "I don't have any problems."

He blew up. "Don't jerk me around, Connie! You think I'm stupid? What do you think Holland told me? You think I didn't go through with erasure, don't you. What kind of bastard do you take me for?"

Through the window that faced the trading room she could see the agents' faces turn toward the office.

"Don't shout. Draw the curtains."

"Screw the curtains! I want to know what's going on in that head of yours."

"That's a first. You never seemed to care much before. You wanted me to wipe out what's in my head. You want it now."

He paced back and forth before the window, hands knotted behind his back. "That's not fair," he said.

She felt vulnerable. "Maybe it's not. This has been rough for me. I can't help wondering about what things were like before I was erased."

"How would I know? Hasn't it been good since? Why rake up the past?"

"I can't change the past, Harry. It happened."

"What do you mean? Why would we get erased if not to change it?"

"So you did get erased?"

He stopped pacing and looked at her. The silence became uncomfortable. But she wouldn't wilt under that stare anymore. He closed his eyes, opened them again.

"That question doesn't deserve an answer," he said. "I'm your husband."

Now she was mad. "I'm your wife. I deserve the truth."

He sat down in the chair meant for her clients. "You really hate me, don't you?"

"You lied to me before. I have to know that you're not lying again."

Harry seemed to relax. It was a comfortable chair—she always treated her clients well.

"I love you," he said. "I've always loved you."

"That's not enough. I have to know the truth."

Instead of rushing to reassure her, he sat in the chair as if he had come there to talk about commodity options. His sudden withdrawal left Connie off-balance, as if a door she had been pushing against had been suddenly opened. "Say something, Harry. For god's sake—"

"Would you believe me if I said yes, I was erased?"

She hesitated. "I think so."

"Yes, I was erased. I don't remember any lies. Now what happens the next time I don't do what you expect? The next time I let you down?"

Connie felt dizzy. "I don't know. We'll have to see. It's not that simple—"

"You can explain it to me sometime." Harry shuddered visibly. He looked at the floor. "Maybe this wasn't such a hot idea."

She didn't know what to say. He stood. "I've got to go. I'm tired. I feel like I'm losing everything."

You squandered it, she thought. "Harry—"

"I'm going to move out for a while, Connie. I'll be gone by the time you get home."

Connie tried to say something, but he was gone. She couldn't say she wanted to see him there that evening, or any other evening. She felt ill. She replayed the scene in her mind, shuddering herself as she thought of Harry sitting impassively in the chair like a stunned animal. The traders were back to staring at their terminals; their curiosity evaporated when Harry left, or perhaps the gossip was put on hold until after hours.

Ten minutes later she went to her own terminal, read in the current market, hooked into Fox and the newsline. There were only forty minutes left in the trading session; the dollar was up against the ECU and off twenty against the yen. Activity was quiet; ninety-two traders in the pit circuit and everybody waiting for the 1500 EST release of the latest U.S. Gross National Product report. Connie evened up several accounts and went long dollars for her own account in anticipation of a positive report, contrary to expectations. At release time the GNP was up, and she made thirty thousand dollars before the close of trading.

After work she went to one of the best restaurants in town, ate alone, had three drinks. She had no desire to get home early. It had started raining by the time she left the restaurant; the lower level of the streetcar was crowded, and it was after eleven when she reached home. She got soaked in the half-block from the stop to her door. Harry wasn't there. She undressed, toweled her hair, and got into a robe. His closet was empty, the drawers of his dresser pulled open and bare, only his spare razor in the bathroom. By this time the wind had picked up and the rain rattled the windowpanes. She ran through the house turning on lights, closing windows, shutting off the lights again.

Harry's workroom was last. His computer was gone; he must have been able to get a van on short notice. The rest of his junk was still there. Maybe he still hoped to come back. The window beside his worktable stood open two inches, and the rain blew in. She ought to just leave it open, let Harry worry about his own machines, if he worried. She realized suddenly that despite all the time he had for them, he might not care about the machines at all. Well, she couldn't leave them at that.

Connie struggled to close the window all the way, but someone had jammed it downward crookedly so that it was caught at an angle in the frame, fighting against itself. It could not be forced closed. She grabbed the handles at the bottom of the frame and jerked upward. Nothing. She bent her knees and pulled with all her strength. It would not budge. When she let off, the muscles of her arms quivered with weakness. Already her slippers and the bottom of her robe were wet. The tree limbs outside the window raged back and forth in the wind; the rain drummed on the roof.

She found a crescent wrench. Using a short length of pipe as a fulcrum, she levered the wrench under the window and leaned all her weight on it. Her wet hands were slick, and the tight grip flushed the blood out of them. She put her shoulders into it and shoved the wrench downward. The window shot up an inch, the wrench slipped, and she fell. A gash in the palm of her hand bled profusely. She got up and pulled the window open, jiggling it when it stuck. The storm was at its height; when she leaned over to draw the window down again, the rain flew into her face. She gritted her teeth; it was almost a smile. The counterweights squeaked in the wall until the window was completely closed.

The drumming of rain on the roof increased. She sat on the floor in her wet robe and sucked the blood from her cut. It was not as bad as she'd thought.

IN INFINITY MEETING IN INFINITY MEETING IN INFINITY MEETIN
TING IN INFINITY MEETING IN INFINITY MEETING IN INFINITY ME
MEETING IN INFINITY MEETING IN INFINITY MEETING IN INFINITY
ITY MEETING IN INFINITY MEETING IN INFINITY MEETING IN INF
INFINITY MEETING IN INFINITY MEETING IN INFINITY MEETING IN
G IN INFINITY MEETING IN INFINITY MEETING IN INFINITY MEETIN
ETING IN INFINITY MEETING IN INFINITY MEETING IN INFINITY M
MEETING IN INFINITY MEETING IN INFINITY MEETING IN INFINIT
NITY MEET   EETING IN INF
INFINITY M   Y MEETING I
G IN INFINITY MEETING IN INFINITY MEETING IN INFINITY MEET
EETING IN INFINITY MEETING IN INFINITY MEETING IN INFINITY M
Y MEETING IN INFINITY MEETING IN INFINITY MEETING IN INFINI
FINITY MEETING IN INFINITY MEETING IN INFINITY MEETING IN IN
N INFINITY MEETING IN INFINITY MEETING IN INFINITY MEETING

faustfeathers

one

I F FRATER ALBERGUS WAS EVER TO DRAW DOCTOR FAUSTUS INTO IN-criminating conversation, the time was now. The afterdinner talk had been light. The Rathaus clock had struck nine, and Faustus's servant Wagner had retired to the student quarters. The doctor seemed at ease. Albergus determined to trick Faustus into some statement that would indicate that he had indeed made a contract with the Fiend.

"So tell me, learned Faustus, how you discovered the secret of this miraculous alembic."

"Just lucky, I guess," Faustus said.

Leaning forward over his glass of hock, he placed one end of a tightly rolled cylinder of brown leaves into his mouth, and the other into the candle's flame. He sucked air through the cylinder until the end caught fire, leaned back, and exhaled a plume of vile smoke. Albergus coughed.

Faustus pushed forward a box full of the cylinders. "Have a cigar."

As Albergus reached out uncertainly, Faustus added, "Just one."

"To be sure."

Faustus had accepted Albergus's letter of introduction from Doctor Phutatorious of Nuremberg at its face value. As far as Faustus knew, then, Albergus was simply a brother logician. The Pope had warned Albergus before he'd left the Holy See that these Protestant academicians were shrewd, and Faustus the shrewdest of them all. But if Albergus could prove that Faustus was behind the practical jokes and infernal assaults the pontiff had recently suffered, much of the Protestant leadership of Germany would be discredited. It would be a great victory for the Roman Church—and for Albergus, the Pope's personal astrologer.

But there was something else: the fires of curiosity burned as brightly in Albergus as in any scholar of the age. If Faustus had made an infernal pact, then he knew things one could know only through the forfeit of one's soul. Knowledge perhaps of the meaning of life itself! Such knowledge might be worth the loss of the soul, but Albergus was too cautious a man to pay in that coin. Faustus, however, had already paid. By clever catechizing perhaps Albergus could steal from him the prize without ever having to risk a wager.

"What is the nature of this—this 'seegar' you burn here, Faustus? Albertus Magnus speaks of securing rooms against evil spirits by burning certain herbs, but he advocates the use of a brazier. Does not this smoke taste noxious to the palate?"

Faustus rested his head in his hand, the cigar jutting from between two fingers beside his ear. His expression was melancholy. "I've had better smokes, but you won't be able to get them for a couple of hundred years. I just burn these ropes to drive the bugs away."

Albergus gingerly held the unlit cigar to his nose. It smelled sweet. "In Nuremberg it is said that you have had some success in conjuring the shades of historical figures."

"Hysterical figures. And I do mean figures. You should meet that Helen."

"Helen of Troy?"

"Troy, Schenectady—one of those cities. I forget."

Albergus leapt at Faustus's indiscretion. "So you have indeed raised the dead?"

"She only seems that way. Are you going to smoke that cigar or eat it? Go ahead; you can pay me later."

"Pay you?"

"Money, money, money!—that's all you care about. It's destroying our marriage!" Faustus blew smoke at him. His large black eyebrows arched. "These cigars would cost a couple of kroner on the open market. Of course it's closed now, so you're left to your own devices. You did bring your devices, didn't you? If not, you'll have to get your brothers to help you."

"I have no brothers—"

"Your father must have been relieved."

"My dear Faustus, do not insult me. I may only be an itinerant scholar, but I've come all the way from Vienna just to sit at your feet and learn."

"As long as you're down there, how about shining those shoes?"

"You treat me as if I were a mountebank."

"Oh, high finance, eh? Well, money means nothing here, my friend. You'll learn soon enough that a little Latin goes a long way in this university. There used to be a little Latin around here, but he went away. That's how I got this job. You look a little Latin yourself, and I wish you'd gone with him. You young scholars want to dance to the music without paying the piper. And what does it get you? Asparagus, or contract bridge. But a card like you could care less who holds the bridge contract, as long as you can pass water under it. Speaking of contracts, do you really think you're going to get your hands on mine?"

Albergus was at a loss. "I'm sure I don't know what you are talking about."

"If you're so sure why aren't you rich? You brute! No, don't try to apologize."

"I didn't come here to be insulted."

"This is a good place for it. Where do you usually go?"

Albergus stood, sweating. He tried conciliation. "I beg your pardon, learned Faustus. I—"

"I can't pardon you. You'll have to talk to the Pope. Too bad, I hear he's not much of an audience. Well, it's certainly been a pleasure talking to myself this evening. I must visit myself more often. As for you, sir, I want you to remember that scholarship is as scholarship does, and neither does my wife, if I had one, which I don't. Nor do my children, if I had any, who would be proud of me for saying so. Now get out!"

Faustus struck a pose of injured dignity and pointed at the door. His lower lip was thrust out beneath his mustache, and his new-fangled spectacles glinted in the candlelight. Thus driven from the field of verbal combat, Frater Albergus could not doubt that this was the greatest alchemist, logician, and philosopher in all of Christendom.

two

Something was rotten in the town of Wittenberg, and Albergus suspected it was in the pocket of the more sloppy of the two sloppy men he summoned to his room at The Boar's Bollocks the next morning. The man's face was round and empty as the full moon, and from ten feet away he smelled like a Sicilian fishmonger. From five feet away he smelled like the fish. Curly red hair exploded from beneath his floppy hat.

His companion's hat was black and came to a point that hinted at a pointed skull beneath it. His coat was shabby and two sizes too small, and he wore a look of small-minded guile.

"Noble Robin and gentle Dicolini, welcome!" Albergus extended his hand.

Robin loped forward and shook it vigorously. His grasp was cold and clammy, and when Albergus got free he found himself holding a dead carp. He recoiled and dropped it onto the floor. Robin looked offended.

"Atsa some joke, eh boss?" Dicolini said.

"Gentlemen, gentlemen." Albergus forced himself to remain calm. "Let us speak of our business. I have called you here because you are brother scholars, acquainted with the university, and students of the renowned Doctor Faustus. I have also heard that you are available for delicate work and for a reasonable fee can keep your mouths shut. I trust I have not been misled?"

"I keepa my mouth shut for nothing," Dicolini said. "Robin, his mouth cost extra."

Robin opened his mouth and stuck out his tongue, which had a price painted on it. He honked like a goose.

"What I want you to do is to keep an eye on Doctor Faustus for me."

"Atsa different story. Eyes cost more."

"No, no. 'Keep an eye on him'—that's just an expression."

"You want the whole expression, it cost you a pretty penny. We give you a pretty expression, though." Robin puffed out his cheeks, pursed his lips, and crossed his eyes.

Albergus swallowed and began again. "I want you to find out how Faustus spends his evenings. Does he practice black magic? Is he in league with infernal forces? And I need proof, the sooner the better. Should you do this for me, your investigation shall receive such thanks as fits a king's remembrance."

Dicolini looked suspicious. "How much you gonna pay?"

Albergus winced: there was no need for subtlety with these two. "I'll pay you ten silver pieces."

"We a-no want no pieces. We want the whole thing." Robin honked agreement.

Albergus was taken aback. "Another ten pieces, then, if you provide me with the information I need. That's all."

"How do we know thatsa all?"

"What?"

"Look, we shadow Faustus for you, how we gonna know when you give us ten pieces thatsa the whole thing?"

"But I'm offering you twenty pieces for shadowing Faustus."

"See what I mean? First you gotta ten pieces, now you gotta twenty pieces, but we no gotta the whole thing."

"You shadow Faustus for me, and then we'll talk about the whole thing."

"You no understand. Suppose I drop a vase, itsa break. How many pieces I got? I don't know; I gotta count them. Now maybe you give me ten pieces, you give me twenty pieces, I still don't have them all, maybe. I shatter vase, we shadow Faustus, itsa same thing: we no gonna do the job unless we know we gotta the whole thing."

As Albergus and Dicolini haggled, Robin crept behind them. He drew another carp from the folds of his ragged cloak and slipped it onto Albergus's chair.

By this time Dicolini had bumped the spy rental-rate up to thirty silver pieces per day. Albergus's face was red from argument. He drew a kerchief from his sleeve, mopped his brow, and sat down to catch his breath. A moment later he let out a strangled cry and leapt from the chair, cracking his knee against the table. He picked up the fish with two fingers and held it out at arm's length.

"What's this?" he demanded.

Robin whipped out his sword and lunged, impaling the carp and the sleeve of Albergus's doublet. Albergus fell back and slipped on the first carp. His arms flew up, jerking Robin toward him. Dicolini caught Albergus under the shoulders, and Robin, with a honk, sprawled on top of him.

"Atsa fish," Dicolini said.

Albergus struggled out of Dicolini's grasp and tried to draw the sword from his sleeve. Unfortunately, Robin's hand was caught in the guard. By the time Robin let go, the sword's pommel was wedged under the clasp that held Albergus's cloak closed around his neck. The guard pressed his throat, and his arm stretched out along the length of the blade as if tied to a splint. The point pricked the palm of his hand. Chin forced high into the air, Albergus whirled about like a manic signpost. The two students eyed him warily.

"Take it easy, boss," Dicolini said. "We get you out."

All he wanted was to get out of this interview alive.

Robin leapt upon Albergus's back and shoved a hand down his collar. Albergus staggered. Dicolini pulled him over onto the table. He lay spread-eagled while Robin got hold of the sword and began to draw it through the collar of his cloak. The blade slid across Albergus's neck. They were going to cut his throat.

"Relax, boss," Dicolini said, sitting on his left arm. "We take care of everything."

Albergus held his breath, not daring to cry out. He felt the rapier tickle his beard. The pressure on his neck eased as the blade slid by. The putrid carp caught against his upthrust chin. Then the sword was gone and the fish lay on his throat. He let out a huge breath. His body was covered with sweat.

Robin shook hands with Dicolini.

"Gentlemen," said Albergus, as he tugged his clothes and his dignity back into order. "I trust we are in agreement now? You'll do this piece of work for me?"

"We do the whole thing," said Dicolini. Robin honked.

"Splendid." He steered them toward the door, his arms across their shoulders.

"We gotta go now," Dicolini said. "We're gonna be late for the classes we wanna miss."

"My apologies. Just make sure you get me something I can use against Faustus."

Robin pulled a red-hot poker out of the pocket of his robe. He gripped the iron in both hands, waving the glowing tip beneath Albergus's nose. Albergus fell back. Robin, grinning wildly, offered him the poker.

Dicolini shoved Robin. "Whatsa matter for you? You crazy? Faustus no play poker, hesa play bridge."

Robin looked hurt. He put the iron back into his pocket.

three

Wagner habitually sat in the front row of Doctor Faustus's afternoon alchemy class. As the doctor's fag, supposedly his favorite student, he was obliged to remain at the scholar's beck and call. It was not easy work. Faustus only seemed interested in Wagner when he could design another humiliation for him.

Doctor Faustus strode back and forth in front of the lecture hall in his queer long-legged lope, his black academic gown swirling behind him. The visiting scholar Albergus, whom Wagner had met the night before while serving at Faustus's table, watched the doctor with rapt attention.

Wagner had thought that being accepted as Faustus's student would be the beginning of the prestige he had dreamt of since boyhood. He longed to command the arcane powers that Faustus alone understood. Then maybe powerful men would cross continents to hear *him* speak! Beautiful women would cross time itself to give him pleasure.

For Wagner was in love. Yes, he wanted to know the secrets of the universe, but he would not have put up with a tenth of the indignities to which Faustus had subjected him had he not by chance glimpsed Helen of Troy in the doctor's bedchamber one evening. From that moment his heart had not been his own. To go back to the women of Wittenberg after seeing fair Helen would be like settling for porridge after the promise of roast mutton. With onions.

Doctor Faustus had drawn a curtain at the front of the hall to expose an elaborate chart of the human head, marked with astrological notation.

"Here we have a diagram of the astral mind in the fourth quarter of the phrenological year." Faustus tapped the top of the skull with a pointer. "You'll note the eruptions at the zenith. These eruptions can be cleared up with fulminate of mercury, but the woman only comes on Tuesday afternoons. The rest of the week you have to take care of yourself, if you know what's good for you. Wagner, tell us what's good for you."

Startled out of daydreams of Helen, Wagner stumbled to his feet. He said the first thing that came into his head. "Chastity, Doctor Faustus."

Faustus rocked back and forth on his heels, his hands folded behind his back. "Chastity, is it? What about obedience?"

"Obedience!"

"Poverty?"

"That too."

"Quit monking around, boy!" Who do you think you're kidding? Why don't you sit down and hibernate until that bonus in your codpiece goes away. Or is that a cod in your bonuspiece?"

There was a crash from the corner of the classroom. Faustus turned on Robin and Dicolini, who sprawled facedown on the floor. One had tripped over the other, who had tripped over his sword while sneaking into the room.

"Late for class again, eh?"

As the two students slid into seats in the front row, a chicken burst out of Robin's cloak. He grabbed for it, but the unfortunate creature shot from his arms and skittered across Faustus's lectern. Robin dove after, scattering Faustus's notes, caught the squawking fowl, and shoved it into an interior pocket.

"We a-no late," Dicolini said.

Faustus stormed over. "Why, the town clock struck not five minutes ago. It's half past three!"

"No it's not."

Robin pulled an hourglass from somewhere in his bottomless cloak and waved it at Faustus. All the sand was in the bottom of the glass.

"See. We're right on time," Dicolini said.

"Not according to that," Faustus said.

"Atsa run a little fast. She'sa use quicksand."

"Oh, no. You can't fool me that easily. It must be four o'clock by that hourglass."

"Then class is over. Let's go, Robbie." Dicolini got up to leave.

"Hold on, Macduff. I'm not done with this lecture yet."

"Too bad. We're done listening."

"Well, you can forget about leaving until *my* clock strikes four. Time is money, and my time is worth at least a couple of marks. You boys look like a couple of marks. Are you brothers?"

Robin was insulted. He huffed and puffed as if he were about to go berserk.

"My friend, hesa get pretty mad," Dicolini said. "You watch out, or he give you a piece of his mind."

"No thanks. I wouldn't want to take the last piece."

"Atsa okay. He won't notice."

"Well, if you say so." Faustus reached for Robin's arm. "Come up here, young man." Somehow, the doctor found himself holding the student's thigh; he dropped it in disgust. "Let's take a look at your skull."

Robin pulled a glowing skull from inside his cloak and presented it to the doctor. The class recoiled in horror—save for Faustus, who calmly popped the jaws open and relit his cigar from the candle burning inside. He tossed the skull over his shoulder, stood Robin in front of the chart, and backed off a step to appraise him. With his round face and drooping lip, Robin looked about as intelligent as a hard-boiled egg.

Faustus tapped the pointer against Robin's head. "The astral mind is responsible for contact with the spiritual world without the intervention of either seraphim or cherubim. You all know what a seraph is, don't you?"

Dicolini stood proudly. "Sure. On my pancakes, I like a maple seraph."

"No, no. Cherubs, seraphs."

"I no like a cherub. I like a maple."

"These aren't food—they're angels."

"I no like angel food, either."

"Well, that takes the cake. Where was I?" Faustus turned back to Robin. "Oh, yes—the astral mind."

Robin was rubbing up against the chart like a cat.

"Let's forget about the astral mind. That's obviously not relevant with this subject. Don't let me wake you, now. I'm not offending you by talking, am I?"

Robin honked.

"Gesundheit. Moving south from the astral mind, we come to the inferior regions of the intellect. And when I say inferior, I mean inferior. The inferior mind, as you'll remember from our last lecture, is responsible for worldly thought, for instance, how did your nose get that way and wasn't that a great plague we had last month. Worldly thought, of course, must be processed by one of the other organs before it becomes definable in emotional terms. The heart, for instance, controls affection, the liver, love, and the spleen, anger. Who can tell us what the kidneys control?"

Dicolini rose again. "The kidneys keep their legs from bending backwards."

Faustus leaned toward Albergus. "Do you hear voices?" Dicolini looked about him to accept the congratulations of his fellow students. Faustus turned on him. "A kid's knees already bend backwards. Do you have any more bright ideas?"

"Not right now. I let you know."

"Do that. Drop me a postcard to warn me when you'll arrive. If I had a couple more students like you boys I could change gold into base metal."

Wagner longed for the end of class so he could return to his room to think his thoughts of Helen in private. Robin, left to himself behind the podium, pretended *he* was the lecturer. He opened the book before him, and a small cloud of dust billowed from the ancient pages. He took out his kerchief with a flourish, sneezed, and then blew his nose with a sound that was not quite as loud as the Emperor's fanfare. At that moment there was a flash of light and a smell of sulphur. When Wagner's vision readjusted, he saw an imp standing on the edge of the podium. Its tiny red eyes glowed, and its barbed tail lashed with impatience. Albergus gasped. Faustus stubbed his cigar out on Dicolini's hat. Robin's face lit with delight. He held out his hand to the imp.

"Oh no you don't!" Faustus said, lunging for the podium.

"Come on, Robbie!" Dicolini yelled.

The imp leapt onto Robin's shoulder. Faustus and Robin danced back and forth on opposite sides of the lectern. Robin made a dash for the door, and once he was through Dicolini slammed it in Faustus's face. Faustus paced angrily back to the lectern, whirled and pointed a finger at Wagner.

"As your punishment, you will bring that demon back to me by midnight."

Dumbfounded, Wagner struggled from his seat. "But, Magister, I didn't do anything!"

Faustus shrugged. "Since when has that made any difference around here?"

four

When he hungers, I'll feed him his own intestines, Mephistophilis thought. Imagining tortures for Faustus had become his only defense.

"Midnight tonight, noble Faustus," he said. "Then do the jaws of hell open to receive thee."

Faustus held out a cigar. "Light it," he commanded.

The cigar's tip caught fire, and Faustus took a few speculative puffs. "And what happens after that?"

Mephistophilis separated his hands, as if parting a curtain, re-

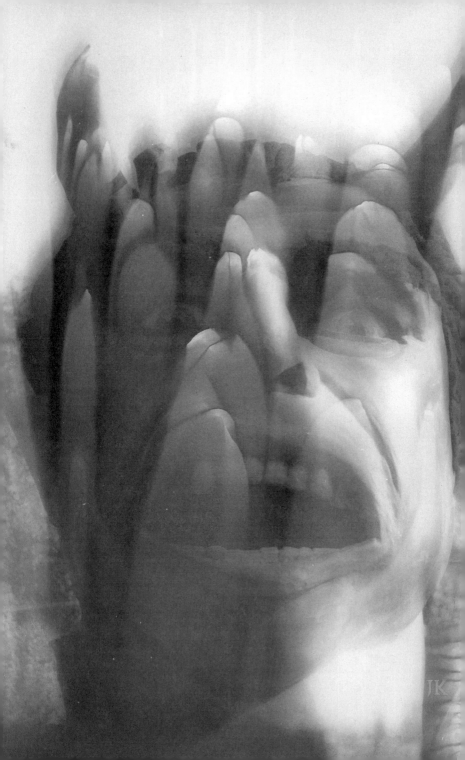

vealing a vision of Dis, the city of hell, and the souls in torment there.

"You will be thrown into this perpetual torture-house. These are the furies, tossing damned souls on burning forks; their bodies boil in lead. Over here are humans broiling on coals that can never die. These souls that are fed with sops of burning fire were gluttons in their lives who laughed to see the poor starve at their gates. But they are nothing. You shall see ten thousand tortures more horrid."

"You're not much of a travel agent. 'See Dis and die.'"

"Usually it's the other way around."

"You're right," Faustus said ruefully. "Dis ain't no joke."

"Fools that will laugh on earth must weep in hell."

"Sure you won't settle for a moan in Cologne?"

Grubs on the eyeballs. Maybe he'd start him with that. In the meantime, there was no sense in reminding Faustus of his fast-approaching damnation. Mephistophilis dissolved the vision of hell. He ought not to do the other side's work for it: Faustus might still repent. But Mephistophilis doubted that he would—Faustus never took anything seriously, and he showed no signs of being about to turn over a new leaf. Instead he insisted on playing more silly pranks.

"Why set Wagner the task of recovering the imp that Robin's tricks have set free? The imp is a creature of fire. Command, and I will retrieve it before the clock has pronounced a single minute."

"That goes without saying. Which you never do. If I'd wanted a course in public speaking I would have conjured up Demosthenes, or Dale Carnegie. How's Dale doing these days, anyway?"

"He has great influence in low places."

"A friend of yours, eh?"

When he thirsts he'll get hot bile. Twenty-four years of Faustus's repartee had taken its toll on such a lover of urbane wit as Mephistophilis. When he fell from heaven, he knew he was in for a poorer class of associate, but he didn't think it could get this low. This was hell, nor was he out of it.

Faustus had spared Mephistophilis no humiliation in the idiocy of the tasks he had put to him. Every time he was summoned, Mephistophilis found himself sticking antlers on some moronic ostler, changing bales of hay into horses, or whacking the Pope on the head with a bladder. There was no subtlety to it. He had expected more from the great scholar.

"By the way," said Faustus, "have you seen Helen lately?"

"In your closet."

"In my closet! What's she doing in there?"

"You told her to get in."

"I did?" Faustus crossed his arms and rubbed his chin. "Oh, yes. Literal girl. Thank heaven for literal girls."

"Heaven had nothing to do with it."

"You're not kidding."

"Shall I have her dress?"

"It wouldn't fit you. Work on your thighs."

When he tires, I'll strap him to a bed of razors.

Faustus paced back and forth. "So she's in the closet, eh? And here I stand bantering with the servants. Get her out here pronto. If she won't come, call for me and I'll go in after her. If I don't come back, you can have my astrolabe."

"Worry not about Helen, Faustus. If she disobeys you, I'll cull thee out the wildest Fräuleins in the north of Europe."

"The cull of the wild, eh? Sounds like a bunch of dogs to me. And who's going to clean up after them, tell me that? If I gave you half a chance, you'd wreck this happy home." He swept out a book of raffle tickets and proffered them. "How about half a chance? Cost you ten marks."

An eon up to his chin in boiling manure. "No, thank you," Mephistophilis said.

"Don't feel lucky, eh? Okay, just keep an eye on Wagner for me then. He wants to examine Helen's thesis. Can you imagine the consequences if she managed to seduce that boy? Why, she's been dead for two thousand years! What would his mother say? What would *I* say?"

Mephistophilis would have sighed had it been necessary for him to breathe. "What would you say?"

"Is it true that you wash your hair in clam broth?"

A codpiece burning iron.

five

Helen had been in the closet for a long time. She could not say exactly how long, for she had seen no sign of day or night during her confinement. Being a shade (albeit a fleshly one), she was not particularly concerned with the passage of time anyway. Mostly, she was bored.

Helen's duty had been to distract Faustus from his damnation, and Mephistophilis could not accuse her of failing to lie down on the job. She had enjoyed Faustus's attentions much of the time. Not all the time, however. She wanted variety. She wanted gaiety, she wanted laughter, she wanted to dance! And although Faustus had allowed her to wear some very interesting garments—garments that might have stirred the passion even of an Achilles (known to have a preference for young soldiers)—she was just as likely, on Faustus's whim, to end up in an uncomfortable position. Such as the closet. How she wished something would happen!

As if the gods were eavesdropping, the door opened and a man rushed in. He fumbled in the darkness, his hands stretched before him as if he were blind. But Helen's eyes were accustomed to the gloom, and she recognized him immediately as Doctor Faustus's servant, Wagner. He tripped over a pair of the boots Faustus had insisted on giving her and fell into her arms.

"Mrrumph!" he cried. "Who is it?"

She helped him up. "It is I, Helen."

"Helen!" Suddenly the young man seemed to have difficulty breathing. "Helen! Just who I've been looking for. I must see you."

"And here I am without a candle."

"No one can hold a candle to you. I need you, Helen. You cannot know the torture I've been through imagining what Faustus has been doing with you."

"Is that why you came into the closet?"

"Faustus sent me on a fool's errand, but now that I've met you I'll never play the fool again. He expects me to find a demon he lost; I snuck in here to search his books for a spell to help me. I don't know why he can't do it himself."

"He knows how to do it himself, believe me," Helen said. "But sometimes he'd rather not. Look at me."

Wagner grasped her shoulders and pulled her to him. "I wish I could. I dashed in here only to escape detection when I heard voices in the next room." His nose wrinkled. "Do you smell burning sulphur?"

"You should never eat radishes."

"Who can he have out there with him?"

Helen could see only one way to keep Wagner from finding out about Mephistophilis and Faustus's contract. And he was not an uncomely lad.

"Some visiting scholar, surely." She drew Wagner's head down to her breast. "I'm so glad you found me. I didn't even suspect that you knew of my existence. But you must go now."

"Go? But I just got here!"

"Nevertheless." She pried him loose. "If Faustus found you here his jealousy would know no bounds. Come back later, fair student. Tonight! Faustus will be gone until midnight. Return at ten, and I will show you arts of which I alone am mistress. Until then you must do his bidding."

"Ten? How can I wait that long, thinking of you?"

"Troilus recommends cold baths and strenuous exercise. Until ten, my love!" She propelled him through the door and shut it.

When she heard him leave the room, Helen smiled. She didn't really know whether Faustus would be out at ten, but she had already forgotten about that. She was going to have some fun at last.

six

Robin's conjuring of the demon had been enough for Frater Albergus: such magical prowess, conferred on an idiot through the mere inspection of Faustus's magical book, indicated that the stories of the scholar's pact with the devil were true. Even granting the dangers of practicing black magic, the thought of the secrets in that book was enough to make Albergus tremble like a stallion in spring.

He sat at a table in the corner of The Boar's Bollocks and plotted how to break into Faustus's rooms that night. As he calculated the best time to make his assault, he was interrupted.

"Pardon me, sir." It was the student, Wagner. "I am looking for my fellow students Robin and Dicolini. Have you seen them?"

"Not since they fled your master's lecture."

Wagner looked melancholy. He sat on the bench next to Albergus. "I've exhausted myself searching. I thought they were my friends, but it seems they are more interested in other matters now."

"A sad breach of faith." Albergus wondered if he might not use this limp fool to his advantage. "Is there anything a fellow scholar can do?"

"Nothing. Unless you can retrieve the imp that Robin called up."

The stars were with him! "I am not without some magical prowess," Albergus said casually. "Perhaps I can locate it. Not only that, but if you'll tell me when Faustus will be away, I can deposit the creature—caged—in his rooms. It would make a good joke, don't you think? Especially after the shameful way he treated you today."

Wagner looked like a puppy in a butcher's shop. "If you could do that, my gratitude would surpass Goneril's to her father."

"You have only to ask."

"Yes, good Frater, please! Faustus told me he would not be home until midnight tonight. If you can arrive before then. . . ."

"I shall be there at ten."

Wagner looked worried. "Better make it eleven. Eleven-thirty? I have affairs—uh—business. I will let you in."

"Leave it to me," Albergus said. "I will be discreet."

Wagner shook Albergus's hand vigorously. He looked as excited as a groom on his wedding day. He left whistling.

There would be nothing Wagner could do when Albergus showed up with a mouthful of excuses instead of the imp. Once Albergus was inside Faustus's apartments, the battle was won, the book was his. Still, it would be a delicate operation; he would have to be careful not to compromise himself. The student Wagner was no problem; Albergus would have him arrested with Faustus, and they would burn on the same pyre. But Albergus could not afford to be recognized by some ostler or servingman when he stole the book. A disguise! He rubbed his hands together and smiled. A false mustache, a change of clothing, and he himself could impersonate Faustus. Brilliant! He was so pleased with himself that he decided to go immediately and ask the Bishop of Wittenberg to assemble an ecclesiastical tribunal. He left a few pfennig and half a tankard of ale on the table.

As soon as he was out the door Robin and Dicolini emerged from beneath the table, where they had been playing cards. Dicolini drained Albergus's ale in two gulps and pocketed the tankard. Robin picked up the coins and bit through one. He chewed thoughtfully for a moment, then pulled a saltshaker from his pocket, gave the remainder a liberal sprinkle, and popped it into his mouth.

"You hear that, Robbie? That Icebergus, hesa cross-double us. Hesa break the case himself and keep alla pieces. We gonna have to get tough."

Robin thrust one fist under Dicolini's nose; his other arm went into a windmill windup. Dicolini kicked him in the shin.

"Whatsa matter for you! Getta tough with him, not me! Now listen, we gotta move fast and get to Faustus's place first, before the boss, before Wagner, before anybody. We get there so early we be there before we arrive."

Robin honked approval.

Little did they know that Faustus himself was relaxing in a private room upstairs with a cigar and a flagon of distilled wine. He has his feet up on the rump of Mephistophilis, who played the part of ottoman that evening, complete to burnoose and scimitar. Mephistophilis remained abjectly subservient, giving no sign of the thoughts that swirled through his mind like acid in an alchemist's flask. Faustus could not know what the archfiend intended to do with that scimitar at the stroke of midnight. Stroke was the proper word.

At that very moment Wagner was lowering himself into a tub in the basement. The innkeeper stared in astonishment: he had had to break a skim of ice on the rain barrel in order to draw this madman's bath. "Th-thank you, good friend," said Wagner. "Th-this is perfect." The innkeeper shook his head and withdrew. The temperature of the water did little to cool Wagner's desire. His thoughts flew to his rendezvous with Helen. He would disguise himself as Faustus and surprise her. How she would laugh, and how sweet his revenge against his taskmaster would be!

Helen, meanwhile, was in the closet.

seven

"Okay, Robbie. You tug onna rope, and I'll get in through the window." Robin and Dicolini had managed to get a rope looped around one of the joists that jutted out below the eaves of the building. One end was tied around Dicolini's belly, and Robin held the other. "Keep a lookout. If anybody comes, whistle."

Robin spat into his palms, rubbed them together, leapt high into the air, and seized hold of the rope. He came down with a jerk. The rope tightened viciously around Dicolini's waist, yanking him two feet into the air. There he hung, unable to draw breath enough to protest. Robin hung on the opposite side, wriggling and tugging in the effort to pull his partner higher. They banged into each other, flopping like hooked fish. The Rathaus clock struck nine forty-five.

∞   ∞   ∞

Wagner arrived at the door to the courtyard and knocked for the porter. Martin, who had been drinking the master's hock since matins, shuffled out of his tiny room into the cold of the evening and opened the door.

"My services are needed in the apartment of Doctor Faustus," Wagner told him. He passed through the courtyard and up the stairs. Quietly, he tried the door to Faustus's rooms and found it unlocked. The common room was dark; he lit a candle and opened the bedroom door a crack. It seemed that no one was about. He closed the door behind him, took the bundle from beneath his arm, and slipped into a nightshirt and cap, painting a broad greasepaint version of Faustus's mustache beneath his nose. He donned a stolen pair of the doctor's spectacles and sidled over to the closet.

"Helen!" He opened the door and stood at the threshold.

"Darling!" Helen gasped, throwing her arms around his neck. Her ardor surprised him; he wondered if she remembered their date. "Don't worry—it's me, Wagner," he said. "You can come out now."

Helen froze. "Oh!"

"What's the matter?"

"I thought you were Faustus. I forgot to tell you that I can't come out of the closet until he says I can. After all, I am his to command." She smiled sheepishly. "Would you like to come in?"

Damn! If only he'd kept his mouth shut! He was pondering his next step when he heard voices in the adjoining room. He rushed into the closet and slammed the door. Helen pressed against him. Maybe the closet wasn't so bad after all.

They listened. Through the closed door they could hear Faustus's muffled voice. "I wish you'd stop following me around," Faustus said. "I just want to get ready for bed."

"You shall not sleep this night, Faustus." A voice like a razor scraping glass.

"I won't if you keep pestering me. Go away." A rush of air. "Now where's my nightshirt? I thought I left it lying around here somewhere. Are you still in there?"

"Who?" Helen said.

"Unless you've got an owl in there, Helen of Troy."

Wagner nudged Helen frantically. "What owl?" she asked. "There's no owl in here."

"Owl take your word for it. Does one of you birds want to hand me my nightshirt?"

Wagner pawed through the clothes until he found a nightshirt.

He gave it to Helen, and she opened the door a crack to hand it out. Faustus peeked in.

"Hope it isn't too boring in there."

"Not yet. I wouldn't mind some fresh air once in a while."

Faustus sniffed. "The air in there smells pretty fresh already. Or maybe it's my undershirt. Would you like a book to read?"

"No, thank you."

Faustus closed the door, and Wagner breathed a sigh of relief. He listened closely and heard Faustus leave the bedroom. Just then the clock struck the quarter hour and he jumped in surprise.

"You said Faustus would be out tonight."

Helen placed her small hands on his chest. "Did I?"

He decided not to pursue her sin of deception but to concentrate on other, more interesting, sins. But the more he warmed to his task, the less Helen responded. "Noble queen—" he said.

"I'm sorry, but I can't get into the mood lying on old shoes. Can't you find some way to let me out?"

Wagner struggled to control his passion. He had no time! He would need a miracle . . . Faustus's magic book! It had to contain a spell to release her. "Wait here," he said, and slipped out.

∞   ∞   ∞

Outside the courtyard gate, Albergus's impatience had overmastered his reason. Though it was only ten-thirty, he had to get that book! He donned his Faustus disguise of greasepaint mustache, spectacles, and black academic robes and pounded on the courtyard door. Martin, woozy with drink, was fooled.

Albergus mounted the stairs, stepped cautiously into Faustus's rooms, and began to search. He poked his head into the bedroom: it appeared empty. The trunk at the foot of the bed held only clothing. He opened the closet door.

"Darling!" Albergus was seized around the neck, smothered by the touch and scent of an almost-naked woman. He recoiled, trembling. Who knew what incubus or succubus this creature—so womanly to the gaze—might be?

"Can I come out of the closet, dearest? Then will I fulfill your every desire."

"Back, hell-fiend!" Albergus squeaked. He slammed the door.

He wiped the sweat from his brow, then stiffened. There was a scraping at the window. Someone was trying to break in! He slipped out of the room.

∞   ∞   ∞

Dicolini fumbled with the window, his feet braced on the snowy sill. It opened, and he fell into the room. He untied himself, peeked out of the bedroom door, then drew back to decide on his next move. On top of the opened trunk lay a long nightshirt. Dicolini snapped his fingers. He removed his boots, rolled up his trousers, and put on the shirt and a stocking cap. Several containers of unguents sat on a bedside table; he chose the blackest and painted a broad mustache under his prominent nose.

Thus disguised, he was about to sneak into the next room when he heard a woman's voice from the closet.

"Is that you?"

He stood stock-still. "Maybe."

"Please let me out of here."

"Who are you?"

"Don't be silly. You know who I am."

"Itsa slip my mind."

"Well," Helen said sarcastically, "I'm the most beautiful woman in history."

"Never mind coming out. I come in." Dicolini climbed into the closet.

"Darling!" She threw her arms around his neck.

∞   ∞   ∞

Wagner frantically searched Faustus's study, every moment expecting to be discovered. His precious hour with Helen was fast evaporating. Albergus was due at eleven-thirty! Wagner would just have to ignore his arrival—but if Faustus answered the door, what would Albergus tell him? For that matter, where *was* Faustus?

The clock in the Rathaus tower struck eleven. Wagner cursed his evil luck and pawed through the papers on Faustus's writing table. He was about to give up when he noticed the corner of a piece of parchment poking up from between the desk and the wall. He drew it out. It was some sort of contract. He was trying to make out the Latin in the dim lamplight when the door opened. He dove under the desk.

Albergus entered the study, peered about cautiously, and began searching the desk. Finding nothing of interest, he turned to the bookshelves. Wagner, watching, wondered why Faustus should creep so stealthily through his own room—unless there was some supernatural danger abroad. He remembered the strange voice in the bedroom, drew farther back beneath the desk, and shoved the contract inside his shirt.

Eleven-fifteen. Albergus had been lost behind the stacks of books for what seemed an eternity. Wagner was gathering his courage to sneak back to the bedroom when another Faustus, in nightshirt and cap, entered the study. Wagner nearly swallowed his tongue. Albergus cursed and watched in silence, hidden by the shelves.

Muttering to himself, Faustus crossed to the desk and searched through the papers. He pulled manuscripts from the scroll rack above the desk; his knees were inches from Wagner's nose. At last he found a bundle of cigars he'd been seeking. There was a crash in the next room.

"Mice!" Faustus exclaimed, dashing behind a table covered with an alchemical experiment.

∞   ∞   ∞

In the bedroom, Dicolini had long since released Helen from the closet. He had forgotten about shadowing Faustus. He was willing to forget about Robin, Faustus, the known world, if only Helen would prove as willing.

"*Bella fellissima ronzoni, alla pacino,*" Dicolini said, pressing her toward the bed.

"My lord, you know I don't understand Latin."

"Atsa not Latin, atsa Italian."

"I don't understand Italian, either."

"Atsa okay. Neither do I."

Helen began to suspect this was not Doctor Faustus. She resisted, wondering if she ought to get back into the closet. The two fell wrestling onto the bed.

∞   ∞   ∞

Down in the alley, Robin was freezing. The horn beneath his cloak felt like an icicle. He had tacked to his cart a page torn from a book: a woodcut depicting a fire in a brick hearth. He huddled next to it. As he flapped his arms before the illustrated flames, the imp, which had taken up residence on his shoulder, inside his shirt, woke and bit Robin's neck. Robin leapt about in agony, slapping his shoulder. The creature popped out of his cloak and raced up the rope. Robin whistled at it to come down. The imp ignored him and scurried through the window.

Robin ran about frantically, then stopped. A wild gleam came into his eyes. He rummaged through the cart until he found a nightshirt, cap, and spectacles. He smeared some grease from the axle beneath his nose and, thus disguised, climbed the rope after his pet.

As he dropped in through the window, his eyes bulged at the sight of Dicolini and Helen on the bed. Dicolini had lost the advantage of surprise in their wrestling match. The most beautiful woman in history had her foot on his neck; his arms were pinned beneath him. Robin approached, trying to figure out what exactly was going on and how he might join in.

"Faustus!" Dicolini exclaimed. Robin looked over his shoulder in alarm. Helen released Dicolini, who scrambled from the room; she smiled tentatively at Robin.

His smile was as wide as the crescent moon.

"Darling!" she said breathlessly, opening her arms.

Robin's horn honked as he leapt on top of her.

∞   ∞   ∞

Mephistophilis had not spent four million years in damnation for nothing. He was getting an early start from hell; he knew how tricky these souls got as their time approached. He materialized, wrapped in flames and clouds of sulphurous smoke, in the common room just as Dicolini hurtled out of the bedroom. Unable to stop, Dicolini ran headlong into him. The two of them sprawled across Faustus's dining table in an explosion of crockery and candlesticks.

Mephistophilis sprang up and ran a claw through the worms sprouting from his scalp. "Your time is nigh, mortal. You will pay dearly for your sins."

Dicolini's face was a mask of dismay. "I never touched her, boss. Shesa better man than I am."

"You insist on playing the fool even now?"

"No. Hesa still down inna street."

Mephistophilis restrained himself: only a few more minutes until midnight. He left the quaking Faustus and went to question Helen.

Robin and Helen were rolling around on the bed. Once more Helen had realized that this Faust was not the genuine article. Their struggles were punctuated by honks of Robin's horn as it was squeezed against her thigh. At least she hoped it was a horn.

Mephistophilis was nonplussed by this second Faustus. He strode over to the bed, his claws clicking on the bare wooden floor. Robin looked up to see the devil's eyes glowing like coals in the darkness. He leapt from the bed and scurried into the closet.

"It will avail Faustus nothing to hide."

Helen was relieved to see the Prince of Darkness instead of another mustached lover. "I don't think that's Faustus," she said.

"Who is it then?"

"I don't know, but I've seen a lot of him lately."

Mephistophilis became suspicious. "Don't tell me *you've* succumbed to Faustus. Are you doing his bidding?"

"You find him and I'll try."

"Where is he?"

"Hang around awhile. He'll turn up. If not him, then at least someone just as good."

Mephistophilis moaned. "'Better to rule in hell than serve in heaven,' ha!"

∞   ∞   ∞

Dicolini had fled from the common to the study. Faustus, seeing his double enter the room, got up from behind the table.

"So it's you, is it?"

"Atsa crazy," Dicolini said. "Itsa no me. Itsa you."

"How do I know it's me?"

"I just told you. I'm not here."

Faustus puffed his cigar and thought about it. "If you're me, then how come you're not smoking a cigar?"

"You no give me one."

Faustus whipped a cigar out of his pocket. "There you go. Let's see you get out of that one."

"You got a match?"

"Never mind." Faustus took the cigar back.

It was too much for Wagner. He saw his chance to escape. He crawled toward the door, and had almost made it when Faustus spotted him.

"Hold on there!" Faustus shouted. "I can't get away from me that easily!"

Wagner scrambled up and shot out through the common to the bedroom. He did not look back.

Albergus had watched all of this with astonishment. Doppelgängers! Faustus was indeed a master of the black arts. Yet he could not fathom the doctor's reason for putting on this show—unless Faustus knew Albergus was in his apartments, disguised as Faustus. Albergus reasoned from this that he must be close to discovering something that Faustus did not want discovered. He was about to renew his search when he saw something move on a bottom shelf. A rat. No. It was the imp! The tiny demon beckoned him with its delicate clawed hand.

∞ ∞ ∞

In his panicked retreat, Wagner went right past Helen on the bed to the closet. "Darling!" he gasped, throwing his arms around the figure in the darkness.

A large sloppy kiss was planted on his neck. She was so much more substantial than he remembered. But there was something queer . . . the closet was filled with the odor of rotting fish. He pulled her closer, and she honked.

He was hugging another Faustus! As he fell back in dismay, he heard Helen's voice from outside. "What are you doing in there?"

He opened the door and dragged Robin out behind him. The latter's face was split by a shy smile; he beamed up at Wagner the way a schoolgirl beams at her secret love. Helen lay on the bed. Wagner booted Robin out of the room and slammed the door.

Helen was his at last! She whispered to him, her breasts heaving like the soft hills of the Peloponnesus during a minor earthquake. Her hips were a lyre playing ancient music. Wagner's vision blurred, and he sank down beside her. The Rathaus clock struck eleven forty-five.

∞ ∞ ∞

Mephistophilis had rendered himself invisible until he could decide which Faustus was his. He let one crawl from the study and stayed to hear the remaining two argue. He wasn't pleased with the possibility that he might take the wrong one. He was sure that the contract had no clause to cover such a contingency, and the power that ruled the universe would probably not accept the excuse that he couldn't tell the difference. As the minutes ticked away, the thought that his revenge might even now be thwarted stoked his anger to an inferno of rage. He could draw blood from each of the contenders and match the type against the signature on the contract. But that would only cause further delay, to say nothing of the cost of the lab report.

There was one quick method—he would have to shock one of them into an admission. He moved between Faustus and Dicolini and materialized.

"Oh, so you're back, eh?" the two said simultaneously.

"Your doom is at hand."

"Never mind that, pick a card." Faustus fanned a tarot deck out before Mephistophilis.

"I picka ace of wands," Dicolini said.

"Wandaful. You win. Does your wormy friend want to try his luck?"

"Hesa outside in the alley."

Robin entered the study carrying a slice of bread. He went over to Faustus's alchemical experiment, dipped his finger into a salve compounded of cinnabar and verdigris, spread it across the bread, and took a bite. He nodded in pleasure and offered it to Faustus.

"No thanks. It's bad enough being damned. Indigestion I don't need."

The clock in the Rathaus tower began to strike midnight.

"Enough!" Mephistophilis shouted. Albergus, who had been so absorbed in the books at the back of the room that he had not paid attention to the fiend's arrival, was jolted by the infernal voice. The imp had directed him to Faustus's magic book, hidden beneath a stack of Greek pornographic scrolls.

"Which one of you is the real Faustus?" Mephistophilis demanded.

The three Faustuses pointed at each other.

Albergus was supremely sure of himself. He held the secrets of life tucked in the crook of his arm, and had reason now to fear no man on earth.

"*I* am the true Faustus!" he said, striding forward from the back of the room.

"Good enough for me," said Mephistophilis.

As the sound of the last stroke of midnight faded away, the floor beneath Albergus opened and all the fiends of hell, laughing, exploded upward to seize his ankles.

eight

Wagner was unsure whether the explosion he heard was in his head or elsewhere in the apartment. He was not capable of accurate observation at just that moment. When he came to his senses, Helen was gone.

He checked the closet. It held only clothes.

Realizing that the smell of smoke was real, he hurried through the common room to Faustus's study. Strewn about were charred papers, shards of glassware, and smoking fragments of meat and bone. A cold wind blew in through the shattered window. Waving his arms to dispel the fumes, Wagner made out two figures sitting on the floor, lighting cigars from a bonfire of burning books. A third was shoveling books onto the blaze. All looked vaguely like Doctor Faustus.

"Atsa good smoke," one of them said.

"Where is she?" Wagner was furious. Then he realized why the triplets were staring at him: he was wearing no breeches. One of the seated Faustuses gestured impolitely at his nakedness. "Cut is the branch that might have grown full straight." Wagner recognized him as the real doctor.

"What have you done with her?"

"She was one helluva wrestler, eh, partner?" said Dicolini.

Robin leaned on his pitchfork and gave a long, low whistle.

"But it's not fair!" said Wagner. "We were just getting started."

Faustus reached up, peeled the sweat-soaked contract from Wagner's chest, glanced at it, and added it to the fire. "My boy, she's a scarlet woman and you're nothing but a green student. She would have made you blue someday."

"Yeah," said Dicolini. "If only Faustus hadn't turned yellow."

"Meanwhile," Faustus added, "how about a little roast scholar?"

"Atsa no roast," Dicolini said. "Atsa friar."

Robin honked.

MEETING IN INFINITY MEETING IN INFINITY

a clean escape

> I've been thinking about devils. I mean, if there are
> devils in the world, if there are people in the world who
> represent evil, is it our duty to exterminate them?
> —JOHN CHEEVER,
> THE FIVE-FORTY-EIGHT

A S SHE SAT IN HER OFFICE, WAITING—FOR EXACTLY WHAT SHE did not know—Dr. Evans hoped that it wasn't going to be another bad day. She needed a cigarette and a drink. She swiveled the chair around to face the closed venetian blinds beside her desk, leaned back, and laced her hands behind her head. She closed her eyes and breathed deeply. The air wafting down from the ventilator in the ceiling smelled of machine oil. It was cold. Her face felt it, but the bulky sweater kept the rest of her warm. Her hair felt greasy. Several minutes passed in which she thought of nothing. There was a knock at the door.

"Come in," she said absently.

Havelmann entered. He had the large body of an athlete gone slightly soft, gray hair, and a lined face. At first glance he didn't look sixty. His well-tailored blue suit badly needed pressing.

"Doctor?"

Evans stared at him for a moment. She would kill him. She

looked down at the desk, rubbed her forehead. "Sit down," she said.

She took the pack of cigarettes from her desk drawer. "Would you care to smoke?"

The old man accepted one. She watched him carefully. His brown eyes were rimmed with red; they looked apologetic.

"I smoke too much," he said. "But I can't quit."

She gave him a light. "More people around here are quitting every day."

Havelmann exhaled smoothly. "What can I do for you?"

What can I do for *you*, sir.

"First, I want to play a little game." Evans took a handkerchief out of her pocket. She moved a brass paperweight, a small model of the Lincoln Memorial, to the center of the desk blotter. "I want you to watch what I'm doing now."

Havelmann smiled. "Don't tell me—you're going to make it disappear, right?"

She tried to ignore him. She covered the paperweight with the handkerchief. "What's under this handkerchief?"

"Can we put a little bet on it?"

"Not this time."

"A paperweight."

"That's wonderful." Evans leaned back. "Now I want you to answer a few questions."

The old man looked around the office curiously: at the closed blinds, at the computer terminal and keyboard against the wall, at the pad of switches in the corner of the desk. His eyes came to rest on the mirror high in the wall opposite the window. "That's a two-way mirror."

Evans sighed. "No kidding."

"Are you videotaping this?"

"Does it matter to you?"

"I'd like to know. Common courtesy."

"Yes, we're being recorded. Now answer the questions."

Havelmann seemed to shrink in the face of her hostility. "Sure."

"How do you like it here?"

"It's okay. A little boring. A man couldn't even catch a disease here, from the looks of it, if you know what I mean. I don't mean any offense, Doctor. I haven't been here long enough to get the feel of the place."

Evans rocked slowly back and forth. "How do you know I'm a doctor?"

"Aren't you a doctor? I thought you were. This is a hospital, isn't it? So I figured when they sent me in to see you, you must be a doctor."

"I am a doctor. My name is Evans."

"Pleased to meet you, Dr. Evans."

She would kill him. "How long have you been here?"

The man tugged on his earlobe. "I must have just got here today. I don't think it was too long ago. A couple of hours. I've been talking to the nurses at their station."

What she wouldn't give for three fingers of Jack Daniel's. She looked at him over the steeple of her fingers. "Such talkative nurses."

"I'm sure they're doing their jobs."

"I'm sure. Tell me what you were doing before you came to this . . . hospital."

"You mean right before?"

"Yes."

"I was working."

"Where do you work?"

"I've got my own company—ITG Computer Systems. We design programs for a lot of people. We're close to getting a big contract with Ma Bell. We swing that and I can retire by the time I'm forty—if Uncle Sam will take his hand out of my pocket long enough for me to count my change."

Evans made a note on her pad. "Do you have a family?"

Havelmann looked at her steadily. His gaze was that of an earnest young college student, incongruous on a man of his age. He stared at her as if he could not imagine why she would ask him these abrupt questions. She detested his weakness; it raised in her a fury that pushed her to the edge of insanity. It was already a bad day, and it would get worse.

"I don't understand what you're after," Havelmann said, with considerable dignity. "But just so your record shows the facts: I've got a wife, Helen, and two kids. Ronnie's nine and Susan's five. We have a nice big house and a Lincoln and a Porsche. I follow the Braves and I don't eat quiche. What else would you like to know?"

"Lots of things. Eventually I'll find them out." Evans tapped her pencil on the edge of the desk. "Is there anything you'd like to ask me? How you came to be here? How long you're going to have to stay? Who you are?"

Havelmann's voice went cold. "I know who I am."

"Who are you, then?"

"My name is Robert Havelmann."

"That's right," Dr. Evans said. "What year is it?"

Havelmann watched her warily, as if he were about to be tricked. "What are you talking about? It's 1984."

"What time of year?"

"Spring."

"How old are you?"

"Thirty-five."

"What do I have under this handkerchief?"

Havelmann looked at the handkerchief on the desk as if noticing it for the first time. His shoulders tightened and he looked suspiciously at her.

"How should I know?"

∞   ∞   ∞

He was back again that afternoon, just as rumpled, just as innocent. How could a person get old and remain innocent? She could not remember things ever being that easy. "Sit down," she said.

"Thanks. What can I do for you, Doctor?"

"I want to follow up on the argument we had this morning."

Havelmann smiled. "Argument? This morning?"

"Don't you remember talking to me this morning?"

"I never saw you before."

Evans watched him coldly. Havelmann shifted in his chair.

"How do you know I'm a doctor?"

"Aren't you a doctor? They told me I should go in to see Dr. Evans in room 10."

"I see. If you weren't here this morning, where were you?"

Havelmann hesitated. "Let's see—I was at work. I remember telling Helen—my wife—that I'd try to get home early. She's always complaining because I stay late. The company's pretty busy right now: big contract in the works. Susan's in the school play, and we have to be there by eight. And I want to get home in time to do some yard work. It looked like a good day for it."

Evans made a note. "What season is it?"

Havelmann fidgeted like a child, looked at the window, where the blinds were still closed.

"Spring," he said. "Sunny, warm—very nice weather. The redbuds are just starting to come out."

Without a word Evans got out of her chair and opened the

blinds, revealing a barren field swept with drifts of snow. Dead grass whipped in the strong wind, and clouds roiled in the sky.

"What about this?"

Havelmann stared. His back straightened. He tugged at his earlobe.

"Isn't that a bitch. If you don't like the weather here—wait ten minutes."

"What about the redbuds?"

"This weather will probably kill them. I hope Helen made the kids wear their jackets."

Evans looked out the window. Nothing had changed. She drew the blinds and sat down again.

"What year is it?"

Havelmann adjusted himself in his chair, calm again. "What do you mean? It's 1984."

"Did you ever read that book?"

"Slow down a minute. What book?"

Evans wondered what he would do if she got up and ground her thumbs into his eyes. "The book by George Orwell titled *1984*." She forced herself to speak slowly. "Are you familiar with it?"

"Sure. We had to read it in college." Was there a trace of irritation beneath Havelmann's innocence? Evans sat as still as she could.

"I remember it made quite an impression on me," Havelmann continued.

"What kind of impression?"

"I expected something different from the professor. He was a confessed liberal. I expected some kind of bleeding-heart book. It wasn't like that at all."

"Did it make you uncomfortable?"

"No. It didn't tell me anything I didn't know already. It just showed what was wrong with collectivism. You know—Communism represses the individual, destroys initiative. It claims it has the interests of the majority at heart. And it denies all human values. That's what I got out of *1984*, though to hear that professor talk about it, it was all about Nixon and Vietnam."

Evans kept still. Havelmann went on.

"I've seen the same mentality at work in business. The large corporations, they're just like the government. Big, slow. You could show them a way to save a billion, and they'd squash you like a bug because it's too much trouble to change."

"You sound like you've got some resentments," said Evans.

The old man smiled. "I do, don't I. I admit it. I've thought a lot about it. But I have faith in people. Someday I may just run for state assembly and see whether I can do some good."

Her pencil point snapped. She looked at Havelmann, who looked back at her. After a moment she focused her attention on the notebook. The broken point had left a black scar across her precise handwriting.

"That's a good idea," she said quietly, her eyes still lowered. "You still don't remember arguing with me this morning?"

"I never saw you before I walked in this door. What were we supposed to be fighting about?"

He was insane. Evans almost laughed aloud at the thought—of course he was insane—why else would he be here? The question, she forced herself to consider rationally, was the nature of his insanity. She picked up the paperweight and handed it across to him. "We were arguing about this paperweight," she said. "I showed it to you, and you said you'd never seen it before."

Havelmann examined the paperweight. "Looks ordinary to me. I could easily forget something like this. What's the big deal?"

"You'll note that it's a model of the Lincoln Memorial."

"You probably got it at some gift shop. D.C. is full of junk like that."

"I haven't been to Washington in a long time."

"I wish I could avoid it. I live there. Bethesda, anyway."

Evans closed her notebook. "I have a possible diagnosis of your condition," she said suddenly.

"What condition?"

This time the laughter was harder to repress. Tears almost came to her eyes. She caught her breath and continued. "You exhibit the symptoms of Korsakov's syndrome. Have you ever heard of that before?"

Havelmann looked as blank as a whitewashed wall. "No."

"Korsakov's syndrome is an unusual form of memory loss. Recorded cases go back to the late 1800s. There was a famous one in the 1970s—famous to doctors, I mean. A Marine sergeant named Arthur Briggs. He was in his fifties, in good health aside from the lingering effects of alcoholism, and had been a career noncom until his discharge in the midsixties after twenty years in the service. He functioned normally until the early seventies, when he lost his memory of any events that occurred to him after September 1944.

He could remember in vivid detail, as if they had just happened, events up until that time. But of the rest of his life—nothing. Not only that, his continuing memory was affected so that he could remember events that occurred in the present only for a period of minutes, after which he would forget totally."

"I can remember what happened to me right up until I walked into this room."

"That's what Sergeant Briggs told his doctors. To prove it he told them that World War II was going strong, that he was stationed in San Francisco in preparation for being sent to the Philippines, that it looked like the St. Louis Browns might finally win a pennant if they could hold on through September, and that he was twenty years old. He had the outlook and abilities of an intelligent twenty-year-old. He couldn't remember anything that happened to him longer than twenty minutes. The world had gone on, but he was permanently stuck in 1944."

"That's horrible."

"So it seemed to the doctor in charge—at first. Later he speculated that it might not be so bad. The man still had a current emotional life. He could still enjoy the present; it just didn't stick with him. He could remember his youth, and for him his youth had never ended. He never aged. He never saw his friends grow old and die; he never remembered that he himself had grown up to be a lonely alcoholic. His girlfriend was still waiting for him back in Columbia, Missouri. He was twenty years old forever. He had made a clean escape."

Evans opened a desk drawer and took out a hand mirror. "How old are you?" she asked.

Havelmann looked frightened. "Look, why are we doing—"

"How old are you?" Evans's voice was quiet but determined. Inside her a pang of joy threatened to break her heart.

"I'm thirty-five. What the hell—"

Shoving the mirror at him was as satisfying as firing a gun. Havelmann took it, glanced at her, then tentatively, like the most nervous of freshmen checking the grade on his final exam, looked at his reflection. "Jesus Christ," he said. He started to tremble.

"What happened? What did you do to me!" He got out of the chair, his expression contorted. "What did you do to me! I'm thirty-five! What happened?"

∞   ∞   ∞

Dr. Evans stood in front of the mirror in her office. She was wearing her uniform. It was as rumpled as Havelmann's suit. She had the tunic unbuttoned and was feeling her left breast. She lay down on the floor and continued the examination. The lump was undeniable. No pain yet.

She sat up, reached for the pack of cigarettes on the desk top, fished out the last one and lit it. She crumpled the pack and threw it at the wastebasket. Two points. She had been quite a basketball player in college, twenty years before. She lay back down and took a long drag on the cigarette, inhaling deeply, exhaling the smoke with force, with a sigh of exhaustion. She probably couldn't make it up and down the court a single time anymore.

She turned her head to look out the window. The blinds were open, revealing the same barren landscape that showed before. There was a knock at the door.

"Come in," she said.

Havelmann entered. He saw her lying on the floor, raised an eyebrow, grinned. "You're Dr. Evans?"

"I am."

"Can I sit here, or should I lie down too?"

"Do whatever you fucking well please."

He sat in the chair. He had not taken offense. "So what did you want to see me about?"

Evans got up, buttoned her tunic, sat in the swivel chair. She stared at him. "Have we ever met before?" she asked.

"No. I'm sure I'd remember."

He was sure he would remember. She would fucking kill him. He would remember that.

She ground out the last inch of cigarette. She felt her jaw muscles tighten; she looked down at the ashtray in regret. "Now I have to quit."

"I should quit. I smoke too much myself."

"I want you to listen to me closely now," she said slowly. "Don't respond until I'm finished."

"My name is Major D. S. Evans, and I am a military psychologist. This office is in the infirmary of NECDEC, the National Emergency Center for Defense Communications, located one thousand feet below a hillside in West Virginia. As far as we know we are the only surviving governmental body in the continental United States. The scene you see through this window is being relayed from a surface monitor in central Nebraska; by computer command I can connect us with any of the twelve monitors still functioning on the surface."

Evans turned to her keyboard and typed in a command; the scene through the window snapped to a shot of broken masonry and twisted steel reinforcement rods. The view was obscured by dust caked on the camera lens and by a heavy snowfall. Evans typed in an additional command and touched one of the switches on her desk. A blast of static, a hiss like frying bacon, came from the speaker.

"That's Dallas. The sound is a reading of the background radiation registered by detectors at the site of this camera." She typed in another command and the image on the "window" flashed through a succession of equally desolate scenes, holding ten seconds on each before switching to the next. A desert in twilight, motionless under low clouds; a murky underwater shot in which the remains of a building were just visible; a denuded forest half-buried in snow; a deserted highway overpass. With each change of scene the loudspeaker stopped for a split second, then the hiss resumed.

Havelmann watched all of this soberly.

"This has been the state of the surface for a year now, ever since the last bombs fell. To our knowledge there are no human beings alive in North America—in the Northern Hemisphere, for that matter. Radio transmissions from South America, New Zealand, and Australia have one by one ceased in the last eight months. We have not observed a living creature above the level of an insect through any of our monitors since the beginning of the year. It is the summer of 2010. Although, considering the situation, counting years by the old system seems a little futile to me."

Dr. Evans slid open a desk drawer and took out an automatic. She placed it in the middle of the desk blotter and leaned back, her right hand touching the edge of the desk near the gun.

"You are now going to tell me that you never heard of any of this, and that you've never seen me before in your life," she said. "Despite the fact that I have been speaking to you daily for two weeks and that you have had this explanation from me at least three times during that period. You are going to tell me that it is 1984 and that you are thirty-five years old, despite the absurdity of such a claim. You are going to feign amazement and confusion; the more I insist that you face these facts, the more you are going to become distressed. Eventually you will break down into tears and expect me to sympathize. You can go to hell."

Evans's voice had grown angrier as she spoke. She had to stop; it was almost more than she could do. When she resumed she was under control again. "If you persist in this sham, I may kill you. I assure you that no one will care if I do. You may speak now."

Havelmann stared at the window. His mouth opened and closed stupidly. How old he looked, how feeble. Evans felt a sudden surge of doubt. What if she were wrong? She had an image of herself as she might appear to him: arrogant, bitter, an incomprehensible inquisitor whose motives for tormenting him were a total mystery. She watched him. After a few minutes his mouth closed; the eyes blinked rapidly and were clear.

"Please. Tell me what you're talking about."

Evans shuddered. "The gun is loaded. Keep talking."

"What do you want me to say? I never heard of any of this. Only this morning I saw my wife and kids, and everything was all right. Now you give me this story about atomic war and 2010. What, have I been asleep for thirty years?"

"You didn't act very surprised to be here when you walked in. If you're so disoriented, how do you explain how you got here?"

The man sat heavily in the chair. "I don't remember. I guess I thought I came here—to the hospital, I thought—to get a checkup. I didn't think about it. You must know how I got here."

"I do. But I think you know too, and you're just playing a game with me—with all of us. The others are worried, but I'm sick of it. I can see through you, so you may as well quit the act. You were famous for your sincerity, but I always suspected that was an act, too, and I'm not falling for it. You didn't start this game soon enough for me to be persuaded you're crazy, despite what the others may think."

Evans played with the butt of her dead cigarette. "Or this could be a delusional system," she continued. "You think you're in a hospital, and your schizophrenia has progressed to the point where you deny all facts that don't go along with your attempts to evade responsibility. I suppose in some sense such an insanity would absolve you. If that's the case, I should be more objective. Well, I can't. I'm failing my profession. Too bad." Emotion had drained away from her until, by the end, she felt as if she were speaking from across a continent instead of a desk.

"I still don't know what you're talking about. Where are my wife and kids?"

"They're dead."

Havelmann sat rigidly. The only sound was the hiss of the radiation detector. "Let me have a cigarette."

"There are no cigarettes left. I just smoked my last one." Evans touched the ashtray. "I made two cartons last a year."

Havelmann's gaze dropped. "How old my hands are! . . . Helen has lovely hands."

"Why are you going on with this charade?"

The old man's face reddened. "God damn you! Tell me what happened!"

"The famous Havelmann rage. Am I supposed to be frightened now?"

The hiss from the loudspeaker seemed to increase. Havelmann lunged for the gun. Evans snatched it and pushed back from the desk. The old man grabbed the paperweight and raised it to strike. She pointed the gun at him.

"Your wife didn't make the plane in time. She was at the western White House. I don't know where your damned kids were—probably vaporized with their own families. You, however, had Operation Kneecap to save you. Mr. President. Now sit down and tell me why you've been playing games, or I'll kill you right here and now. Sit down!"

A light seemed to dawn on Havelmann. "You're insane."

"Put the paperweight back on the desk."

He did. He sat.

"But you can't simply be crazy," Havelmann continued. "There's no reason why you should take me away from my home and subject me to this. This is some kind of plot. The government. The CIA."

"And you're thirty-five years old?"

Havelmann examined his hands again. "You've done something to me."

"And the camps? Administrative Order 31?"

"If I'm the president, then why are you quizzing me here? Why can't I remember a thing about it?"

"Stop it. Stop it right now," Evans said. She heard her voice for the first time. It sounded more like that of an old man than Havelmann's. "I can't take any more lies. I swear that I'll kill you. First it was the commander-in-chief routine, calisthenics, stiff upper lips and discipline. Then the big brother, let's have a whiskey and talk it over, son. Yessir, Mr. President." Havelmann stared at her. He was going to make her kill him, and she knew she wouldn't be strong enough not to.

"Now you can't remember anything," she said. "Your boys are confused, they're fed up. Well, I'm fed up too."

"If this is true, you've got to help me!"

"I don't give a rat's ass about helping you!" Evans shouted. "I'm interested in making you tell the truth! Don't you realize that we're dead? I don't care about your feeble sense of what's right and wrong; just tell me what's keeping you going. Who do you think you're going to impress? You think you've got an election to win? A place in history to protect? There isn't going to be any more history! History ended last August!

"So spare me the fantasy about the hospital and the nonexistent nurses' station. Someone with Korsakov's wouldn't make up that story. He would recognize the difference between a window and an HDTV screen. A dozen other slips. You're not a good enough actor."

Her hand trembled. The gun was heavy. Her voice trembled, too, and she despised herself for it. "Sometimes I think the only thing that's kept me alive is knowing I had half a pack of cigarettes left. That and the desire to make you crawl."

The old man sat looking at the gun in her hand. "I was the president?"

"No," said Evans. "I made it up."

His eyes seemed to sink farther back in the network of lines surrounding them.

"I started a war?"

Evans felt her heart race. "Stop lying! You sent the strike force; you ordered the preemptive launch."

"I'm old. How old am I?"

"You know how old—" She stopped. She could hardly catch her breath. She felt a sharp pain in her breast. "You're sixty-one."

"Jesus, Mary, Joseph."

"That's it? That's all you can say?"

Havelmann stared hollowly, then slowly, so slowly that at first it was not apparent what he was doing, lowered his head into his hands and began to cry. His sobs were almost inaudible over the hiss of the radiation detector. Evans watched him. She rested her elbows on the desk, steadying the gun with both hands. Havelmann's head shook in front of her. Despite his age, his gray hair was thick.

After a moment Evans reached over and switched off the loudspeaker. The hissing stopped.

Eventually Havelmann stopped crying. He raised his head. He looked dazed. His expression became unreadable. He looked at the doctor and the gun. "My name is Robert Havelmann," he said. "Why are you pointing that gun at me?"

"Don't do this," said Evans. "Please."

"Do what? Who are you?"

Evans watched his face blur. Through her tears he looked like a much younger man. The gun drooped. She tried to lift it, but it was as if she were made of smoke—there was no substance to her, and it was all she could do to keep from dissipating, let alone kill anyone as clean and innocent as Robert Havelmann. He reached forward. He took the gun from her hand. "Are you all right?" he asked.

∞ ∞ ∞

Dr. Evans sat in her office, hoping that it wasn't going to be a bad day. The pain in her breast had not come that day, but she was out of cigarettes. She searched the desk on the odd chance she might have missed a pack, even a single butt, in the corner of one of the drawers. No luck.

She gave up and turned to face the window. The blinds were open, revealing the snow-covered field. She watched the clouds roll before the wind. It was dark. Winter. Nothing was alive.

"It's cold outside," she whispered.

There was a knock at the door. Dear god, leave me alone, she thought. Please leave me alone.

"Come in," she said.

The door opened and an old man in a rumpled suit entered. "Dr. Evans? I'm Robert Havelmann. What did you want to talk about?"

IN INFINITY MEETING IN INFINITY MEETING IN INFINITY MEETING
TING IN INFINITY MEETING IN INFINITY MEETING IN INFINITY MEE
MEETING IN INFINITY MEETING IN INFINITY MEETING IN INFINITY
TY MEETING IN INFINITY MEETING IN INFINITY MEETING IN INFI
NFINITY MEETING IN INFINITY MEETING IN INFINITY MEETING IN
G IN INFIN   TY MEETIN
TING IN INFI   NFINITY ME
MEETING IN INFIN   MEETING IN INFINITY   G IN INFINITY
NITY MEE   ETING IN INF
INFINITY   park and lock it!   MEETING I
G IN INFINITY MEETING IN INFINITY MEETING IN INFINITY MEETI
ETING IN INFINITY MEETING IN INFINITY MEETING IN INFINITY M
J MEETING IN INFINITY MEETING IN INFINITY MEETING IN INFINIT
INITY MEETING IN INFINITY MEETING IN INFINITY MEETING IN IN
J INFINITY MEETING IN INFINITY MEETING IN INFINITY MEETING

**not responsible!
park and lock it!**

AVID BAKER WAS BORN IN THE BACKSEAT OF HIS PARENTS' CHEVY in the great mechanized lot at mile 1.375×10^{25}. "George, we need to stop," his mother Polly said. "I'm having pains." She was a week early.

They had been cruising along pretty well at twilight, his father concentrating on getting in another fifty miles before dark, when they were cut off by the big two-toned Mercury and George had to swerve four lanes over into the far right. George and Polly later decided that the near-accident was the cause of the premature birth. They even managed to laugh at the incident in retrospect— they ruefully retold the story many times, so that it was one of the family fables David grew up with—but David always suspected his father pined after those lost fifty miles. In return he'd gotten a son.

"Not responsible! Park and lock it!" the loudspeakers at the tops of the poles in the vast asphalt field shouted, over and over. For a first birth Polly's labor was surprisingly short, and the robot doctor emerged from the Chevy in the gathering evening with a healthy seven-pound boy. George Baker flipped his cigarette away nervously, the butt glowing as it spun into the night. He smiled.

In the morning George stepped into the bar at the first rest stop, had a quick one, and registered his name: David John Baker. Born 8:15 Standard Westbound Time, June 13 . . .

"What year is it?" George asked the bartender.

"802,701." The robot smiled benignly. It could not do otherwise.

"802,701." George repeated it aloud and punched the keys of the terminal. "Eight hundred two thousand, seven hundred and one." The numbers spun themselves out like a song. Eight-oh-two, seven-oh-one.

David's mother had smiled weakly, reclining in the passenger's seat, when they'd started again. Her smile had never been strong. David slept on her breast.

Much later Polly told David what a good baby he'd been, not like his younger sister Caroline, who had the colic. David took satisfaction in that: he was the good one. It made the competition between him and Caroline even more intense. But that was later. As a baby David slept to the steady thrumming of the V-8 engine, the gentle rocking of the car. He was cooed at by the android attendants at the camps where they pulled over at the end of the day. His father would chat with the machine that came over to check the odometer and validate their mileage card. George would tell about any of the interesting things that had happened on the road—and he always seemed to have something—while Polly fixed supper at one of the grills and the ladies from the other cars sat around in a circle in front of the komfy kabins and talked about their children, their husbands, about their pregnancies and how often they got to drive. David sat on Polly's lap or played with the other kids. Once past the toddler stage he followed his dad around and watched, a little scared, as the greasy self-assured robots busied themselves about the service station. They were large and composed. The young single drivers tried hard to compete with their mechanical self-containment. David hung on everything his dad said.

"The common driving man," George Baker said, hands on the wheel, "the good average driver—doesn't know his asshole from a tail pipe."

Polly would draw David to her, as if to blot out the words. "George—"

"All right. The kid will know whether you want him to or not."

But David didn't know, and they wouldn't tell him. That was the way of parents: they never told you even when they thought they were explaining everything, and so David was left to wonder and learn as best he could. He watched the land speed by long before he had words to say what he saw; he listened to his father tell his mother what was wrong and right with the world. And the sun set every night at the other end of that world, far ahead of them still, beyond the gas stations and the wash-and-brushup buildings and the quietly deferential androids that always seemed the same no matter how far they'd gone that day, Westbound.

When David was six he got to sit on George's lap, hold the wheel in his hands, and "drive the car." With what great chasms of anticipation and awe did he look forward to those moments! His father would say suddenly, after hours of driving in silence, "Come sit on my lap, David. You can drive."

Polly would protest feebly that he was too young. It was dangerous. David would clamber into his dad's lap and grab the wheel. How warm it felt, how large, and how far apart he had to put his hands! The indentations on the back were too wide for his fingers, so that two of his fit into the space meant for one adult's. George would move the seat up and scrunch his thin legs together so that David could see over the hood of the car. His father operated the pedals and gearshift, and most of the time he kept his left hand on the wheel too—but then he would slowly take it away and David would be steering all by himself. His heart had beaten fast. At those moments the car had seemed so large. The promise and threat of its speed had been almost overwhelming. He knew that by a turn of the wheel he could be in the high-speed lane; he knew, even more amazingly, that he held in his hands the potential to steer them off the road, into the gully, and death. The responsibility was great, and David took it seriously. He didn't want to do anything foolish, he didn't want to make George think him any less a man. He knew his mother was watching. Whether she had love or fear in her eyes he could not know, because he couldn't take his eyes from the road to see.

When David was seven there was a song on the radio that Polly sang to him, "We all drive on." That was his song. David sang it back to her, and his father laughed and sang it too, badly, voice hoarse and off-key, not like his mother, whose voice was sweet. "We all drive on," they sang together.

> "You and me and everyone
> Never ending, just begun
> Driving, driving on."

"Goddamn right we drive on," George said. "Goddamn pack of maniacs."

David remembered clearly the first time he became aware of the knapsack and the notebook. It was one evening after they'd eaten supper and were waiting for Polly to get the cabin ready for bed. George went around to the trunk to check the spare, and this time he took a green knapsack out and, in the darkness near the edge of the campground, secretively opened it.

"Watch, David, and keep your mouth shut about what you see."

David watched.

"This is for emergencies." George, one by one, set the things on the ground: first a rolled oilcloth, which he spread out, then a line of tools, then a gun and boxes of bullets, a first-aid kit, some packages of crackers and dried fruit, and some things David didn't know. One thing had a light and a thick wire and batteries.

"This is a metal detector, David. I made it myself." George took a black book from the sack. "This is my notebook." He handed it to David. It was heavy and smelled of the trunk.

"Maps of the Median, and—"

"George!" Polly's voice was a harsh whisper, and David jumped a foot. She grabbed his arm. George looked exasperated and a little guilty—though David did not identify his father's reaction as guilt until he thought about it much later. He was too busy trying to avoid the licking he thought was coming. His mother marched him back to the cabin after giving George her best withering gaze.

"But Mom—"

"To sleep! Don't puzzle yourself about things you aren't meant to know, young man."

David puzzled himself. At times the knapsack and the notebook filled his thoughts. His father would give him a curious glance and tantalizingly vague answers whenever he asked about them—safely out of earshot of Polly.

Shortly after that Caroline was born. This time the Bakers were not caught by surprise, and Caroline came into the world at the hospital at mile 1.375×10^{25}, where they stopped for three whole days for Polly's lying in. Nobody stopped for three whole days, for anything. David was impatient. They'd never *get* anywhere waiting, and the androids in the hospital were all boring, and the comic books in the motionless waiting room he had all read before.

This time the birth was a hard one. George sat hunched forward in a plastic chair, and David paced around, stomping on the cracks in the linoleum. He leaned on the windowsill and watched all the cars fly by on the highway, Westbound, and in the distance, beyond the barbed wire, sentry towers and minefields, mysterious, ever unattainable—Eastbound.

After what seemed like a very long time, the white porcelain doctoroid came back to them. George stood up as soon as he appeared. "Is she—"

"Both fine. A little girl. Seven pounds, five ounces," the doctoroid reported, grille gleaming.

George didn't say anything then, just sat down in the chair. After a while he came over to David, put his hand on the boy's shoulder, and they both watched the cars moving by, the light of the bright midsummer's sun flashing off the windshields as they passed, blinding them.

∞   ∞   ∞

David was nine when they bought the Nash. It had a big chrome grille that stretched like a bridge across the front, the vertical bars bulging outward in the middle, so that, with the headlights, the car looked to be grinning a big nasty grin.

David went with George through the car lot while Polly sat with Caroline in the lounge of the dealership. He watched his father dicker with the bow-tied salesdroid. George acted as if he seriously meant to buy a new car, when in fact his yearly mileage average would entitle him to no more than a second-hand, second-rank sedan, unless he intended for them all to go hungry. He wouldn't have done that, however. Whatever else Polly might say about her husband, she could not say he wasn't a good provider.

"So why don't you show us a good used car," George said, running his hand through his thinning hair. "Mind you, don't show us any piece of junk."

The salesdroid was, like his brothers, enthusiastic and unreadable. "Got just the little thing for you, Mr. Baker—a snappy number. C'mon," it said, rolling down toward the back of the lot.

"Here you go." It opened the door of the blue Nash with its amazingly dextrous hand. David's father got in. "Feel that genuine vinyl upholstery. Not none of your cheap plastics, that'll crack in a week of direct sun." The salesdroid winked its glassy eye at David. "Hop in, Son. See how you like it."

David started to, then saw the look of warning on George's face.

"Let's have a look at the engine," George said.

"Righto." The droid rolled around the fat front fender, reached through the grille, and tripped the latch. The engine was clean as a whistle, the cylinder heads painted cherry red, the spark plug leads numbered for easy changes. It was like the pictures out of David's schoolbooks.

The droid started up the Nash; the motor gave out a rumble and vibrated ever so slightly. David smelled the clean tang of evaporating gasoline.

"Only one owner," the droid said, volume turned up now so it could be heard over the sound of the engine.

George looked uncertain.

"How much?"

"Book says it's worth 200,000 validated miles. You can drive her out, with your Chevy in trade, for . . . let me calculate . . . 174,900."

Just then David noticed something in the engine compartment. On either side over the wheel wells there were cracks in the metal that had been painted over so you could only see them from the reflection of the sunlight where the angle of the surface changed. That was where the shocks connected up with the car's body.

He tugged at his father's sleeve. "Dad," he said, pointing.

George ran a hand over the metal. He looked serious. David thought he was going to get mad. Instead he straightened up and smiled.

"How much did you say?"

The android stood stock-still. "150,000 miles."

"But Dad—"

"Shut up, David," he said. "I'll tell you what, Mr. Sixty. 100,000. And you reweld those wheel wells before we drive it an inch."

That was how they bought the Nash. The first thing George said when they were on their way again was, "Polly, that boy of ours is smart as a whip. The shocks were about to rip through the bodywork, and we'd of been scraping down the highway with our nose to the ground like a basset. David, you're a born driver, or else too smart to waste yourself on it."

David didn't quite follow that, but it made him a little more content to move into the backseat. At first he resented it that Caroline had taken his place in the front. She got all the attention, and David only got to sit and look out at where they had been, or what they were going by, never getting a good look at where they were going. If he leaned over the back of the front seat, his father would say, "Quit breathing down my neck, David. Sit down and behave yourself. Do your homework."

After a while he wouldn't have moved into the front if they'd asked him to: that was for babies. Instead he watched raptly out the left side-window for fleeting glimpses of Eastbound, wondering always about what it was, how it got there, and about the no-man's-land and the people they said had died trying to cross. He asked George about it, and that started up the biggest thing they were ever to share together.

"They've told you about Eastbound in school, have they?"

"They told us we can't go there. Nobody can."

"Did they tell you why?"

"No."

His father laughed. "That's because they don't know why! Isn't that incredible, David? They teach a thing in school, and everybody believes it, and nobody knows why or even thinks to ask. But you wonder, don't you? I've seen it."

He did wonder. It scared him that his father would talk about it.

"Men are slipstreamers, David. Did you ever see a car follow close behind a big truck to take advantage of the windbreak to make the driving easier? That's the way people are. They'll follow so close they can't see six inches beyond their noses, as long as it makes things easier. And the schools and the teachers are the biggest windbreaks of all. You remember that. Do you remember the knapsack in the trunk?"

"*George,*" Polly said.

"Be quiet, Polly. The boy's growing up." To David he said, "You know what it's for. You know what's inside."

"To go across . . .," David hesitated, his heart leaping.

"To cross the Median! We can do it. We don't have to be like everybody else, and when the time comes, when we need to get away the most, when things are really bad—we can do it! I'm prepared to do it."

Polly tried to shush him, and it became an argument. But David was thrilled at the new world that had opened. His father was a criminal—but he was right! From then on they worked on the preparations together. They would have long talks on what they would do and how they would do it. David drew maps on graph paper, and sometimes he and George would climb to the highest spot available by the roadside at the day's end, to puzzle out once again the defenses of the Median.

"Don't tell your mother about this," George would say. "You know she doesn't understand."

∞   ∞   ∞

Each morning, before they had gone very far at all, David's father would stop the car and let David out at a bus stop to be picked up by the school bus, and eight hours later the bus would let him out again some hundreds of miles farther west. Soon his parents would be there to pick him up, if they were not there already when he got off with the other kids. More than once David overheard drivers at the camps in the evening complaining about how having kids really slowed a man down in his career, so he'd never get as far as he would have if he'd had the sense to stay single. Whenever some young man whined about waiting around half his life for a school bus, George Baker would only light another cigarette and be very quiet.

In school David learned the principles of the internal combustion engine. Internal Combustion was his favorite class. Other boys and girls would shoot paperclips at each other over the backseats of the bus, or fall asleep staring out the windows, but David sat in a middle seat (he would not move to the front and be accused of being teacher's pet) and, for the most part, paid good attention. His favorite textbook was one they used both in history and social studies; it had a blue cloth cover. The title, pressed into the cover in faded yellow, was *Heroes of the Roads.* On the bus, during recess, David and the other boys argued about who was the greatest driver of them all.

To most of them Alan "Lucky" Totter was the only driver. He'd made 10,220,796 miles when he tried to pass a Winnebago on the right at 85 miles per hour in a blinding snowstorm. Some people thought that showed a lack of judgment, but Lucky Totter didn't give a damn for judgment, or anything else. Totter was the classic lone-wolf driver. Born to respectable middle-class parents who drove a Buick with holes in its sides, Totter devoured all he could find out about cars. At the age of thirteen he deserted his parents at a rest stop at mile 1.375×10^{25}, hot-wired a Bugatti-Smith that the owner had left unlocked, and made 8,000 miles before the Trooperbots brought him to justice. After six months in the paddy wagon he came out with a new resolve. He worked for a month at a service station at jobs even the androids would shun, getting nowhere. At the end of that time he'd rebuilt a junked Whippet roadster and was on his way, hell-bent for leather. Every extra mile he drove he plowed back into financing a newer and faster car. Tirelessly, it seemed, Totter kept his two-tones to the floorboards, and the pavement fairly flew beneath his wheels. No time for a wife or family, 1,000 miles a day was his only satisfaction, other than the quick comforts of any of the fast women he might pick up who wanted a chance to say they'd been for a ride with Lucky Totter. The solitary male to the end, it was a style guaranteed to earn him the hero worship of boys all along the world.

But Totter was not the all-time mileage champion. That pinnacle of glory was held by Charles Van Huyser, at a seemingly unassailable 11,315,201 miles. It was hard to see how anyone could do better, for Van Huyser was the driver who had everything: good reflexes, a keen eye, iron constitution, wherewithal, and devilish good looks. He was a child of the privileged classes, scion of the famous Van Huyser drivers, and had enjoyed all the advantages the boys on a middle-lane bus like David's would never see. His father had been one of the premier drivers of his generation, and had made more than seven million miles himself, placing him a respectable twelfth on the all-time list. Van Huyser rode the most exclusive of preparatory buses, and was outfitted from the beginning with the best made-to-order Mercedes that android hands could fashion. He was in a lane by himself. Old-timers would tell stories of the time they had been passed by the Van Huyser limo and the distinguished, immaculately tailored man who sat behind the wheel. Perhaps he had even tipped his homburg as he flashed by. Spartan in his daily regimen, invariably kind, if a little condescending, to lesser drivers, he never forgot his position in society, and died at the respectable age of eighty-six, peacefully, in the private washroom of the Drivers' Club dining room at mile 1.375×10^{25}.

There were scores of others in *Heroes of the Road*, all of their stories inspiring, challenging, even puzzling. There was Ailene Stanford, at six-million-plus miles the greatest female driver ever, carmaker and mother and credit to her sex. And Reuben Jefferson, and the Kosciusco brothers, and the mysterious trance driving of Akira Tedeki. The chapter "Detours" held frightening tales of abject failure, and of those who had wasted their substance and their lives trying to cross the Median.

"You can't believe everything you read, David," George told him. "They'll tell you Steve Macready was a great man."

It was like George Baker to make statements like that and then never explain what he meant. It got on David's nerves sometimes, though he figured his dad did it because he had more important things on his mind.

But Steve Macready was David's personal favorite. Macready was third on the all-time list behind Van Huyser and Totter, at 8,444,892 miles. Macready hadn't had the advantages of Van Huyser, and he scorned the reckless irresponsibility of Totter. He was an average man, to all intents and purposes, and he showed just how much an average guy could do if he had the willpower. Born into an impoverished hundred-mile-a-day family that couldn't seem to keep a car on the road three days in a row before it broke down, one of eight brothers and sisters, Macready studied quietly when he could, watched the ways of the road with an intelligent eye, and helped his father and mother keep the family rolling. Compelled to leave school early because the family couldn't keep up with the slowest of school buses, he worked on his own, managed to get hold of an old junker that he put on the road, and set off at the age of sixteen, taking two of his sisters with him. In those first years his mileage totals were anything but spectacular. But he kept plugging away, taking care of his sisters, seeing them married off to two respectable young drivers along the way, never hurrying. At the comparatively late age of thirty he married a simple girl from a family of Ford owners and fathered four children. He saw to his boys' educations. He drove on, making a steady 500 miles a day, and 200 on each Saturday and Sunday. He did not push himself or his machine; he did not lag behind. Steadiness was his watchword. His sons grew up to be fine drivers themselves, always ready to lend the helping hand to the unfortunate motorist. When he died at the age of eighty-two, survived by his wife, children, eighteen grandchildren, and twenty-six great-grandchildren, drivers all, he had become something of a legend in his own quiet time. Steve Macready.

George Baker never said much when David talked about the arguments the kids had over Macready and the other drivers. When he talked about his own youth, he would give only the most tantalizing hints of the many cars he had driven before he picked up Polly, of the many places he'd stopped and people he'd ridden with. David's grandfather had been something of an inventor, he gathered, and had modified his pickup with an extralarge tank and a small, efficient engine to get the most mileage for his driving time. George didn't say much about his mother or brothers, though he said some things that indicated that his father's plans for big miles never panned out, and about how it was not always pleasant to ride in the back of an open pickup with three brothers and a sick mother.

Eventually David saw that the miles were taking something out of his father. George Baker conversed less with Polly and the kids, and talked more at them.

Once, in a heavy rainstorm after three days of rolling hill country, forests that encroached on the edges of the pavement and fell like a dark wall between Westbound and forgotten Eastbound, the front end of the Nash had jumped suddenly into a mad vibration that threw David's heart into his throat.

"George!" Polly shouted.

"Shut up!" he yelled, trying to steer the bucking car to the roadside.

And then they were stopped, and breathing heavily, and the only sound was the drumming of the rain, the ticking of the car as it settled into motionlessness, and the hissing of the cars that still sped by them over the wet pavement. David's father, slow and bearlike, opened the door and pulled himself out. David got out too. Under the hood they saw where the rewelded wheel well had given way, and the shock was ripping through the metal. "Shit," George muttered.

As they stood there a gunmetal gray Cadillac pulled over to stop behind them, its flashing amber signal warm as fire under the leaden skies. A stocky man in an expensive raincoat got out. "Can I help you?" he asked.

George stared at him for a good ten seconds. He looked back at the Cadillac, looked at the man again.

"No thanks," he said.

The man hesitated, then turned, went back to his car and drove off.

So they had to wait three hours in the broken-down Nash as darkness fell and George trudged off down the highway for the next rest stop. He returned with an android serviceman, and they were towed to the nearest station. David, never patient at his best, grew more and more angry. His father offered not a word of explanation, and his mother tried to keep David from getting after him about his refusing help. But David finally challenged his father on the plain stupidity of his actions, which would mystify any sensible driver.

At first George acted as if he didn't hear David. Then he exploded.

"Don't tell me about sensible drivers! I don't need it, David! Don't tell me about your Van Huysers, and don't give me any of that Steve Macready crap, either. Your Van Huysers never did anything for the common driving man, despite all their extra miles. Nobody gives it away. That's just the way this road works."

"What about Macready?" David asked. He didn't understand what his father was talking about. You didn't have to run someone else down in order to be right. "Look at what Macready did."

"You don't know what you're talking about," George said. "You get older, but you still think like a kid. Macready sucked up to every tinman on the road. I wouldn't stoop so low as that. Half the time he let his *wife* drive! They don't tell you about that in that damn school, do they?

"Wake up and look at this road the way it is, David. People will use you like a chamois if you don't. Take my word for it. *Damn* it! If I could just get a couple of good months out of this heap and get back on my feet. A couple of good months!" He laughed scornfully.

It was no use arguing with George when he was in that mood. David shut up, inwardly fuming.

"Follow the herd!" George yelled. "That's all people ever do. Never had an original thought in their life."

"George, you don't need to shout at the boy," Polly said.

"Shout! I'm not shouting!" he shouted. George looked at her as if she were a hitchhiker. "Why don't you shut up. The boy and I were just having an intelligent conversation. A fat lot you know about it." He gripped the wheel as if he meant to grind it into powder. A deadly silence ensued.

"I need to stop," he said a couple of miles later, pulling off the road into a bar and grill.

They sat in the car, ears ringing.

"I'm hungry," Caroline said.

"Let's get something to eat, then." Polly leapt at the opportunity to do something normal. "Come on, David. Let's go in."

"You go ahead. I'll be there in a minute."

After they left David stared out the car window for a while. He reached under the seat and took out the notebook, which he had moved there a long time before. The spine was almost broken through now, with some of the leaves loose and water-stained. The paper was worn with writing and rewriting. David leafed through the sketches of watchtowers, the maps, the calculations. In the margin of page six his father had written, in handwriting so faded now that it was like the pale voice of years speaking, from far away, "Keep your ass down. Low profile."

∞   ∞   ∞

David was sixteen. His knees were crowded by the back of the car's front seat, and he stared sullenly out the window at the rolling countryside and the gathering night.

Caroline, having just concluded her fight with him with a belligerent "Oh, yeah!" was leaning forward, her forearms flat against the top of the front seat, her chin resting on them as she stared grimly ahead. Polly was knitting a cover for the box of kleenex that rested on the dashboard, muffling the radio speaker.

"I'm tired," George said. "I'm going to stop here for a quick one." He pulled the ancient Nash over into the exit lane, downshifted, and the car lurched forward more slowly, the engine rattling in protest of the increased rpms. David could have done it better himself.

They pulled into the parking lot of Fast Ed's Bar and Grill. "You go back and order a fish fry," George said, slamming the car door and turning his back on them. Polly put aside the knitting, picked up her purse, and took them in the side door to the dining room. There was no one else there, but they could hear the TV and the loud conversations from the front. After a while a waitress robot rolled back to them. Its porcelain finish was chipped, and the hands were stained rusty brown, like an old bathtub.

They ordered, the food came, and they ate. Still George did not return from the bar.

"Go get your father, David," his mother said. He could tell she was mad.

"I'll go, Ma," Caroline said.

"Stay still! It's bad enough he takes us to his gin mills, without you becoming a barfly's pet. Go ahead, David."

David went. His father was sitting at the far end of the bar, near the windows that faced the highway. The late afternoon sun gleamed along the polished wood, glinted harshly from the bottles racked on the shelves behind it, turned the mirror against the wall and the brass spigots of the taps into fire. George Baker was talking loudly with two other middle-aged drivers. His legs looked amazingly scrawny as he perched on the stool. Suddenly David was very angry.

"Are you going to come and eat?" he demanded.

George turned to him, his sloppy good humor stiffening to ire. "What do you want?"

"We're eating. Mom's waiting."

He leaned over to the man on the next stool. "See what I mean?" he said. To David he said, much more boldly, "Go and eat. I'm not hungry." He picked up his shot, downed it in one swallow, and took another draw on the beer setup.

Rage and humiliation burned in David. He did not recognize the man at the bar as his father—and then, shuddering, he did.

"Are you coming?" David could hardly speak. The other men at the bar were quiet now. Only the television continued to babble.

"Go away," his father said.

David wanted to kick over the stool and see him sprawled on the floor. Instead he turned and walked stiffly back to the dining room, past the table where his mother and sister sat. He stalked out to the lot, slamming the screen door behind him. He stood looking at the beat-up Nash in the red-and-white light of Fast Ed's sign. The sign buzzed, and night was coming, and clouds of insects swarmed around the neon in the darkness. A hundred yards away, on the highway, the drivers had their lights on, fanning before them. The air smelled of exhaust.

He couldn't go back into the bar. He would never step back into a place like that again. The world seemed all at once immensely old, immensely cheap, immensely tawdry. David looked over his shoulder at the vast woods that started just beyond the back of Fast Ed's. Then he walked to the front of the lot and stared across the highway toward the distant lights that marked Eastbound. How very far away they seemed.

David went back to the car and got the knapsack out of the trunk. He stepped over the rail at the edge of the lot, crossed the gully beside the road, and waiting for his chance, dashed across the twelve lanes of Westbound to the Median. A hundred yards ahead of him lay the beginning of no-man's-land. Beyond that, where those distant lights swept by in their retrograde motion—what?

But he would never get into a car with George Baker again.

∞   ∞   ∞

There were three levels of defenses between Westbound and Eastbound, or so they had surmised. The first was biological, the second was mechanical, and the third and most important, psychological.

As David moved farther from the highway the ground, which was more or less level near the shoulders, grew uneven. The field was unmowed, thick with nettles and coarse grass, and in the increasing darkness he stumbled more than once. Because the land sloped downward as he advanced, the lights ahead of him became obscured by the foliage.

He thought once that he heard his name called above the faint rushing of the cars behind him, but when he turned he could see nothing but Westbound. It seemed remarkably far away already. His progress became slower. He knew there were snakes in the open fields. The mines could not be far ahead. He could be in the minefield at that very moment.

He stopped, heart racing. Suddenly he knew he was in a minefield, and his next step would blow him to pieces. He saw the shadow of the first line of barbed wire ahead of him, and for the first time he considered going back. But the thought of his father and his mother stopped him. They would be glad to take him back and smother him.

David crouched, swung the pack from his shoulder, and took out the metal detector. Sweeping it a few inches above the ground in front of him, he crawled forward on his hands and knees. It was slow going. There was something funny about the air: he didn't smell anything but field and earth—no people, no rubber, no gasoline. He eyed the nearest watchtower, where he knew infrared scanners swept the Median and automatic rifles nosed about incuriously. Whenever the light in his palm went red, David slid slowly to one side or the other and went on. Once he had to flatten himself suddenly to the earth as some object—animal or search mech—rustled through the dry grass not ten yards away. He waited for the bullet in his neck.

He came to the first line of barbed wire. It was rusty and overgrown. Weeds had used it for a trellis, and when David clipped through the wire the overgrowth held the gap closed. He had to tear the opening wider with his hands, and the cheap work gloves he wore were next to no protection.

He lay in the dark, sweating. He would never last at this rate. He decided to take the chance of moving ahead in short, crouching runs, ignoring the mines. For a while it seemed to ease the pressure, until his foot slipped on some metal object and he leapt away, crying aloud, waiting for the blast that didn't come. Crouched in the grass, panting, he saw that he had stepped on a hubcap.

David began to wonder why the machines hadn't spotted him yet. He was far beyond the point any right-thinking driver might pass. Then he realized that he could hear nothing of either Westbound or Eastbound. He had no idea how long it had been since he'd left the parking lot, but the gibbous moon was coming down through the clouds. David wondered what his mother had done after he'd taken the pack and left; he could imagine his father's drunken amazement as she told him. Maybe even Caroline was worried. He was far beyond them now. He was getting away, amazed at how easy it was, once you made up your mind, amazed at how few had the guts to try it. If they'd even told him the truth.

A perverse idea hit him: maybe the teachers and drivers, like sheep huddled in their trailer beds, had never tried to see what lay in the Median. Maybe all the servodefenses had rotted like the barbed wire, and it was only the pressure of their dead traditions that kept people glued to their westward course. Suddenly twelve lanes, which had seemed a whole world to him all his life, shrank to the merest thread. Who could say what Eastbound might be? Who could predict how much better men had done for themselves there? Maybe it was the Eastbounders who had built the roads, who had created the defenses and myths that kept them all penned in filthy Nashes, rolling west.

David laughed aloud. He stood up. He slung the pack over his shoulder again, and this time boldly struck out for the new world.

"Halt!"

A figure stood erect before him, and a blinding light shone from its head. The confidence drained from David instantly; he dropped to the ground.

"Please stand." David was pinned in the center of the search beam. He reached into the knapsack for the revolver. "This is a restricted area, intruder," the machine said. "Please return to your assigned role."

David blinked in the glare. He could see nothing of the thing's form. "Role?"

"I am sure that the first thing they taught you was that entry into this area is forbidden. Am I right?"

"What?" David had never heard this kind of talk from a machine.

"Your elders have said that you should not come here. That is one very good reason why you should not be here. I'm sure you'll agree. The requests of the society that, in a significant way, created us, if not unreasonable, ought to be given considerable thought before we reject them. This is the result of evolution. The men and women who went before you had to concern themselves with survival in order to live long enough to bear the children who eventually became the present generation. Their rules are engineering-tested. Such experience, let alone your intelligence working *within* the framework of evolution, ought not to be lightly discarded. We are not born into a vacuum. Am I right?"

David wasn't sure the gun was going to do him any good. "I guess so. I never thought about it."

"Precisely. Think about it."

David thought. "Wait a minute! How do I know *people* made the rules? I don't have any proof. I never see people making rules now."

"On the contrary, intruder, you see it every day. Every act a person performs is an act of definition. We create what we are from moment to moment. The future before us is merely the emptiness of time that does not exist without events to fill it. The greatest of changes is possible: in theory you are just as likely to turn into an aimless collection of molecules in this next instant as you are to remain a human being. That is, unless you believe that human beings are fated and possess no free will. . . ."

"People have free will." David knew that, if he knew anything. "And they ought to use it."

"That's right." The machine's light was as steady as the sun. "You wouldn't be in a forbidden area if people did not have free will. You yourself, intruder, are a proof of mankind's freedom."

"Okay. Now let me go by—"

"So we have established that human beings have free will. We

will assume that they follow rules. Now, having free will, and as-
suming that by some mischance one of these rules is distasteful to
them—we leave aside for the moment who made the rule—then
one would expect people to disobey it. They need not even have an
active purpose to disobey; in the course of a long enough time
many people will break this burdensome rule for the best—or worst
—of reasons. The more unacceptable the rule, the greater the
number of people who will discard it at one time or another. They
will, as individuals or groups, consciously or unconsciously, create
a new rule. This is change through human free will. So, even if the
rules were not originated by humans, in time change would ensue
given the merits of the 'system,' as we may call it, and the system
will *become* human-created. My earlier evolutionary argument
then follows as the night the day. Am I right?"

If a robot could sound triumphant, this one did.

"Ah—"

"So one good reason for doing only what you're told is that you
have the free will to do otherwise. Another good reason is God."

"God?"

"The Supreme Being, the Life Force, that ineluctable, undefin-
able spiritual presence that lies—or perhaps lurks—within the
substance of things. The Holy Father, the First—"

"What about Him?"

"God doesn't want you to cross the Median."

"I bet He doesn't," David said sarcastically.

"Have you ever seen an automobile accident?"

The robot was going too fast, and the light made it hard for
David to think. He closed his eyes and tried to fight back. "Everybody's seen accidents. People get killed. Don't go telling me God
killed them because they did something wrong."

"Don't be absurd!" the robot said. "You must try to stretch your
mind, intruder; this is not some game we're playing. This is real
life. Not only do actions have consequences, but consequences are
pregnant with Meaning.

"In the auto accident we have a peculiar sequence of events. The
physicist tells us that heat and vibration cause a weakening of the
molecular bonds between certain long-chain hydrocarbons that
comprise the substance of the tire of a car traveling at sixty miles
per hour. The tire blows. As a result of the sudden change in the
moment of inertia of this wheel, certain complex analyzable oscilla-
tions occur. The car swerves to the left, rolls over six times, tossing

people! Right, MILO?" I leaned over, taking my eyes off the road, and blew smoke into his face, screaming, "ARE YOU LISTENING, MILO? MARK MY WORDS!"

"Y-yes."

"GOO, GOO, GA-GA-GAA!"

I put my foot all the way to the floor. The wind howled through the window, the gray highway flew beneath us.

"Mark my words, Milo," I whispered. He never heard me. "Twenty-five across. Eight letters. N-i-h-i-l—"

My pulse roared in my ears, there joining the drowned choir of the fields and the roar of the engine. Body slimy with sweat, fingers clenched through the cigar, fists clamped on the wheel, smoke stinging my eyes. I slammed on the brakes, downshifting immediately, sending the transmission into a painful whine as the car slewed and skidded off the pavement, clipping a reflecting marker and throwing Milo against the windshield. The car stopped with a jerk in the gravel at the side of the road, just shy of a sign announcing, WELCOME TO OHIO.

There were no other lights on the road. I shut off my own and sat behind the wheel, trembling, the night air cool on my skin. The insects wailed. The boy was slumped against the dashboard. There was a star fracture in the glass above his head, and warm blood came away on my fingers when I touched his hair. I got out of the car, circled around to the passenger's side, and dragged him from the seat into the field adjoining the road. He was surprisingly light. I left him there, in a field of Ohio soybeans on the evening of a summer's day.

∞   ∞   ∞

The city of Detroit was founded by the French adventurer Antoine de la Mothe Cadillac, a supporter of Comte de Pontchartrain, minister of state to the Sun King, Louis XIV. All of these men worshiped the Roman Catholic god, protected their political positions, and let the future go hang. Cadillac, after whom an American automobile was named, was seeking a favorable location to advance his own economic interests. He came ashore on July 24, 1701, with fifty soldiers, an equal number of settlers, and about one hundred friendly Indians near the present site of the Veteran's Memorial Building, within easy walking distance of the Greyhound Bus Terminal.

The car did not run well after the accident, developing a reluc-

to Jesus; some devote their lives to artwork. It all comes to pretty much the same thing. You get old. You die."

"Tell me something I don't already know."

"Why do you think I picked you up, Milo? I saw your question mark and it spoke to me. You probably think I'm some pervert out to take advantage of you. I have a funny name. I don't talk like your average middle-aged businessman. Forget about that." The old excitement was upon me; I was talking louder and louder, leaning on the accelerator. The car sped along. "I think you're as troubled by the materialism and cant of life in America as I am. Young people like you, with orange hair, are trying to find some values in a world that offers them nothing but crap for ideas. But too many of you are turning to extremes in response. Drugs, violence, religious fanaticism, hedonism. Some, like you I suspect, to suicide. Don't do it, Milo. Your life is too valuable." The speedometer touched eighty, eighty-five. Milo fumbled for his seat belt but couldn't find it.

I waved my hand, holding the cigar, at him. "What's the matter, Milo? Can't find the belt?" Ninety now. A pickup went by us going the other way, the wind of its passing beating at my head and shoulder. Ninety-five.

"Think, Milo! If you're upset with the present, with your parents and the schools, think about the future. What will the future be like if this trend toward valuelessness continues in the next hundred years? Think of the impact of the new technologies! Gene splicing, gerontology, artificial intelligence, space exploration, biological weapons, nuclear proliferation! All accelerating this process! Think of the violent reactionary movements that could arise —are arising already, Milo, as we speak—from people's desire to find something to hold on to. Paint yourself a picture, *Milo*, of the kind of man or woman another hundred years of this process might produce!"

"What are you talking about?" He was terrified.

"I'm talking about the survival of values in America! Simply that." Cigar smoke swirled in front of the dashboard lights, and my voice had reached a shout. Milo was gripping the sides of his seat. The speedometer read 105. "And you, *Milo*, are at the heart of this process! If people continue to think the way you do, *Milo*, throwing their crossword puzzle books out the windows of their Audis all across America, the future will be full of absolutely valueless

"That's right. How about 'widespread'; four letters."

"Rife."

"You're pretty good." He stared at the crossword for a minute, then rolled down his window and threw the book, and the pencil, out of the car. He rolled up the window and stared at his reflection in it. I couldn't let him get off that easily. I turned off the interior light, and the darkness leapt inside.

"What's your name, son? What are you so mad about?"

"Milo. Look are you queer? If you are, it doesn't matter to me but it will cost you . . . if you want to do anything about it."

I smiled and adjusted the rearview mirror so I could watch him —and he could watch me. "No, I'm not queer. The name's Loki." I extended my right hand, keeping my eyes on the road.

He looked at the hand. "Loki?"

As good a name as any. "Yes. Same as the Norse god."

He laughed. "Sure, Loki. Anything you like. Fuck you."

Such a musical voice. "Now there you go. Seems to me, Milo— if you don't mind my giving you my unsolicited opinion—that you have something of an attitude problem." I punched the cigarette lighter, reached back and pulled a cigar from my jacket on the back-seat, in the process weaving the car all over Highway 6. I bit the end off the cigar and spat it out the window, stoked it up. My insects wailed. I cannot explain to you how good I felt.

"Take for instance this crossword puzzle book. Why did you throw it out the window?"

I could see Milo watching me in the mirror, wondering whether he should take me seriously. The headlights fanned out ahead of us, the white lines at the center of the road pulsing by like a rapid heartbeat. Take a chance, Milo. What have you got to lose?

"I was pissed," he said. "It's a waste of time. I don't care about stupid games."

"Exactly. It's just a game, a way to pass the time. Nobody ever really learns anything from a crossword puzzle. Corporation lawyers don't get their Porsches by building their word power with crosswords, right?"

"I don't care about Porsches."

"Neither do I, Milo. I drive an Audi."

Milo sighed.

"I know, Milo. That's not the point. The point is that it's all a game, crosswords or corporate law. Some people devote their lives

haps he found it in his heart to smile. Laughter—the Best Medicine.

A bit of a racing shift, then back to Interstate 70. My hip twinged all the way across Illinois.

∞ ∞ ∞

I had originally intended to work my way east to Buffalo, New York, but after the Oak Hill business I wanted to cut it short. If I stayed on the interstate I was sure to get caught; I had been lucky to get as far as I had. Just outside of Indianapolis I turned onto Route 37 north to Fort Wayne and Detroit.

I was not, however, entirely cowed. Twenty-five years in one time had given me the right instincts, and with the coming of the evening and the friendly insects to sing me along, the boredom of the road became a new recklessness. Hadn't I already been seen by too many people in those twenty-five years? Thousands had looked into my honest face—and where were they? Ruth had reminded me that I was not stuck here. I would soon make an end to this latest adventure one way or another, and once I had done so, there would be no reason in God's green world to suspect me.

And so: north of Fort Wayne, on Highway 6 east, a deserted country road (what was he doing there?), I pulled over to pick up a young hitchhiker. He wore a battered black leather jacket. His hair was short on the sides, stuck up in spikes on top, hung over his collar in back; one side was carrot-orange, the other brown with a white streak. His sign, pinned to a knapsack, said "?" He threw the pack into the backseat and climbed into the front.

"Thanks for picking me up." He did not sound like he meant it. "Where you going?"

"Flint. How about you?"

"Flint's as good as anywhere."

"Suit yourself." We got up to speed. I was completely calm. "You should fasten your seat belt," I said.

"Why?"

The surly type. "It's not just a good idea. It's the law."

He ignored me. He pulled a crossword puzzle book and a pencil from his jacket pocket. "How about turning on the light."

I flicked on the dome light for him. "I like to see a young man improve himself," I said.

His look was an almost audible sigh. "What's a five-letter word for 'the lowest point'?"

"Nadir," I replied.

its three passengers, a man and two women, about like tomatoes in a blender, and collides with a bridge abutment, exploding into flame. To the scientist, this is a simple cause-and-effect chain. The accident has a rational explanation: the tire blew."

David felt queasy. His hand, in the knapsack, clutched the gun.

"You see right away what's wrong with this explanation. It explains nothing. We know the rational explanation is inadequate without having to be able to say how we know. Such knowledge is the doing of God. God and His merciful Providence set the purpose behind the fact of our existence, and is it possible to believe that a sparrow can fall without His holy cognizance and will?"

"I don't believe in God."

"What does that matter, intruder?" The thing's voice now oozed angelic understanding. "Need you believe in gravity for it to be an inescapable fact of your existence? God does not demand your belief; He merely requests that you, of your own inviolate free will and through the undeserved gift of His grace, come to acknowledge and obey Him. Who can understand the mysteries of faith? Certainly not I, a humble mechanism. *Knowledge* is what matters, and if you open yourself to the currents that flow through the interstices of the material and immaterial universe, that knowledge will be vouchsafed *you*, intruder. You do not belong here. God knows who you are, and He saw what you did. Am I right?"

David was getting mad. "What has this got to do with car accidents?"

"The auto accident does not occur without the knowledge and permission of the Lord. This doesn't mean that He is responsible for it. He accepts the responsibility without accepting the Responsibility. This is a mystery."

"Bull!" David had heard enough talk. It was time to act.

"Be silent, intruder! Where were you when He laid the asphalt of Westbound? Who set up the mileage markers, and who painted the line upon it? On what foundation was its reinforced concrete sunk, and who made the komfy kabins, when the morning stars sang together, and all the droids and servos shouted for joy?"

It was his chance. The machine was still motionless, its mad light trained on him. A mist had sprung from the no-man's-land. Poison gas? He had no gas mask; speed was his only hope. He couldn't move. He hefted the gun. He felt dizzy, a little numb, steeling himself to move. He had to be stronger than the robot! It was just a machine!

"So that is the second good reason why you should not proceed with your ill-advised adventure," it droned on. "God is telling you to go back."

God. Rifles. He had to go! Now! Still he couldn't move. The fog grew, and its smell was strangely pungent. Once past the robot, who knew what he could find. But the machine's voice exuded self-confidence.

"A third and final good reason why you should return to your assigned role, intruder, is this:

"If you take another step, I will kill you."

∞   ∞   ∞

David woke. He was cold, and he was being shaken by a sobbing man. It was his father.

"Not responsible! Park and lock it!" For the first time in as long as he could remember, David actually heard the crying of the loud-speakers in the parking lot. He struggled to sit up. His mouth tasted like a thousand miles of road grime.

George Baker held his shoulders and looked into his face. He didn't say anything. He stood up and went to stand by the car. Shakily, he lit a cigarette. David's mother crouched over him. "David—David, are you all right?"

"What happened?"

"Your father went after you. We didn't know what happened, and I was so afraid I'd lose both of you—and then he came back carrying you in his arms."

"Carrying me? That's ridiculous." George wasn't capable of carrying a wheel hub fifty yards. David looked at the potbellied man leaning against the front fender of their car. His father was staring off across the lot. Suddenly David felt ashamed of himself. He didn't know what it was in his chest striving to express itself, but sitting there in the parking lot at mile 1.375×10^{25}, looking at the middle-aged man who was his father, he began to cry.

George never said a word to David after that day about how he had managed to follow his son into the Median, about what a struggle it must have been to make himself do that, about how and where he had found the boy, and how he had managed to bring him back, or about what it all meant to him. David never told his father about the robot and what it had said. It was all a little unreal to him. The boy who had stood there, desperately trying to get somewhere else, and the words the robot had spoken, all seemed terribly remote, as if the whole incident were something he had read about. It was a fantasy that could not have occurred in the real world of pavement and gasoline.

Father and son did not speak about it. They didn't say anything much at first, as they tentatively felt out the boundaries of what seemed to be a new relationship. Even Caroline recognized that a change had taken place, and she didn't taunt David the way she had before. Unstated was the fact that David was no longer a boy.

A month later and many thousand miles farther along, George nervously broached the subject of buying David a car. It was a shock for David to hear that, and he knew they could hardly afford it, but he also knew there was a rightness to it. And so they found themselves in the lot of Gears MacDougal's New and Used Autos.

George was too loud, too jocular. "How about this Chevy, David? A Chevy's a good driving man's car." He looked embarrassed.

David got down and felt a tire. "She's got good rubber on her."

The salesdroid was rolling up to greet them as George opened the hood of the Chevy. "Looks pretty clean," he said.

"They clean them all up."

"They sure do. You can't trust them as far as you'd . . . ah, hello."

"Good morning," the droid said, coming to rest beside them. "That's just the little thing for you. One owner, and between you and me, he didn't drive her too hard. He wasn't much of a driver."

George looked at the machine soberly. "Is that so."

"That is so, sir."

"My son's buying this car, not me," George said suddenly, loudly, as if shaking away the dust of his thoughts. "You should talk to him. And don't try to put anything over on him; he knows his stuff and . . . well, you just talk to him, not me, see?"

"Certainly, sir." The droid rolled between them and told David about the Chevy's V-8. David hardly listened. He watched his father step quietly to the side and light a cigarette. George stood with Polly and Caroline and looked ill at ease, quieter than David could ever remember. As the robot took David around the car, pointing out its extras, it came to him just what his father was: not a strong man, not a special man, not a particularly smart man. He was the same man he had been when David had sat on his lap years before; he was the same man who had taken him on his strolls around the rest stops so many times. He was the drunk who had slouched on the stool in Fast Ed's. He was a good driving man.

"I'll take it," David said, breaking off the salesdroid in midsentence.

"Righto," the machine said, its hard smile unvarying. It did not miss a beat. Within seconds a hard copy of the title had emerged from the slot in its chest. Within minutes the papers had been signed, the mileage validated and subtracted from George Baker's yearly total, and David stood beside his car. It was not a very good car to start out with, but many had started with less, and it was the best his father could do. Polly hugged him and cried. Caroline reached up and kissed him on the cheek; she cried too. George shook his hand, and did not seem to want to let go.

"Remember now, take it easy for the first thousand or so, until you get the feel of her. Check the oil, see if it burns oil. I don't think it will. It's got a good spare, doesn't it?"

"It does, Dad."

"Good. That's good." George stood silent for a moment, looking up at his son. The day was bright, and the breeze disarrayed the thinning hair he had combed over his bald spot. "Good-bye, David. Maybe we'll see you on the road?"

"Sure you will."

David got into the Chevy and turned the key in the ignition. The motor started immediately and breathed its low and steady rumble. The seat was very hot against his back. The windshield was spotless, and beyond the nose of the car stretched the access ramp to Westbound. The highway swarmed with the cars that were moving while they dawdled there still. David put the car in gear, stepped slowly on the accelerator, released the clutch, and moved smoothly down the ramp, gathering speed. He shifted up, moving faster, and then quickly once again. The force of the wind streaming in through the window increased from a breeze to a gale, and its sound became a continuous buffeting as it whipped his hair about his ear. Flicking the turn signal, David merged into the flow of traffic, the sunlight flashing off the hood ornament that led him on toward the distant horizon, just out of his reach, but attainable he knew, as he pressed his foot to the accelerator, hurrying on past mile 1.375×10^{25}.

IN INFINITY MEETING IN INFINITY MEETING IN INFINITY MEETING
TING IN INFINITY MEETING IN INFINITY MEETING IN INFINITY MEE
MEETING IN INFINITY MEETING IN INFINITY MEETING IN INFINITY
ITY MEETING IN INFINITY MEETING IN INFINITY MEETING IN INFI
NFINITY MEETING IN INFINITY MEETING IN INFINITY MEETING IN
G IN INFINITY MEETING IN INFINITY MEETING IN INFINITY MEETIN
ETING IN INFINITY MEETING IN INFINITY MEETING IN INFINITY M
MEETING IN INFINITY MEETING IN INFINITY MEETING IN INFINIT
NITY MEETING IN INFINIT **man** IN INFINITY MEETING IN IN
INFINITY MEETING IN INFINITY MEETING IN INFINITY MEETING I
G IN INFINITY MEETING IN INFINITY MEETING IN INFINITY MEET
EETING IN INFINITY MEETING IN INFINITY MEETING IN INFINITY M
J MEETING IN INFINITY MEETING IN INFINITY MEETING IN INFINI
FINITY MEETING IN INFINITY MEETING IN INFINITY MEETING IN IN
N INFINITY MEETING IN INFINITY MEETING IN INFINITY MEETING

WHEN IT WOKE US IN THE PREDAWN OF THAT FALL MORNING, I thought the sound in the basement was only the cat— but Linda, who worries about these things, insisted that I check it out. Besides, there sat Groucho our Siamese, ears pricked, on the bookshelf. The weather had turned cold just four days ago, and maybe an oppossum had managed to find its way into the house. But as I pulled on my slippers and robe there came a rustling from directly beneath us so distinct that I shivered, despite my determination to be the calm one, the one in control.

Flashlight in hand, I went to the basement stairs. I flipped on the light and limped down the steps. Groucho, alert and curious, tangled himself underfoot. About halfway down I crouched and looked, eyes level with the floor joists, around the cluttered room. At first I saw nothing unusual, but then noticed, huddled near the sacks of peat moss and pine bark mulch, a third baggy shape. I turned to Linda, who trembled at the top of the stairs. "It's a man," I said.

Linda watched me for a second. "What should we do?"

"Maybe I can scare him away."

"Be careful."

I went back to the bedroom and pulled on the jeans and sweat-shirt I'd worn the day before while changing the car's oil. Linda hovered nervously about the basement door. When I went back down he was still where I'd found him. The morning light was coming up through the basement windows; the one on the south wall was pried open. I wondered whether he might be asleep, but then I saw the gleam of his eyes watching me. He didn't move as I picked up a rake and approached. I stood five feet away, trying to seem assured and strong, feeling vulnerable. I waved the rake at him. "Get out. Come on, out!"

His dark eyes watched me. He remained still.

I stepped forward and poked the rake handle at him. At first he didn't react, then his hand flashed out from beneath his rotten coat and he grabbed the end of it. I felt the strength of his grip, like electricity, run up the handle to me. "Get out," I said.

"I'm hungry," he said, getting up. "I need something to eat."

"I don't care whether you're hungry."

We stood there, two men joined by the handle of the rake stiff as a regulation. He was about my size, dark unkempt hair in his eyes, dressed in khakis with the knees worn through, filthy once-white running shoes, several layers of T-shirts with a wide-lapelled pin-striped suit coat over them. The top T-shirt had writing on it: I'M WITH STUPID.

He smiled at me. "New Orleans?"

"What?"

"The whores on Canal Street. Hurricanes in plastic cups. Fat tourists from Texarkana, wearing masks. The whole sleazy scene."

"I don't know what you're talking about."

"You remind me of somebody I knew there. Farmer Brown, we called him." He let go of the rake handle, shoving it away disdainfully, as if he'd played this game many times before and was tired of it. "He had a rake, too."

"Get out of my basement."

"'Get out of my basement,' he mocked. "Get serious, Farmer Brown."

Groucho brushed against my leg, then moved forward to sniff the man's shoes. He crouched down, picked up the cat and held him in his lap, scratching him gently behind the ears. Groucho stretched and settled down, purring audibly.

"I want you out of here."

"I want a cigarette holder and a vacation in Portugal." He addressed the cat. "Think it's likely I'll get them, puss-puss?"

I looked over my shoulder. Linda stood halfway down the stairs, watching. "Go back up," I told her. Clutching the rake, I followed her up to the kitchen.

"Tom, you've got to do something."

My gut was already tied in a knot, and Linda's pushing only wrenched it further. "I don't know what to do."

"Well, you can't just leave him down there." Linda turned her back on me and started banging last night's dishes in the sink. "The Criswells had a man in their garage last winter, and it took three months before they could get him out. The place still smells like an outhouse. What if he comes upstairs while we're asleep?"

"He's not going to come upstairs. He's probably as scared of us as we are of him." Even as I spoke I knew it was an evasion.

"I don't care whether *he's* scared. I want him out of here."

I ran my hand through my hair. "Look. For now we can lock the basement door. There's not much he can get into. He can use the bathroom down there. Maybe he'll go away if we don't feed him. If he's still here when we come back from work, then I promise you, I'll get him out."

Linda just stared at me. I could tell she was furious, but also scared, wanting to cry but damned if she would. Her jaw clenched, and she stalked back to the bedroom. I heard water run in the bathroom. I stared out the window over the kitchen sink, then turned on the coffee maker. Groucho rubbed against my ankles, begging for breakfast. Aside from Linda and the chirping of birds in the yard, there was no sound. I wondered who Farmer Brown was.

∞　　∞　　∞

I've never been to New Orleans, but what I hear of it does not appeal to me. Sleazy bars, sex for money, the American version of the fevered exoticism of some Caribbean tourist town.

I'm a quiet man, and I've led a quiet life. The one way in which my childhood might be said to have differed from most was in its loneliness. I was an only child of elderly parents. My father and mother owned a drugstore in Tampa, where most of the people are old. Our neighborhood had few children. On top of that, when I was eight I broke my leg bicycling and was out of school, in a chest-to-knee cast, for five months. I came out of it with a right leg an inch shorter than my left and a permanent limp. Add to this a reticent nature, and the result was that I never seemed to develop any lasting friendships.

This solitude followed me into adulthood; aside from Linda, I had no close friends.

The neighborhood where we lived was old and well-established. A man in the basement was a fairly unusual occurrence, though since the new subdivisions had sprouted north of the city limits there had been increased numbers of cases even in the heart of town. It had not gotten to be a big enough problem that the city council had paid any attention to it, though Mr. Rappoport, the cranky retiree who lived behind us, had raised the issue at the last meeting of the neighborhood association.

At the studio that day I concentrated on finishing the Hayes Engineering Group annual report I'd been working on for the last twelve weeks. The project was due at the printer by Thursday. As usual, the client had dawdled on giving the necessary approvals and now was insisting on last-minute changes after the type had been set, yet still expected me to meet the deadline. Still, Horowitz, the printing rep at Athena Graphics, assured me that they would go to press by the weekend even if it meant in the middle of the night. Just before lunch I got a call from Hayes himself. "Larson?"

"Yes?"

"I was just looking over the proofs you sent me again, and it struck me that it might be more effective if you put all the figures in boldface. It would make them stand out more."

"I couldn't do that without compromising the entire design, Mr. Hayes. You can't just change one element like that without rethinking everything else."

"I'm not talking about changing a single word. Just the typeface."

I counted to three. "If you insist, I'll do it. But I can't guarantee we'll get done on time."

"Such a simple change? I thought you were a resourceful young man."

I was up against it. Hayes was a new client, and I expected to get a lot of business from him over the next years. I had lowballed my bid to get my foot in the door, promising first-class design and first-class service. "I'll have to talk this over with the printer. I'll get back to you."

"You do that."

It was all I could do to keep from slamming down the phone. If the printer got rushed, he'd screw up for sure and my whole plan would go down the tubes. My life was turning to shit.

Halfway through lunch I remembered the man in the basement and hurried over to the Hardware Warehouse at the Wonderlands Mall. After letting me wander around the home and garden section long enough to feel totally self-conscious, a salesman came up. He had the professionally competent manner of his breed; his name-plate read ROGER. I was already faintly annoyed. "Well, Roger, what have you got to help me get rid of a man in my basement?"

"Man in the basement? How old?"

"I can't tell how old he is, exactly. I didn't ask. He's not small—probably six feet tall, one-seventy or so."

The conversation turned into a manhood challenge. Roger wasn't going to help me until I admitted I was incompetent and needed his help. He was the expert, and I was the one who didn't know how to take care of myself. As we stood there in the aisle I got more and more angry, yet felt unable to escape.

"He's the violent type?"

"Yes. No question about it."

"You want to kill him?" Roger finally asked.

"Of course." I tried to act like there was never any question.

Roger turned and led me, limping more obviously in the effort to keep up with him, to another quarter of the store, beneath a big red banner hanging from the rafters reading HOME IMPROVEMENTS. He took a clear plastic bag from a shelf. *Quietus*, it said in bright red letters. The powder inside might have been brown sugar.

"This here's the quality product on the market right now. Cou-ple of tablespoonfuls in some food—peanut butter or oatmeal work good. The stuff's tasteless, but it has a texture to it, so it should be something that will disguise that. But usually these guys are so hun-gry it doesn't much matter."

When I got home there was music playing on the stereo. Nick Lowe's "Cruel to Be Kind." I heard sounds from the kitchen. "Linda?" I called.

He stuck his head through the doorway into the living room. "Howdy, Farmer Brown," he said, then ducked back into the kitchen. I followed. He stood at the counter making a peanut butter and jelly sandwich.

I don't know why I should have felt shocked, but it was as if I'd found a large cockroach in the bathtub. I hesitated in the doorway. He looked at me, finished spreading peanut butter on a slice of wheat bread, joined the halves of the sandwich, and took a bite. Crumbs were scattered all over the counter, and he'd left the tops off the jars. He nodded at the paper bag in my hand, still chewing. "Did you buy me something?"

I put the bag of poison into the pantry. "Brown sugar," I said. "How did you get upstairs?"

"Not much of a lock on that basement door. You should take care of that."

"What gives you the idea you can just come in here and use our things, eat our food?"

"Is this your food? Are these your things?"

"Well, they aren't yours."

"Possession is nine-tenths of the law." He took another bite of the sandwich. "And in my experience, possession is a matter of character."

I went to the liquor cabinet and poured myself a scotch. It burned going down, warmed my belly, its scent backing up my nose. Instantly I felt the beginning of a headache. I picked up the mail from the kitchen table. The man drew himself a glass of water and sat down opposite me. Just two old friends, long separated, sitting around the house having a chat. "Tough day?" he said.

"None of your business."

"You know, in my mind I can visualize what it must be like to have a job like yours. I have a very powerful mind. And it seems to me, in my mind, that it's only after you stop taking other people's shit that you start to taste life." He took another bite of the sandwich, and grinned.

In the living room Lowe was singing about making an American squirm. I sucked down the scotch, trying to figure out what to do next. When I heard Linda's car in the driveway my anxiety came back. I looked at the basement door.

"Don't worry," he said. "I won't tell her you couldn't face me."

"I am facing you."

He watched me, took a sip of water. Something in the way he did this was so fastidious that it stood out in contrast to his shabby clothes, rude manner. "Of course you are, Farmer Brown," he said. I heard the front door open.

"She won't leave you just because you're scared," the man said softly. "I am, after all, an unpleasant reality."

He went down the stairs to the basement.

Linda came into the kitchen. She looked at the drink in my hand. "Is he still down there?"

"He's still there," I said.

She went into the living room and turned down the stereo. She came back into the kitchen, grim-faced, and screwed the top back on the jar of peanut butter. Brushing crumbs off the counter into her hand, she said, "I wish you'd put things away after you use them, Tom."

∞ ∞ ∞

By midevening the headache was going strong. I hadn't felt like eating, and we'd passed supper in silence.

"Just don't press me about this," I told her later. "Trust me: I'll get him out." We were undressing for bed; we'd not exchanged three sentences that evening. She slipped on the T-shirt and shorts she wore instead of pajamas. Her shoulders were still slender as a girl's. I wanted her; we hadn't made love for weeks, but Linda's manner was as cold as if sex had not been invented yet. "He's not dangerous," I insisted.

"I don't care if he isn't." Her voice was brittle. "He scares me."

"He scares me, too. I want him out of here. But let it be for a while. I'll get him out." She got into bed; I reached over to touch her shoulder. She pulled away. "Linda?"

She didn't answer. My stomach churned. I turned off the light and lay there silently for a long time. Lying there, I thought about him. I pictured him crouched in the dark of the basement, the musty smell, the crickets and spiders. He was alone down there; I was alone up here. I imagined getting up, going to the refrigerator, popping the tops on two beers, and going down to visit him. We might sit on the old lawn chairs and talk, in low whispers, careful not to wake Linda. We would tell each other our stories. Groucho would come down and curl up on my lap. Our eyes, the man's and mine, would glint in the darkness like those of two untamed and sullen beasts.

Eventually, thinking of him, I fell asleep.

In the morning I got up before Linda and made myself some oatmeal. I sliced a banana into it and sprinkled it with brown sugar. The bag of poison lay on the pantry shelf like an accusation. I poured a cup of coffee and turned on the stereo. U2: *Rattle and Hum.* I kept the volume down, ate my oatmeal, and listened to the music.

Afterward I went downstairs to check up on him. He'd cleared out one end of the basement, found the old canvas cot from among the camping equipment, and set it up. But he wasn't there, and the basement window was opened wide. I felt relief, to be sure, but also a vague disappointment.

When I turned to go back upstairs he entered from the basement bathroom. He had my briefcase and car keys in his hand and acted as if he was about to step out the door. The jeans and shirt he was wearing he must have taken from the laundry room. Although he seemed to have showered and washed his hair, he had not shaved and, with the rumpled clothes, looked more like somebody going on vacation than to work. "What do you think you're doing?" I asked him.

"I'm going down to your studio. You look like you could use a day off."

"You can't go to work dressed like that!"

"What's the use of being your own boss if you have to invent a dress code?"

"You don't know the first thing about my work."

"I know more than you think. I've looked through the stuff in here," he said, hefting the briefcase. "Besides, what's there to know? No sense throwing a veil of mystery over what must be mostly a matter of snowing the people who pay you. It's all in your attitude."

I followed him, ineffectual as smoke, as he went upstairs and out the door. He climbed into my car and drove away.

I stood there stunned until Linda came into the room. She looked over at the stereo, which had gotten as far as "Love Rescue Me."

"I thought I heard you leave. Aren't you going to work today?"

"No. You're so damned hot about me getting rid of that man in the basement, then I'm going to have to stay home and work on it."

She looked at me, surprised at my anger. For a moment I could see the absolute weariness and disgust in her face. Not only did she dislike me, she had absolutely no respect for me and was tired of putting up with the charade. While she went into the kitchen to make her breakfast, I slumped onto the sofa and pretended to read the sports page. The gray lines of newsprint slid past my eyes unread. The CD cycled to "God Part II." I turned up the volume to window-shaking levels. The phase-distorted guitar bounced the knickknacks on the mantel.

Linda came out and shouted something at me. I shook my head and pointed at my deaf ears. She stalked out of the house, slamming the front door. I tried not to imagine what she'd make of my missing car. The stereo wailed. I believed in love, but it wasn't working.

∞   ∞   ∞

So I got drunk. After I polished off the bottle of scotch I switched to brandy. I played loud music, stared at Linda's books crowding the living-room shelves, and felt alternately sorry for myself and murderously angry. At Linda, at my clients, at the man in the basement.

Except he wasn't down there anymore. Brandy in my hand, unshaven and rank, I stumbled downstairs to his lair. You would hardly have known that anyone had been there. It suddenly hit me to wonder whether he was going to come meekly back down when he returned from my studio.

It ought not to have been so hard to get rid of him. He was not a family member. He was not a guest. We didn't owe him anything. We had gotten along fine without him for many years. If any of the neighbors had men in their basements it was not a fact they advertised. And who knew what damage he was doing to the business I had labored over the last six years to erect?

Around five he pulled into the driveway and sauntered in, whistling. He tossed my briefcase onto the ottoman, flopped down on the sofa, and put his feet up on the big coffee table Linda had brought with her from before we got married. "Howdy, Farmer Brown. Where's your rake?"

He looked so relaxed there, and I was so drunk, that instead of getting angry I felt sad. I sat down next to him. "What happened at the studio today? Did you really go there?"

"Nowhere else. You can stop worrying about the Hayes Group report."

"What do you mean?"

"I fired the printer. Horowitz was lying to you all along. He wasn't going to meet the deadline, and while he put you off with excuses the bastard went behind your back to Hayes and blamed the delays and mistakes on you."

"You can't fire him! It's too late! I can't find another printer on such short notice. Hayes is already breathing down my neck."

"Right. So I told Hayes that under the circumstances I'd understand if he went elsewhere."

"You *what?* Hayes is my biggest client. If I could satisfy him I'd double my income in the next twelve months."

"At the cost of an ulcer. And your balls. Hayes is a petty tyrant and a coward. A man with a bank account and no integrity. Do you really need the money that bad?"

I started to protest, but then the thought of never having to suck up to Hayes, or deal with the printer's lies, sank in. My shoulders already felt less tight. "I don't know," I said.

"You don't know. But I do."

I took another sip of brandy. Groucho came by, hopped onto my lap, and began butting my hand. I heard Linda's car in the driveway. She came in laden with books, briefcase, staggering as she dangled two recyclable sacks of groceries from her fingertips. She saw us on the sofa and dropped the groceries.

I sat there. The man leapt up and took one bag from her arms, scooped the fallen one from the floor. "I was just helping Tom," he said. "I might as well help you, too."

Staring at me as if she could not believe, a little dazed, she said, "I guess so."

∞   ∞   ∞

That was the beginning. In a week he had come to be a part of our lives. I still went to work, but when I felt bad or woke up late or was hung over or didn't feel like shaving, he filled in. I can't tell you that, along with the worry, I didn't feel relief. I can't say, honestly, that he did a worse job than I would have. He did a different one.

Linda at first was nervous around him. She never gave him the opportunity to touch her, even the most casual of contacts. I remember once when she was washing out the coffeepot and he took it from her to dry. He touched her wrist, and she shuddered visibly. I took this for distaste and felt guilty about it, acted apologetic around her as if the man were my idea, as if I had brought him into the house and was the one responsible for keeping him. I can't even say that wasn't true, although it's not all of the truth. Linda didn't let me touch her, either.

The man treated me with playful contempt through which I read some other attitude. An attitude I could not define. I found myself becoming more antisocial. I no longer gladly put up with the hypocrisies necessary to do business. If people asked me a question, I told them the truth, regardless of the reaction. If they didn't want an answer, then why did they ask? I watched people in the streets, at restaurants, in movie theaters. How many women had some shrill madwoman in their attics? How many men had a man in their basement, calling them mocking names, making himself indispensable? Did they summon him upstairs when they felt the need, regretting and needing him at the same time, humiliated yet queerly pleased?

I let my hair grow long and stopped shaving. The man got his hair cut. He began to wear my clothes, which fit him, more or less. Cleaned up, smelling of cologne and wearing my suit, he resembled me—except for my limp—though no one who knew me would mistake us for each other. On days when I did go to work I would come home to find him sitting around the living room, reading Linda's books, playing my CDs. He said he was getting a good picture of our characters.

"And what do you think of us?" I asked.

"I think you are more or less what you expect to be."

Things got pretty slow at my studio. I spent some long hours there trying to please the clients I had left, repeatedly calculating my monthly overhead and eyeing the incredible shrinking balance in my business account. I made call after call to former clients, always on some flimsy pretext, pretending to be casual, hoping they might throw me some business. When this got to be too much for me, I'd walk across the street to the park and feed nuts to the squirrels.

One lunchtime, to my surprise, I found Simpson Hayes sitting out there on one of the benches. For a minute I thought about circling behind to the other side of the park, but then he looked up and saw me. I sat down beside him. "Fancy meeting you here," I said.

"Larson," he said. There were dark circles under his eyes. "How's business?"

"Business is just fine."

"That's not what Horowitz tells me."

"If you still believe what he tells you, then there's no point in us talking."

To my surprise, Hayes smiled—a trifle grimly. "Horowitz really screwed you over there, didn't he? He was lying to you."

"You figured that out. Maybe you've caught on that you can't trust Athena Graphics?"

"So what? I can't say I have much sympathy for you. You can't let anyone get the advantage over you. Not if you're a professional."

"A professional."

"A pro sees what has to be done, then he does it. It doesn't matter how he feels about it. That's why you're a lousy businessman."

I thought of a dozen defensive replies, started to speak, said nothing. I opened my bag of peanuts and scattered a few on the path in front of us. "You look worn out, Hayes. Is being such a macho man hard work?"

He looked at me sharply. "You're the one who's going out of business."

I was tired of him. "That's right, I almost forgot. Thanks for reminding me." I got up and crossed back to my office.

I was in no mood to face my empty drafting table, so I decided to call it a day. The encounter with Hayes was the last straw. The more I thought about him, the madder I got. The guy as much as admitted he was getting fucked by Horowitz, he looked like he hadn't slept in three days, and still his only reaction to seeing me was to try to make me feel like shit.

On the way home it occurred to me that Hayes might be fighting a man in his basement. What would he do? Kill him, probably, in short order. Hayes and the man were birds of a feather, both followers of the Attila the Hun school of interpersonal relations. For them, there were no limits. If the world were made of people like them, we'd still be dodging spears.

I was the one in trouble, not Hayes.

To my surprise, when I reached home Linda's car was in the driveway. I panicked when I thought of her alone with the man. He was capable of anything. I hurried to the door, rushed in. Silently I moved down the hall. The bedroom door stood open. I heard a rustling of bedclothes. I came in on them naked in each other's arms, caught a glimpse of Linda's face, eyes closed and lips parted, cheeks flushed as he rocked her in his arms, her head almost off the side of the bed. The man glanced up at me; the corner of his mouth quirked upward in a grin. Linda's eyes came open, and I turned and stumbled from the room.

If I'd thought my intrusion might have disturbed them, I was sadly mistaken. I'd sat for forty minutes, fuming, in the den before either of them came to face me. It was Linda, wearing her blue terry-cloth bathrobe. Her cheeks were still flushed, her hair tangled. "What are you doing back so early?"

"What am *I* doing?"

She sat down on the love seat. "I'm sorry, Tom. I told you to get rid of him. I told you he was dangerous."

"You didn't tell me that you were."

"No I didn't. You just assumed I was harmless."

"Where is he?"

She smoothed the robe over her leg. I ached to touch her. "He went back into the basement."

"That's not good enough, Linda. None of this is. You owe me better than this."

"So? This is a two-way street."

"Shut up! Just shut up! I'm the one who's been betrayed here."

"Don't be too sure of that. It took more than just me for things to get so bad between us before he showed up."

I couldn't stand it. I stormed into the kitchen, kicked open the basement door, and stalked down the stairs. He was lounging on the old lawn chair, sipping a scotch.

"Well, if it isn't Farmer Brown," he said. "Hello, Farmer Brown."

"Don't call me that."

"What shall I call you, Farmer Brown?"

"You slept with my wife."

"Actually, we hadn't gotten around to the sleeping part, yet."

I paced around the basement. It hardly seemed like the place it had been before he'd come. It looked like a shabby apartment in some third world country. Some student's room, halfway between a hovel and the lower middle class, partway up the evolutionary scale but not there yet.

"All right," I said. "You've screwed up our lives enough. I want you out of here—right now."

"You don't want me out of here. If I left, you'd be a lump of clay, without me. That's all, a lump of clay."

"Better a lump of clay and peaceful. You're ripping me apart! I didn't ask for this."

"Yes you did. We both know you wanted me here, you called me up, and after I leave you'll be dead. You want me gone? Here, take this." He reached behind him on the floor, picked something up, and held it out to me. It was the bag of poison. "It would be more honest to just kill yourself."

I just stood there. "That's what you want me to think—that I can't live without you. But who says I can't?"

"She's never going to give you what you want, Tom. Love without any responsibilities? It doesn't exist in the real world, once we leave the womb. And you can't even handle the affection you're getting now—pitiful as it is."

"Stop it!"

"What's the matter—hitting too close to home? I know you.
The reason I'm here is to make up for all that. For you to live without me would be for you to eat all the shit the world offers, and call
it whipped cream. It would mean you'd accept it all. You'd be saying it never could be any better."

"Maybe it can't."

"Suit yourself. That's not my department. I'm only the alternative."

My eyes were burning. "Okay, okay," I said. "Maybe you're
right. But does it have to be so painful? I can't go on living like this.
I fooled myself for years, living half-alive, growing a tumor because that's all I knew. I don't want to live that way anymore. I
can't. I'll do myself in. I want some peace."

"What do I know about peace? I'm just the man in your basement." He drained the last of the scotch, leaned back calm as a
millionaire on permanent vacation.

I caught my breath. "Fuck you," I said, rage erasing the humiliation. "I don't believe I've put up with you for so long. I don't even
know your name."

"My name is Tom."

That was it. I grabbed the rake and swung round on him, whip-
ping it level like a baseball bat. Quick as thought, he caught the
handle and wrenched it out of my hands. He stood up. Not even
breathing hard, he tossed the rake onto the floor. He flipped the
bag of poison at me. I caught it, fumbling.

"You are truly pitiful," he said. "Do something constructive.
Use it."

∞   ∞   ∞

I turned and limped up the stairs, past Linda where she waited in
the kitchen, out the front door and into my car. I drove around for
a while, barely able to see the streets through my tears, the bag of
poison on the passenger's seat beside me.

Unconsciously I found myself downtown, driving toward my
studio. I couldn't face that. Instead I pulled into the Saratoga Street
ramp. I sat in my parked car, hands gripping the wheel, crying out
loud now, for a long time. Eventually I stopped. I sat back, breathing hard, and took the bag onto my lap. *Quietus.* I could tear it
open right there, take a good healthy mouthful. I squeezed the bag
with my thumbs, feeling the moist powder inside, and gradually all
thought drained from my mind.

It was four-thirty, and the ramp started to get busy with people heading out for an early start on the weekend. I saw Clarice Ward, an architect who worked in the Hayes Engineering Group. The group's office was in the Columbia Tower attached to the deck.

I got out of the car. Ignoring the elevator in order to avoid facing anyone, I took the stairs up to the Hayes Group office. It was hard work making it up ten flights of stairs with my bum leg.

Hayes's secretary, who had put me off dozens of times over the phone, was cleaning up her desk. "Mr. Hayes is gone," she said.

"Then he won't mind my dropping something off in his office," I said, and pushed past her through the door.

Hayes was leaning back in his chair, gazing out the window at the skyline. "Time to go home, Hayes," I said. "Don't be a workaholic. It's Friday."

He swiveled around, face creased with annoyance. "What do you want?"

"I want to help you out."

He stared up at me. He really did look exhausted. "Look, if I hurt your feelings this afternoon, I'm sorry."

"I appreciate the sentiment. But I didn't come here looking for an apology, either. Are you having some trouble at home?"

"Nothing I can't handle." He played with the Waterman pen on his desk blotter, spinning it like a pinwheel. "Look, Tom. If you need work I'll think about it. I'll call you."

"I don't need work, I'm just paying a social call. That problem at home? Maybe you've got some vermin in the basement?" I slapped the bag of *Quietus* down on the desk. "You might have use for this."

He looked at me with new interest. "You've had trouble with— intruders?"

"Just one."

He picked up the poison. "This bag hasn't been opened."

"Because my troubles are over. Use it if you can't think of anything better. Then give me a call and maybe I can help you salvage your report."

I left him there, turning the bag over in his hands. I walked back down the stairs to the parking deck, and it did not seem to me that my leg bothered me much at all.

∞   ∞   ∞

When I came back home, the house was dark. I considered confronting them, but the thought of another ugly scene, and the pain it would inevitably cause me—and Linda—kept me away from the bedroom. I would save that for tomorrow. It was not that I could put it off forever—I was through putting things off—but I didn't need it now. The question for now was, where would I sleep?

The place was silent, and I didn't turn on any lights. Streetlight coming through the blinds threw lines of light and shadow across the furniture, casting everything into high relief. Sleeping on the sofa, an antique Linda had picked out for us, would be like spending the night on broken ground. Instead I walked from room to room, seeing our house as I had not seen it before. There were the oak bookshelves Linda had picked out, lining the living-room wall. On the shelves were ranked the spines of her books, English and American literature, political science, philosophy, religion. How many of them were mine?—there, in the lower corner of the last shelf, a pile of AIGA annuals and *Communication Arts.* Not an impressive showing.

Here was Linda's coffee table. The stereo cabinet—I remembered us going to pick it out, how she had stated unequivocally what she wanted while I kept my mouth shut. The pictures on the wall—her choice, too.

It was not a bad-looking home, or an uncomfortable one. It was very livable. But it did not look like the home of a graphic designer, and it hit me that, if I were to leave and never come back, Linda would not have to change the house in any significant way to make it completely hers. I wasn't evident in our home at all.

Well, that didn't have to be. I went over to the shelf, took out my books, and laid them on the coffee table. The armchair—I had never liked the way it sat across from the window, throwing the late afternoon light into your eyes. I moved the lamp, the chair. I shoved the sofa away from the wall, took down Linda's photos from Oxford that hung above the stereo cabinet, and replaced them with the Magritte print from my study. By the entryway I piled the knickknacks from the mantel that would have to go elsewhere.

It ended up an hour of sweaty work in the dark, and I made some noise, but if they heard any of this in the bedroom they did not bother about it. Groucho came out, miaowed once, and sat on the ottoman to watch. As I worked it seemed to me that my leg did not ache as it often had before under stress. It tingled. When I was done I sat in the armchair, in its new place, and looked around the still-dark room. It was recognizably the same room, but at least now I could point in it to those things that were mine. Paint the walls and bookshelves white, and it would be an entirely brighter place.

Now where to sleep? Not the sofa. Then I had an idea, the most natural idea in the world. I went down to the basement, to the cot where the man had been. It did not look half so strange as it had the other times I'd been there. I lay down. It smelled familiar, not so musty. It felt more comfortable than I remembered. As I lay there I imagined how it would be to live down here for years, ignored, unable to affect what went on upstairs, barely surviving, limping along alive but unheard. I thought about New Orleans and Mardi Gras, the masked and drunken people in the streets, spending a night on pleasure because they owed that to some part of themselves that would be stifled by the sacrifices of Lent. Eventually I fell asleep, and slept more restfully than I had for weeks.

In the morning I was wakened, in the predawn, by the footsteps of someone on the stairs.

It was Linda. She stood there uncertainly, the flashlight in her hand. "I woke up and no one was there," she said. "I was so afraid I was alone, and I looked all through the house. Why did you come back down here?"

Still fuddled by sleep, I held up my hand to shield my eyes from the light. I was not entirely sure where I was or how I had come to be there. Cold morning air flowed in through the open window. "I thought you didn't want me up there."

"Of course I want you. It scared me when I woke and you weren't next to me."

"I guess I didn't know that." I sat up on the edge of the cot. Groucho hopped up beside me and rubbed my hand. I took him in my arms, stood and went to Linda.

She watched me soberly, her eyes glistening. "You changed everything around. It's different up there now."

I held Groucho out to her, and she scratched him under the chin. He purred. She took my arm, and we climbed the stairs together. My limp was entirely gone.

IG IN INFINITY MEETING IN INFINITY MEETING IN INFINITY MEET
EETING IN INFINITY MEETING IN INFINITY MEETING IN INFINITY M
Y MEETING IN INFINITY MEETING IN INFINITY MEETING IN INFINI
FINITY MEETING IN INFINITY MEETING IN INFINITY MEETING IN IN
N INFINITY MEETING IN INFINITY MEETING IN INFINITY MEETING
NG IN INFINITY MEETING IN INFINITY MEETING IN INFINITY MEE
IEETING IN INFINITY MEETING IN INFINITY MEETING IN INFINITY
TY MEETING IN INFINITY MEETING IN INFINITY MEETING IN INFIN
IFINITY MEETING IN IN INFINITY MEETING IN
IN INFINITY MEETING MEETING IN INFINITY MEETIN
TING IN INFINITY MEETING IN INFINITY MEETING IN INFINITY ME
MEETING IN INFINITY MEETING IN INFINITY MEETING IN INFINITY
IITY MEETING IN INFINITY MEETING IN INFINITY MEETING IN INF
INFINITY MEETING IN INFINITY MEETING IN INFINITY MEETING IN
G IN INFINITY MEETING IN INFINITY MEETING IN INFINITY MEETI

invaders

15 NOVEMBER 1532: THAT NIGHT NO ONE SLEPT. ON THE HILLS outside Cajamarca, the campfires of the Inca's army shone like so many stars in the sky. De Soto had reported that Atahualpa had perhaps forty thousand troops under arms, but looking at the myriad lights spread across those hills, de Candia realized that estimate was, if anything, low.

Against them, Pizarro could throw one hundred foot soldiers, sixty horse, eight muskets, and four harquebuses. Pizarro, his brother Hernando, de Soto, and Benalcázar laid out plans for an ambush. De Candia and his artillery would be hidden in the building along one side of the square, the cavalry and infantry along the others. De Candia watched Pizarro prowl through the camp that night, checking the men's armor, joking with them, reminding them of the treasure they would have, and the women. The men laughed nervously and whetted their swords.

They might sharpen them until their hands fell off; when morning dawned, they would be slaughtered. De Candia breathed deeply of the thin air and turned from the wall.

Ruiz de Arce, an infantryman with a face like a clenched fist, hailed him as he passed. "Are those guns of yours ready for some work tomorrow?"

"We need prayers more than guns."

"I'm not afraid of these brownies," de Arce said.

"Then you're a half-wit."

"Soto says they have no swords."

The man was probably just trying to reassure himself, but de Candia couldn't abide it. "Will you shut your stinking fool's trap! They don't need swords! If they only spit all at once, we'll be drowned."

Pizarro overheard him. He stormed over, grabbed de Candia's arm, and shook him. "Have they ever seen a horse, Candia? Have they ever felt steel? When you fired the harquebus on the seashore, didn't the town chief pour beer down its barrel as if it were a thirsty god? Pull up your balls and show me you're a man!"

His face was inches away. "Mark me! Tomorrow, Saint James sits on your shoulder, and we win a victory that will cover us in glory for five hundred years."

∞   ∞   ∞

2 December 2001: "DEE-fense! DEE-fense!" the crowd screamed. During the two-minute warning, Norwood Delacroix limped over to the Redskins' special conditioning coach.

"My knee's about gone," said Delacroix, an outside linebacker with eyebrows that ran together and all the musculature that modern pharmacology could load onto his six-foot-five frame. "I need something."

"You need the power of prayer, my friend. Stoner's eating your lunch."

"Just do it."

The coach selected a popgun from his rack, pressed the muzzle against Delacroix's knee, and pulled the trigger. A flood of well-being rushed up Delacroix's leg. He flexed it tentatively. It felt better than the other one now. Delacroix jogged back onto the field. "DEE-fense!" the fans roared. The overcast sky began to spit frozen rain. The ref blew the whistle, and the Bills broke huddle.

Delacroix looked across at Stoner, the Bills' tight end. The air throbbed with electricity. The quarterback called the signals; the ball was snapped; Stoner surged forward. As Delacroix backpedaled furiously, sudden sunlight flooded the field. His ears buzzed. Stoner jerked left and went right, twisting Delacroix around like a cork in a bottle. His knee popped. Stoner had two steps on him. TD for sure. Delacroix pulled his head down and charged after him.

But instead of continuing downfield, Stoner slowed. He looked straight up into the air. Delacroix hit him at the knees, and they both went down. He'd caught him! The crowd screamed louder, a scream edged with hysteria.

Then Delacroix realized the buzzing wasn't just in his ears. Elation fading, he lifted his head and looked toward the sidelines. The coaches and players were running for the tunnels. The crowd boiled toward the exits, shedding thermoses and beer cups and radios. The sunlight was harshly bright. Delacroix looked up. A huge disk hovered no more than fifty feet above, pinning them in its spotlight. Stoner untangled himself from Delacroix, stumbled to his feet, and ran off the field.

Holy Jesus and the Virgin Mary on toast, Delacroix thought.

He scrambled toward the end zone. The stadium was emptying fast, except for the ones who were getting trampled. The throbbing in the air increased in volume, lowered in pitch, and the flying saucer settled onto the NFL logo on the forty-yard line. The sound stopped as abruptly as if it had been sucked into a sponge.

Out of the corner of his eye, Delacroix saw an NBC cameraman come up next to him, focusing on the ship. Its side divided, and a ramp extended itself to the ground. The cameraman fell back a few steps, but Delacroix held his ground. The inside glowed with the bluish light of a UV lamp.

A shape moved there. It lurched forward to the top of the ramp. A large manlike thing, it advanced with a rolling stagger, like a college freshman at a beer blast. It wore a body-tight red stretchsuit, a white circle on its chest with a lightning bolt through it, some sort of flexible mask over its face. Blond hair covered its head in a kind of brush cut, and two cup-shaped ears poked comically out of the sides of its head. The creature stepped off onto the field, nudging aside the football that lay there.

Delacroix, who had majored in public relations at Michigan State, went forward to greet it. This could be the beginning of an entirely new career. His knee felt great.

He extended his hand. "Welcome," he said. "I greet you in the name of humanity and the United States of America."

"Cocaine," the alien said. "We need cocaine."

∞   ∞   ∞

Today: I sit at my desk writing a science-fiction story, a tall, thin man wearing jeans, a white T-shirt with the abstract face of a man printed on it, white high-top basketball shoes, and gold-plated wire-rimmed glasses.

In the morning I drink coffee to get me up for the day, and at night I have a gin and tonic to help me relax.

∞   ∞   ∞

16 November 1532: "What are they waiting for, the shitting dogs!" the man next to de Arce said. "Are they trying to make us suffer?"

"Shut up, will you?" De Arce shifted his armor. Wedged into the stone building on the side of the square, sweating, they had been waiting since dawn, in silence for the most part except for the creak of leather, the uneasy jingle of cascabels on the horses' trappings. The men stank worse than the restless horses. Some had pissed themselves. A common foot soldier like de Arce was lucky to get a space near enough to the door to see out.

As noon came and went with still no sign of Atahualpa and his retinue, the mood of the men went from impatience to near panic. Then, late in the day, word came that the Indians again were moving toward the town.

An hour later, six thousand brilliantly costumed attendants entered the plaza. They were unarmed. Atahualpa, borne on a golden litter by eight men in cloaks of green feathers that glistened like emeralds in the sunset, rose above them. De Arce heard a slight rattling, looked down, and found that his hand, gripping the sword so tightly the knuckles stood out white, was shaking uncontrollably. He unknotted his fist from the hilt, rubbed the cramped fingers, and crossed himself.

"Quiet now, my brave ones," Pizarro said.

Father Valverde and Felipillo strode out to the center of the plaza, right through the sea of attendants. The priest had guts. He stopped before the litter of the Inca, short and steady as a fence post. "Greetings, my lord, in the name of Pope Clement VII, His Majesty the Emperor Charles V, and Our Lord and Savior Jesus Christ."

Atahualpa spoke and Felipillo translated: "Where is this new god?"

Valverde held up the crucifix. "Our God died on the cross many years ago and rose again to Heaven. He appointed the Pope as His viceroy on earth, and the Pope has commanded King Charles to subdue the peoples of the world and convert them to the true faith. The king sent us here to command your obedience and to teach you and your people in this faith."

"By what authority does this pope give away lands that aren't his?"

Valverde held up his Bible. "By the authority of the word of God."

The Inca took the Bible. When Valverde reached out to help him get the cover unclasped, Atahualpa cuffed his arm away. He opened the book and leafed through the pages. After a moment he threw it to the ground. "I hear no words," he said.

Valverde snatched up the book and stalked back toward Pizarro's hiding place. "What are you waiting for?" he shouted. "The saints and the Blessed Virgin, the bleeding wounds of Christ himself, cry vengeance! Attack, and I'll absolve you!"

Pizarro had already stridden into the plaza. He waved his kerchief. "Santiago, and at them!"

On the far side, the harquebuses exploded in an enfilade. The lines of Indians jerked like startled cats. Bells jingling, de Soto's and Hernando's cavalry burst from the lines of doorways on the adjoining side. De Arce clutched his sword and rushed out with the others from the third side. He felt the power of God in his arm. "Santiago!" he roared at the top of his lungs, and hacked halfway through the neck of his first Indian. Bright blood spurted. He put his boot to the brown man's shoulder and yanked free, lunged for the belly of another wearing a kilt of bright red-and-white checks. The man turned, and the sword caught between his ribs. The hilt was almost twisted from de Arce's grasp as the Indian went down. He pulled free, shrugged another man off his back, and daggered him in the side.

After the first flush of glory, it turned to filthy, hard work, an hour's wade through an ocean of butchery in the twilight, bodies heaped waist-high, boots skidding on the bloody stones. De Arce alone must have killed forty. Only after they'd slaughtered them all and captured the Sapa Inca did it end. A silence settled, broken only by the moans of dying Indians and distant shouts of the cavalry chasing the ones who had managed to break through the plaza wall to escape.

Saint James had indeed sat on their shoulders. Six thousand dead Indians, and not one Spaniard nicked. It was a pure demonstration of the power of prayer.

∞   ∞   ∞

31 January 2002: It was Colonel Zipp's third session interrogating the alien. So far the thing had kept a consistent story, but not a credible one. The only consideration that kept Zipp from panic at the thought of how his career would suffer if this continued was the rumor that his fellow case officers weren't doing any better with any of the others. That, and the fact that the Krel possessed technology that would reestablish American superiority for another two hundred years. He took a drag on his cigarette, the first of his third pack of the day.

"Your name?" Zipp asked.

"You may call me Flash."

Zipp studied the red union suit, the lightning bolt. With the flat chest, the rounded shoulders, pointed upper lip, and pronounced underbite, the alien looked like a cross between Wally Cleaver and the Mock Turtle. "Is this some kind of joke?"

"What is a joke?"

"Never mind." Zipp consulted his notes. "Where are you from?"

"God has ceded us an empire extending over sixteen solar systems in the Orion arm of the galaxy, including the systems around the stars you know as Tau Ceti, Epsilon Eridani, Alpha Centauri, and the red dwarf Barnard's star."

"God gave you an empire?"

"Yes. We were hoping He'd give us your world, but all He kept talking about was your cocaine."

The alien's translating device had to be malfunctioning. "You're telling me that God sent you for cocaine?"

"No. He just told us about it. We collect chemical compounds for their aesthetic interest. These alkaloids do not exist on our world. Like the music you humans value so highly, they combine familiar elements—carbon, hydrogen, nitrogen, oxygen—in pleasing new ways."

The colonel leaned back, exhaled a cloud of smoke. "You consider cocaine like—like a symphony?"

"Yes. Understand, Colonel, no material commodity alone could justify the difficulties of interstellar travel. We come here for aesthetic reasons."

"You seem to know what cocaine is already. Why don't you just synthesize it yourself?"

"If you valued a unique work of aboriginal art, would you be satisfied with a mass-produced duplicate manufactured in your hometown? Of course not. And we are prepared to pay you well, in a coin you can use."

"We don't need any coins. If you want cocaine, tell us how your ships work."

"That is one of the coins we had in mind. Our ships operate according to a principle of basic physics. Certain fundamental physical reactions are subject to the belief system of the beings promoting them. If I believe that X is true, then X is more probably true than if I did not believe so."

The colonel leaned forward again. "We know that already. We call it the 'observer effect.' Our great physicist Werner Heisenberg—"

"Yes. I'm afraid we carry this principle a little further than that."

"What do you mean?"

Flash smirked. "I mean that our ships move through interstellar space by the power of prayer."

∞ ∞ ∞

13 May 1533: Atahualpa offered to fill a room twenty-two feet long and seventeen feet wide with gold up to a line as high as a man could reach, if the Spaniards would let him go. They were skeptical. How long would this take? Pizarro asked. Two months, Atahualpa said.

Pizarro allowed the word to be sent out, and over the next several months, bearers, chewing the coca leaf in order to negotiate the mountain roads under such burdens, brought in tons of gold artifacts. They brought plates and vessels, life-sized statues of women and men, gold lobsters and spiders and alpacas, intricately fashioned ears of maize, every kernel reproduced, with leaves of gold and tassels of spun silver.

Martin Bueno was one of the advance scouts sent with the Indians to Cuzco, the capital of the empire. They found it to be the legendary city of gold. The Incas, having no money, valued precious metals only as ornament. In Cuzco the very walls of the Sun Temple, Coricancha, were plated with gold. Adjoining the temple was a ritual garden where gold maize plants supported gold butterflies, gold bees pollinated gold flowers.

"Enough loot that you'll shit in a different gold pot every day for the rest of your life," Bueno told his friend Diego Leguizano upon his return to Cajamarca.

They ripped the plating off the temple walls and had it carried to Cajamarca. There they melted it down into ingots.

The huge influx of gold into Europe was to cause an economic catastrophe. In Peru, at the height of the conquest, a pair of shoes cost $850, and a bottle of wine $1,700. When their old horseshoes wore out, iron being unavailable, the cavalry shod their horses with silver.

∞   ∞   ∞

21 April 2003: In the executive washroom of Bellingham, Winston, and McNeese, Jason Prescott snorted a couple of lines and was ready for the afternoon. He returned to the brokerage to find the place in a whispering uproar. In his office sat one of the Krel. Prescott's secretary was about to piss himself. "It asked specifically for you," he said.

What would Attila the Hun do in this situation? Prescott thought. He went into the office. "Jason Prescott," he said. "What can I do for you, Mr. . . .?"

The alien's bloodshot eyes surveyed him. "Flash. I wish to make an investment."

"Investments are our business." Rumors had flown around the New York Merc for a month that the Krel were interested in investing. They had earned vast sums selling information to various computer, environmental, and biotech firms. Several of the aliens had come to observe trading in the currencies pit last week, and only yesterday Jason had heard from a reliable source that they were considering opening an account with Merrill Lynch. "What brings you to our brokerage?"

"Not the brokerage. You. We heard that you are the most ruthless currencies trader in this city. We worship efficiency. You are efficient."

Right. Maybe there was a hallucinogen in the toot. "I'll call in some of our foreign-exchange experts. We can work up an investment plan for your consideration in a week."

"We already have an investment plan. We are, as you say in the markets, 'long' in dollars. We want you to sell dollars and buy francs for us."

"The franc is pretty strong right now. It's likely to hold for the next six months. We'd suggest—"

"We wish to buy $50 billion worth of francs."

Prescott stared. "That's not a very good investment." Flash said nothing. The silence grew uncomfortable. "I suppose if we stretch it out over a few months, and hit the exchanges in Hong Kong and London at the same time—"

"We want these francs bought in the next week. For the week after that, a second $50 billion. Fifty billion a week until we tell you to stop."

Hallucinogens for sure. "That doesn't make any sense."

"We can take our business elsewhere."

Prescott thought about it. It would take every trick he knew—and he'd have to invent some new ones—to carry this off. The dollar was going to drop through the floor, while the franc would punch through the sell-stops of every trader on ten world markets. The exchanges would scream bloody murder. The repercussions would auger holes in every economy north of Antarctica. Governments would intervene. It would make the historic Hunt silver squeeze look like a game of Monopoly.

Besides, it made no sense. Not only was it criminally irresponsible, it was stupid. The Krel would squander every dime they'd earned.

Then he thought about the commission on $50 billion a week.

Prescott looked across at the alien. From the right point of view, Flash resembled a barrel-chested college undergraduate from Special Effects U. He felt an urge to giggle, a euphoric feeling of power. "When do we start?"

∞   ∞   ∞

19 May 1533: In the fields the *puric*s, singing praise to Atahualpa, son of the sun, harvested the maize. At night they celebrated by getting drunk on *chicha*. It was, they said, the most festive month of the year.

Pedro Sancho did his drinking in the dark of the treasure room, in the smoke of the smelters' fire. For months he had been troubled by nightmares of the heaped bodies lying in the plaza. He tried to ignore the abuse of the Indian women, the brutality toward the men. He worked hard. As Pizarro's squire, it was his job to record daily the tally of Atahualpa's ransom. When he ran low on ink, he taught the *puric*s to make it for him from soot and the juice of berries. They learned readily.

Atahualpa heard about the ink and one day came to him. "What are you doing with those marks?" he said, pointing to the scribe's tally book.

"I'm writing the list of gold objects to be melted down."

"What is this 'writing'?"

Sancho was nonplussed. Over the months of Atahualpa's captivity, Sancho had become impressed by the sophistication of the Incas. Yet they were also queerly backward. They had no money. It was not beyond belief that they should not know how to read and write.

"By means of these marks, I can record the words that people speak. That's writing. Later other men can look at these marks and see what was said. That's reading."

"Then this is a kind of quipu?" Atahualpa's servants had demonstrated for Sancho the quipu, a system of knotted strings by which the Incas kept talleys. "Show me how it works," Atahualpa said.

Sancho wrote on the page: *God have mercy on us.* He pointed. "This, my lord, is a representation of the word 'God.'"

Atahualpa looked skeptical. "Mark it here." He held out his hand, thumbnail extended.

Sancho wrote "God" on the Inca's thumbnail.

"Say nothing now." Atahualpa advanced to one of the guards, held out his thumbnail. "What does this mean?" he asked.

"God," the man replied.

Sancho could tell the Inca was impressed, but he barely showed it. That the Sapa Inca had maintained such dignity throughout his captivity tore at Sancho's heart.

"This writing is truly a magical accomplishment," Atahualpa told him. "You must teach my *amautas* this art."

Later, when the viceroy Estete, Father Valverde, and Pizarro came to chide him for the slow pace of the gold shipments, Atahualpa tested each of them separately. Estete and Valverde each said the word "God." Atahualpa held his thumbnail out to the conquistador.

Estete chuckled. For the first time in his experience, Sancho saw Pizarro flush. He turned away. "I don't waste my time on the games of children," Pizarro said.

Atahualpa stared at him. "But your common soldiers have this art."

"Well, I don't."

"Why not?"

"I was a swineherd. Swineherds don't need to read."

"You are not a swineherd now."

Pizarro glared at the Inca. "I don't need to read to order you put to death." He marched out of the room.

After the others had left, Sancho told Atahualpa, "You ought not to humiliate the governor in front of his men."

"He humiliates himself," Atahualpa said. "There is no skill in which a leader ought to let himself stand behind his followers."

∞   ∞   ∞

Today: The part of this story about the Incas is as historically accurate as I could make it, but this Krel business is science fiction. I even stole the name "Krel" from a 1950s SF flick. I've been addicted to SF for years. In the evening my wife and I wash the bad taste of the news out of our mouths by watching old movies on videotape.

A scientist, asked why he read SF, replied, "Because in science fiction the experiments always work." Things in SF stories work out more neatly than in reality. Nothing is impossible. Spaceships move faster than light. Atomic weapons are neutralized. Disease is abolished. People travel in time. Why, Isaac Asimov even wrote a story once that ended with the reversal of entropy!

The descendants of the Incas, living in grinding poverty, find their most lucrative crop in coca, which they refine into cocaine and sell in vast quantities to North Americans.

∞   ∞   ∞

23 August 2008: "Catalog number 208," said John Bostock. "Georges Seurat, *Bathers.*"

FRENCH GOVERNMENT FALLS, the morning *Times* had announced. JAPAN BANS U.S. IMPORTS. FOOD RIOTS IN MADRID. But Bostock had barely glanced at the newspaper over his coffee; he was buzzed on caffeine and adrenaline, and it was too late to stop the auction, the biggest day of his career. The lot list would make an art historian faint. *Guernica. The Potato Eaters. The Scream.* Miró, Rembrandt, Vermeer, Gauguin, Matisse, Constable, Magritte, Pollock, Mondrian. Six desperate governments had contributed to the sale. And rumor had it the Krel would be among the bidders.

The rumor proved true. In the front row, beside the solicitor Patrick McClannahan, sat one of the unlikely aliens, wearing red tights and a lightning-bolt insignia. The famous Flash. The creature leaned back lazily while McClannahan did the bidding with a discreetly raised forefinger.

Bidding on the Seurat started at ten million and went orbital. It soon became clear that the main bidders were Flash and the U.S. government. The American campaign against cultural imperialism was getting a lot of press, ironic since the Yanks could afford to

challenge the Krel only because of the technology the Krel had lav-
ished on them. The probability suppressor that prevented the deto-
nation of atomic weapons. The autodidactic antivirus that cured
most diseases. There was talk of an immortality drug. Of a time
machine. So what if the European Community was in the sixth
month of an economic crisis that threatened to dissolve the unify-
ing efforts of the past twenty years? So what if Krel meddling
destroyed humans' capacity to run the world? The Americans were
making money, and the Krel were richer than Croesus.

The bidding reached $1.2 billion, at which point the American
ambassador gave up. Bostock tapped his gavel. "Sold," he said in
his most cultured voice, nodding toward the alien.

The crowd murmured. The American stood. "If you can't see
what they're doing to us, then you don't deserve our help!"

For a minute Bostock thought the auction was going to turn into
a riot. Then the new owner of the pointillist masterpiece stood,
smiled. Ingenuous, clumsy. "We know that there has been considerable disquiet over our purchase of these historic works of art,"
Flash said. "Let me promise you, they will be displayed where all
humans—not just those who can afford to visit the great museums
—can see them."

The crowd's murmur turned into applause. Bostock put down
his gavel and joined in. The American ambassador and his aides
stalked out. Thank God, Bostock thought. The attendants brought
out the next item.

"Catalog number 209," Bostock said. "Leonardo da Vinci,
Mona Lisa."

∞   ∞   ∞

26 July 1533: The soldiers, seeing the heaps of gold grow, became
anxious. They consumed stores of coca meant for the Inca messengers. They fought over women. They grumbled over the airs of
Atahualpa. "Who does he think he is? The governor treats him like
a hidalgo."

Father Valverde cursed Pizarro's inaction. That morning, after
matins, he spoke with Estete. "The governor has agreed to meet
and decide what to do," Estete said.

"It's about time. What about Soto?" De Soto was against harm-
ing Atahualpa. He maintained that, since the Inca had paid the ransom, he should be set free, no matter what danger this would present. Pizarro had stalled. Last week he had sent de Soto away to

check out rumors that the Tahuantinsuyans were massing for an attack to free the Sapa Inca.

Estete smiled. "Soto's not back yet."

They went to the building Pizarro had claimed as his, and found the others already gathered. The Incas had no tables or proper chairs, so the Spaniards were forced to sit in a circle on mats as the Indians did. Pizarro, only a few years short of threescore, sat on a low stool of the sort that Atahualpa used when he held court. His left leg, whose old battle wound still pained him at times, was stretched out before him. His loose white shirt had been cleaned by some *puric*'s wife. Valverde sat beside him. Gathered were Estete, Benalcázar, Almagro, de Candia, Riquelme, Pizarro's young cousin Pedro, the scribe Pedro Sancho, Valverde, and the governor himself.

As Valverde and Estete had agreed, the viceroy went first. "The men are jumpy, Governor," Estete said. "The longer we stay cooped up here, the longer we give these savages the chance to plot against us."

"We should wait until Soto returns," de Candia said, already looking guilty as a dog. "We've got nothing but rumors so far. I won't kill a man on a rumor."

Silence. Trust de Candia to speak aloud what they were all thinking but were not ready to say. The man had no political judgment—but maybe it was just as well to face it directly. Valverde seized the opportunity. "Atahualpa plots against us even as we speak," he told Pizarro. "As governor, you are responsible for our safety. Any court would convict him of treason, and execute him."

"He's a king," de Candia said. Face flushed, he spat out a cud of leaves. "We don't have authority to try him. We should ship him back to Spain and let the emperor decide what to do."

"This is not a king," Valverde said. "It isn't even a man. It is a creature that worships demons, that weaves spells about half-wits like Candia. You saw him discard the Bible. Even after my months of teaching, after the extraordinary mercies we've shown him, he doesn't acknowledge the primacy of Christ! He cares only for his wives and his pagan gods. Yet he's satanically clever. Don't think we can let him go. If we do, the day will come when he'll have our hearts for dinner."

"We can take him with us to Cuzco," Benalcázar said. "We

don't know the country. His presence would guarantee our safe conduct."

"We'll be traveling over rough terrain, carrying tons of gold, with not enough horses," Almagro said. "If we take him with us, we'll be ripe for ambush at every pass."

"They won't attack if we have him."

"He could escape. We can't trust the rebel Indians to stay loyal to us. If they turned to our side, they can just as easily turn back to his."

"And remember, he escaped before, during the civil war," Valverde said. "Huascar, his brother, lived to regret that. If Atahualpa didn't hesitate to murder his own brother, do you think he'll stop for us?"

"He's given us his word," Candia said.

"What good is the word of a pagan?"

Pizarro, silent until now, spoke. "He has no reason to think the word of a Christian much better."

Valverde felt his blood rise. Pizarro knew as well as any of them what was necessary. What was he waiting for? "He keeps a hundred wives! He betrayed his brother! He worships the sun!" The priest grabbed Pizarro's hand, held it up between them so they could both see the scar there, where Pizarro had gotten cut preventing one of his own men from killing Atahualpa. "He isn't worth an ounce of the blood you spilled to save him."

"He's proved worth twenty-four tons of gold." Pizarro's eyes were hard and calm.

"There is no alternative!" Valverde insisted. "He serves the Antichrist! God demands his death."

At last Pizarro seemed to have gotten what he wanted. He smiled. "Far be it from me to ignore the command of God," he said. "Since God forces us to it, let's discuss how He wants it done."

∞ ∞ ∞

5 October 2009: "What a lovely country Chile is from the air. You should be proud of it."

"I'm from Los Angeles," Leon Sepulveda said. "And as soon as we close this deal, I'm going back."

"The mountains are impressive."

"Nothing but earthquakes and slag. You can have Chile."

"Is it for sale?"

Sepulveda stared at the Krel. "I was just kidding."

They sat at midnight in the arbor, away from the main buildings of Iguassu Microelectronics of Santiago. The night was cold and the arbor was overgrown and the bench needed a paint job— but then, a lot of things had been getting neglected in the past couple of years. All the more reason to put yourself in a financial situation where you didn't have to worry. Though Sepulveda had to admit that, since the advent of the Krel, such positions were harder to come by, and less secure once you had them.

Flash's earnestness aroused a kind of horror in him. It had something to do with Sepulveda's suspicion that this thing next to him was as superior to him as he was to a guinea pig, plus the alien's aura of drunken adolescence, plus his own willingness, despite the feeling that the situation was out of control, to make a deal with it. He took another Valium and tried to calm down.

"What assurance do I have that this time-travel method will work?"

"It will work. If you don't like it in Chile, or back in Los Angeles, you can use it to go into the past."

Sepulveda swallowed. "Okay. You need to read and sign these papers."

"We don't read."

"You don't read Spanish? How about English?"

"We don't read at all. We used to, but we gave it up. Once you start reading, it gets out of control. You tell yourself you're just going to stick to nonfiction—but pretty soon you graduate to fiction. After that, you can't kick the habit. And then there's the oppression."

"Oppression?"

"Sure. I mean, I like a story as much as the next Krel, but any pharmacologist can show that arbitrary cultural, sexual, and economic assumptions determine every significant aspect of a story. Literature is a political tool used by ruling elites to ensure their hegemony. Anyone who denies that is a fish who can't see the water it swims in. Or the fascist who tells you, as he beats you, that those blows you feel are your own delusion."

"Right. Look, can we settle this? I've got things to do."

"This is, of course, the key to temporal translation. The past is another arbitrary construct. Language creates reality. Reality is smoke."

"Well, this time machine better not be smoke. We're going to find out the truth about the past. Then we'll change it."

"By all means. Find the truth." Flash turned to the last page of the contract, pricked his thumb, and marked a thumbprint on the signature line.

After they sealed the agreement, Sepulveda walked the alien back to the courtyard. A Krel flying pod with Vermeer's *The Letter* varnished onto its door sat at the focus of three spotlights. The painting was scorched almost into unrecognizability by atmospheric friction. The door peeled downward from the top, became a canvas-surfaced ramp.

"I saw some interesting lines inscribed on the coastal desert on the way here," Flash said. "A bird, a tree, a big spider. In the sunset, it looked beautiful. I didn't think you humans were capable of such art. Is it for sale?"

"I don't think so. That was done by some old Indians a long time ago. If you're really interested, though, I can look into it."

"Not necessary." Flash waggled his ears, wiped his feet on Mark Rothko's *Earth and Green*, and staggered into the pod.

∞   ∞   ∞

26 July 1533: Atahualpa looked out of the window of the stone room in which he was kept, across the plaza where the priest Valverde stood outside his chapel after his morning prayers. Valverde's chapel had been the house of the virgins; the women of the house had long since been raped by the Spanish soldiers, as the house had been by the Spanish god. Valverde spoke with Estete. They were getting ready to kill him, Atahualpa knew. He had known ever since the ransom had been paid.

He looked beyond the thatched roofs of the town to the crest of the mountains, where the sun was about to break in his tireless circuit of Tahuantinsuyu. The cold morning air raised dew on the metal of the chains that bound him hand and foot. The metal was queer, different from the bronze the *puric*s worked or the gold and silver Atahualpa was used to wearing. If gold was the sweat of the sun, and silver the tears of the moon, what was this metal, dull and hard like the men who held him captive, yet strong, too—stronger, he had come to realize, than the Inca. It, like the men who brought it, was beyond his experience. It gave evidence that Tahuantinsuyu, the Four Quarters of the World, was not all the world after all. Atahualpa had thought none but savages lived beyond their lands. He'd imagined no man readier to face ruthless necessity than himself. He had ordered the death of Huascar, his own brother. But he was learning that these men were capable of enormities against which the Inca civil war would seem a minor discomfort.

That evening they took him out of the building to the plaza. In the plaza's center, the soldiers had piled a great heap of wood on flagstones, some of which were still stained with the blood of the six thousand slaughtered attendants. They bound him to a stake amid the heaped fagots, and Valverde appealed one last time for the Inca to renounce Satan and be baptized. He promised that if Atahualpa would do so, he would earn God's mercy: they would strangle him rather than burn him to death.

The rough wood pressed against his spine. Atahualpa looked at the priest, and the men gathered around, and the women weeping beyond the circle of soldiers. The moon, his mother, rode high above. Firelight flickered on the breastplates of the Spaniards, and from the waiting torches drifted the smell of pitch. The men shifted nervously. Creak of leather, clink of metal. Men on horses shod with silver. Sweat shining on Valverde's forehead. Valverde stared at Atahualpa as if he desired something, but was prepared to destroy him without getting it if need be. The priest thought he was showing Atahualpa resolve, but Atahualpa saw that beneath Valverde's face he was a dead man. Pizarro stood aside, with the Spanish viceroy Estete and the scribe. Pizarro was an old man. He ought to be sitting quietly in some village, outside the violence of life, giving advice and teaching the children. What kind of world did he come from, that sent men into old age still charged with the lusts and bitterness of the young?

Pizarro, too, looked as if he wanted this to end.

Atahualpa knew that it would not end. This was only the beginning. These men would suffer for this moment as they had already suffered for it all their lives, seeking the pain blindly over oceans, jungles, deserts, probing it like a sore tooth until they'd found and grasped it in this plaza of Cajamarca, thinking they sought gold. They'd come all this way to create a moment that would reveal to them their own incurable disease. Now they had it. In a few minutes, they thought, it would at last be over, that once he was gone, they would be free—but Atahualpa knew it would be with them ever after, and with their children and grandchildren and the million others of their race in times to come, whether they knew of this hour in the plaza or not, because they were sick and would pass the sickness on with their breath and semen. They could not burn out the sickness so easily as they could burn the Son of God to ash. This was a great tragedy, but it contained a huge jest. They were caught in a wheel of the sky and could not get out. They must destroy themselves.

"Have your way, priest," Atahualpa said. "Then strangle me, and bear my body to Cuzco, to be laid with my ancestors." He knew they would not do it, and so would add an additional curse to their faithlessness.

He had one final curse. He turned to Pizarro. "You will have responsibility for my children."

Pizarro looked at the pavement. They put up the torch and took Atahualpa from the pyre. Valverde poured water on his head and spoke words in the tongue of his god. Then they sat him upon a stool, bound him to another stake, set the loop of cord around his neck, slid the rod through the cord, and turned it. His women knelt at his side and wept. Valverde spoke more words. Atahualpa felt the cord, woven by the hands of some faithful *puric* of Cajamarca, tighten. The cord was well made. It cut his access to the night air; Atahualpa's lungs fought, he felt his body spasm, and then the plaza became cloudy and he heard the voice of the moon.

∞ ∞ ∞

12 January 2011: Israel Lamont was holding big-time when a Krel monitor zipped over the alley. A minute later one of the aliens lurched around the corner and approached him. Lamont was ready.

"I need to achieve an altered state of consciousness," the alien said. It wore a red suit, a lightning bolt on its chest.

"I'm your man," Lamont said. "You just try this. Best stuff on the street." He held the vial out in the palm of his hand. "Go ahead, try it." The Krel took it.

"How much?"

"One million."

The Krel gave him a couple hundred thousand. "Down payment," it said. "How does one administer this?"

"What, you don't know? I thought you guys were hip."

"I have been working hard, and am unacquainted."

This was ripe. "You burn it," Lamont said.

The Krel started toward the trash-barrel fire. Before he could empty the vial into it, Lamont stopped him. "Wait up, homes! You use a pipe. Here, I'll show you."

Lamont pulled a pipe from his pocket, torched up, and inhaled. The Krel watched him. Brown eyes like a dog's. Goofy honkie face. The rush took him, and Lamont saw in the alien's face a peculiar need. The thing was hungry. Desperate.

"I may try?" The alien reached out. Its hand trembled.

Lamont handed over the pipe. Clumsily, the creature shook a block of crack into the bowl. Its beaklike upper lip, however, prevented it from getting its mouth tight against the stem. It fumbled with the pipe, from somewhere producing a book of matches. "Shit, I'll light it," Lamont said.

The Krel waited while Lamont held his Bic over the bowl. Nothing happened. "Inhale, man."

The creature inhaled. The blue flame played over the crack; smoke boiled through the bowl. The creature drew in steadily for what seemed to be minutes. Serious capacity. The crack burned totally through. Finally the Krel exhaled.

It looked at Lamont. Its eyes were bright.

"Good shit?" Lamont said.

"A remarkable stimulant effect."

"Right." Lamont looked over his shoulder toward the alley's entrance. It was getting dark. Yet he hesitated to ask for the rest of the money.

"Will you talk with me?" the Krel asked, swaying slightly.

Surprised, Lamont said, "Okay. Come with me."

Lamont led the Krel back to a deserted store that abutted the alley. They went inside and sat down on some crates against the wall.

"Something I been wondering about you," Lamont said. "You guys are coming to own the world. You fly across the planets, Mars and that shit. What you want with crack?"

"We seek to broaden our minds."

Lamont snorted. "Right. You might as well hit yourself in the head with a hammer."

"We seek escape," the alien said.

"I don't buy that, neither. What you got to escape from?"

The Krel looked at him. "Nothing."

They smoked another pipe. The Krel leaned back against the wall, arms at its sides like a limp doll. It started a queer coughing sound, chest spasming. Lamont thought it was choking and tried to slap it on the back. "Don't do that," it said. "I'm laughing."

"Laughing? What's so funny?"

"I lied to Colonel Zipp," it said. "We want cocaine for kicks."

Lamont relaxed a little. "I hear you now."

"We do everything for kicks."

"Makes for hard living."

"Better than maintaining consciousness continuously without interruption."

"You said it."

"Human beings cannot stand too much reality," the Krel said. "We don't blame you. Human beings! Disgust, horror, shame. Nothing personal."

"You bet."

"Nonbeing penetrates that in which there is no space."

"Uh-huh."

The alien laughed again. "I lied to Sepulveda, too. Our time machines take people to the past they believe in. There is no other past. You can't change it."

"Who the fuck's Sepulveda?"

"Let's do some more," it said.

They smoked one more. "Good shit," it said. "Just what I wanted."

The Krel slid off the crate. Its head lolled. "Here is the rest of your payment," it whispered, and died.

Lamont's heart raced. He looked at the Krel's hand, lying open on the floor. In it was a full-sized ear of corn, fashioned of gold, with tassels of finely spun silver wire.

∞   ∞   ∞

Today: It's not just physical laws that science-fiction readers want to escape. Just as commonly, they want to escape human nature. In pursuit of this, SF offers comforting alternatives to the real world. For instance, if you start reading an SF story about some abused wimp, you can be pretty sure that by chapter two he's going to discover he has secret powers unavailable to those tormenting him, and by the end of the book, he's going to save the universe. SF is full of this sort of thing, from the power fantasy of the alienated child to the alternate history where Hitler is strangled in his cradle and the Library of Alexandria is saved from the torch.

Science fiction may in this way be considered as much an evasion of reality as any mind-distorting drug. I know that sounds a little harsh, but think about it. An alkaloid like cocaine or morphine invades the central nervous system. It reduces pain, produces euphoria, enhances our perceptions. Under its influence we imagine we have supernormal abilities. Limits dissolve. Soon, hardly aware of what's happened to us, we're addicted.

Science fiction has many of the same qualities. The typical reader comes to SF at a time of suffering. He seizes on it as a way to deal with his pain. It's bigger than his life. It's astounding. Amazing. Fantastic. Some grow out of it; many don't. Anyone who's been around SF for a while can cite examples of longtime readers as hooked and deluded as crack addicts.

Like any drug addict, the SF reader finds desperate justifications for his habit. SF teaches him science. SF helps him avoid "future shock." SF changes the world for the better. Right. So does cocaine.

Having been an SF user myself, however, I have to say that, living in a world of cruelty, immersed in a culture that grinds people into fish meal like some brutal machine, with histories of destruction stretching behind us back to the Pleistocene, I find it hard to sneer at the desire to escape. Even if escape is delusion.

∞   ∞   ∞

18 October 1527: Timu drove the foot plow into the ground, leaned back to break the crust, drew out the pointed pole, and backed up a step to let his wife, Collyur, turn the earth with her hoe. To his left was his brother, Okya; and to his right, his cousin, Tupa; before them, their wives planting the seed. Most of the *puric*s of Cajamarca were there, strung out in a line across the terrace, the men wielding the foot plows, and the women or children carrying the sacks of seed potatoes.

As he looked up past Collyur's shoulders to the edge of the terrace, he saw a strange man approach from the post road. The man stumbled into the next terrace up from them, climbed down steps to their level. He was plainly excited.

Collyur was waiting for Timu to break the next row; she looked up at him questioningly.

"Who is that?" Timu said, pointing past her at the man.

She stood up straight and looked over her shoulder. The other men had noticed, too, and stopped their work.

"A *chasqui* come from the next town," said Okya.

"A *chasqui* would go to the *curaca*," said Tupa.

"He's not dressed like a *chasqui*," Timu said.

The man came up to them. Instead of a cape, loincloth, and flowing *onka*, the man wore uncouth clothing: cylinders of fabric that bound his legs tightly, a white short-sleeved shirt that bore on its front the face of a man, and flexible white sandals that covered all his foot to the ankle. He shivered in the spring cold.

He was extraordinarily tall. His face, paler than a normal man's, was long, his nose too straight, mouth too small, and lips too thin. Upon his face he wore a device of gold wire that, hooking over his ears, held disks of crystal before his eyes. The man's hands were large, his limbs long and spiderlike. He moved suddenly, awkwardly.

Gasping for air, the stranger spoke rapidly the most abominable Quechua Timu had ever heard.

"Slow down," Timu said. "I don't understand."

"What year is this?" the man asked.

"What do you mean?"

"I mean, what is the year?"

"It is the thirty-fourth year of the reign of the Sapa Inca Huayna Capac."

The man spoke some foreign word. "Goddamn," he said in a language foreign to Timu, but which you or I would recognize as English. "I made it."

Timu went to the *curaca*, and the *curaca* told Timu to take the stranger in. The stranger told them that his name was "Chuan." But Timu's three-year-old daughter, Curi, reacting to the man's sudden gestures, unearthly thinness, and piping speech, laughed and called him "the Bird." So he was ever after to be known in that town.

There he lived a long and happy life, earned trust and respect, and brought great good fortune. He repaid them well for their kindness, alerting the people of Tahuantinsuyu to the coming of the invaders. When the first Spaniards landed on their shores a few years later, they were slaughtered to the last man, and everyone lived happily ever after.

NG IN INFINITY MEETING IN INFINITY MEETING IN INFINITY MEE
EETING IN INFINITY MEETING IN INFINITY MEETING IN INFINITY
Y MEETING IN INFINITY MEETING IN INFINITY MEETING IN INFIN
FINITY MEETING IN INFINITY MEETING IN INFINITY MEETING IN
IN INFINITY MEETING IN INFINITY MEETING IN INFINITY MEETING
ING IN INFINITY MEETING IN INFINITY MEETING IN INFINITY MEI
MEETING IN INFINITY MEETING IN INFINITY MEETING IN INFINITY
TY MEETING IN INFINITY MEETING IN INFINITY MEETING IN INFI
NFINITY MEETIN   MEETING IN
G IN INFINITY ME   ITY MEETIN
TING IN INFINITY MEETING IN INFINITY MEETING IN INFINITY M
MEETING IN INFINITY MEETING IN INFINITY MEETING IN INFINIT
ITY MEETING IN INFINITY MEETING IN INFINITY MEETING IN INF
INFINITY MEETING IN INFINITY MEETING IN INFINITY MEETING
G IN INFINITY MEETING IN INFINITY MEETING IN INFINITY MEET

judgment call

BOTTOM OF THE FIRST, NO SCORE, DUTCH ON FIRST, SIMONETTI ON second, two outs. In the bar afterward, Sandy replayed it in his head.

Sandy had faced this Louisville pitcher maybe twice before. He had a decent fastball and a good curve, enough so he'd gotten Sandy out more than his share. And Sandy was in a slump (three for eighteen in the last five games), and the count was one and two; and the Louisville catcher was riding him. The ump was real quiet, but Sandy knew he was just waiting to throw his old rabbit punch to signal the big K—fist punching the air, but it might as well be Sandy's gut. It was hot. His legs felt rubbery.

Old War Memorial was quiet. There weren't more than fifteen hundred people there, tops; Louisville was leading the American Association, and the Bisons were dead last. The steel struts holding up the roof in right were ranked in the distance like the trees of the North Carolina pine forest where he grew up, lost in the haze and shadows of the top rows where nobody ever sat. The sky was overcast, and a heavy wind from the lake snapped the flag out in left center, but it was very hot for Buffalo, even for June. People were saying the climate was changing: it was the ozone layer, the Japs, the UFOs, the end of the world. Some off-duty cop or sanitation worker with a red face was ragging him from the stands. Sandy would have liked to deck him, but he had to ignore it because the pitcher was crouched over, shaking off signals. He went into his stretch.

Then something happened: suddenly Sandy knew, he just knew he could hit this guy. The pitcher figured he had Sandy plugged—curveball, curveball, outside corner and low, then high and tight with the fastball to keep him from leaning—but it hit Sandy like a line drive between the eyes that he had the *pitcher* plugged, he *knew* where the next pitch was going to be. And there it was, fastball inside corner, and he turned on it and *bye-bye baby!* That sweet crack of the ash. Sandy watched it sail out over the left field fence; saw the pitcher, head down, kick dirt from the mound—sorry, guy; could be you won't see the majors as soon as you thought—and jogged around the bases feeling so *good*. He was going to live forever. He was going to get laid every night.

That was just his first at bat. In the top of the sixth he made a shoestring catch in right center, and in the second and the seventh he threw out runners trying to go from first to third. At the plate he went four for five, bringing his average up to a tantalizing .299. And number five was an infield bouncer that Sandy was sure he'd beat out, but the wop ump at first called him out. A judgment call. The pud-knocker. But it was still the best game Sandy had ever played.

And Aronsen, the Sox general manager, was in town to take a look at the Bisons in the hope of finding somebody they could bring up to help them after the bad start they'd had. After the game he came by in the locker room. He glanced at Sandy's postgame blood panel. Sandy played it cool: he was at least 0.6 under the limit on DMD, not even on scale for steroids. Sandy should get ready right away, Aronsen told him, to catch the morning train to Chicago. They were sending Estivez down and bringing him up. They were going to give him a chance to fill the hole in right field. Yes sir, Sandy said, polite, eager.

Lordy, lordy—yes sir, he'd thought as he walked down Best with Dutch and Leon toward the Main Street tramway—good-bye, War Memorial. The hulk of the stadium, the exact color of a Down East dirt farmer's tobacco-stained teeth, loomed above them, the Art Deco globes that topped its corners covered with pigeon shit. Atop the corroded limestone wall that ran along the street was a chain-link fence, rusted brown, and atop the fence glistened new coils of barbed wire. The barbed wire was supposed to keep vagrants from living in the stadium. It made the place look like a prison.

Now it was a few hours later, and Sandy was having a drink with Dutch and Leon at the Ground Zero on Delaware. He'd already stopped by a machine and withdrawn the entire six hundred dollars in his account, had called up the rental office and told them he was leaving and they could rent the place because he wasn't coming back. Chalk up one for his side. Sandy paid for the first round. He had it figured: you paid for the first stiff one, you didn't hesitate a bit, and the others would remember that much better than how slow you were on the second or third; so if you played it right, you came out ahead on drinks when the evening was done. Even when you didn't, you got the rep with the regulars at the bar of being a generous kind of guy. Sure enough, Dutch paid for the second round and Leon for the third, and then some fans came by and got the next two. So Sandy was way ahead. His day. Only one thing was needed to make it complete.

"You lucky sonofabitch," Dutch shouted over the din of the talk and the flatscreen behind the bar. "You haven't played that well in a month. The Killer decides to go crazy on the day that Aronsen's in town."

There was more than kidding in Dutch's voice. "That's when it pays to look your best," Sandy said.

Dutch stared at the screen, where a faggot VJ with a wig and ruffles and lace cuffs was counting down the Top 100 videos of the twentieth century. Most of them were from the past two years. "Wouldn't do me any good," Dutch said. "They've got two first basemen ahead of me. I could hit .350, and I wouldn't get a shot at the majors."

"Playin' the wrong position, man," said Leon. His high eyebrows gave him a perpetually innocent expression.

Dutch didn't have the glove to play anywhere else but first. Sandy felt a little sorry for Dutch, who had wrecked his chances with HGH. At eighteen he had been a pretty hot prospect, a first baseman who could hit for average and field okay. But he didn't have any power, so he'd taken the hormone in order to beef up. He'd beefed up, all right—going to six-five, 230—but his reflexes got shot to hell in the process. Now he could hit twenty home runs in triple-A ball, but he struck out too much and his fielding was mediocre and he was slow as an ox. And the American League had abandoned the DH rule just about the time Dutch went off the drug.

It was a sad story. But Sandy got tired of his bitching, too. A real friend didn't bitch at you when you got called up. "You ought to work on the glove," he said.

A glint of hate showed in Dutch's face for a second, then he said, "I got to piss," and headed for the men's room.

"Sometimes he gets to me," Sandy said.

Leon lazily watched the women in the room, leaning his back against the bar, elbows resting on the edge, his big, gnarled catcher's hands hanging loosely from his wrists. On the screen behind him, a naked girl was bouncing up and down on a pink neon pogo stick. Sandy couldn't tell if she was real or vidsynthed.

"Got to admit, Killer, you ain't been playin' that good lately," Leon said over his shoulder. They called Sandy "The Killer" because of the number of double plays he hit into: Killer as in rally killer. "You been clutched out. Been tryin' too hard."

Now it was Leon, too. Leon had grown up in Fayetteville, not ten miles from Sandy's dad's farm, but Sandy would not have hung around with Leon back there. Leon was ten years older, his father was a noncom at Fort Bragg, and he was the wrong color. Sandy always felt like blacks were keeping secrets that he would just as soon not know.

Sandy finished his bourbon and ordered another. "You don't win without trying."

Leon just nodded. "Look at that talent there." He pointed his chin toward a table in the corner.

At the table, alone, sat a woman. He wondered how she had got there without him noticing her: she had microshort blonde hair and a pale oval face with a pointed chin. Blue lips. Her dark eyelashes were long enough so that he could see them from the bar. But what got him was her body. Even from across the room, Sandy could tell she was major league material. She wore a tight blue dress and was drinking something pale, on the rocks.

She looked over at them and calmly locked glances with Sandy. Something strange happened then. He had a feeling of vertigo, and then was overwhelmed by a vivid memory, a flashback to something that had happened to him long before.

It's the end of the summer of your junior year of high school, and you're calling Jocelyn from the parking lot of the Dairy King out near Highway 95. Brutal heat. Tapping your car keys impatiently on the dented metal shelf below the phone. Jocelyn is going to Atlantic Beach with Sid Phillips, and she hasn't even told you. Five rings, six. You had to get the news from Trudy Jackson and act like you knew all about it when it was like you'd been kneed in the groin.

An answer. "Hello?"

"Miz James, this is Sandy Ellison. Can I talk to Jocelyn?"

"Just a minute." Another wait. The sun burns the back of your neck.

"Hello." Jocelyn's voice sounds nervous.

The anger explodes in your chest. "What the fuck do you think you're doing?"

A semi blasts by on Highway 95, kicking up a cloud of dust and gravel. You turn your back to the road and hold your hand over your other ear.

"What are you talking about?"

"You better not fuck with me, Jocelyn. I won't take it."

"Slow down, Sandy. I—"

"If you go to the beach with him, it's over." You try to make it sound like a threat instead of a plea.

At first Jocelyn doesn't answer. Then she says, "You always were a jerk." She hangs up.

You stand there with the receiver in your hand. It feels hot and greasy. The dial tone mocks you. Then Jeff Baxter and Jack Stubbs drive up in Jeff's Trans Am, and the three of you cruise out to the lake and drink three six-packs. "Bitch," you call her. "Fucking bitch."

The woman was still staring at him. She didn't look at all like Jocelyn. Sandy broke eye contact. He realized that Dutch had come back, had been back for a while while Sandy was spaced-out. Fucking Jocelyn.

Sandy made a decision. "One hundred says I boost her tonight."

Leon regarded him coolly. Dutch snorted. "Gonna pull down your batting average, boy."

"Definitely a tough chance," Leon said.

"You think so? It's my day. We'll see who's trying too hard, Leon."

"You got a bet."

Sandy pulled the wad of bills out of his shirt pocket and laid two fifties on the bar. "You hold it, Dutch. I'll get it back tomorrow when I pick up my gear." Dutch stuffed the redbucks into his shirt pocket. Sandy picked up his drink and went over to the table.

The woman watched him the whole way. Up close she was even more spectacular. "Hey," he said.

"Hello. It's about time. I've been waiting for you."

He pulled out a chair and sat down. "Sure you have."

"I never lie." Her smile was a dare. "How much is riding on this?"

He couldn't tell whether she was hostile or just a tease. Well, he could go with the pitch. "One hundred," Sandy said. "That's a week's pay in triple-A."

"What is triple-A?" Her husky voice had some trace of accent to it—Hispanic?

"Baseball. My name is Sandy Ellison. I play for the Bisons."

She sipped her drink. Her ears were small and flat against her head. The shortness of her hair made her head seem large and her violet eyes enormous. He would die if he didn't have her that night. "Are you a good player?" she asked.

"I just got called up to the majors. Monday night I'll be starting for Chicago."

"You are a lucky man."

Luck again. The way she said it made Sandy think for a moment he was being set up: Leon and Dutch and all that talk about luck. But Dutch was too dumb to pull some elaborate practical joke. Leon was smart enough, but he wasn't mean enough. Still, it would be a good idea to stay on his guard. "Not luck; skill."

"Oh, skill. I thought you were lucky."

"How come I've never seen you here before?"

"I'm from out of town."

"I figured as much. Where?"

"Lexington."

Sandy ran his finger around the rim of his glass. "Kentucky? We just played Louisville. You follow the Cards on their road trips?"

"Road trips?"

"The game we played today was against the Louisville Cardinals. They're in town on a road trip."

"What a coincidence." Again the smile. "I'm on a road trip, too. But I'm not following this baseball team. I came to Buffalo for another reason, and I'm leaving tomorrow."

"It's a good town to be leaving. You help me celebrate, and I'll help you."

"That's why I'm here."

Right. Sandy glanced over at the bar. Leon and Dutch were talking to a couple of women. On the flatscreen was a newsflash about the microwave deluge in Arizona. Shots of househubs at the supermarket wearing their aluminized suits. He turned back to the woman and smiled. "Run that by me again."

The woman gazed at him calmly over her high cheekbones. "Come on, Sandy. Read my lips. This is your lucky day, and I'm here to celebrate it with you. A skillful man like you must understand what that means."

"Did Leon put you up to this? If he did, the bet's off."

"Leon is one of those two men at the bar? I don't know him. If I were to guess, I would guess that he is the black man. I'd also guess that you proposed the bet to him, not he to you. Am I right?"

"I made the bet."

"You see. My lucky guess. Well, if you made the bet with Leon, then it's unlikely that Leon hired me to trick you. It is unlikely for other reasons, too."

This was the weirdest pickup talk Sandy had ever heard. "Why do I get the feeling there's a proposition coming?"

"Don't tell me you didn't expect a proposition to pass between us sometime during this conversation."

"For sure. But I expected to be making it."

"Go ahead."

Sandy studied her. "You northern girls are different."

"I'm not from the North."

"Then you're from a different part of the South than I grew up in."

"It takes all kinds. May I ask you a question?"

"Sure."

"Why the bet?"

"I just wanted to make it interesting."

"I'm not interesting enough unless there's money riding on me?"

Riding on her. Sandy smiled. The woman smiled back. "I just like to raise the stakes," he said. "But the bet is between me and them, to prove a point. It has nothing to do with you."

"You're not very flattering."

"That's not what I meant."

"Yes. We can make it even more interesting. You think you can please me?"

Sandy finished his bourbon. "If you can be pleased."

"Good. So let's make it very interesting." She opened her clutch purse and tilted it toward him. She reached inside and held something so that Sandy could see it. A glint of metal. It was a straight razor.

"If you don't please me, I get to hurt you. Just a little."

Sandy stared at her. "Are you kidding?"

She stared back. Her look was steady.

"Maybe you're not as good as you tell me. Maybe you'll need to have some luck."

She had to be teasing. Sandy considered the odds. Even if she wasn't, he thought he could handle her. Sandy stood up. "It's a deal."

She didn't move. "You're sure you want to try this?"

"I know what I want when I see it."

"You already know enough to make a decision?"

He came around to her side of the table. "Let's go," he said. She closed her purse and led him toward the door. Sandy winked at Leon as they passed the bar; Leon's face looked as surprised and skeptical as ever. The girl's hips, swaying as she walked ahead of him, pulled him along the way the smell of food in the dumpster by the concession stand drew the retirees living in the cardboard boxes on Jefferson Avenue.

Once in the street he slipped an arm around her waist and nudged her over to the side of the building. Her perfume was dizzying. "What's your name?" he asked her.

"Judith," she said.

"Judith." It sounded so old-fashioned. There was a Judith in the Bible, he thought. But he had never paid attention in Bible class.

He kissed her. He had to force his tongue between her lips. Then she bit it, lightly. Her mouth was strong and wet. She moved her hips against him.

You are twelve. You're sitting in the Beulah Land Baptist Church with your mother. She must be thirty-five or so, a pretty woman with blonde hair, putting on a little weight. Your father doesn't go to church. Lately your mother has been going more often and reading from the Bible after supper.

Some of your classmates, including Carrie Ford and Sue Harvey, are being baptized that Sunday. The two girls ride the bus with you, and Carrie has the biggest tits in the seventh grade.

The choir sings a hymn while the Reverend Mr. Foster takes the girls into the side room; and when the song is done, the curtains in front of the baptismal font open and there stand the minister and

Carrie, waist-deep in the water. Carrie is wearing a blue robe, try-
ing nervously not to smile. Behind them is a painting of the lush
green valley of the Promised Land and the shining City on the Hill.
The strong light from the spot above them makes Carrie's golden
hair shine, too.

The Reverend Mr. Foster puts his hand on Carrie's shoulder,
lifts his other hand toward heaven, and calls on the Lord.

"Do you renounce Satan and all his ways?" he asks Carrie.

"Yes," she says, looking holy. She crosses her hands at the
wrists, palms in, and folds her hands over those tits, as if to hold
them in.

The minister touches the back of her neck. She jumps a bit, and
you know she didn't expect that, but then lets him duck her head
beneath the surface of the water. He holds her down for a long
time, making sure she knows who's boss. You like that. The minis-
ter says the words of the baptism and pulls her up again.

Carrie gasps and sputters. She lifts her hands to push the hair
away from her eyes. The robe clings to her chest. You can see
everything. As she tries to catch her breath, you feel yourself get-
ting an erection.

You put your hand on your lap and try to make the erection go
away, but the mere contact with your pants leg makes you get even
harder. You can't help it; your dick has run away with you. You
turn red and shift uncomfortably in the pew, and your mother
looks at you. She sees your hand on your lap.

"Sandy!" she hisses. A woman in front of you looks around.

Your mother tries to ignore you. The curtains close. You wish
you were dead. At the same time you want to get up, go to the side
room, and watch Carrie Ford take off her wet robe and towel her-
self dry.

He felt the warmth of Judith's lips on his, her arms around his
neck. He pushed away from her, staring. This was no time for some
drug flashback. After a moment he placed his hands on either side
of her head against the wall and leaned toward her. She bit her
lower lip. He had an erection after all. Whether it was because of
the memory or Judith, he couldn't tell; he felt the embarrassment
and guilt that had burned in him at the church. He felt mad.
"Listen," he said. "Let's go to my place."

"Whatever you like." They walked down the block to the tram
station. Sandy lived in one of the luxury condos that had been built
on the Erie Basin before the market crash. He had an expensive

view across the lake. It was even more high-rent now that the Sunbelters were moving North to escape the drought.

They got off downtown and walked up River Street to the apartment; he inserted his ID card and punched in the security code. The lock snapped open, and Sandy ushered her in.

The place was wasted on Judith. She walked through his living room, the moon through the skylight throwing triangular shadows against the cathedral ceiling and walls, and thumbed on the bedroom light as if she had been there before. When he followed her, he found her standing just inside the door. She began to unbutton his shirt. He felt hot. He tried to undress her, but she pushed his hands away, pushed him backward until he fell awkwardly onto the water bed. She stood above him. The expression on her face was very grave.

She knelt on the undulating bed and rested her hands on his chest. He fumbled on the headboard shelf for the amyl nitrite. She pushed his hand away, took one of the caps, and broke it under his nose. His heart slammed against his ribs as if it would leap out of his chest; the air he breathed was hot and dry, and the tightness of the crotch of his jeans was agony. Eventually she helped him with that, but not before she had spent what seemed like an eternity making it worse.

The sight of her naked almost made him come right then. But she knew how to control that. She seemed to know everything in his mind before he knew it himself; she responded or didn't respond as he needed, precisely, kindly. She became everything that he wanted. She took him to the brink again and again, stopped just short, brought him back. She seemed hooked into the sources of his desire: his pain, his fear, his hope, all translated into the simple, slow motions of her sex and his. He forgot to worry about whether he was pleasing her. He forgot who he was. For an hour he forgot everything.

It was dark. Sandy lay just on the edge of sleep with his eyelids sliding closed and the distant sound of a siren in the air. The siren faded.

"You're beautiful, Sandy," Judith said. "I may not cut you after all."

Sandy felt so groggy he could hardly think. "Nobody cuts the Killer," he mumbled, and laughed. He rolled onto his stomach. The bed undulated; he felt dizzy.

"Such a wonderful body. Such a hard dick."

She slid her hand down his backbone, and as she did, all the muscles of his back relaxed, as if it were a twisted cord that she was unwinding. It was almost a dream. In the interior of his mind was a tiny alarm, like the siren that had passed into another part of the city.

"Now," said Judith, "I want to tell you a story."

"Sure."

Lightly stroking his back, Judith said, "This is the story of Yancey Camera."

"Funny name." He felt so sleepy.

"It is. To begin with, Yancey Camera was a young man of great promise and trustful good nature. Would you believe me if I told you that he was as handsome as the leading man in a black-and-white movie? He was that handsome, and was as smart as he was handsome, and as rich as he was smart. His dick was as reliable as his credit rating. He was a lucky young man.

"But Yancey did not believe in luck. Oh, he gave lip service to luck; when people said, 'Yancey, you're a lucky boy,' he said, 'Yes, I guess I am.' But when he thought about it, he understood that when they told him how lucky he was, they were really saying that he did not deserve his good fortune; had done nothing to earn it; and in a more rationally ordered universe he would not be handsome, smart, or rich, and his dick would be no more reliable than any other man's. Yancey came to realize that when people commented on his luck, they were really expressing their envy, and he immediately suspected those people. This lack of trust enabled him to spot more than a few phonies, for there was a large degree of truth in Yancey Camera's analysis.

"The problem was that as time went on and Yancey saw how much venality was concealed by people's talk of luck, he forgot that he had not initially done anything to earn the good looks, intellect, wealth, and hard dick that he possessed. In other words, Sandy, he came to disbelieve in luck. He thought that a man of his skills could control every situation. He forgot about the second law of thermodynamics, which tells us that we all lose, and that those times when we win are merely local statistical deviations in a universal progress from a state of lower to a state of higher entropy. Yancey's own luck was just such a local deviation. As time passed and Yancey's good fortune continued, he began ultimately to think that he was beyond the reach of the second law of thermodynamics."

Forget the alarm; forget the razor. The second law of sexual dynamics. First you screw her, then she talks. Sandy thought about the instant he had hit the home run, the feel of the bat in his hands, the contact with the ball so pure and sweet he knew it was out of the park even before he had finished following through.

"This is a sin that the Fates call hubris," Judith said, "and as soon as they realized the extent of Yancey Camera's error, they set about to rectify the situation. Now, there are several ways in which such an imbalance can be restored. It can be done in stages, or it can be done in one sudden, enormous stroke.

"And here my story divides: in one version of the story, Yancey Camera marries a beautiful young woman, fathers four sons, and opens an automobile dealership. Unfortunately, because Yancey's home is built on the site of a chemical waste dump, one of his boys is born with spina bifida and is confined to a wheelchair. The child dies at the age of twelve. One of his other boys is unable to compete in school and becomes a behavior problem. A third is brilliant but commits suicide at the age of fourteen when his girlfriend goes to the beach with another boy. Under the pressure of these disappointments, Yancey's wife becomes a shrill harridan. She gets fat and drinks and embarrasses him at parties. Yancey gets fat, too, and loses his hair. He is left with the consolation of his auto dealership, but then there is a war in the Middle East in which the oil fields are destroyed with atomic weapons. Suddenly there is no more oil. Yancey goes bankrupt. A number of other things happen that I will not tell you about. Suffice it to say that by the end of this version of the story, Yancey has lost his good looks, his money, and finally his fine mind, which becomes unhinged by the pressures of his misfortune. In the end he loses his hard dick, too, and dies cursing his bad luck. For in the end he is certain that bad luck, and not his own behavior, is responsible for his destruction. And he is right."

"That's too bad."

"That is too bad, isn't it?" Judith lifted the hair from the back of his neck with the tips of her fingers. It tickled.

"The other version of the story, Sandy, is even more interesting. Yancey Camera grows older, and success follows success in his life. He marries a beautiful young woman who does not get fat, and fathers four completely healthy and well-adjusted sons. He becomes a successful lawyer and enters politics. He wins every election he enters. Eventually he becomes the President of the Entire

Country. As president he visits every state capital. Everywhere he goes the people of the nation gather to meet him, and when Yancey departs, he leaves two groups of citizens behind. The first group goes home saying, 'What a fortunate people we are to have such a handsome, smart, and wealthy president.' Others say, 'What a smart, handsome, and wealthy people we are to have elected such a handsome, smart, and wealthy leader.' What a skilled nation, they tell themselves, they must be. Like their president, they assume that their gifts are not the result of good luck but of their inherent virtue. Therefore, all who point out this good luck must be jealous. And so the Fates or the second law of thermodynamics deal with Yancey's nation as they dealt with Yancey in the other version of this story. In their arrogance, Yancey Camera and his people, in the effort to maintain an oil supply for their automobiles, provoke a war that destroys all life on earth, including the lives, good looks, wealth, and hard dicks of all the citizens of that country, lucky and unlucky. The end.

"What do you think of that, Sandy?"

Sandy was on the verge of sleep. "I think you're hung up on dicks," he mumbled, smiling to himself. "All you women."

"Could be," Judith whispered. Her breath was warm on his ear. He fell asleep.

He woke with a start. She was no longer lying beside him. How could he have let down his guard so easily? She could have ripped him off—or worse. Where had he put the cash from the bank? He rolled over and reached for his pants on the floor beside the bed, then poked his index finger into the hip pocket. It was empty. He felt an adrenal surge, lurched out of bed, and began to haul on his pants. He was hopping toward the hallway, tugging on his zipper, when he saw her through the open bathroom door.

She turned toward him. The light behind her was on. Her face was totally in shadow, and her voice, when she spoke, was even huskier than the voice he had heard before.

"Did you find it?" she asked.

He felt afraid. "Find what?"

"Your money."

Then he remembered he had stuck the crisp bills, fresh from the machine, into the button-flap pocket of his shirt. He ran back to the bed, found the shirt on the floor, and fumbled at it. The money was there.

When he turned back to her, she was standing over him. She

reached down and touched his face.

You're fifteen. You are sitting at the chipped Formica table in the kitchen of the run-down farmhouse, sweating in the ninety-degree heat, eating a peanut butter sandwich and drinking a glass of sweet tea. The air is damp and hot as a fever compress. Through the patched screen door you can see the porch, the dusty red-clay yard, and a corner of the tobacco field, vivid green, running down toward the even darker line of trees along the bend of the Cape Fear that marks the edge of the farm. The air is full of the sweet smell of the tobacco. Even the sandwich tastes of it.

You're wearing your high school baseball uniform. Your spikes and glove—a Dale Murphy autograph—rest on the broken yellow vinyl of the only other serviceable kitchen chair. You're starting in right today, at two o'clock, in the first round of the Cumberland County championships, and afterward you're going out for pizza with Jocelyn. Your heart is pulling you away from the farm, your thoughts fly through a jumble of images: Jocelyn's fine blonde hair, the green of the infield grass, the brightly painted ads on the outfield fence, the way the chalk lines glow blinding white in the summer sun, the smell of Jocelyn's shoulders when you bury your face in the nape of her neck. If you never have to suffer through another summer swamped under the sickly sweet smell of tobacco, it will be all right with you.

You finish eating and are washing out the glass and plate in the sink when you hear your father's boots on the porch and the screen door slams behind him. You ignore the old man. He comes over to the counter, opens the cupboard, and takes out the bottle of sour mash bourbon and a drinking glass. Less than an inch is left in the bottom of the bottle. He curses and pours the bourbon into the glass, then drinks it off without putting down the bottle. He sighs heavily and leans against the counter.

You dry your hands quickly and get your glove and spikes.

"Where you going?" your father asks, as if the uniform and equipment are not enough.

"We got a game today."

He looks at you. His eyes are set in a network of wrinkles that come from squinting against the sun. Mr. Witt, the high school coach, has the same wrinkles around his eyes, but his are from playing outfield when he was with Atlanta. And Mr. Witt's eyes are not bloodshot.

Your father doesn't say anything. He takes off his billed cap and wipes his forearm across his brow. He turns and reaches into the sugar canister he keeps in the cupboard next to his bottles. You try to leave, but are stopped by his voice again. "Where's the sugar-bowl money?"

"I don't know."

His voice is heavy, slow. "There was another twelve dollars in here. What did you do with it?"

You stand in the door, helpless. "I didn't touch your money."

"Liar. What did you do with it!"

Pure hatred flares in you. "I didn't take your fucking money, you old drunk!"

You slam out the screen door and stalk over to the beat-up Maverick that you worked nights and weekends saving up to buy. You grind the gearshift into first, let the engine roar through the rotten muffler, spin the tires on the dirt in the yard. In the side mirror you see the old man standing on the porch shouting at you. But you can't hear what he's shouting, and the image shakes crazily as you bounce up the rutted drive.

Sandy flinched. He was crouched in his apartment, and the woman was standing over him. He still shook with anger at his father's accusation, still sweated from the heat; he could still smell the tobacco baking in the sun. How he hated the old man and his suspicion. For the first time in years he felt the vivid contempt he'd had then for the smallness that made his father that way.

He backed away from Judith, shaking. She reached out and touched him again.

You're in this same bedroom, leaning half out of bed where you've just gotten your ashes hauled better than you have in your entire life, in order to stick your finger into a pocket to see whether you've been robbed. On the day that you made the majors, on the day that you played better than you have in your entire life, on the day you played better than, in truth, you know you are really able to play. Sticking your finger into your pants pocket like a half-wit sticking his finger up his ass because it feels so good. A pitiful loser. Just like your father.

Sandy jerked away from her. He scrambled toward the bed, suddenly terrified. His knees were so weak he couldn't pull himself into the bed.

"What's the matter, Sandy?" She stepped toward him.

"Don't touch me!"

"You don't like my touch?"

"You're going to kill me." He said it quietly, amazed; and as he spoke, he realized it was true.

She moved closer. "That remains to be seen, Sandy."

"Don't touch me again! Please!"

"Why not?"

Cowering, he looked up at her, trying to make out her face in the darkness. It wasn't fair. But then something welled up in him, and he knew it *was* fair, and that was almost more than he could stand. "I'm sorry," he said.

She knelt beside him, wrapped her arms around him, and said nothing.

After a while he stopped crying. He wiped his eyes and nose with the corner of the bed sheet, ashamed. He sat on the edge of the bed, back to her. "I'm sorry," he said.

"Yes," she said. Then he saw that in her other hand, the one she had not touched him with, she held the straight razor. She had been holding it all the time.

"I didn't realize I might be hurting your feelings," he said.

"You can't hurt my feelings." There was no emotion in her voice. There was nothing. Looking at her face was like looking at an empty room.

"Don't worry," she said, folding the blade back into the handle. "I won't hurt you."

It was a blind voice. Sandy shuddered. She leaned toward him. Her body was excruciatingly beautiful, yet he stumbled back from the bed, grabbing for his shirt, as if the pants weren't enough, as if it were January and he was lost on the lakefront in a blizzard.

"You don't have to be afraid," she said. "Come to bed."

He stood there, indecisive. He had to get out of there. She was insane—fuck insane; she wasn't even human. He looked into her cold face. It was not dead. It was like the real woman was in another place and this body was a receiver over which she was bringing him a message from a far distance—from another country, from across the galaxy. If he left now, he would be okay, he knew. But something that might have happened to him would not happen, and in order to find out what that was, he would have to take a big chance. He looked up at the moon through the skylight. The clouds passed steadily across it, making it seem like it was moving. The moon didn't move that fast; it moved so slowly that you couldn't tell, except Sandy knew that in five minutes the angle of the shadows on the wall and chair and bed would be all different. The room would be changed.

She was still in bed. Sandy came back, dropped the shirt, took off his pants, and got in beside her. Her skin was very smooth.

∞   ∞   ∞

The clock read 8:45; he would have to hurry. He felt good. He got his bags out of the closet and began to pack. Halfway through, he stopped to get the shirt he had left on the floor. He picked it up and shoved it into his laundry bag, then remembered the cash and pulled it out again. She had left him fifteen dollars. One ten, five ones.

He pushed the shirt down into the bottom of the bag and finished packing. He called a cab and rode over to War Memorial.

On the Hitachi in the cab he watched the morning news, hoping to get the baseball scores. Nothing. The Reverend Mr. Gilray declares the Abomination of Desolation has begun, the Judgment is at hand. Reports the Israelis have used tactical nukes in the Djibouti civil war. Three teenagers spot another UFO at Chestnut Ridge.

When he got to the park, Sandy tipped the cabbie a redbuck and went directly to the locker room and cleaned out his locker. He was hoping to avoid Leon or Dutch, but just as he was getting ready to leave, Dutch showed up to take some hitting before the Sunday afternoon game.

"Looks like I underrated you, sport. Just like on the field." He hauled out his wallet and began to get the bills.

"Keep it," Sandy said.

"Huh?" Dutch, surprised, looked like a vanilla imitation of Leon's perpetual innocence.

"Leon won the bet."

Dutch snickered. "She got wise to you, huh?"

Sandy zipped his bag shut and picked up his glove and bats. He smiled. "You could say that. I got to go—cab's waiting. Wish me luck."

"Thought you didn't need luck."

"Goes to show you what I know. Say good-bye to Leon for me, okay?" He shook Dutch's hand and left.

MEETING IN INFINITY MEETING IN INFINITY MEETING IN INFINITY MEETIN
TING IN INFINITY MEETING IN INFINITY MEETING IN INFINITY ME
MEETING IN INFINITY MEETING IN INFINITY MEETING IN INFINITY
ITY MEETING IN INFINITY MEETING IN INFINITY MEETING IN INF
INFINITY MEETING IN INFINITY MEETING IN INFINITY MEETING IN
G IN INFINITY MEETING IN INFINITY MEETING IN INFINITY MEETI
ETING IN INFINITY MEETING IN INFINITY MEETING IN INFINITY M
MEETING IN INFINITY MEETING IN INFINITY MEETING IN INFINI
ITY MEETING IN INFINITY MEETING IN INFINITY MEETING IN IN
INFINITY MEETING IN INFINITY MEETING IN INFINITY MEETING
NG IN INFINITY MEETING IN INFINITY MEETING IN INFINITY MEE
EETING IN INFINITY MEETING IN INFINITY MEETING IN INFINITY
Y MEETING IN INFINITY MEETING IN INFINITY MEETING IN INFIN
FINITY MEETING IN INFINITY MEETING IN INFINITY MEETING IN
IN INFINITY MEETING IN INFINITY MEETING IN INFINITY MEETIN

buddha nostril bird

AFTER WE KILLED THE GUARD, GLAUCON AND I RAN DOWN THE corridor away from the Well. Glaucon had been seriously aged in the fight. He limped and cursed, a piece of dying meat and he knew it. I brushed my hand along the wall looking for a door.

"We'll make it," I said.

"Sure," he said. He held his arm against his side.

We ran past a series of ontological windows: a forest fire, a sun in space, a factory refashioning children into flowers. I worried that the corridor might be a loop. For all I knew, the sole purpose of such corridors was to confuse and recapture escapees. Or maybe the corridors were just for fun. The Relativists delight in such absurdities.

More windows: a snowstorm, a cloudy seascape, a corridor exactly like the one we were in, in which two men wearing yellow robes—prison kosodes like ours—searched for a way out. Glaucon stopped. The hand of his double reached out to meet his. The face of mine stared at me angrily; a strong face, an intelligent one. "It's just a mirror," I said.

"Mirror?"

"A mirror," a voice said. Protagoras appeared ahead of us in the corridor. "Like sex, it reproduces human beings."

An old joke, and typical of Protagoras to quote it without attribution.

Glaucon raised his clock. In the face of Protagoras's infinite mutability it was less than useless: there was no way Glaucon would even get a shot off. My spirit sank as I watched the change come over him. Protagoras dripped fellowship. Glaucon liked him. Nobody but a maniac could dislike Protagoras.

It took all my will to block the endorphin assault, but Glaucon was never as strong as I. A lot of talk about brotherhood had passed between us, but if I'd had my freedom I would have crisped him on the spot. Instead I hid myself from Protagoras's blue eyes, as cold as chips of aquamarine in a mosaic.

"Where are you going?" Protagoras said.

"We were going—" Glaucon started.

"—nowhere," I said.

"A hard place to get to," said Protagoras.

Glaucon's head bobbed like a dog's.

"I know a short way," Protagoras said. "Come along with me."

"Sure," said Glaucon.

I struggled to maintain control. If you had asked him, Protagoras would have denied controlling anyone: "The Superior Man rules by humility." Another sophistry.

We turned back down the corridor. If I stayed with them until we got to the center, there would be no way I could escape. Desperation forced me to test the reality of one of the windows. As we passed the ocean scene, I pushed Glaucon into Protagoras and threw my shoulder against the glass. The window shattered; I was falling. My kosode flapped like the melting wings of Icarus as sky and sea whirled around me, and I hit the water. My breath exploded from me. I flailed and tumbled. At last I found the surface. I sputtered and gasped, my right arm in agony; my ribs ached. I kicked off my slippers and leaned onto my back. The waves rolled me up and down. The sky was low and dark. At the top of each swell I could see to the storm-clouded horizon, flat as a psychotic's affect —but in the other direction was a beach.

I swam. The bad shoulder and the kosode made it hard, but at that moment I would not have traded places with Glaucon for all the enlightenment of the ancients.

∞   ∞   ∞

When they sent me to the penal colony they told me, "Prisons ought to be places where people are lodged only temporarily, as guests are. They must not become dwelling places."

Their idea of temporary is not mine. Temporary doesn't mean long enough for your skin to crack like the dry lakebed outside your window, for the memory of your lover's touch to recede until it's only a torment in your dreams, as distant as the mountains that surround the penal colony. These distinctions are lost on Relativists, as are all distinctions. Which, I suppose, is why I was sent there.

They keep you alone, mostly. I didn't mind the isolation—it gave me time to understand exactly how many ways I had been betrayed. I spent hours thinking of Areté, etching her ideal features in my mind. I remembered how they'd ripped me away from her. I wondered if she still lived, and if I would ever see her again. Eventually, when memory had faded, I conquered the passage of time itself: I reconstructed her image from incorruptible ideas and planned the revenge I would take once I was free again, so that the past and the future became more real to me than the endless, featureless present. Such is the power of idea over reality. To the guards I must have looked properly meditative. Inside I burned.

Each day at dawn we would be awakened by the rapping of sticks on our iron bedsteads. In the first hour we drew water from the Well of Changes. In the second we were encouraged to drink (I refused). In the third we washed floors with the water. From the fourth through the seventh we performed every other function that was necessary to maintain the prison. In the eighth we were tortured. At the ninth we were fed. At night, exhausted, we slept.

The torture chamber is made of ribbed concrete. It is a cold room, without windows. In its center is a chair, and beside the chair a small table, and on the table the hood. The hood is black and appears to be made of ordinary fabric, but it is not. The first time I held it, despite the evidence of my eyes I thought it had slipped through my fingers. The hood is not a material object: you cannot feel it, and it has no texture, and although it absorbs all light it is neither warm nor cold.

Your inquisitor invites you to sit in the chair and slip the hood over your head. You do so. He speaks to you. The room disappears. Your body melts away, and you are made into something else. You are an animal. You are one of the ancients. You are a stone, a drop of rain in a storm, a planet. You are in another time and place. This may sound intriguing, and the first twenty times it is. But it never ends. The sessions are indiscriminate. They are deliberately pointless. They continue to the verge of insanity.

I recall one of these sessions, in which I lived in an ancient city and worked a hopeless routine in a store called the "World of Values." The values we sold were merchandise. I married, had children, grew old, lost my health and spirit. I worked forty years. Some days were happy, others sad; most were neither. The last thing I remembered was lying in a hospital bed, unable to see, dying, and hearing my wife talk with my son about what they should have for dinner. When I came out from under the hood, Protagoras yanked me from the chair and told me this poem:

> *Out from the nostrils of the Great Buddha*
> *Flew a pair of nesting swallows.*

I could still hear my phantom wife's cracking voice. I was in no mood for riddles. "Tell me what it means."

"Drink from the Well and I'll tell you."

I turned my back on him.

It was always like that. Protagoras had made a career out of tormenting me. I had known him for too many years. He put faith in nothing, was totally without honor, yet he had power. His intellect was available for any use. He wasted years on banalities. He would argue any side of a case, not because he sought advantage, but because he did not care about right or wrong. He was intolerably lucky. Irresponsible as a child. Inconstant as the wind. His opaque blue gaze could be as witless as a scientist's.

And he had been my first teacher. He had introduced me to Areté, offered me useless advice throughout our stormy relationship, given ambiguous testimony at my trial, and upon the verdict abandoned the university in order to come to the prison and become my inquisitor. The thought that I had once idolized him tormented me more than any session under the hood.

After my plunge through the window into the sea, I fought my way through the surf to the beach. For an unknown time I lay gasping on the wet sand. When I opened my eyes I saw a flock of gulls had waddled up to me. An arm's length away the lead gull, a great bull whose ragged feathers stood out from his neck in a ruff, watched me with beady black eyes. Others of various sizes and markings stood in a wedge behind him. I raised my head; the gulls retreated a few steps, still holding formation. I understood immediately that they were ranked according to their stations in the flock. Thus does nature shadow forth fundamental truth: the rule of the strong over the weak, the relation of one to the many in hierarchical order.

Off to the side stood a single scrawny gull, quicker than the rest, but separate, aloof. I supposed him to be a gullish philosopher. I saluted him, my brother.

A sandpiper scuttled along the edge of the surf. Dipping a handful of seawater, I washed sand and pieces of shell from my cheek. Up the slope, saw grass and sea oats held the dunes against the tides. The scene was familiar. With wonder and some disquiet I understood that the window had dumped me into the Great Water quite near the Imperial City.

I stumbled up the sand to the crest of the dunes. In the east, beneath piled thunderheads, lightning flashed over the dark water. To the west, against the sunset's glare, the sand and scrub turned into fields. I started inland. Night fell swiftly. From behind me came clouds, strong winds, then rain. I trudged on, singing into the downpour. The thunder sang back. Water streamed down the creases of my face, the wet kosode weighed on my chest and shoulders, the rough grass cut my feet. In the profound darkness I could continue only by memorizing the landscape revealed by flashes of lightning. Exhilarated, I hurried toward my lover. I shouted at the raindrops, any one of which might be one of my fellow prisoners under the hood. "I'm free!" I told them. I forded the swollen River of Indifference. I stumbled through Iron Tree Forest. Throughout the night I put one foot before the other, and some hours before dawn, in a melancholy drizzle, passed through the Heron's Gate into the city.

In the Processor's Quarter I found a doorway whose overhang kept out the worst of the rain. Above hung the illuminated sign of the Rat. In the corner of this doorway, under this sign, I slept.

∞   ∞   ∞

I was awakened by the arrival of the owner of the communications shop in whose doorway I had slept.

"I am looking for the old fox," I said. "Do you know where I can find him?"

"Who are you?"

"You may call me the little fox."

He pushed open the door. "Well, Mr. Fox, I can put you in touch with him instantly. Just step into one of our booths."

He must have known I had no money. "I don't want to communicate. I want to see him."

"Communication is much better," the shop owner said. He took a towel, a copper basin, and an ornamental blade from the cupboard beneath his terminal. "No chance of physical violence. No distress other than psychological. Completely accurate reproduction. Sensory enhancement: olfactory, visual, auditory." He opened a cage set into the wall and seized a docile black rat by the scruff of the neck. "Recordability. Access to a network of supporting information services. For slight additional charge we offer intelligence augmentation and instant semiotic analysis. We make the short man tall. Physical presence has nothing to compare."

"I want to speak with him in private."

Not looking at me, he took the rat to the stone block. "We are bonded."

"I don't question your integrity."

"You have religious prejudices against communication? You are a Traveler?"

He would not rest until he forced me to admit I was penniless. I refrained from noting that, if he was such a devout communicator, he could easily have stayed home. Yet he had walked to his shop in person. Swallowing my rage, I said, "I have no money."

He sliced the rat's neck open. The animal made no sound.

After he had drained the blood and put the carcass into the display case, he washed his hands and turned to me. He seemed quite pleased with himself. He took a small object from a drawer. "He is to be found at the university. Here is a map of the maze." He slipped it into my hand.

For this act of gratuitous charity, I vowed that one day I would have revenge. I left.

The streets were crowded. Dusty gold light filtered down between the ranks of ancient buildings. Too short to use the moving ways, I walked. Orange-robed messengers threaded their way through the crowd. Sweating drivers in loincloths pulled pedicabs; I imagined the perfumed lottery winners who reclined behind the opaqued glass of their passenger compartments. In the Medical Quarter, street-side surgeons hawked their services in front of racks of breasts and penises of prodigious size. As before, the names of the streets changed hourly to mark the progress of the sun across the sky. All streets but one, and I held my breath when I came to it: the Way of Enlightenment, which ran between the reform temple

and the Imperial Palace. As before, metamorphs entertained the faithful on the stage outside the temple. One of them changed shape as I watched, from a dog-faced man wearing the leather skirt of an athlete to a tattooed CEO in powered suit. "Come drink from the Well of Changes!" he called ecstatically to passersby. "Be reformed!"

The Well he spoke of is both literal and symbolic. The prison Well was its brother; the preachers of the temple claim that all the Wells are one Well. Its water has the power to transform both body and mind. A scientist could tell you how it is done: viruses, brain chemistry, hypnosis, some insane combination of the three. But that is all a scientist could tell you. Unlike a scientist, I could tell you why its use is morally wrong. I could explain that some truths are eternal and ought to be held inviolate, and why a culture that accepts change indiscriminately is rotten at its heart. I could demonstrate, with inescapable logic, that reason is better than emotion. That spirit is greater than flesh. That Relativism is the road to hell.

Instead of relief at being home, I felt distress. The street's muddle upset me, but it was not simply that: the city was exactly as I had left it. The wet morning that dawned on me in the doorway might have been the morning after I was sent away. My absence had made no discernible difference. The tyranny of the Relativists that I and my friends had struggled against had not culminated in the universal misery we had predicted. Though everything changed minute to minute, it remained the same. The one thing that ought to remain constant, Truth, was to them as chimerical as the genechangers of the temple.

They might have done better, had they had teachers to tell them good from bad.

Looking down the boulevard, in the distance, at the heart of the city, I could see the walls of the palace. By midday I had reached it. Vendors of spiced cakes pushed their carts among the petitioners gathered beneath the great red lacquered doors. One, whose cakes each contained a free password, did a superior business. That the passwords were patent frauds was evident by the fact that the gatekeeper ignored those petitioners who tried using them. But that did not hurt sales. Most of the petitioners were halflings, and a dim-witted rabbit could best them in a deal.

I wept for my people, their ignorance and illogic. I discovered that I was clutching the map in my fist so tightly that the point of it had pierced my skin. I turned from the palace and walked away, and did not feel any relief until I saw the towers of the university rising above Scholars' Park. I remembered my first sight of them, a young boy down from the hills, the smell of cattle still about me, come to study under the great Protagoras. The meticulously kept park, the calm proportions of the buildings, spoke to the soul of that innocent boy: here you'll be safe from blood and passion. Here you can lose yourself in the world of the mind.

The years had worn the polish off that dream, but I can't say that, seeing it now, once more a fugitive from a dangerous world, I did not feel some of the same joy. I thought of my mother, a loutish farmer who would whip me for reading; of my gentle father, brutalized by her, trying to keep the flame of truth alive in his boy.

On the quadrangle I approached a young woman wearing the topknot and scarlet robe of a humanist. Her head bounced to some inner rhythm, and as I imagined she was pursuing some notion of the Ideal, my heart went out to her. I was about to ask her what she studied when I saw the pin in her temple. She was listening to transtemporal music: her mind eaten by puerile improvisations played on signals picked up from the death agonies of the cosmos. Generations of researchers had devoted their lives to uncovering these secrets, only to have their efforts used by "artists" to erode people's connections with reality. I spat on the walk at her feet; she passed by, oblivious.

At the entrance to the humanities maze I turned on the map and followed it into the gloom. Fifteen minutes later it guided me into the Department of Philosophy. It was the last place I expected to find the fox—the nest of our enemies, the place we had plotted against tirelessly. The secretary greeted me pleasantly.

"I'm looking for a man named Socrates," I said. "Some call him 'the old fox.'"

"Universe of Discourse 3," she said.

I walked down the hall, wishing I had Glaucon's clock. The door to the hall stood open. In the center of the cavelike room, in a massive support chair, sat Socrates. At last I had found a significant change: he was grossly obese. The ferretlike features I remembered were folded in fat. Only the acute eyes remained. I was profoundly shaken. As I approached, his eyes followed me.

"Socrates."

"Blume."

"What happened to you?"

Socrates lifted his dimpled hand, as if to wave away a triviality. "I won."

"You used to revile this place."

"I reviled its usurpers. Now I run it."

"You run it?"

"I'm the dean."

I should have known Socrates had turned against our cause, and perhaps at some level I had. If he had remained true, he would have ended up in a cell next to mine. "You used to be a great teacher," I said.

"Right. Let me tell what happens when a man starts claiming he's a great teacher. First he starts wearing a brocade robe. Then he puts lifts in his sandals. The next thing you know the department's got a nasty paternity suit on its hands."

His senile chuckle was like the bubbling of water in an opium pipe.

"How did you get to be dean?"

"I performed a service for the Emperor."

"You sold out!"

"Blume the dagger," he said. Some of the old anger shaded his voice. "So sharp. So rigid. You always were a prig."

"And you used to have principles."

"Ah, principles," he said. "I'll tell you what happened to my principles. You heard about Philomena the Bandit?"

"No. I've been somewhat out of touch."

Socrates ignored the jab. "It was after you left. Philomena invaded the system, established her camp on the moon, and made her living raiding the empire. The city was at her mercy. I saw my opportunity. I announced that I would reform her. My students outfitted a small ship, and Areté and I launched for the moon."

"Areté!"

"We landed in a lush valley near the camp. Areté negotiated an audience for me. I went, alone. I described to Philomena the advantages of politic behavior. The nature of truth. The costs of living in the world of shadows and the glory of moving into the world of light. How, if she should turn to Good, her story would be told for generations. Her fame would spread throughout the world and her honor outlast her lifetime by a thousand years.

"Philomena listened. When I was finished she drew a knife and asked me, 'How long is a thousand years?'

"Her men stood all around, waiting for me to slip. I started to speak, but before I could she pulled me close and pushed the blade against my throat.

"'A thousand years,' Philomena said, 'is shorter than the exposure of a neutrino passing through a world. How long is life?'

"I was petrified. She smiled. 'Life,' she said, 'is shorter than this blade.'

"I begged for mercy. She threw me out. I ran to the ship, in fear for my life. Areté asked what happened: I said nothing. We set sail for home.

"We landed amid great tumult. I first thought it was riot but soon found it celebration. During our voyage back Philomena had left the moon. People assumed I had convinced her. The Emperor spoke. Our enemies in philosophy were shortened, and the regents stretched me into dean.

"Since then," Socrates said, "I have had trouble with principles."

"You're a coward," I said.

Despite the mask of suet, I could read the ruefulness in Socrates's eyes. "You don't know me," he said.

"What happened to Areté?"

"I have not seen her since."

"Where is she?"

"She's not here." He shifted his bulk, watching the screen that encircled the room. "Turn yourself in, Blume. If they catch you, it will only go harder."

"Where is she?"

"Even if you could get to her, she won't want to see you."

I seized his arm, twisted. "Where is Areté!"

Socrates inhaled sharply. "In the palace," he said.

"She's a prisoner?"

"She's the Empress."

∞   ∞   ∞

That night I took a place among the halflings outside the palace gate. Men and women regrown from seed after their deaths, imprinted with stored files of their original personalities, all of them had lost resolution, for no identity file could encapsulate human complexity. Some could not speak, others displayed features too stiff to pass for human, and still others had no personalities at all. Their only chance for wholeness was to petition the Empress to perform a transfinite extrapolation from their core data. To be miraculously transformed.

An athlete beside me showed me his endorsements. An actress showed me her notices. A banker showed me his lapels. They asked me my profession. "I am a philosopher," I said.

They laughed. "Prove it," the actress said.

"In the well-ordered state," I told her, "there will be no place for you." To the athlete I said, "Yours is a good and noble profession." I turned to the banker. "Your work is more problematical," I said. "Unlike the actress, you fulfill a necessary function, but unlike the athlete, by accumulating wealth you are likely to gain more power than is justified by your small wisdom."

This speech was beyond them: the actress grumbled and went away. I left the two men and walked along below the battlements. Two bartizans framed the great doors, and archers strolled along the ramparts or leaned through the embrasures to spit on the petitioners. For this reason the halflings camped as far back from the walls as they might without blocking the street. The archers, as any educated man knew, were there for show: the gates were guarded only by a single gatekeeper, a monk who could open the door if bested in a battle of wits, but without whose acquiescence the door could not be budged.

He sat on his stool beside the gate, staring quietly ahead. Those who tried to talk to him could not tell whether they'd get a cuff on the ear or a friendly conversation. His flat, peasant's face was so devoid of intellect that it was some time before I recognized him as Protagoras.

His disguised presence could be one of his whims. Or it could be he was being punished for letting me escape; it could be that he waited for me. I felt an urge to run. But I would not duplicate Socrates's cowardice. If Protagoras recognized me he did not show it, and I resolved to get in or get caught. I was not some half-wit, and I knew him. I approached. "I wish to see the Empress," I said.

"You must wait."

"I've been waiting for years."

"That doesn't matter."

"I have no more time."

He studied me. His manner changed. "What will you pay?"

"I'll pay you a story that will make you laugh until your head aches."

He smiled. I saw that he recognized me; my stomach lurched. "I know many such stories," he said.

"Not like mine."

"Yes. I can see you are a great breeder of headaches."

Desperation drove me forward. "Listen, then: once there was a warlord who discovered that someone had stolen his most precious possession, a jewel of power. He ordered his servants to scour the fortress for strangers. In the bailey they found a beggar heading for the gate. The lord's men seized him and carried him to the well. 'The warlord's great jewel is lost,' they said to him. They thrust the beggar's head beneath the water. He struggled. They pulled him up and asked, 'Where is the jewel?'

" 'I don't know,' he said.

"They thrust him down again, longer this time. When they pulled him up he sputtered like an old engine. 'Where is the jewel?' they demanded. 'I don't know!' he replied.

"Furious at his insolence, fearful for their lives if they should rouse their lord's displeasure, the men pushed the beggar so far into the well that a bystander thought, 'He will surely drown.' The beggar kicked so hard it took three strong men to hold him. When at last they pulled him up he coughed and gasped, face purple, struggling to speak. They pounded him on the back. Finally he drew breath enough for words.

" 'I think you should get another diver,' the beggar said. 'I can't see it anywhere down there.' "

Protagoras smiled. "That's not funny."

"What?"

"Maybe for us, but not for the beggar. Or the bystander. Or the servants. The warlord probably had them shortened."

"Don't play games. What do you really think?"

"I think of poor Glaucon. He misses you."

Then I saw that Protagoras only meant to torment me, as he had so many times before. He would answer my desperate need with feeble jokes until I wept or went mad. A fury more powerful than the sun itself swept over me, and I lost control. I fell on him, kicking, biting. The petitioners looked on in amazement. Shouts echoed from the ramparts. I didn't care. I'd forgotten everything but my rage; all I knew was that at last I had him in my hands. I scratched at his eyes, I beat his head against the pavements. Protagoras struggled to speak. I pulled him up and slammed his head against the doors. The tension went out of his muscles. Cross-legged, as if preparing to meditate, he slid to the ground. Blood glistened in the torchlight on the lacquered doors. "Now that's funny," he whispered, and died.

The weight of his body against the door pushed it ajar. It had been open all along.

∞   ∞   ∞

No one came to arrest me. Across the inner ward, at the edge of an ornamental garden, a person stood in the darkness beneath a plane tree. Most of the lights of the palace were unlit, but radiance from the clerestory above heightened the shadows. Hesitantly I drew closer, too unsteady after my sudden fit of violence to hide. In my confusion I could think to do no more than approach the figure in the garden, who stood patiently as if in long expectation of me. From ten paces away I saw it was a woman dressed as a clown. From five I saw it was Areté.

Her laughter, like shattering crystal, startled me. "How serious you look!"

My head was full of questions. She pressed her fingers against my lips, silencing them. I embraced her. Red circles were painted on her cheeks, and she wore a crepe beard, but her skin was still smooth, her eyes bright, her perfume the same. She was not a day older.

The memory of dead Protagoras's slack mouth marred my triumph. She ducked out of my arms, laughing again. "You can't have me unless you catch me!"

"Areté!"

She darted through the trees. I ran after her. My heart was not in it, and I lost her until she paused beneath a tree, hands on knees, panting. "Come on! I'm not so hard to catch."

The weight was lifted from my heart. I dodged after her. Beneath the trees, through the hedge maze, among the night-blooming jasmine and bougainvillea, the silver moon tipping the edges of the leaves, I chased her. At last she let herself be caught; we fell together into a damp bed of ivy. I rested my head on her breast. The embroidery of her costume was rough against my cheek.

She took my head in her hands and made me look her in the face. Her teeth were pearly white, breath sweet as the scented blossoms around us.

We kissed, through the ridiculous beard (I could smell the spirit gum she'd used to affix it), and the goal they had sought to instill in me at the penal colony was attained: my years of imprisonment vanished into the immediate moment as if they had never existed.

∞   ∞   ∞

That kiss was the limit of our contact. I expected to spend the night with her; instead, she had a slave take me to a guesthouse for visiting dignitaries, where I was quartered with three minor landholders from the mountains. They were already asleep. After my day of confusion, rage, desire, and fear, I lay there weary but hard awake, troubled by the sound of my own breathing. My thoughts were jumbled white noise. I had killed him. I had found her. Two of the fantasies of my imprisonment fulfilled in a single hour. Yet no peace. The murder of Protagoras would not long go unnoticed. I assumed Areté already knew but did not care. But if she was truly the Empress, why had he not been killed years before? Why had I rotted in prison under him?

I had no map for this maze and eventually fell asleep.

In the morning the slave, Pismire, brought me a wig of human hair, a green kimono, a yellow silk sash, and solid leather sandals: the clothes of a prosperous nonentity. My roommates appeared to be barely lettered country bumpkins, little better than my parents, come to court seeking a judgment against a neighbor or a place for a younger child or protection from some bandit. One of them wore the colors of an inferior upland collegium; the others no colors at all.

I suspected at least one of them was Areté's spy; they might have thought me one as well. We looked enough alike to be brothers.

We ate in a dining room attended by machines. I spent the day studying the public rooms of the palace, hoping to get some information. At the tolling of sixth hour Pismire found me in the vivarium. He handed me a message under the Imperial seal, and left. I turned it on.

"You are invited to an important meeting," the message said.

"With whom?" I asked. "For what purpose?"

The message ignored me. "The meeting begins promptly at ninth hour. Prepare yourself." There followed directions to the place.

When I arrived, the appointed room was empty. A long oak table, walls lined with racks of document spindles. At the far end, French doors gave onto a balcony overlooking an ancient city of glass and metal buildings. I could hear the faint sounds of traffic below.

A side door opened and a woman in the blue suit of the Lawyer entered, followed by a clerk. The woman's glossy black hair was stranded with gray, but her face was smooth. She wore no makeup. She stood at the end of the table, back to the French doors, and set down a leather box. The clerk sat at her right hand. I realized that this forbidding figure was Areté. She had become as mutable as Protagoras.

"Be seated," she said. "We are here to take your deposition."

"Deposition?"

"Your statement on the matter at hand."

"What matter?"

"Your escape from the penal colony. Your murder of the gate-keeper, the honored philosopher Protagoras."

The injustice of this burned through my dismay. "Not murder. Self-defense. Or better still, euthanasia."

"Don't quibble with us. We are deprived of his presence."

"Grow a duplicate. Bring him back to life."

For reply she merely stared at me across the table. The air tasted stale, and I felt a bead of sweat run down my breast beneath my robe. "Is this some game?"

"You may well wish it a game."

"Areté!"

"I am not Areté. I am a Lawyer." She leaned toward me. "Why were you sent to prison?"

"You were with me! You know."

"We are taking your version of events for the record."

"You know as well as I that I was imprisoned for seeking the Truth."

"Which truth?"

There was only one. "The one that people don't want to hear," I said.

"You had access to a truth people did not acknowledge?"

"They are blinded by custom and self-interest."

"You were not?"

"I had, through years of self-abnegation and study, risen above them. I had broken free of the chains of prejudice, climbed out of the cave of shadows that society lives in, and looked at the sun direct."

The clerk smirked as I made this speech. It was the first expression he'd shown.

"And you were blinded by it," Areté said.

"I saw the truth. But when I came back they said I was blind. They would not listen, so they put me away."

"The trial record says that you assisted in the corruption of youth."

"I was a teacher."

"The record says you refused to listen to your opponents."

"I refuse to listen to ignorance and illogic. I refuse to submit to fools, liars, and those who let passion overcome reason."

"You have never been fooled?"

"I was, but not now."

"You never lie?"

"If I do, I still know the difference between a lie and the truth."

"You never act out of passion?"

"Only when supported by reason."

"You never suspect your own motives?"

"I know my motives."

"How?"

"I examine myself. Honestly, critically. I apply reason."

"Spare me your colossal arrogance, your revolting self-pity. Eyewitnesses say you killed the gatekeeper in a fit of rage."

"I had reason. Do you presume to understand my motives better than I? Do you understand your own?"

"No. But that's because I am dishonest. And totally arbitrary." She opened the box and took out a clock. Without hesitation she pointed it at the clerk. His smugness punctured, he stumbled back, overturning his chair. She pressed the trigger. The weapon must have been set for maximum entropy: before my eyes the clerk aged ten, twenty, fifty years. He died and rotted. In less than a minute he was a heap of bones and gruel on the floor.

"You've been in prison so long you've invented a harmless version of me," Areté said. "I am capable of anything." She laid the clock on the table, turned and opened the doors to let in a fresh night breeze. Then she climbed onto the table and crawled toward me. I sat frozen. "I am the Destroyer," she said, loosening her tie as she approached. Her eyes were fixed on mine. When she reached me she pushed me over backward, falling atop me. "I am the force that drives the blood through your dying body, the nightmare that wakes you sweating in the middle of the night. I am the fiery caldron within whose heat you are reduced to a vapor, extended from the visible into the invisible, dissipated on the winds of time, of fading memory, of inevitable human loss. In the face of me, you are incapable of articulate speech. About me you understand nothing."

She wound the tie around my neck, drew it tight. "Remember that," she said, strangling me.

∞   ∞   ∞

I passed out on the floor of the interview room and awoke the next morning in a bed in a private chamber. Pismire was drawing the curtains on a view of an ocean beach: half-asleep, I watched the tiny figure of a man materialize in a spray of glass, in midair, and fall precipitously into the sea.

Pismire brought me a breakfast of fruit and spiced coffee. Touching the bruises on my neck, I watched the man resurface in the sea and swim ashore. He collapsed on the sand. A flock of gulls came to stand by his head. If I broke through this window, I could warn him. I could say: Socrates is fat. Watch out for the gatekeeper. Areté is alive, but she is changed.

But what could I tell him for certain? Had Areté turned Relativist, like Socrates? Was she free, or being made to play a part? Did she intend to prosecute me for the murder of Protagoras? But if so, why not simply return me to the penal colony?

I did not break through the window, and the man eventually moved up the beach toward the city.

That day servants followed me everywhere. Minor lords asked my opinions. Evidently I was a taller man than I had been the day before. I drew Pismire aside and asked him what rumors were current. He was a stocky fellow with a topknot of coarse black hair and shaved temples, silent, but when I pressed him he opened up readily enough. He said he knew for a fact that Protagoras had set himself up to be killed. He said the Emperor was dead and the Empress was the focus of a perpetual struggle. That many men had sought to make Areté theirs, but none had so far succeeded. That disaster would surely follow any man's success.

"Does she always change semblance from day to day?"

He said he had never noticed any changes.

In midafternoon, at precisely the same time I had yesterday received the summons to the deposition, a footman with the face of a frog handed me an invitation to dine with the Empress that evening.

Three female expediters prepared a scented bath for me; a fourth laid out a kimono of blue crepe embroidered with gold fishing nets. The mirror they held before me showed a man with wary eyes. At the tolling of ninth hour I was escorted to the banquet hall. The room was filled with notables in every finery. A large, low table stretched across the tesselated floor, surrounded by cushions. Before each place was an enamel bowl, and in the center of the table was a large three-legged brass caldron. Areté, looking no more than twenty, stood talking to an extremely handsome man near the head of the table.

"I thank you for your courtesy," I told her.

The man watched me impassively. "No more than is your due," Areté replied. She wore a bright costume of synthetics with pleated shoulders and elbows. She looked like a toy. Her face was painted into a hard mask.

She introduced me to the man, whose name was Meno. I drew her away from him. "You frightened me last night," I said. "I thought you had forgotten me."

Only her soft brown eyes showed she wasn't a pleasure surrogate. "What makes you think I remember?"

"You could not forget and still be the one I love."

"That's probably true. I'm not sure I'm worth such devotion."

Meno watched us from a few paces away. I turned my back to him and leaned closer to her. "I can't believe you mean that," I said quickly. "I think you say such things because you have been imprisoned by liars and self-aggrandizers. But I am here for you now. I am an objective voice. Just give me a sign, and I will set you free."

Before she could answer, a bell sounded and the people took their places. Areté guided me to a place beside her. She sat, and we all followed suit.

The slaves stood ready to serve, waiting for Areté's command. She looked around the table. "We are met here to eat together," she said. "To dine on ambrosia, because there has been strife in the city, and ambition, and treachery. But now it is going to stop."

Meno now looked openly angry. Others were worried.

"You are the favored ones," said Areté. She turned to me. "And our friend here, the little fox, is the most favored of all. Destiny's author—our new and most trusted adviser."

Several people started to protest. I seized the opportunity given by their shock. "Am I indeed your adviser?"

"You may test it by deeds."

"You and you—" I beckoned to the guards. "Clear these people from the room."

The guests were in turmoil. Meno tried to speak to Areté, but I stepped between them. The guards came forward and forced the men and women to leave. After they were gone, I had the guards and slaves leave as well. The doors closed and the hall was silent. I turned. Areté had watched it all calmly, sitting cross-legged at the head of the table.

"Now, Areté, you must listen to me. Your commands have been twisted throughout this city. You and I have an instinctive sympathy. You must let me determine who sees you. I will interpret your words. The world is not ready to understand without an interpreter; they need to be educated."

"And you are the teacher."

"I am suited to it by temperament and training."

She smiled meekly.

I told Areté that I was hungry. She rose and prepared a bowl of soup from the caldron. I sat at the head of the table. She came and set the bowl before me, then kneeled and touched her forehead to the floor.

"Feed me," I said.

She took the bowl and a napkin. She blew on the ambrosia to cool it, lips pursed. Like a serving girl, she held the bowl to my lips. Areté fed me all of it, like mother to child, lover to lover. It tasted better than anything I had ever eaten. It warmed my belly and inflamed my desire. When the bowl was empty I pushed it away, knocking it from her hand. It clattered on the marble floor. I would be put off no longer. I took her right there, amid the cushions.

She was indeed the hardest of toys.

∞   ∞   ∞

It had taken me three days from my entrance to the palace to become Areté's lover and voice. The Emperor over the Empress. On the first day of my reign I had the shopkeeper who had insulted me whipped the length of the Way of Enlightenment. On the second I ordered that only those certified in philosophy be qualified to vote. On the third I banished the poets.

Each evening Areté fed me ambrosia from a bowl. Each night we shared the Imperial bed. Each morning I awoke calmer, in more possession of myself. I moved more slowly. The hours of the day were drained of their urgency. Areté stopped changing. Her face settled with a quiet clarity into my mind, a clarity unlike the burning image I had treasured up during my years in the prison.

On the morning of the third day I awoke fresh and happy. Areté was not there. Pismire entered the room bearing a basin, a towel, a razor, a mirror. He washed and shaved me, then held the mirror before me. For the first time I saw the lines about my eyes and mouth were fading, and realized that I was being reformed.

I looked at Pismire. I saw him clearly: eyes cold as aquamarines.

"It's time for you to come home, Blume," he said.

No anger, no protest, arose in me. No remorse. No frustration. "I've been betrayed," I said. "Some virus, some drug, some notion you've put in my head."

Protagoras smiled. "The ambrosia. Brewed with water from the Well."

∞　　∞　　∞

Now I am back in the prison. Escape is out of the question. Every step outward would be a step backward. It's all relative.

Instead I draw water from the Well of Changes. I drink. Protagoras says whatever changes will happen to me will be a reflection of my own psyche. That my new form is not determined by the water, but by me. How do I control it, I ask. You don't, he replies.

Glaucon has become a feral dog.

Protagoras and I go for long walks across the dry lake. He seldom speaks. I am not angry. Still, I fear a relapse. I am close to being nourished, but as yet I am not sure I am capable of it. I don't understand, as I never understood, where the penal colony is. I don't understand, as I never understood, how I can live without Areté.

Protagoras sympathizes. "Can't live with her, can't live without her," he says. "She's more than just a woman, Blume. You can experience her, but you can't own her."

Right. When I complain about such gnomic replies, Protagoras only puts me under the hood again. I think he knows some secret he wants me to guess, yet he gives no hints. I don't think that's fair.

After our most recent session, I told Protagoras my latest theory of the significance of the poem about the swallows. The poem, I told him, was an emblem of the ultimate and absolute truth of the universe. All things are determined by the ideas behind them, I said. There are three orders of existence, the Material (represented by the physical statue of the Buddha), the Spiritual (represented by its form), and the highest, which transcends both the Physical and the Spiritual, the Ideal (represented by the flight of the birds). Humbly I begged Protagoras to tell me whether my analysis was true.

Protagoras said, "You are indeed an intellectual. But in order for me to reveal the answer to a question of such profound spiritual significance, you must first bow down before the sacred Well."

At last I was to be enlightened. Eyes brimming with tears of hope, I turned to the Well and, with the utmost sincerity, bowed.

Then Protagoras kicked me in the ass.

MEETING IN INFINITY MEETING IN INFINITY MEETING IN INFINITY MEE
EETING IN INFINITY MEETING IN INFINITY MEETING IN INFINITY
Y MEETING IN INFINITY MEETING IN INFINITY MEETING IN INFIN
FINITY MEETING IN INFINITY MEETING IN INFINITY MEETING IN
IN INFINITY MEETING IN INFINITY MEETING IN INFINITY MEETING
ING IN INFINITY MEETING IN INFINITY MEETING IN INFINITY MEE
MEETING IN INFINITY MEETING IN INFINITY MEETING IN INFINITY
ITY MEETING IN INFINITY MEETING IN INFINITY MEETING IN INFI
NFINITY MEE
G IN INFINITY
ETING IN
TING IN INFINITY MEETING IN INFINITY MEETING IN INFINITY M
MEETING IN INFINITY MEETING IN INFINITY MEETING IN INFINIT
NITY MEETING IN INFINITY MEETING IN INFINITY MEETING IN IN
INFINITY MEETING IN INFINITY MEETING IN INFINITY MEETING
NG IN INFINITY MEETING IN INFINITY MEETING IN INFINITY MEE

another orphan

And I only am escaped alone to tell thee.
—Job

one

HE WOKE TO DARKNESS AND SWAYING AND THE STINK OF MANY bodies. He tried to lift his head and reach across the bed and found he was not in his bed at all. He was in a canvas hammock that rocked back and forth in a room of other hammocks.

"Carol?" Still half-asleep, he looked around, then lay back, hoping that he might wake and find this just a dream. He felt the distance from himself he often felt in dreams. But the room did not go away, and the smell of sweat and salt water and some overwhelming stink of oil became more real. The light slanting down through a latticed grating above became brighter; he heard the sound of water and the creak of canvas, and the swaying did not stop, and the men about him began to stir. It came to him, in that same dreamlike calm, that he was on a ship.

A bell sounded twice, then twice again. Most of the other men were up, grumbling, and stowing away the hammocks.

"What ails you, Fallon?" someone called. "Up, now."

two

His name was Patrick Fallon. He was thirty-two years old, a broker for a commission house at the Chicago Board of Trade. He played squash at an athletic club every Tuesday and Thursday night. He lived with a woman named Carol Bukaty.

The night before, he and Carol had gone to a party thrown by one of the other brokers and his wife. As sometimes happened with these parties, this one had degenerated into an exchange of sexual innuendo, none of it apparently serious, but with undertones of suspicion and the desire to hurt. Fallon had had too much wine and had said a few things to the hostess and about Carol that he had immediately wanted to retract. They'd driven back from the party in silence, but the minute they'd closed the door it had been a fight. Neither of them shouted, but his quiet statement that he did not respect her at all and hers that she was sickened by his excess, managed quite well. They had become adept at getting at each other. They had, in the end, made up, and had made love.

As Fallon had lain there on the edge of sleep, he had had the idle thought that what had happened that evening was silly, but not funny. That something was wrong.

Fallon had the headache that was the residue of the wine; he could still smell Carol. He was very hungry and dazed as he stumbled into the bright sunlight on the deck of the ship. It was there. It was real. He was awake. The ocean stretched flat and empty in all directions. The ship rolled slightly as it made way with the help of a light wind, and despite the early morning it was already hot. He did not hear the sound or feel the vibration of an engine. Fallon stared, unable to collect the scattered impressions into coherence; they were all consistent with the picture of an antiquated sailing ship on a very real ocean, all insane when compared with where his mind told him he ought to be.

The men had gone to their work as soon as they'd stretched into the morning light. They wore drab shirts and canvas trousers; most were barefoot. Fallon walked unsteadily along the deck, trying to keep out of their way as they set to scrubbing the deck. The ship was unlike anything he had ever seen on Lake Michigan; he tried to ignore the salt smell that threatened to make it impossible for him to convince himself this was Lake Michigan. Yet it seemed absurd for such a small vessel to be in the middle of an ocean. He knew that the Coast Guard kept sailing ships for training its cadets, but these were no cadets.

The deck was worn, scarred, and greasy with a kind of oily, clear lardlike grease. The rail around the deck was varnished black and weather-beaten, but the pins set through it to which the rigging was secured were ivory. Fallon touched one—it was some kind of tooth. More ivory was used for rigging-blocks and on the capstan around which the anchor chain was wound. The ship was a thing of black wood fading to white under the assault of water and sun, and of white ivory corroding to black under the effect of dirt and hard use. Three longboats, pointed at both ends, hung from arms of wood and metal on the left—the port—side; another such boat was slung at the rear of the deck on the starboard side, and on the raised part of the deck behind the mainmast two other boats were turned turtle and secured. Add to this the large hatch on the main deck and a massive brick structure that looked like some old-fashioned oven just behind the front mast, and there hardly seemed room for the fifteen or twenty men on deck to go about their business. There was certainly no place to hide.

"Fallon! Set your elbows to that deck, or I shall have to set your nose to it!" A short sandy-haired man accosted him. Stocky and muscular, he was some authority; there was insolence in his grin, and some seriousness. The other men looked up.

Fallon got out of the man's way. He went over to one of the groups washing down the deck with salt water, large scrub brushes, and what looked like push brooms with leather flaps instead of bristles, like large versions of the squeegees used to clean windows. The sandy-haired man watched him as he got down on his hands and knees and grabbed one of the brushes.

"There's a good lad, now. Ain't he, fellows?"

A couple of them laughed. Fallon started scrubbing, concentrating on the grain of the wood, at first fastidious about not wetting the already damp trousers he had apparently slept in, soon realizing that that was a lost cause. The warm water was sloshed over them, the men leaned on the brushes, and the oil slowly flaked up and away through the spaces in the rail into the sea. The sun rose, and it became even hotter. Now and then one of the men tried to say a word or two to him, but he did not answer.

"Fallon here's got the hypos," someone said.

"Or the cholera," another said. "He does look a bit bleary about the eye. Are you thirsty, Fallon? D'your legs ache? Are your bowels knotted?"

"My bowels are fine," he said.

That brought a good laugh. "Fine, he says! Manxman!" The sailor called to a decrepit old man leaning on his squeegee. "Tell the King-Post that Fallon's bowels are fine, now! The scrubbing does seem to have eased them."

"Don't ease them here, man!" the old man said seriously. The men roared again, and the next bucket of water was sloshed up between Fallon's legs.

three

In the movies men had faced similar situations. The amnesiac soldier came to on a farm in Wales. But invariably the soldier would give evidence of his confusion, challenging the farm owner, pestering his fellow workers with questions about where he was and how he got there, telling them of his persistent memory of a woman in white with golden hair. Strangely—strangely even to Fallon—he did not feel that way. Confusion, yes, dread, curiosity —but no desire to call attention to himself, to try to make the obvious reality of his situation give way to the apparent reality of his memories. He did not think this was because of any strength of character or remarkable powers of adaptation. In fact, everything he did that first day revealed his ignorance of what he was supposed to know and do on the ship. He did not feel any great presence of mind; for minutes at a time he would stop working, stunned with awe and fear at the simple alienness of what was happening. If it was a dream, it was a vivid dream. If anything was a dream, it was Carol and the Chicago Board of Trade.

The soldier in the movie always managed, despite the impediments of his amnesia and the ignorance of those around him, to find the rational answer to his mystery. The shell fragment that had grazed his forehead in Normandy had sent him back to a Wessex sanitorium, from which he had wandered during an air raid, to be picked up by a local handyman driving his lorry to Llanelly, who in the course of the journey decided to turn a few quid by leasing the poor soldier to a farmer as his half-wit cousin laborer. So it had to be that some physicist at the University of Chicago, working on the modern equivalent of the Manhattan Project, had accidentally created a field of gravitational energy so intense that a vagrant vortex had broken free from it and, in its lightning progress through the city on its way to extinction, plucked Fallon from his bed in the suburbs, sucked him through a puncture in the fabric of space and time, to deposit him in a hammock on a midnineteenth-century sailing ship. Of course.

Fallon made a fool of himself ten times over during the day. Despite his small experience with fresh-water sailing, he knew next to nothing about the work he was meant to do on this ship. Besides cleaning the deck and equipment, the men scrubbed a hard black soot from the rigging and spars. Fallon would not go up into the rigging. He was afraid, and tried to find work enough on the deck. He did not ask where the oil and soot had come from; it was obvious the source had been the brick furnace that was now topped by a tight-fitting wooden cover. Some of the cracks in the deck were filled with what looked like dried blood, but it was only the casual remark of one of the other men that caused him to realize, shocked at his own slowness, that this was a whaling ship.

The crew was an odd mixture of types and races; there were white and black, a group of six Orientals who sat apart on the rear deck and took no part in the work, men with British and German accents, and an eclectic collection of others—Polynesians, an Indian, a huge shaven-headed black African, and a mostly naked man covered from head to toe with purple tattoos, whorls and swirls and vortexes, images and symbols, none of them quite decipherable as a familiar object or person. After the decks had been scrubbed to a remarkable whiteness, the mate named Flask set Fallon to tarring some heavy ropes in the forepart of the ship, by himself, where he would be out of the others' way. The men seemed to realize that something was wrong with him, but said nothing and apparently did not take it amiss that one of their number should begin acting strangely.

Which brought him, hands and wrists smeared with warm tar, to the next question: how did they know who he was? He was Fallon to all of them. He had obviously been there before he awakened; he had been a regular member of the crew with a personality and role to fill. He knew nothing of that. He had the overwhelming desire to get hold of a mirror to see whether the face he wore was indeed the face he had worn in Chicago the night before. The body was the same, down to the appendix scar he'd carried since he was nine years old. His arms and hands were the same; the fatigue he felt and the rawness of his skin told him he had not been doing this type of work long. So assume he was there in his own person, his Chicago person, the *real* Fallon. Was there now some confused nineteenth-century sailor wandering around a brokerage house on Van Buren? The thought made him smile. The sailor at the Board of Trade would probably get the worse of it.

So they knew who he was, even if he didn't remember ever having been here before. There was a Patrick Fallon on the ship, and *he* had somehow been brought here to fill that role. Reasons unknown. Method unknown. Way out . . .

Think of it as an adventure. How many times as a boy had he dreamed of similar escapes from the mundane? Here he was, the answer to a dream, twenty-five years later. It would make a tremendous story when he got back, if he could find someone he could trust enough to tell it to—if he could get back.

There was a possibility that he tried to keep himself from dwelling on. He had come here while asleep, and though this reality gave no evidence of being a dream, if there was a symmetry to insanity, then on waking the next morning, might he not be back in his familiar bed? Logic presented the possibility. He tried not to put too much faith in logic. Logic had not helped him when he was on the wrong side of the soybean market in December 1980.

The long tropic day declined; the sunset was a travel agent's dream. They were traveling east, by the signpost of that light. Fallon waited, sitting by a coil of rope, watching the helmsman at the far end of the ship lean, dozing, on the long ivory tiller that served this ship in place of the wheel with handspikes he was familiar with from Errol Flynn movies. It had to be a bone from some long-dispatched whale, another example of the savage Yankee practicality of whoever had made this whaler. It was a queerly innocent, gruesome artistry. Fallon had watched several idle sailors in the afternoon carving pieces of bone while they ate their scrap of salt pork and hard bread.

"Fallon, you can't sleep out here tonight, unless you want the Old Man to find you lying about." It was a tall sailor of about Fallon's age. He had come down from aloft shortly after Fallon's assignment to the tar bucket, had watched him quietly for some minutes before giving him a few pointers on how the work was done. In the falling darkness Fallon could not make out his expression, but the voice held a quiet distance that might mask just a trace of kindness. Fallon tried to get up and found his legs had grown so stiff he failed on the first try. The sailor caught his arm and helped him to his feet. "You're all right?"

"Yes." Fallon was embarrassed.

"Let's get below, then." They stepped toward the latticed hatch near the bow.

"And there he is," the sailor said, pausing, lifting his chin aft.

"Who?" Fallon looked back with him and saw the black figure there, heavily bearded, tall, in a long coat, steadying himself by a hand in the rigging. The oil lamp above the compass slightly illuminated the dark face—and gleamed deathly white along the ivory leg that projected from beneath his black coat. Fixed, immovable, the man leaned heavily on it.

"Ahab," the sailor said.

four

Lying in the hammock, trying to sleep, Fallon was assaulted by the feverish reality of where he was. The ship rocked him like a gentle parent in its progress through the calm sea; he heard the rush of water breaking against the hull as the *Pequod* made headway, the sighing of the breeze above, heard the steps of the night watch on deck, the occasional snap of canvas, the creaking of braces; he sweated in the oppressive heat belowdecks; he drew heavy breaths, trying to calm himself, of air laden with the smell of mildewed canvas and what he knew to be whale oil. He held his hands before his face and in the profound darkness knew them to be his own. He touched his neck and felt the slickness of sweat beneath the beard. He ran his tongue over his lips and tasted salt. Through the open hatch he could make out stars that were unchallenged by any other light. Would the stars be the same in a book as they were in reality?

In a book. Any chance he had to sleep flew from him whenever he ran up against that thought. Any logic he brought to bear on his situation crumbled under the weight of that absurdity. A time machine he could accept, some chance cosmic displacement that sucked him into the past. But not into a book. That was insanity; that was hallucination. He knew that if he could sleep now, he would wake once more in the real world. But he had nothing to grab hold of. He lay in the darkness listening to the ship and could not sleep at all.

They had been compelled to read *Moby Dick* in the junior-year American Renaissance class he'd taken to fulfill the last of his humanities requirements. Fallon remembered being bored to tears by most of Melville's book, struggling with his interminable sentences, his woolly speculations that had no bearing on the story; he remembered being caught up by parts of that story. He had seen the movie with Gregory Peck. Richard Basehart, king of the sci-fi flicks, had played Ishmael. Fallon had not seen anyone who looked like Richard Basehart on the ship. The mate, Flask—he remembered that name now. He remembered that all the harpooners were savages. Queequeg.

He remembered that in the end, everyone but Ishmael died.

He had to get back. Sleep, sleep, you idiot, he told himself. He could not keep from laughing; it welled up in his chest and burst through his tightly closed lips. Fallon's laugh sounded more like a man gasping for breath than one overwhelmed by humor: he barked, he chuckled, he sucked in sudden drafts of air as he tried to control the spasms. Tears were in his eyes, and he twisted his head from side to side as if he were strapped to a bed in some ward. Some of the others stirred and cursed him, but Fallon, a character in a book where everyone died on the last page, shook with helpless laughter, crying, knowing he would not sleep.

five

With a preternatural clarity born of the sleepless night, Fallon saw the deck of the *Pequod* the next morning. He was a little stunned yet, but if he kept his mind in tight check the fatigue would keep him from thinking, and he would not feel the distress that was waiting to burst out again. Like a man carrying a bowl filled with acid, Fallon carried his knowledge tenderly.

He observed with scientific detachment, knowing that sleep would ultimately come, and with it perhaps escape. The day was bright and fair, a duplicate of the previous one. The whaler was clean and prepared for her work; all sails were set to take advantage of the light breeze, and the mastheads were manned with lookouts. Men loitered on deck. On the rear deck—the quarterdeck, they called it—Ahab paced, with remarkable steadiness for a man wearing an ivory leg, between the compass in its box and the mainmast, stopping for seconds to stare pointedly at each end of his path. Fallon could not take his eyes off the man. He was much older than Fallon had imagined him from his memories of the book. Ahab's hair and beard were still black, except for the streak of white that ran through them as the old scar ran top to bottom across his face, but the face itself was deeply worn, and the man's eyes were sunken in wrinkles, hollow. Fallon remembered Tigue, who had traded in the gold pit, who had once been the best boy on the floor—the burnout, they called him now, talking a very good game about shorting the market. Tigue's eyes had the same hollow expectation of disaster waiting inevitably for him—just him—that Ahab's held. Yet when Fallon had decided Ahab had to be the same empty nonentity, the man would pause at the end of his pathway and stare at the compass, or the gold coin that was nailed to the mast, and his figure would tighten in the grip of some stiffening passion, as if he were shot through with lightning. As if he were at the focal point of some cosmic lens that concentrated all the power of the sun on him, so that he might momentarily burst into spontaneous flame.

Ahab talked to himself, staring at the coin. His voice was conversational, and higher pitched than Fallon had imagined it would be. Fallon was not the only man who watched him in wonder and fear.

"There's something ever egotistical in mountaintops and towers, and all other grand and lofty things; look here—three peaks as proud as Lucifer. The firm tower, that is Ahab; the volcano, that is Ahab; the courageous, the undaunted, and victorious fowl, that, too, is Ahab; all are Ahab; and this round gold is but the image of the rounder globe, which, like a magician's glass, to each and every man in turn but mirrors back his own mysterious self. . . ."

All spoken in the tone of a man describing a minor auto accident (the brown Buick swerved to avoid the boy on the bicycle, crossed over the yellow line, and hit the milk truck, which was going south on Main Street). As soon as he had stopped, Ahab turned and, instead of continuing his pacing, went quietly below.

One of the ship's officers—the first mate, Fallon thought—who had been talking to the helmsman before Ahab began to speak, now advanced to look at the coin. Fallon began to remember what was going to happen. Theatrically, though there was nobody there to listen to him, the mate began to speak aloud about the Trinity and the sun, hope and despair. Next came another mate, who talked of spending the doubloon quickly, then gave a reading comparing the signs of the zodiac to a man's life. Overwritten and silly, Fallon thought.

Flask now came to the doubloon and figured out how many cigars he could buy with it. Then came the old man who had sloshed the water all over Fallon the previous morning, who gave a reading of the ship's doom under the sign of the lion. Then Queequeg, then one of the Orientals, then a black boy—the cabin boy.

The boy danced around the mast twice, crouching low, rising on his toes, and each time around stared at the doubloon with comically bugged eyes. He stopped. "I look, you look, he looks, we look, ye look, they look."

I look, you look, he looks, we look, ye look, they look.

They all looked at it; they all spouted their interpretations. That was what Melville had wanted them to do to prove his point. Fallon did not feel like trying to figure out what that point was. After the dramatics, the *Pequod* went back to dull routine, and he to cleanup work on the deck, to tarring more ropes. They had a lot of ropes.

He took a break and walked up to the mast to look at the coin himself. Its surface was stamped with the image of three mountains, with a flame, a tower, and a rooster at their peaks. Above were the sun and the signs of the zodiac. REPUBLICA DEL EQUADOR: QUITO, it said. A couple of ounces, worth maybe $1,300 on the current gold market, according to the London fix Fallon last remembered. It wouldn't be worth as much to these men, of course; this was preinflation money. He remembered that the doubloon had been nailed there by Ahab as a reward to whoever spotted Moby Dick first.

I look, you look, he looks, we look, ye look, they look.

Fallon looked, and nothing changed. His tiredness grew as the day wore through a brutally hot afternoon. When evening at last came and the grumbling of his belly had been at least partially assuaged by the meager meal served the men, Fallon fell exhausted into the hammock. He did not worry about not sleeping this time; consciousness fell away as if he had been drugged. He had a vivid dream. He was trying, under cover of darkness, to pry the doubloon away from the mast so that he might throw it into the sea. Anxiously trying not to let the helmsman at the tiller spot him, he heard the step, tap, step, tap, of Ahab's pacing a deck below. It was one of those dreams where one struggles in unfocused terror to accomplish some simple task. He was afraid he might be found any second by Ahab. If he were caught, then he would be exposed and vilified before the crew's indifferent gaze.

He couldn't do it. He couldn't get his fingers under the edge of the coin, though he bruised them bloody. He heard the knocking of Ahab's whalebone step ascending to the deck; the world contracted to the coin welded to the mast, his broken nails, the terrible fear. He heard the footsteps drawing nearer behind him as he frantically tried to free the doubloon, yet he could not run, and he would not turn around. At the last, after an eternity of anxiety, a hand fell on his shoulder and spun him around, his heart leaping into his throat. It was not Ahab, but Carol.

He woke breathing hard, pulse pounding. He was still in the hammock, in the forecastle of the *Pequod*. He closed his eyes again, dozed fretfully through the rest of the night. Morning came: he was still there.

The next day several of the other men prodded him about not having taken a turn at the masthead for a long time. He stuck to mumbled answers and hoped they would not go to any of the officers. He wanted to disappear. He wanted it to be over. The men treated him more scornfully as the days passed. And the days passed, and still nothing happened to free him. The doubloon glinted in the sun each morning, at the center of the ship, and Fallon could not get away. I look, you look, he looks, we look, ye look, they look.

six

Fallon had assumed his sullen station by the tar bucket. There he felt at least some defense from his confusion. He could concentrate on the smell and feel of the tar; he remembered the summers on the tarred road in front of his grandparents' house in Elmira, how the sun would raise shining bubbles of tar at the edges of the resurfaced country road, how the tar would stick to your sneakers and get you a licking if you tracked it into Grandmother's immaculate kitchen. He and his cousin Seth had broken the bubbles with sticks and watched them slowly subside into themselves. The tar bucket on the *Pequod* was something Fallon could focus on. The tar was real; the air he breathed was real—Fallon himself was real.

Stubb, the second mate, stood in front of him, arms akimbo. He stared at Fallon; Fallon lifted his head and saw the man's small smile. There was no charity in it.

"Time to go aloft, Fallon. You've been missing your turn, and we won't have any slackers aboard."

Fallon couldn't think of anything to say. He stumbled to his feet, wiping his hands on a piece of burlap. A couple of the other sailors were watching, waiting for Fallon to shy off or for Stubb to take him.

"Up with ye!" Stubb shoved Fallon's shoulder, and he turned, fumbling for the rigging. Fallon looked momentarily over the side of the ship to the sea that slid calmly by them; the gentle rolling of the deck that he had in so short a time become accustomed to now returned to him with frightening force. Stubb was still behind him. Taking a good breath, he pulled himself up and stepped barefoot onto the rail. Facing inward now, he tried to climb the rigging. Stubb watched him with dispassion, waiting, it seemed, for his failure. Expecting it. It was like trying to climb one of those rope ladders at the county fair: each rung he took twisted the ladder in the direction of his weight, and the rocking of the ship, magnified as he went higher, made it hard for his feet to find the next step. He had never been a particularly self-conscious man, but felt he was being watched by them all now and was acutely conscious of how strange he must seem. How touched with idiocy and fear.

Nausea rose, the deck seemed farther below than it had any reason to be, the air was stifling; the wind was without freshness and did not cool the sweat from his brow and neck. He clutched the ropes desperately; he tried to take another step, but the strength seemed drained from his legs. Humiliated, burning with shame yet at the same time mortally afraid of falling—and of more than that, of the whole thing, of the fact that here he was where he ought not to be, cheated, abused, mystified—he wrapped his arms around the rigging, knees wobbly, sickness in his gut, bile threatening to heave itself up the back of his throat. Crying, eyes clenched tight, he wished it would all go away.

"Fallon! Fallon, you dog, you dog*fish*, why don't you climb! You had better climb, weak-liver, for I don't want you down on my deck again if you won't!" Stubb roared his rage. Fallon opened his eyes, saw the red-faced man staring furiously up at him. Perhaps he'll have a stroke, Fallon thought.

He hung there, half-up, half-down, unable to move. I want to go home, he thought. Let me go home. Stubb raged and ridiculed him; others gathered to laugh and watch. Fallon closed his eyes and tried to go away. He heard a sound like the wooden mallet of the carpenter.

"What is the problem here, Mr. Stubb?" A calm voice. Fallon looked down again. Ahab stood with his hand on the mainmast to steady himself, looking up. His thumb was touching the doubloon.

Stubb was taken by surprise, as if Ahab were some apparition that had been called up by an entirely inappropriate spell. He jerked his head upward to indicate Fallon.

Squinting against the sun, Ahab studied Fallon for some time. His face was unnaturally pale in comparison to the tanned faces of the others turned up to look at him. Yet against the pallor, the white scar ran, a deathlike sign, down the side of his face. His dark hair was disarrayed in the hot breeze. He was an old man; he swayed in the attempt to steady himself.

"Why don't ye go up?" Ahab called to Fallon.

Fallon shook his head. He tried to step up another rung, but though his foot found the rope, he didn't seem to have the strength he needed to pull himself up.

Ahab continued to regard him. He did not seem impatient or angry, only curious, as if Fallon were an animal sitting frozen on a traffic mall, afraid of the cars that passed. He seemed content to stand watching Fallon indefinitely. Stubb shifted nervously from foot to foot, his anger displaced and negated. The crewmen simply watched. Some of them peered above Fallon in the rigging; the ropes he clung to jerked, and he looked up himself to see that the man who had been standing at the masthead was coming down to help him.

"Bulkington!" Ahab cried, waving to the man to stop. "Let him be!" The sailor retreated upward and swung himself onto the yard-arm above the mainsail. The *Pequod* waited. If there were whales to be hunted, they waited too.

Very distinctly, so that Fallon heard every word, Ahab said, "You must go up. You have taken the vow with the rest, and I will not have you go back on it. Would you go back on it? You must go up, or else you must come down, and show yourself for the coward and weakling you would then be."

Fallon clung to the rigging. He had taken no vow. It was all a story. What difference did it make what he did in a story? If he was to be a character in a book, why couldn't he defy it, do what he wanted instead of following the path they indicated? By coming down he could show himself as himself.

"Have faith!" Ahab called.

Above him, Bulkington hawked and spat, timing it so that with the wind and the rocking of the *Pequod*, he hit the sea and not the deck. Fallon bent his head back and looked up at him. It was the kind sailor who had helped him below on that first night. He hung suspended. He looked down and watched Ahab sway with the rolling of the deck, his eyes still fixed on Fallon. The man was crazy. Melville was crazy for inventing him.

Fallon clenched his teeth, pulled on the ropes, and pushed himself up another step toward the masthead. He was midway up the mainsail, thirty feet above the deck. He concentrated on one rung at a time, breathing steadily, and pulled himself up. When he reached the level of the main yard, Bulkington swung himself below Fallon and helped him along. The complicated motion that came when the sailor stepped onto the ropes had Fallon clinging once again, but this time he was out of it fairly quickly. They ascended, step by dizzying step, to the masthead. The sailor got into the port masthead hoop, helping Fallon into the starboard. The *Pequod*'s flag snapped in the wind a couple of feet above their heads.

"And here we are, Fallon," Bulkington said. Immediately he dropped himself down into the rigging again, so nimbly and suddenly that Fallon's breath was stopped in fear for the man's fall.

Way below, the men were once more stirring. Ahab exchanged some words with Stubb; then, moving out to the rail and steadying himself by a hand on one of the stays, a foreshortened black puppet far below, he turned his white face up to Fallon once again. Cupping his hand to his mouth, he shouted, "Keep a steady eye, now! If ye see fin or flank of him, call away!"

Call away. Fallon was far above it all now, alone. He had made it. He had taken no vow and was not obligated to do anything he did not wish to. He had ascended to the masthead of his own free will, but, if he was to become a whaler, then what harm would there be in calling out whales—normal whales? Not literary ones. Not white ones.

He looked out to the horizon. The sea stretched out to the utmost ends of the world, covering it all, every secret, clear and blue and a little choppy under the innocent sky.

seven

Fallon became used to the smell of the *Pequod*. He became accustomed to feeling sweaty and dirty, to the musty smell of mildew and the tang of brine trying to push away the stench of the packing plant.

He had not always been fastidious in his other life. In the late sixties, after he had dropped out of Northwestern, he had lived in an old house in a rundown neighborhood with three other men and a woman. They had called it "The Big House," and to the outside observer they must have been hippies. "Hair men." "Freaks." "Dropouts." It was a vocabulary that seemed quaint now. The perpetual pile of dirty dishes in the sink, the Fillmore West posters, the black light, the hot and cold running roaches, the early-fifties furniture with corners shredded to tatters by their three cats. Fallon realized that that life had been as different from his world at the Board of Trade as the deck of the *Pequod* was now.

Fallon had dropped out because, he'd told himself, there was nothing he wanted from the university that he couldn't get from its library, or by hanging around the student union. It was hard for him to believe how much he had read then: Skinner's behaviorism, Spengler's history, pop physics and Thomas Kuhn, Friedman and Galbraith, Shaw, Conrad, Nabokov, and all he could find of Hammett, Chandler, Macdonald, and their imitators. Later he had not been able to figure out just why he had forsaken a degree so easily; he didn't know if he was too irresponsible to do the work, or too slow, or above it all and following his own path. Certainly he had not seen himself as a rebel, and the revolutionary fervor his peers affected (it had seemed affectation ninety percent of the time) never took hold of Fallon completely. He had observed, but not taken part in, the melee at the Democratic Convention. But he put in his time in the back bedroom listening to The Doors and blowing dope until the world seemed no more than a slightly bigger version of the Big House and his circle of friends. He read *The Way of Zen*. He knew Hesse and Kerouac. He hated Richard Nixon and laughed at Spiro Agnew. Aloft in the rigging of the *Pequod*, those years came back to Fallon as they never had in his last five years at the CBT. What a different person he had been at twenty. What a strange person, he realized, he had become at twenty-eight. What a marvelous —and frightening—metamorphosis.

He had gotten sick of stagnating, he told himself. He had seen one or another of his friends smoke himself into passivity. He had seen through the self-delusions of the other cripples in the Big House: cripples was what he had called them when he'd had the argument with Marty Solokov and had stalked out. Because he broke from that way of living did not mean he was selling out, he'd told them. He could work any kind of job; he didn't want money or a house in the suburbs. He had wanted to give himself the feeling of getting started again, of moving, of putting meaning to each day. He had quit washing dishes for the university, moved into a dingy flat closer to the center of the city, and scanned the help-wanted columns. He still saw his friends often and got stoned maybe not quite so often, and listened to music and read. But he had had enough of "finding himself," and he recognized in the others how finding yourself became an excuse for doing nothing.

Marty's cousin was a runner for Pearson Joel Chones on the Chicago Mercantile Exchange who had occasionally come by the house, gotten high, and gone to concerts. Fallon had slept with her once. He called her up, and she asked around, and eventually he cut his hair short—not too short—and became a runner for Pearson, too. He became marginally better groomed. He took a shower and changed his underwear every day. He bought three ties and wore one of them on the trading floor because that was one of the rules of the exchange.

∞   ∞   ∞

It occurred to Fallon to find Ishmael, if only to see the man who would live while he died. He listened and watched; he learned the name of every man on the ship—he knew Flask and Stubb and Starbuck and Bulkington, Tashtego, Daggoo and Queequeg, identified Fedallah, the lead Philippine boatsman. There *was* no Ishmael. At first Fallon was puzzled, then came the beginnings of hope. If the reality he was living in could be found to differ from the reality of Melville's book in such an important particular, then could it not differ in some other way—some way that would at least lead to his survival? Maybe this Ahab caught his white whale. Maybe Starbuck would steel himself to the point where he could defy the madman and take over the ship. Perhaps they would never sight Moby Dick.

Then an unsettling realization smothered the hope before it could come fully to bloom: there was not necessarily an Ishmael in the book. "*Call* me Ishmael," it started. Ishmael was a pseudonym for some other man, and there would be no one by that name on the *Pequod*. Fallon congratulated himself on a clever bit of literary detective work.

Yet the hope refused to remain dead. Yes, there was no Ishmael on the *Pequod*; or anyone on the ship not specifically named in the book might be Ishmael, any one of the anonymous sailors, within certain broad parameters of age and character—and Fallon racked his brain trying to remember what the narrator said of himself— might be Ishmael. He grabbed at that; he breathed in the possibility and tried on the suit for size. Why not? If absurdity were to rule to the extent that he had to be there in the first place, then why couldn't he be the one who lived? More than that, why couldn't he make himself that man? No one else knew what Fallon knew. He had the advantage over them. Do the things that Ishmael did, and you may be him. If you have to be a character in a book, why not be the hero?

∞   ∞   ∞

Fallon's first contact with the heart of capitalism at the CME had been frightening and amusing. Frightening when he screwed up and delivered a May buy-order as a July trade and cost the company ten thousand dollars. It was only through the grace of God and his own guts in facing it out that he had made it through the disaster. He had, he discovered, the ability to hide himself behind a facade that, to the self-interested observer, would appear to be whatever that observer wished it to be. If his superior expected him to be respect- ful and curious, then Fallon was respectfully curious. He did it without having to compromise his inner self. He was not a hypo- crite.

The amusing part came after he had it all down and he began to watch the market like an observer at a very complex Monopoly game. Or, more accurately, like a baseball fan during a pennant race. There were at least as many statistics as in a good baseball season, enough personalities, strategies, great plays, blunders, risk, and luck. Fallon would walk onto the floor at the beginning of the day—the huge room with its concert-hall atmosphere, the banks of price boards around the walls, the twilight, the conditioned air, the hundreds of bright-coated traders and agents—and think of half- time at homecoming. The floor at the end of the day, as he walked across the hardwood scattered with mounds of paper scraps like so much confetti, was a basketball court after the NCAA finals. Top- ping it all off, giving it that last significant twist that was necessary to all good jokes, was the fact that this was all supposed to mean something; it was real money they were playing with, and one tick of the board in Treasury Bills cost somebody eleven hundred dollars. This was serious stuff, kid. The lifeblood of the nation—of the free world. Fallon could hardly hold in his laughter, could not stop his fascination.

∞   ∞   ∞

Fallon's first contact with the whale—his first lowering—was in Stubb's boat. The man at the forward masthead cried out, "There she blows! Three points off starboard! There she blows! Three—no, four of 'em!"

The men sprang to the longboats and swung them away over the side. Fallon did his best to look as if he was helping. Stubb's crew leapt into the boat as it was dropped into the swelling sea, heedless to the possibility of broken bones or sprained ankles. Fallon hesitated a second at the rail, then threw himself off with the feeling of a man leaping off the World Trade Center. He landed clumsily and half bowled over one of the men. He took his place at a center oar and pulled away. Like the man falling off the building, counting off the stories as they flew past him, Fallon thought, "So far, so good." And waited for the crash.

"Stop snoring, ye sleepers, and pull!" Stubb called, halfway between jest and anger. "Pull, Fallon! Why don't you pull? Have you never seen an oar before? Don't look over your shoulder, lad, *pull!* That's better. Don't be in a hurry, men—softly, softly now—but damn ye, pull until you break something! Tashtego! Can't you harpoon me some men with backs to them? *Pull!*"

Fallon pulled until he thought the muscles in his arms would snap, until the small of his back spasmed as if he were indeed being harpooned by the black-haired Indian behind him in the bow. The sea was rough, and they were soon soaked with spray. After a few minutes Fallon forgot the whales they pursued, merged into the rhythm of the work, fell in with the cunning flow of Stubb's curses and pleas, the crazy sermon, now whispered, now shouted. He concentrated on the oar in his hands, the bite of the blade into the water, the simple mechanism his body had become, the working of his lungs, the dry rawness of the breath dragged in and out in time to their rocking, backbreaking work. Fallon closed his eyes, heard the pulse in his ears, felt the cool spray and the hot sun, saw the rose fog of the blood in his eyelids as he faced into the bright and brutal day.

∞   ∞   ∞

At twenty-five, Fallon was offered a position in the office upstairs. At twenty-seven, he had an offer from DCB International to become a broker. By that time he was living with Carol. Why not? He was still outside it all, still safe within. Let them think what they would of him; he was protected, in the final analysis, by that great indifference he held to his breast the way he held Carol close at night. He was not a hypocrite. He said nothing he did not believe in. Let them project upon him whatever fantasies they might hold dear to themselves. He was outside and above it all, analyzing futures for DCB International. Clearly, in every contract that crossed his desk, it was stated that DCB and its brokers were not responsible for reverses that might be suffered as a result of suggestions they made.

So he had spent the next four years apart from it, pursuing his interests, which, with the money he was making, he found were many. Fallon saw very little of the old friends now. Solokov's cousin told him he was now in New York, cadging money from strangers in Times Square. Solokov, she said, claimed it was a pretty good living. He claimed he was still beating the system. Fallon had grown up enough to realize that no one really beat any system—as if there were a system. There was only buying and selling, subject to the forces of the market and the infirmities of the players. Fallon was on the edges of it, could watch quietly, taking part as necessary (he had to eat), but still stay safe. He was no hypocrite.

∞   ∞   ∞

"To the devil with ye, boys, will ye be outdone by Ahab's heathens? Pull, spring it, my children, my fine hearts-alive, smoothly, smoothly, bend it hard starboard! Aye, Fallon, let me see you sweat, lad, can you sweat for me?"

They rose on the swell, and it was like rowing uphill; they slid down the other side, still rowing, whooping like children on a toboggan ride, all the time Stubb calling on them. Fallon saw Starbuck's boat off to his right; he heard the rush of water beneath them, and the rush of something faster and greater than their boat.

Tashtego grunted behind him.

"A hit, a hit!" Stubb shouted, and beside Fallon the whaleline was running out with such speed that it sang and hummed and smoked. One of the men sloshed water over the place where it slid taut as a wire over the gunnel. Then the boat jerked forward so suddenly that Fallon was nearly knocked overboard when his oar, still trailing in the water, slammed into his chest. Gasping at the pain, he managed to get the oar up into the air. Stubb had half risen from his seat in the stern.

They flew through the water. The whaleboat bucked as it slapped the surface of every swell the whale pulled them through. Fallon held on for dear life, not sure whether he ought to be grateful he hadn't been pitched out when the ride began. He tried to twist around to see the monster that was towing them, but able to turn only halfway, all he could see for the spray and the violent motion was the swell and rush of white water ahead of them. Tashtego, crouched in the bow, grinned wickedly as he tossed out wooden blocks tied to the whaleline in order to tire the whale with their drag. You might as well try to tire a road grader.

Yet he could not help but feel exhilarated, and he saw that the others in the boat, hanging on or trying to draw the line in, were flushed and breathing as hard as he.

He turned again and saw the whale.

∞ ∞ ∞

Fallon had been a good swimmer in high school. He met Carol Bukaty at a swimming pool about a year after he had gone to work at the CME. Fallon first noticed her in the pool, swimming laps. She was the best swimmer there, better than he, though he might have been stronger than she in the short run. She gave herself over to the water and did not fight it; the kick of her long legs was steady and strong. She breathed easily and her strokes were relaxed, yet powerful. She did not swim for speed, but she looked as if she could swim for days, so comfortable did she seem in the water. Fallon sat on the steps at the pool's edge and watched her for half an hour without once getting bored. He found her grace in the water arousing. He knew he had to speak to her. He slid into the pool and swam laps behind her.

At last she stopped. Holding on to the trough at the end of the pool, she pushed her goggles up onto her forehead and brushed the wet brown hair away from her eyes. He drew up beside her.

"You swim very well," he said.

She was out of breath. "Thank you."

"You look as if you wouldn't ever need to come out of the

water. Like anything else might be a comedown after swimming."
It was a strange thing for him to say, it was not what he wanted to
say, but he did not know what he wanted, besides her.

She looked puzzled, smiled briefly, and pulled herself onto the
side of the pool, letting her legs dangle in the water. "Sometimes
I feel that way," she said. "I'm Carol Bukaty." She stuck out her
hand, very businesslike.

"Pat Fallon."

She wore a gray tank suit; she was slender and small-breasted,
tall, with a pointed chin and brown eyes. Fallon later discovered
that she was an excellent dancer, that she purchased women's
clothing for one of the major Chicago department stores, that she
traveled a great deal, wrote lousy poetry, disliked cooking, liked
children, and liked him. At first he was merely interested in her sex-
ually, though the first few times they slept together it was not very
good at all. Gradually the sex got better, and in the meantime
Fallon fell in love.

She would meet him at the athletic club after work; they would
play racquetball in the late afternoon, go out to dinner, and take in
a movie, then spend the night at his or her apartment. He met her
alcoholic father, a retired policeman who told endless stories about
ward politics and the Daley machine, and Carol spent a Christmas
with him at his parents'. After they moved in together, they settled
into a comfortable routine. He felt secure in her affection for him.
He did not want her, after a while, as much as he had that first day,
those first months, but he still needed her. It still mattered to him
what she was doing and what she thought of him. Sometimes it
mattered to him too much, he thought. Sometimes he wanted to be
without her at all, not because he had anything he could only do
without her, but only because he wanted to *be* without her.

He would watch her getting dressed in the morning and wonder
what creature she might be, and what that creature was doing in
the same room with him. He would lie beside her as she slept,
stroking the short brown hair at her temple with his fingertips, and
be overwhelmed with the desire to possess her, to hold her head between his hands and know everything that she was; he would shake
with the sudden frustration of its impossibility until it was all he
could do to keep from striking her. Something was wrong with him,
or with her. He had fantasies of how much she would miss him if he
died, of what clothes she would wear to the funeral, of what stories
she would tell her lovers in the future after he was gone.

If Carol felt any of the same things about him, she did not tell him. For Fallon's part, he did not try to explain what he felt in any but the most oblique ways. She should know how he felt, but of course she did not. So when things went badly, and they began to do so more and more, it was not possible for him to explain to her what was wrong, because he could not say it himself, and the pieces of his discontent were things that he was too embarrassed to admit. Yet he could not deny that sometimes he felt as if it was all over between them, that he felt nothing—and at others he would smile just to have her walk into the room.

∞   ∞   ∞

Remarkable creature though the whale was, it was not so hard to kill one after all. It tired, just as a man would tire under the attack of a group of strangers. It slowed in the water, no longer able so effortlessly to drag them after it. They pulled close, and Stubb drove home the iron, jerked it back and forth, drew it out and drove it home again, fist over fist on the hilt, booted foot over the gunnel braced against the creature's flesh, sweating, searching for the whale's hidden life. At last he found it, and the whale shuddered and thrashed a last time, spouting pink mist, then dark blood, where once it spouted feathery white spray. Like a man, helpless in the end, it rolled over and died. Stubb was jolly, and the men were methodical; they tied their lines around the great tail and, as shadows grew long and the sun fell perpendicularly toward the horizon, drew the dead whale to the *Pequod*.

eight

During the cutting up and boiling down of the whale that night, Fallon, perhaps in recognition of his return to normality as indicated by his return to the masthead, was given a real job: slicing the chunks of blubber that a couple of other sailors were hewing out of the great strips that were hauled over the side, into "bible leaves." Fallon got the hang of it pretty quickly, though he was not fast, and Staley, the British sailor who was cutting beside him, kept poking at him to do more. "I'm doing all the work, Fallon," he said, as if his ambition in life were to make sure that he did no more than his own share of the work.

Using a sharp blade like a long cleaver, Fallon would position the chunk of blubber, skin-side down on the cutting table, and imitating Staley, cut the piece into slices like the pages of a book, with the skin as its spine. The blubber leaves flopped outward or stuck to each other, and the table became slick with grease. Fallon was at first careful about avoiding his hands, but the blubber would slide around the table as he tried to cut it if he didn't hold it still. Staley pushed him on, working with dexterity, though Fallon noted that the man's hands were scarred, with the top joint of the middle finger of his left hand missing.

His back and shoulders ached with fatigue, and the smoke from the try-works stung his eyes. When he tried to wipe the tears away, he only smeared his face with grease. But he did a creditable job, cursing all the time. The cursing helped, and the other men seemed to accept him more for it. When finally they were done, and the deck was clean the next day, they were issued a tot of grog and allowed to swim within the lee of the stationary ship. The men were more real to him than when he had sat and watched from the outcast's station of the tar bucket. He was able to speak to them more naturally than he had ever done. But he did not forget his predicament.

"Ye are too serious, Fallon," Staley told him, offering Fallon some of his grog. "I can see you brooding there, and look how it set you into a funk. Ye are better now, perhaps, but mind you, stick to your work and ye may survive this voyage."

"I won't survive it. Neither will you—unless we can do something about Captain Ahab."

Bulkington, who had been watching them, came by. "What of Captain Ahab?"

Fallon saw a chance in this. "Does his seeking after this white whale seem right to you?"

"The whale took his leg," Staley said.

"Some say it unmanned him," the other said, lower. "That's two legs you'd not like to lose yourself, I'll daresay."

Fallon drew them aside, more earnest now. "We will lose more than our balls if we do nothing about this situation. The man is out of his mind. He will drag us all down with him, and this ship with all of us, if we can't convince Starbuck to do something. Believe me, I know."

Friendly Bulkington did not look so friendly. "You do talk strange, Fallon. We took an oath, and we signed the papers before we even sailed a cable from shore. A captain is a captain. You are talking mutiny."

He had to go carefully.

"No, wait. Listen to me. Why are we sent on this trip? Think of the—the stockholders, or whatever you call them. The owners. They sent us out to hunt whales."

"The white whale is a whale." Staley looked petulant.

"Yes, of course it's a whale. But there are hundreds of whales to be caught and killed. We don't need to hunt that one. Hasn't he set his sights on just Moby Dick? What about that oath? That gold piece on the mast? That says he's just out for vengeance. There was nothing about vengeance in the papers we signed. What do you think the owners would say if they knew about what he plans? Do you think they would approve of this wild-goose chase?"

Staley was lost. "Goose chase?"

Bulkington was interested. "Go on."

Fallon had his foot in the door; he marshaled the arguments he had rehearsed over and over again. "There's no more oil in Moby Dick than in another whale. . . ."

"They say he's monstrous big," Staley interjected.

Fallon looked pained. "Not so big as any two whales, then. Ahab is not after any oil you can boil out of the whale's flesh. If the owners knew what he intended, the way I do, if they knew how sick he was the week before he came out of that hole of a cabin he lives in, if they saw that light in his eye and the charts he keeps in his cabinet. . . ."

"Charts? What charts? Have you been in his cabin?"

"No, not exactly," Fallon said. "Look, I know some things, but that's just because I keep my eyes open and I have some sources."

"Fallon, where do you hail from? I swear that I cannot half the time make out what you are saying. Sources? What do you mean by that?"

"Oh, Jesus!" He had hoped for better from Bulkington.

Staley darkened. "Don't blaspheme, man! I'll not take the word of a blasphemer."

Fallon saw another opening. "You're right! I'm sorry. But look, didn't the old man himself blaspheme more seriously than I ever could the night of that oath? If you are a God-fearing man, Staley, you'll know that that is true. Would you give your obedience to such a man? Moby Dick is just another of God's creatures, a dumb animal. Is it right to seek vengeance on an animal? Do you want to be responsible for that? God would not approve."

Staley looked troubled, but stubborn. "Do not tell me what the

Almighty approves. That is not for the likes of you to know. And Ahab is the captain." With that he walked to the opposite side of the deck and stood there watching them as if he wanted to separate himself as much as possible from the conversation, yet still know what was going on.

Fallon was exasperated and tired.

"Why don't you go with Staley, Bulkington? You don't have to stick around with me, you know. I'm not going to do your reputation any good."

Bulkington eyed him steadily. "You are a strange one, Fallon. I did not think anything of you when I first saw you on the *Pequod*. But you may be talking some sense."

"Staley doesn't think so."

Bulkington took a pull on his grog. "Why did you try to persuade Staley of Ahab's madness? You should have known that you couldn't convince such a man that the sky is blue, if it were written in the articles he signed that it was green. Starbuck perhaps, or me. Not Staley. Don't you listen to the man you are talking to?"

Fallon looked at Bulkington; the tall sailor looked calmly back at him, patient, waiting.

"Okay, you're right," Fallon said. "I have the feeling I would not have a hard time convincing you, anyway. You know Ahab's insane, don't you?"

"It's not for me to say. Ahab has better reasons than those you give to him." He drew a deep breath, looked up at the sky, down at the men who swam in the shadow of the ship. He smiled. "They should be more wary of sharks," he said.

"The world does look a garden today, Fallon. But it may be that the old man's eyes are better than ours."

"You know he's mad, and you won't do anything?"

"The matter will not bear too deep a looking into." Bulkington was silent for a moment. "You know the story about the man born with a silver screw in his navel? How it tasked him, until one day he unscrewed it to divine its purpose?"

Fallon had heard the joke in grade school on the South Side. "His ass fell off."

"You and Ahab are too much like that man."

They both laughed. "I don't have to unscrew my navel," Fallon said. "We're all going to lose our asses anyway."

They laughed again. Bulkington put his arm around his shoulders, and they toasted Moby Dick.

nine

There came a morning when, on pumping out the bilge, someone noticed that considerable whale oil was coming up with the water. Starbuck was summoned and, after descending into the hold himself, emerged and went aft and below to speak with Ahab. Fallon asked one of the others what was going on.

"The casks are leaking. We're going to have to lay up and break them out. If we don't, we stand to lose a lot of oil."

Sometime later Starbuck reappeared. His face was red to the point of apoplexy, and he paced around the quarterdeck with his hands knotted behind his back. They waited for him to tell them what to do; he stared at the crewmen, stopped, and told them to be about their business. "Keep pumping," he told the others. "Maintain the lookout." He then spoke briefly to the helmsman leaning on the whalebone tiller, and retreated to the corner of the quarterdeck to watch the wake of the ship. After a while Ahab himself staggered up onto the deck, found Starbuck, and spoke to him. He then turned to the men on deck.

"Furl the t'gallantsails," he called, "and close reef the topsails, fore and aft; back the main yard; up Burtons, and break out in the main hold."

Fallon joined the others around the hold. Once the work had commenced, he concentrated on lifting, hauling, and not straining his back. The Manxman told them that he had been outside Ahab's cabin during the conference and that Ahab had threatened to shoot Starbuck dead on the spot when the mate demanded they stop chasing the whale to break out the hold. Fallon thought about the anger in Starbuck's face when he'd come up again. It struck him that the Starbuck of Melville's book was pretty ineffectual; he had to be to let that madman go on with the chase. But this Starbuck— whether like the one in the book or not—did not like the way things were going. There was no reason why Fallon had to sit around and wait for things to happen. It was worth a shot.

But not that afternoon.

Racism assured that the hardest work in the dank hold was done by the colored men—Daggoo, Tashtego, and Queequeg. They did not complain. Up to their knees in the bilge, clambering awkwardly over and about the barrels of oil in the murderous heat and unbreathable air of the hold, they did their jobs.

It was evening before the three harpooners were told they could halt for the day, and they emerged, sweaty, covered with slime, and bruised. Fallon collapsed against the side of the try-works; others sat beside him. Tall Queequeg was taken by a coughing fit, then went below to his hammock. Fallon gathered his strength, felt the sweat drying stickily on his arms and neck. There were few clouds, and the moon was waxing full. He saw Starbuck then, standing at the rear of the quarterdeck, face toward the mast. Was he looking at the doubloon?

Fallon got shakily to his feet; his legs were rubbery. The first mate did not notice him until he was close. He looked up.

"Yes?"

"Mr. Starbuck, I need to speak to you."

Starbuck looked at him as if he saw him for the first time. Fallon tried to look self-confident, serious. He'd gotten that one down well at DCB.

"Yes?"

Fallon turned so that he was facing inward toward the deck and Starbuck had his back to it to face him. He could see what was happening away from them and would know if anyone came near.

"I could not help but see that you were angry this morning after speaking to Captain Ahab."

Starbuck looked puzzled.

"I assume that you must have told Ahab about the leaking oil, and he didn't want to stop his hunt of the whale long enough to break out the hold. Am I right?"

The mate watched him guardedly. "What passed between Captain Ahab and me was none of your affair, or of the crew's. Is that what you've come to trouble me with?"

"It is a matter that concerns me," Fallon said. "It concerns the rest of the crew, and it ought to concern you. We are being bound by his orders, and what kind of orders is he giving? I know what you've been thinking; I know that this personal vengeance he seeks frightens and repulses you. I *know* what you're thinking. I could see what was in your mind when you stood at this rail this afternoon. He is not going to stop until he kills us all."

Starbuck seemed to draw back within himself. Fallon saw how beaten the man's eyes were; he did not think the mate was a drinker, but he looked like someone who had just surfaced after a long weekend. He could almost see the clockwork turning within Starbuck, a beat too slow, with the belligerence of the drunk being told the truth about himself that he did not want to admit. Fallon's last fight with Stein Jr. at the brokerage had started that way.

"Get back to your work," Starbuck said. He started to turn away.

Fallon put his hand on his shoulder. "You have to—"

Starbuck whirled with surprising violence and pushed Fallon away so that he nearly stumbled and fell. The man at the tiller was watching them.

"To work! You do not know what I am thinking! I'll have you flogged if you say anything more! A man with a three-hundredth lay has nothing to tell me. Go on, now."

Fallon was hot. "God damn you. You stupid—"

"Enough!" Starbuck slapped him with the back of his hand, the way Stein had tried to slap Fallon. Stein had missed. It appeared that Mr. Starbuck was more effectual than Stein Jr. Fallon felt his bruised cheek. The thing that hurt the most was the way he must have looked, like a hangdog insubordinate who had been shown his place. As Fallon stumbled away, Starbuck said, in a steadier voice, "Tend to your own conscience, man. Let me tend to mine."

ten

Lightning flashed again.

"I now know that thy right worship is defiance. To neither love nor reverence wilt thou be kind; and even for hate thou canst but kill, and all are killed!"

Ahab had sailed them into the heart of a typhoon. The sails were in tatters, and the men ran across the deck shouting against the wind and trying to lash the boats down tighter before they were washed away or smashed. Stubb had gotten his left hand caught between one of the boats and the rail; he now held it with his right and grimaced. The mastheads were touched with St. Elmo's fire. Ahab stood with the lightning rod in his right hand and his right foot planted on the neck of Fedallah, declaiming at the lightning. Fallon held tightly to a shroud to keep from being thrown off his feet. The scene was ludicrous; it was horrible.

"No fearless fool now fronts thee!" Ahab shouted at the storm. "I own thy speechless, placeless power; but to the last gasp of my earthquake life will dispute its unconditional, unintegral mastery in me! In the midst of the personified impersonal, a personality stands here!"

Terrific, Fallon thought. Psychobabble. Melville writes in a storm so Ahab can have a backdrop against which to define himself. They must not have gone in for realism much in Melville's day. He turned and tried to lash the rear quarter boat tighter; its stern had already been smashed in by a wave that had just about swept three men, including Fallon, overboard. Lightning flashed, followed a split second later by the rolling thunder. Fallon recalled that five seconds' count meant the lightning was a mile away; by that measure the last bolt must have hit them in the ass. Most of the crew were staring openmouthed at Ahab and the glowing, eerie flames that touched the masts. The light had the bluish tinge of mercury-vapor lamps in a parking lot. It sucked the color out of things; the faces of the frightened men were the sickly hue of fish bellies.

"Thou canst blind, but I can then grope. Thou canst consume, but I can then be ashes!" You bet. "Take the homage of these poor eyes, and shutter-hands. I would not take it . . . ," Ahab ranted on. Fallon hardly gave a damn anymore. The book was too much. Ahab talked to the storm and the God behind it; the storm answered him back, lightning flash for curse. It was dramatic, stagy; it was real: Melville's universe was created so that such dialogues could take place; the howling gale and the tons of water, the crashing waves, flapping canvas, the sweating, frightened men, the blood and seawater—all were created to have a particular effect, to be sure, but it was the real universe, and it would work that way because that was the way it was set up to work by a frustrated, mystified man chasing his own obsessions, creating the world as a warped mirror of his distorted vision.

"There is some unsuffusing thing beyond thee, thou clear spirit, to whom all thy eternity is but time, all thy creativeness mechanical. . . ."

There is an ex-sailor on a farm in Massachusetts trying to make ends meet while his puzzled wife tries to explain him to the relatives.

"The boat! The boat!" cried Starbuck. "Look at thy boat, old man!"

Fallon looked, and backed away. A couple of feet from him the harpoon that was lashed into the bow was tipped with the same fire that illuminated the masts. Silently within the howling storm, from its barbed end twin streamers of electricity writhed. Fallon backed away to the rail, heart beating quickly, and clutched the slick whalebone.

Ahab staggered toward the boat; Starbuck grabbed his arm. "God! God is against thee, old man! Forbear! It's an ill voyage! Ill begun, ill continued; let me square the yards while we may, old man, and make a fair wind of it homewards, to go on a better voyage than this."

Yes, yes, at last Starbuck had said it! Fallon grabbed one of the braces; he saw others of the crew move to the rigging as if to follow Starbuck's order before it was given. They cried, some of them in relief, others in fear, others as if ready at last to mutiny. Yes!

Ahab threw down the last links of the lightning rod. He grabbed the harpoon from the boat and waved it like a torch about his head; he lurched toward Fallon.

"You!" he shouted, staggering to maintain his balance on the tossing deck, hoisting the flaming harpoon to his shoulder as if he meant to impale Fallon on the spot. "But cast loose that rope's end and you will be transfixed—by this clear spirit!" The electricity at the barb hummed inches before him; Fallon could feel his skin prickling and smelled ozone. He felt the rail at the small of his back, cold. The other sailors fell away from the ropes; Starbuck looked momentarily sick. Fallon let go of the brace.

Ahab grinned at him. He turned and held the glowing steel before him with both hands like a priest holding a candle at mass on a feast day.

"All your oaths to hunt the white whale are as binding as mine; and heart, soul, and body, lung and life, old Ahab is bound. And that you may know to what tune this heart beats; look ye here! Thus I blow out the last fear!"

He blew out the flame.

∞   ∞   ∞

They ran out the night without letting the anchors over the side, heading due into the gale instead of riding with the wind at their backs, with tarpaulins and deck truck blown or washed overboard, with the lightning rod shipped instead of trailing in the sea as it ought to, with the man at the tiller beaten raw about the ribs trying to keep the ship straight, with the compass spinning round like a top, with the torn remains of the sails not cut away until long after midnight.

By morning the storm had much abated, the wind had come around, and they ran before it in heavy seas. Fallon and most of the other common sailors, exhausted, were allowed to sleep.

eleven

The argument with Starbuck and his attempts to rouse others to defy Ahab had made Fallon something of a pariah. He was now as isolated as he had been when he'd first come to himself aboard the *Pequod*. Only Bulkington did not treat him with contempt or fear, but Bulkington would do nothing about the situation. He would rather talk, and they often discussed what a sane man would do in their situation, given the conflicting demands of reason and duty. Fallon's ability to remain detached always failed him somewhere in the middle of these talks.

So Fallon came to look upon his stints at the masthead as escape of a sort. It was there that he had first realized that he could rise above the deck of the *Pequod*, both literally and figuratively, for some moments; it was there that he had first asserted his will after days of stunned debility. He would not sing out for the white whale, if it should be his fortune to sight it, but he did sing out more than once for lesser whales. The leap of his heart at the sight of them was not feigned.

They were sailing the calm Pacific east and south of Japan. They had met the *Rachel*, and a thrill had run through the crew at the news that she had encountered Moby Dick and had failed to get him, losing several boats, and the captain's son, in the process. Fallon's memory was jogged. The *Rachel* would pick up Ishmael at the end of the book, when all the others were dead.

They met the *Delight*, on which a funeral was in progress. From the mainmast lookout, Fallon heard the shouted talk between Ahab and her captain about another failed attempt at the white whale. He watched as the dead man, sewn up in his hammock, was dropped into the sea.

It was a clear steel-blue day. The sea rolled in long, quiet swells; the *Pequod* moved briskly ahead before a fair breeze, until the *Delight* was lost in the distance astern. The air was fresh and clear out to the rim of the world, where it seemed to merge with the darker sea. It was as fair a day as they had seen since Fallon had first stood a watch at the masthead.

Up above the ship, almost out of the world of men entirely, rolling at the tip of the mast in rhythm to the rolling of the sea swells, which moved in time with his own easy breathing, Fallon lost his fear. He seemed to lose even himself. Who was he? Patrick Fallon, analyst for a commodities firm. Perhaps that had been some delusion; perhaps that world had been created somewhere inside of him, pressed upon him in a vision. He was a sailor on the *Pequod*. He thought that this was part of some book, but he had not been a reader for many years.

Memories of his other life persisted. He remembered the first time he had ever made love to a woman—to Sally Torrance, in the living room of her parents' house while they were away skiing in Minnesota. He remembered cutting his palm playing baseball when the bat shattered in his hand. The scar in the middle of his hand could not be denied.

Who denied it? He watched an albatross swoop down from above him to skim a few feet above the water, trying to snag some high-leaping fish. It turned away, unsuccessful, beating its wings slowly as it climbed the air. There was rhythm to its unconscious dance. Fallon had never seen anything more beautiful. He hung his arms over the hoop that surrounded him, felt the hot sun beating on his back, the band of metal supporting him.

This was the real world; he accepted it. He accepted the memories that contradicted it. I look, you look, he looks. Could his mind and heart hold two contradictory things? What would happen to him then? He accepted the albatross, the fish, the sharks he could see below the water's surface from his high vantage point. He accepted the grace of the sea, its embrace on this gentlest of days, and he accepted the storm that had tried to kill them only days before. The *Delight*, reason told him—let reason be; he could strain reason no further than he had—the *Delight* might perhaps have been a ship from a story he had read, but he had no doubt that the man who had been dropped to his watery grave as Fallon watched had been a real man.

The blue of sky and sea, the sound of the flag snapping above him, the taste of the salt air, the motion of the sea and earth itself as they swung Fallon at the tip of the mast, the memories and speculations, the feel of warm sun and warm iron—all the sensual world flowed together for Fallon then. He could not say what he felt. Joy that he could hardly contain swelled in his chest. He was at one with all his perceptions, with all he knew and remembered, with Carol, wherever or whatever she might be, with Bulkington and Daggoo and Starbuck and Stein Jr. and the Big House and Queequeg and the CBT and Ahab. Ahab.

Why had Fallon struggled so long against it? He was alive. What thing had driven him to fight so hard? What had happened to

him was absurd, but what thing was not absurd? What thing had
made him change from the student to the dropout to the analyst to
the sailor? Who might Patrick Fallon be? He stretched out his right
arm and turned his hand in the sun.

"Is it I, or God, or who, that lifts this arm?" Fallon heard the
words quite distinctly, as if they were spoken only for him, as if
they were not spoken at all but were only thoughts. God perhaps
did lift Fallon's arm, and if that were so, then who was Fallon to
question the wisdom or purpose of the motion? It was his only to
move.

A disturbance in the blue of the day.

Why should he not have a choice? Why should that God give
him the feeling of freedom if in fact He was directing Fallon's every
breath? Did the Fates weave this trancelike calm blue day to lead
Fallon to these particular conclusions, so that not even his thoughts
in the end were his own, but only the promptings of some force beyond him? And what force could that be if not the force that created this world, and who created this world but Herman Melville, a
man who had been dead for a very long time, a man who had no
possible connection with Fallon? And what could be the reason for
the motion? If this was the real world, then why had Fallon been
given the life he had lived before, tangled himself in, felt trapped
within, only to be snatched away and clumsily inserted into a different fantasy? What purpose did it serve? Whose satisfaction was
being sought?

The moment of wholeness died; the world dissolved into its dis-
parate elements. The sea rolled on. The ship fought it. The wind
was opposed by straining canvas. The albatross dove once again,
and skimming over the surface so fast it was a white blur, snatched
a gleam of silver—a flying fish—from midflight. It settled to the
ocean's surface, tearing at its prey.

The day was not so bright as it had been. Fallon tried to accept
it still. He did not know if there was a malign force behind the motion of the earth in its long journey, or a beneficent one whose purpose was merely veiled to men such as himself—or no force at all.
Such knowledge would not be his. He was a sailor on the *Pequod*.

∞   ∞   ∞

Upon descending, Fallon heard from Bulkington that Starbuck and
Ahab had had a conversation about turning back to Nantucket,

that the mate had seemed almost to persuade the captain to give up the hunt, but that he had failed.

Fallon knew then that they must be coming to the end of the story. It would not be long before they spotted the white whale, and three days after that the *Pequod* would go down with all hands not previously killed in the encounter with the whale—save one. But Fallon had given up the idea that he might be that one. He did not, despite his problems, qualify as an Ishmael. That would be overstating his importance, he thought.

twelve

He woke suddenly to the imperative buzzing of his alarm clock. His heart beat very fast. He tried to slow it by breathing deeply. Carol stirred beside him, then slept again.

He felt disoriented. He walked into the bathroom, staring, as if he had never seen it before. He slid open the mirrored door of the medicine chest and looked inside at the almost-empty tube of toothpaste, the old safety razor, the pack of double-edged blades, the Darvon and tetracycline capsules, the foundation makeup. When he slid the door shut again, his tanned face looked back at him.

He was slow getting started that morning; when Carol got up, he was still drinking his coffee, with the radio playing an old Doors song in the background. Carol leaned over him, kissed the top of his head. It appeared that she loved him.

"You'd better get going," she said. "You'll be late."

He hadn't worried about being late, and it hit him for the first time what he had to do. He had to get to the Board of Trade. He'd have to talk to Stein Jr., and there would be a sheaf of notes on his desk asking him to return calls to various clients who would have rung him up while he was gone. He pulled on the jacket of his pin-striped suit, brushed back his hair, and left.

Waiting for the train, he realized that he hadn't gone anywhere to return from.

He had missed his normal train and arrived late. The streets were nowhere near as crowded as they would have been an hour earlier. He walked north on La Salle Street between the staid, dark old buildings. The sky that showed between them was bright, and already the temperature was rising; it would be a hot one. He wished it were the weekend. Was it Thursday? It couldn't still be Wednesday. He was embarrassed to realize he wasn't sure what day it was.

He saw a very pretty girl in the lobby of the Board of Trade as he entered through the revolving doors. She was much prettier than Carol, and had that unselfconscious way of walking. But she was around the corner before he had taken more than a few steps inside. He ran into Joe Wendelstadt in the elevator, and Joe began to tell him a story about Raoul Lark from Brazil who worked for Cacex in Chicago, and how Lark had tried to pick up some feminist the other night. And succeeded. Those Brazilians.

Fallon got off before Joe could reach the climax. In his office Molly, the receptionist, said Stein wanted to see him. Stein smelled of cigarettes, and Fallon suddenly became self-conscious. He had not brushed his own teeth. When did he ever forget that? Stein had an incipient zit on the end of his nose. He didn't really have anything to talk to Fallon about; he was just wasting time as usual.

Tigue was sick or on vacation.

Fallon worked through the morning on various customer accounts. He had trouble remembering where the market had closed the day before. He had always had a trick memory for such figures, and it had given him the ability to impress a lot of people who knew just as much about the markets as he did. He spent what was left of the morning on the phone to his clients, with a quick trip down to the trading floor to talk to Parsons in the soybean pit.

Carol called and asked him if he could join her for lunch. He remembered he had a date with Kim, a woman from the CME he had met just a week before. He made his excuses to Carol and took off for the Merc.

Walking briskly west on Jackson, coming up on the bridge across the river, he realized he had been rushing around all day and yet could hardly remember what he'd done since he had woken up. He still couldn't remember whether it was Wednesday or Thursday.

As he crossed the bridge with the crowds of lunch-hour office workers, the noontime sun glared brightly for a second from the oily water of the river. Fallon's eyes did not immediately recover. He stopped walking, and somebody bumped into him.

"Excuse me," he said unconsciously.

There was a moment of silence, then the noise of the city resumed and he could see again. He stood at the side of the bridge and looked down at the water. The oil on the surface made rainbow-colored swirls. Fallon shook his head and went on.

Kim stood him up at the restaurant. He waited a long time by the cashier. Finally he made the woman seat him at a table for two. He looked at his watch but had some trouble reading the time. Was he due back at the office?

Just then someone sat down opposite him. It was an old man in a dark suit who had obviously undergone some great ordeal. His face held a look of great pain or sorrow—with hate burning just beneath it. Though his hair was black (and quite unforgivably unkempt for midtown Chicago, as was his rough suit), a shock of white fell across his forehead, and a scar ran from the roots of that white hair straight down the man's face, leaping the brow and eye to continue across the left cheek, sinewing down the jaw and neck to disappear beneath his shirt collar.

He looked strangely familiar.

"It won't work," the man said. "You cannot get away. You have signed the articles, like the rest, and are in for a three-hundredth lay."

"Three-hundredth lay?" Fallon was bewildered.

"A three-hundredth part of the general catastrophe is yours. Don't thank me. It isn't necessary." The old man looked even more sorrowful and more wild, if it were possible to combine those seemingly incompatible emotions.

"To tell you the truth," he said, "I wouldn't hold you to the contract if it were strictly up to me." He shrugged his shoulders and opened his palms before him. "But it isn't."

Fallon's heart was beating fast again. "I don't remember any contract. You're not one of my clients. I don't trade for you. I've been in this business for a long time, mister, and I know better than to sign. . . ."

The wildness swelled in the man. There was something burning in him, and he looked about to scream, or cry.

"*I* have been in the business longer than *you!*" He swung his leg out from beneath the table and rapped it loudly with his knuckle. Fallon saw that the leg was of white bone. "And I can tell *you* that you signed the contract when you signed aboard this ship—there's no other way to get aboard—and you must serve until you strike land again or it sinks beneath you!"

The diners in the restaurant dined on, oblivious. Fallon looked toward the plate glass at the front of the room and saw the water rising rapidly up it, sea-green and turbid, as the restaurant and the city fell to the bottom of the sea.

thirteen

Once again he was jerked awake, this time by the din of someone beating the deck of the forecastle above them with a club. The other sleepers were as startled as Fallon. He rolled out of the hammock with the mists of his dream still clinging to him, pulled on his shirt, and scrambled up to the deck.

Ahab was stalking the quarterdeck in a frenzy of impatience. "Man the mastheads!" he shouted.

The men who had risen with Fallon did just that, some of them only half-dressed. Fallon was one of the first up and gained one of the hoops at the main masthead. Three others stood on the main yard below him. Fallon scanned the horizon and saw off to starboard and far ahead of them the jet of mist that indicated a whale. As it rose and fell in its course through the rolling seas, Fallon saw that it was white.

"What d'ye see?" Ahab called from far below. Had he noticed Fallon's gaze fixed on the spot in front of them?

"Nothing! Nothing, sir!" Fallon called. Ahab and the men on deck looked helpless so far below him. Fallon did not know if his lying would work, but there was the chance that the other men in the rigging, not being as high as he, would not be able to make out Moby Dick from their lower vantage points. He turned away from the whale and made a good show of scanning the empty horizon.

"Top gallant sails!—stunsails! Alow and aloft, and on both sides!" Ahab ordered. The men fixed a line from the mainmast to the deck, looped its lower end around Ahab's rigid leg. Ahab wound the rope around his shoulders and arm, and they hoisted him aloft, twisting with the pressure on the hemp, toward the masthead. He twirled slowly as they raised him up, and his line of sight was obscured by the rigging and sails he had to peer through.

Before they had lifted him two-thirds of the way up, he began to shout.

"There she blows!—there she blows! A hump like a snow-hill! It is Moby Dick!"

Fallon knew enough to begin shouting and pointing immediately, and the men at the other two masts did the same. Within a minute everyone who had remained on the deck was in the rigging trying to catch a glimpse of the creature they had sought, half of them doubting his existence, for so many months.

Fallon looked down toward the helmsman, who stood on his toes, the whalebone tiller under his arm, arching his neck trying to see the whale.

The others in the rigging were now arguing about who had spotted Moby Dick first, with Ahab the eventual victor. It was his fate, he said, to be the one to first spot the whale. Fallon couldn't argue with that.

Ahab was lowered to the deck, giving orders all the way, and three boats were swung outboard in preparation for the chase. Starbuck was ordered to stay behind and keep the ship.

As they chased the whale, the sea became calmer, so the rowing became easier—though just as backbreaking—and they knifed through the water, here as placid as a farm pond, faster than ever. Accompanying the sound of their own wake, Fallon heard the wake of the whale they must be approaching. He strained arms, back, and legs, pulling harder in time to Stubb's cajoling chant, and the rushing grew. He snatched a glance over his shoulder, turned to the rowing, then looked again.

The white whale glided through the sea smoothly, giving the impression of immeasurable strength. The wake he left was as steady as that of a schooner; the bow waves created by the progress of his broad, blank brow through the water fanned away in precise lines whose angle with respect to the massive body did not change. The three whaleboats rocked gently as they broke closer through these successive waves; the foam of Moby Dick's wake was abreast of them now, and Fallon saw how quickly it subsided into itself, giving the sea back its calm face, innocent of knowledge of the creature that had passed. Attendant white birds circled above their heads, now and then falling to or rising from the surface in busy flutterings of wings and awkward beaks. One of them had landed on the broken shaft of a harpoon that protruded from the snow-white whale's humped back; it bobbed up and down with the slight rocking of the whale in its long, muscular surging through the sea. Oblivious. Strangely quiet. Fallon felt as if they had entered a magic circle.

He knew Ahab's boat, manned by the absurd Filipinos, was ahead of them and no doubt preparing to strike first. Fallon closed his eyes, pulled on his oar, and wished for it not to happen. For it to stop now, or just continue without any change. He felt as if he could row a very long time; he was no longer tired or afraid. He just wanted to keep rowing, feeling the rhythm of the work, hearing the low and insistent voice of Stubb telling them to break their backs. Fallon wanted to listen to the rushing white sound of the whale's wake in the water, to know that they were perhaps keeping pace with it, to know that, if he should tire, he could look for a second over his shoulder and find Moby Dick there still. Let the monomaniac stand in the bow of his boat—if he was meant to stand there, if it was an unavoidable necessity—let him stand there with the raised lance and concentrate his hate into one purified moment of will. Let him send that will into the tip of that lance so that it might physically glow with the frustrated obtuseness of it. Let him stand there until he froze from the suspended desire, and let the whale swim on.

Fallon heard a sudden increase in the rushing of the water, several inarticulate cries. He stopped pulling, as did the others, and turned to look in time to see the whale lift itself out of the water, exposing flanks and flukes the bluish white of cemetery marble, and flip its huge tail upward to dive perpendicularly into the sea. Spray drenched them, and sound returned with the crash of the waves coming together to fill the vacuum left by the departure of the creature that had seconds before given weight and direction, place, to the placeless expanse of level waters. The birds circled above the subsiding foam.

They lifted their oars. They waited.

"An hour," Ahab said.

They waited. It was another beautiful day. The sky was hard and blue as the floor of the swimming pool where he had met Carol. Fallon wondered again if she missed him, if he had indeed disappeared from that other life when he had taken up residence in this one—but he thrust those thoughts away. They were meaningless. There was no time in that world after his leaving it; that world did not exist, or if it existed, the order of its existence was not of the order of the existence of the rough wood he sat on, the raw flesh of his hands and the air he breathed. Time was the time between the breaths he drew. Time was the duration of the dream he had had about being back in Chicago, and he could not say how long that had been, even if it had begun or ended. He might be dreaming still. The word *dream* was meaningless, and *awake*. And *real*, and *insane*, and *known*, and all those other interesting words he had once accepted without questioning. Time was waiting for Moby Dick to surface again.

The breeze freshened. The sea began to swell.

"The birds!—the birds!" Tashtego shouted, so close behind Fallon's ear that he winced. The Indian half stood, rocking the whaleboat as he pointed to the seabirds, which had risen and were flying toward Ahab's boat twenty yards away.

"The whale will breach there," Stubb said.

Ahab was up immediately. Peering into the water, he leaned on the steering oar and reversed the orientation of his boat. He then exchanged places with Fedallah, the other men reaching up to help him through the rocking boat. He picked up the harpoon, and the oarsmen stood ready to row.

Fallon looked down into the sea, trying to make out what Ahab saw. Nothing, until a sudden explosion of white as the whale, rocketing upward, turned over as it finally hit the surface. In a moment Ahab's boat was in the whale's jaws, Ahab in the bows almost between them. Stubb was shouting and gesturing, and Fallon's fellows fell to the oars in a disorganized rush. The Filipinos in the lead boat crowded into the stern while Ahab, like a man trying to open a recalcitrant garage door, tugged and shoved at Moby Dick's jaw, trying insanely to dislodge the whale's grip. Within seconds filled with crashing water, cries, and confusion, Moby Dick had bitten the boat in two, and Ahab had belly-flopped over the side like a swimming-class novice.

Moby Dick then began to swim tight circles around the smashed boat and its crew. Ahab struggled to keep his head above water. Neither Stubb nor Flask could bring his boat close enough to pick him up. The *Pequod* was drawing nearer, and finally Ahab was able to shout loudly enough to be heard, "Sail on the whale—drive him off!"

It worked. The *Pequod* picked up the remnants of the whaleboat while Fallon and the others dragged its crew and Ahab into their own boat.

The old man collapsed in the bottom of the boat, gasping for breath, broken and exhausted. He moaned and shook. Fallon was sure he was finished whale chasing, that Stubb and the others would see the man was used up, that Starbuck would take over and sail them home. But in a minute or two Ahab was leaning on his elbow asking after his boat's crew, and a few minutes after that they had resumed the chase with double oarsmen in Stubb's boat.

Moby Dick drew steadily away as exhaustion wore them down. Fallon did not feel he could row any more after all. The *Pequod* picked them up, and they gave chase in vain under all sail until dark.

fourteen

On the second day's chase all three boats were smashed in. Many suffered sprains and contusions, and one was bitten by a shark. Ahab's whalebone leg was shattered, with a splinter driven into his own flesh. Fedallah, who had been the captain's second shadow, was tangled in the line Ahab had shot into the white whale, dragged out of the boat, and drowned. Moby Dick escaped.

fifteen

It came down to what Fallon had known it would come down to eventually.

In the middle of that night he went to talk to Ahab, who slept in one of the hatchways as he had the night before. The carpenter was making him another leg, wooden this time, and Ahab was curled sullenly in the dark lee of the afterscuttle. Fallon did not know whether he was waiting or asleep.

He started down the stairs, hesitated on the second step. Ahab lifted his head. "What do you need?" he asked.

Fallon wondered what he wanted to say. He looked at the man huddled in the darkness and tried to imagine what moved him, tried to see him as a man instead of a thing. Was it possible he was only a man, or had Fallon himself become stylized and distorted by living in the book of Melville's imagination?

"You said—talking to Starbuck today—you said that everything that happens is fixed, decreed. You said it was rehearsed a billion years before any of it took place. Is it true?"

Ahab straightened and leaned toward Fallon, bringing his face into the dim light thrown by the lamps on deck. He looked at him for a moment in silence.

"I don't know. So it seemed as the words left my lips. The Parsee is dead before me, as he foretold. I don't know."

"That is why you're hunting the whale."

"That is why I'm hunting the whale."

"How can this hunt, how can killing an animal tell you anything? How can it justify your life? What satisfaction can it give you in the end, even if you boil it all down to oil, even if you cut Moby Dick into bible leaves and eat him? I don't understand it."

The captain looked at him earnestly. He seemed to be listening, and leaping ahead of the questions. It was very dark in the scuttle, and they could hardly see each other. Fallon kept his hands folded tightly behind him. The blade of the cleaver he had shoved into his belt lay cool against the skin at the small of his back; it was the same knife he used to butcher the whale.

"If it is immutably fixed, then it does not matter what I do. The purpose and meaning are out of my hands, and thine. We have only to take our parts, to be the thing that it is written for us to be. Better to live that role given us than to struggle against it or play the coward, when the actions must be the same nonetheless. Some say I am mad to chase the whale. Perhaps I am mad. But if it is my destiny to seek him, to tear, to burn and kill those things that stand in my path—then the matter of my madness is not relevant, do you see?"

He was not speaking in character.

"If these things are not fixed, and it was not my destiny to have my leg taken by the whale, to have my hopes blasted in this chase, then how cruel a world it is. No mercy, no power but its own, controls it; it blights our lives out of merest whim. No, not whim, for there would then be no will behind it, no builder of this Bedlam hospital, and in the madhouse, when the keeper is gone, what is to stop the inmates from doing as they please? In a universe of cannibals, where all creatures have preyed upon each other, carrying on an eternal war since the world began, why should I not exert my will in whatever direction I choose? Why should I not bend others to my will?" The voice was reasonable, and tired. "Have I answered your question?"

Fallon felt the time drawing near. He felt light, as if the next breeze might lift him from the deck and carry him away. "I have an idea," he said. "My idea is—and it is an idea I have had for some time now, and despite everything that has happened, and what you say, I can't give it up—my idea is that all that is happening . . ." Fallon waved his hand at the world, ". . . is a story. It is a book written by a man named Herman Melville and told by a character named Ishmael. You are the main character in the book. All the things that have happened are events in the book.

"My idea also is that I am not from the book, or at least I wasn't originally. Originally I lived a different life in another time and place, a life in the real world and not in a book. It was not ordered and plotted like a book, and. . . ."

Ahab interrupted in a quiet voice: "You call this an ordered book? I see no order. If it were so orderly, why would the whale task me so?"

Fallon knotted his fingers tighter behind him. Ahab was going to make him do it. He felt the threads of the situation weaving together to create only that bloody alternative, of all the alternatives that might be. In the open market, the price for the future and price for the physical reality converged on delivery day.

"The order's not an easy thing to see, I'll admit," Fallon said. He laughed nervously.

Ahab laughed louder. "It certainly is not. And how do you know this other life you speak of was not a play? A different kind of play. How do you know your thoughts are your own? How do you know that this dark little scene was not prepared just for us, or perhaps for someone who is reading about us at this very moment and wondering about the point of the drama just as much as we wonder at the pointlessness of our lives?" Ahab's voice rose, gaining an edge of compulsion. "How do we know anything?" He grabbed his left wrist, pinched the flesh and shook it.

"How do we know what lies behind this matter? This flesh is a wall, the painting over the canvas, the mask drawn over the player's face, the snow fallen over the fertile field, or perhaps the scorched earth. I know there is something there; there must be something, but it cannot be touched because we are smothered in this flesh, this life. How do we know—"

"Stop it! Stop it!" Fallon shouted. "Please stop asking things! You should not be able to say things like that to me! Ahab does not talk to me!"

"Isn't this what I am supposed to say?"

Fallon shuddered.

"Isn't this scene in your book?"

He was dizzy, sick. "No! Of course not!"

"Then why does that disturb you? Doesn't this prove that we are not pieces of a larger dream, that this is a real world, that the blood that flows within our veins is real blood, that the pain we feel has meaning, that the things we do have consequence? We break the mold of existence by existing. Isn't that reassurance enough?" Ahab was shouting now, and the men awake on deck trying to get the boats in shape for the last day's chase and the *Pequod*'s ultimate destruction put aside their hammers and rope and listened to his justification.

It was time. Fallon, shaking with anger and fear, drew the knife from behind him and leapt at the old man. In bringing up the blade for the attack he hit it against the side of the narrow hatchway. His grip loosened. Ahab threw up his hands and, despite the difference in age and mobility between them, managed to grab Fallon's wrist before he could strike the killing blow. Instead, the deflected cleaver struck the beam beside Ahab's head and stuck there. As Fallon tried to free it, Ahab brought his forearm up and smashed him beneath the jaw. Fallon fell backward, striking his head with stunning force against the opposite side of the scuttle. He momentarily lost consciousness.

When he came to himself again, Ahab was sitting before him with his strong hands on Fallon's shoulders, supporting him, not allowing him to move.

"Good, Fallon, good," he said. "You've done well. But now, no more games, no more dramas, no easy way out. Admit that this is not the tale you think it is! Admit that you do not know what will happen to you in the next second, let alone the next day or year! Admit that we are both free and unfree, alone and crowded in by circumstance in this world that we indeed did not make, but indeed have the power to affect! Put aside those notions that there is another life somehow more real than the life you live now, another air to breathe somehow more pure, another love or hate somehow more vital than the love or hate you bear me. Put aside your fantasy and admit that you are alive, and thus may momentarily die. Do you hear me, Fallon?"

Fallon heard, and saw, and felt and touched, but he did not know. The *Pequod*, freighted with savages and isolatoes, sailed into the night, and the great shroud of the sea rolled on as it rolled five thousand years ago.

MEETING IN INFINITY MEETING IN INFINITY MEETING IN INFINITY MEETI
ETING IN INFINITY MEETING IN INFINITY MEETING IN INFINITY M
G MEETING IN INFINITY MEETING IN INFINITY MEETING IN INFINIT
INITY MEETING IN INFINITY MEETING IN INFINITY MEETING IN IN
N INFINITY MEETING IN INFINITY MEETING IN INFINITY MEETING
NG IN INFINITY MEETING IN INFINITY MEETING IN INFINITY MEET
EETING IN INFINITY MEETING IN INFINITY MEETING IN INFINITY
TY MEETING IN INFINITY MEETING IN INFINITY MEETING IN INFIN
FINITY MEETING IN INFINITY MEETING IN INFINITY MEETING IN I
IN INFINITY MEETING IN INFINITY MEETING IN INFINITY MEETING
TING IN INFINITY MEETING IN INFINITY MEETING IN INFINITY ME
MEETING IN INFINITY MEETING IN INFINITY MEETING IN INFINITY
ITY MEETING IN INFINITY MEETING IN INFINITY MEETING IN INFI
INFINITY MEETING IN INFINITY MEETING IN INFINITY MEETING IN
G IN INFINITY MEETING IN INFINITY MEETING IN INFINITY MEETI

buffalo

I N APRIL 1934 H. G. WELLS MADE A TRIP TO THE UNITED STATES, WHERE he visited Washington, D.C., and met with President Franklin Delano Roosevelt. Wells, sixty-eight years old, hoped the New Deal might herald a revolutionary change in the U.S. economy, a step forward in an "Open Conspiracy" of rational thinkers that would culminate in a world socialist state. For forty years he'd subordinated every scrap of his artistic ambition to promoting this vision. But by 1934 Wells's optimism, along with his energy for saving the world, was waning.

While in Washington he requested to see something of the new social welfare agencies, and Harold Ickes, Roosevelt's Interior Secretary, arranged for Wells to visit a Civilian Conservation Corps camp at Fort Hunt, Virginia.

It happens that at that time my father was a CCC member at that camp. From his boyhood he had been a reader of adventure stories; he was a big fan of Edgar Rice Burroughs, and of H. G. Wells. This is the story of their encounter, which never took place.

∞   ∞   ∞

In Buffalo it's cold, but here the trees are in bloom, the mockingbirds sing in the mornings, and the sweat the men work up clearing brush, planting dogwoods, and cutting roads is wafted away by warm breezes. Two hundred of them live in the Fort Hunt barracks high on the bluff above the Virginia side of the Potomac. They wear surplus army uniforms. In the morning, after a breakfast of grits, Sergeant Sauter musters them up in the parade yard, they climb onto trucks and are driven by Forest Service men out to wherever they're to work that day.

For several weeks Kessel's squad has been working along the river road, clearing rest stops and turnarounds. The tall pines have shallow root systems, and spring rain has softened the earth to the point where wind is forever knocking trees across the road. While most of the men work on the ground, a couple are sent up to cut off the tops of the pines adjoining the road, so if they do fall, they won't block it. Most of the men claim to be afraid of heights. Kessel isn't. A year or two ago back in Michigan he worked in a logging camp. It's hard work, but he is used to hard work. And at least he's out of Buffalo.

The truck rumbles and jounces out the river road, which is going to be the George Washington Memorial Parkway in our time, once the WPA project that will build it gets started. The humid air is cool now, but it will be hot again today, in the eighties. A couple of the guys get into a debate about whether the feds will ever catch Dillinger. Some others talk women. They're planning to go into Washington on the weekend and check out the dance halls. Kessel likes to dance; he's a good dancer. The fox-trot, the lindy hop. When he gets drunk he likes to sing, and has a ready wit. He talks a lot more, kids the girls.

When they get to the site the foreman sets most of the men to work clearing the roadside for a scenic overlook. Kessel straps on a climbing belt, takes an ax, and climbs his first tree. The first twenty feet are limbless, then climbing gets trickier. He looks down only enough to estimate when he's gotten high enough. He sets himself, cleats biting into the shoulder of a lower limb, and chops away at the road side of the trunk. There's a trick to cutting the top so that it falls the right way. When he's got it ready to go he calls down to warn the men below. Then a few quick bites of the ax on the opposite side of the cut, a shove, a crack, and the top starts to go. He braces his legs, ducks his head, and grips the trunk. The treetop skids off, and the bole of the pine waves ponderously back and forth, with Kessel swinging at its end like an ant on a metronome. After the pine stops swinging he shinnies down and climbs the next tree.

He's good at this work, efficient, careful. He's not a particularly strong man—slender, not burly—but even in his youth he shows the attention to detail that, as a boy, I remember seeing when he built our house.

The squad works through the morning, then breaks for lunch from the mess truck. The men are always complaining about the food, and how there isn't enough of it, but until recently a lot of them were living in Hoovervilles—shack cities—and eating nothing at all. As they're eating, a couple of the guys rag Kessel for working too fast. "What do you expect from a Yankee?" one of the southern boys says.

"He ain't a Yankee. He's a Polack."

Kessel tries to ignore them.

"Whyn't you lay off him, Turkel?" says Cole, one of Kessel's buddies.

Turkel is a big blond guy from Chicago. Some say he joined the CCCs to duck an armed robbery rap. "He works too hard," Turkel says. "He makes us look bad."

"Don't have to work much to make you look bad, Lou," Cole says. The others laugh, and Kessel appreciates it. "Give Jack some credit. At least he had enough sense to come down out of Buffalo." More laughter.

"There's nothing wrong with Buffalo," Kessel says.

"Except fifty thousand out-of-work Polacks," Turkel says.

"I guess you got no out-of-work people in Chicago," Kessel says. "You just joined for the exercise."

"Except he's not getting any exercise, if he can help it!" Cole says.

The foreman comes by and tells them to get back to work. Kessel climbs another tree, stung by Turkel's charge. What kind of man complains if someone else works hard? It only shows how even decent guys have to put up with assholes dragging them down. But it's nothing new. He's seen it before, back in Buffalo.

Buffalo, New York, is the symbolic home of this story. In the years preceding the First World War it grew into one of the great industrial metropolises of the United States. Located where Lake Erie flows into the Niagara River, strategically close to cheap electricity from Niagara Falls and cheap transportation by lake boat from the Midwest, it was a center of steel, automobiles, chemicals, grain milling, and brewing. Its major employers—Bethlehem Steel, Ford, Pierce-Arrow, Gold Medal Flour, the National Biscuit Company,

Ralston Purina, Quaker Oats, National Aniline—drew thousands of immigrants like Kessel's family. Along Delaware Avenue stood the imperious and stylized mansions of the city's old money, ersatz-Renaissance homes designed by Stanford White, huge Protestant churches, and a Byzantine synagogue. The city boasted the first modern skyscraper, designed by Louis Sullivan in the 1890s. From its productive factories to its polyglot work force to its class system and its boosterism, Buffalo was a monument to modern industrial capitalism. It is the place Kessel has come from—almost an expression of his personality itself—and the place he, at times, fears he can never escape. A cold, grimy city dominated by church and family, blinkered and cramped, forever playing second fiddle to Chicago, New York, and Boston. It offers the immigrant the opportunity to find steady work in some factory or mill, but, though Kessel could not have put it into these words, it also puts a lid on his opportunities. It stands for all disappointed expectations, human limitations, tawdry compromises, for the inevitable choice of the expedient over the beautiful, for an American economic system that turns all things into commodities and measures men by their bank accounts. It is the home of the industrial proletariat.

It's not unique. It could be Youngstown, Akron, Detroit. It's the place my father, and I, grew up.

The afternoon turns hot and still; during a work break Kessel strips to the waist. About two o'clock a big black De Soto comes up the road and pulls off onto the shoulder. A couple of men in suits get out of the back, and one of them talks to the Forest Service foreman, who nods deferentially. The foreman calls over to the men.

"Boys, this here's Mr. Pike from the Interior Department. He's got a guest here to see how we work, a writer, Mr. H. G. Wells from England."

Most of the men couldn't care less, but the name strikes a spark in Kessel. He looks over at the little potbellied man in the dark suit. The man is sweating; he brushes his mustache.

The foreman sends Kessel up to show them how they're topping the trees. He points out to the visitors where the others with rakes and shovels are leveling the ground for the overlook. Several other men are building a log-rail fence from the treetops. From way above, Kessel can hear their voices between the thunks of his ax. H. G. Wells. He remembers reading "The War of the Worlds" in *Amazing Stories*. He's read *The Outline of History*, too. The stories, the history, are so large, it seems impossible that the man who wrote them could be standing not thirty feet below him. He tries to concentrate on the ax, the tree.

Time for this one to go. He calls down. The men below look up. Wells takes off his hat and shields his eyes with his hand. He's balding, and looks even smaller from up here. Strange that such big ideas could come from such a small man. It's kind of disappointing. Wells leans over to Pike and says something. The treetop falls away. The pine sways like a bucking bronco, and Kessel holds on for dear life.

He comes down with the intention of saying something to Wells, telling him how much he admires him, but when he gets down the sight of the two men in suits and his awareness of his own sweaty chest make him timid. He heads down to the next tree. After another ten minutes the men get back in the car, drive away. Kessel curses himself for the opportunity lost.

∞   ∞   ∞

That evening at the New Willard hotel, Wells dines with his old friends Clarence Darrow and Charles Russell. Darrow and Russell are in Washington to testify before a congressional committee on a report they have just submitted to the administration concerning the monopolistic effects of the National Recovery Act. The right wing is trying to eviscerate Roosevelt's program for large-scale industrial management, and the Darrow Report is playing right into their hands. Wells tries, with little success, to convince Darrow of the shortsightedness of his position.

"Roosevelt is willing to sacrifice the small man to the huge corporations," Darrow insists, his eyes bright.

"The small man? Your small man is a romantic fantasy," Wells says. "It's not the New Deal that's doing him in—it's the process of industrial progress. It's the twentieth century. You can't legislate yourself back into 1870."

"What about the individual?" Russell asks.

Wells snorts. "Walk out into the street. The individual is out on the street corner selling apples. The only thing that's going to save him is some coordinated effort, by intelligent, selfless men. Not your free market."

Darrow puffs on his cigar, exhales, smiles. "Don't get exasperated, H. G. We're not working for Standard Oil. But if I have to choose between the bureaucrat and the man pumping gas at the filling station, I'll take the pump jockey."

Wells sees he's got no chance against the American mythology of the common man. "Your pump jockey works for Standard Oil. And the last I checked, the free market hasn't expended much energy looking out for his interests."

"Have some more wine," Russell says.

Russell refills their glasses with the excellent Bordeaux. It's been a first-rate meal. Wells finds the debate stimulating even when he can't prevail; at one time that would have been enough, but as the years go on the need to prevail grows stronger in him. The times are out of joint, and when he looks around he sees desperation growing. A new world order is necessary—it's so clear that even a fool ought to see it—but if he can't even convince radicals like Darrow, what hope is there of gaining the acquiescence of the shareholders in the utility trusts?

The answer is that the changes will have to be made over their objections. As Roosevelt seems prepared to do. Wells's dinner with the president has heartened him in a way that his debate cannot negate.

Wells brings up an item he read in the *Washington Post*. A lecturer for the Communist party—a young Negro—was barred from speaking at the University of Virginia. Wells's question is, was the man barred because he was a Communist or because he was Negro?

"Either condition," Darrow says sardonically, "is fatal in Virginia."

"But students point out the university has allowed Communists to speak on campus before, and has allowed Negroes to perform music there."

"They can perform, but they can't speak," Russell says. "This isn't unusual. Go down to the Paradise Ballroom, not a mile from here. There's a Negro orchestra playing there, but no Negroes are allowed inside to listen."

"You should go to hear them anyway," Darrow says. "It's Duke Ellington. Have you heard of him?"

"I don't get on with the titled nobility," Wells quips.

"Oh, this Ellington's a noble fellow, all right, but I don't think you'll find him in the peerage," Russell says.

"He plays jazz, doesn't he?"

"Not like any jazz you've heard," Darrow says. "It's something totally new. You should find a place for it in one of your utopias."

All three of them are for helping the colored peoples. Darrow has defended Negroes accused of capital crimes. Wells, on his first visit to America almost thirty years ago, met with Booker T. Washington and came away impressed, although he still considers the peaceable coexistence of the white and colored races problematical.

"What are you working on now, Wells?" Russell says. "What new improbability are you preparing to assault us with? Racial equality? Sexual liberation?"

"I'm writing a screen treatment based on *The Shape of Things to Come*," Wells says. He tells them about his screenplay, sketching out for them the future he has in his mind. An apocalyptic war, a war of unsurpassed brutality that will begin, in his film, in 1939. In this war, the creations of science will be put to the services of destruction in ways that will make the horrors of the Great War pale in comparison. Whole populations will be exterminated. But then, out of the ruins will arise the new world. The orgy of violence will purge the human race of the last vestiges of tribal thinking. Then will come the organization of the directionless and weak by the intelligent and purposeful. The new man. Cleaner, stronger, more rational. Wells can see it. He talks on, supplely, surely, late into the night. His mind is fertile with invention, still. He can see that Darrow and Russell, despite their Yankee individualism, are caught up by his vision. The future may be threatened, but it is not entirely closed.

∞   ∞   ∞

Friday night, back in the barracks at Fort Hunt, Kessel lies on his bunk reading a secondhand *Wonder Stories*. He's halfway through the tale of a scientist who invents an evolution chamber that progresses him through fifty thousand years of evolution in an hour, turning him into a big-brained telepathic monster. The evolved scientist is totally without emotions and wants to control the world. But his body's atrophied. Will the hero, a young engineer, be able to stop him?

At a plank table in the aisle a bunch of men are playing poker for cigarettes. They're talking about women and dogs. Cole throws in his hand and comes over to sit on the next bunk. "Still reading that stuff, Jack?"

"Don't knock it until you've tried it."

"Are you coming into D.C. with us tomorrow? Sergeant Sauter says we can catch a ride in on one of the trucks."

Kessel thinks about it. Cole probably wants to borrow some money. Two days after he gets his monthly pay he's broke. He's always looking for a good time. Kessel spends his leave more quietly; he usually walks into Alexandria—about six miles—and sees a movie or just strolls around town. Still, he would like to see more of Washington. "Okay."

Cole looks at the sketchbook poking out from beneath Kessel's pillow. "Any more hot pictures?"

Immediately Kessel regrets trusting Cole. Yet there's not much he can say—the book is full of pictures of movie stars he's drawn. "I'm learning to draw. And at least I don't waste my time like the rest of you guys."

Cole looks serious. "You know, you're not any better than the rest of us," he says, not angrily. "You're just another Polack. Don't get so high-and-mighty."

"Just because I want to improve myself doesn't mean I'm high-and-mighty."

"Hey, Cole, are you in or out?" Turkel yells from the table.

"Dream on, Jack," Cole says, and returns to the game.

Kessel tries to go back to the story, but he isn't interested anymore. He can figure out that the hero is going to defeat the hyper-evolved scientist in the end. He folds his arms behind his head and stares at the knots in the rafters.

It's true, Kessel does spend a lot of time dreaming. But he has things he wants to do, and he's not going to waste his life drinking and whoring like the rest of them.

Kessel's always been different. Quieter, smarter. He was always going to do something better than the rest of them; he's well-spoken, he likes to read. Even though he didn't finish high school he reads everything: *Amazing, Astounding, Wonder Stories.* He believes in the future. He doesn't want to end up trapped in some factory his whole life.

Kessel's parents emigrated from Poland in 1911. Their name was Kisiel, but his got Germanized in Catholic school. For ten years the family moved from one to another middle-sized industrial town, as Joe Kisiel bounced from job to job. Springfield. Utica. Syracuse. Rochester. Kessel remembers them loading up a wagon in the middle of night with all their belongings in order to jump the rent on the run-down house in Syracuse. He remembers pulling a cart down to the Utica Club brewery, a nickel in his hand, to buy his father a keg of beer. He remembers them finally settling in the First Ward of Buffalo. The First Ward, at the foot of the Erie Canal, was an Irish neighborhood as far back as anybody could remember, and the Kisiels were the only Poles there. That's where he developed his chameleon ability to fit in, despite the fact he wanted nothing more than to get out. But he had to protect his mother, sister, and little brothers from their father's drunken rages. When Joe Kisiel died in 1924 it was a relief, despite the fact that his son ended up supporting the family.

For ten years Kessel has strained against the tug of that responsibility. He's sought the free and easy feeling of the road, of places different from where he grew up, romantic places where the sun shines and he can make something entirely American of himself.

Despite his ambitions, he's never accomplished much. He's been essentially a drifter, moving from job to job. Starting as a pinsetter in a bowling alley, he moved on to a flour mill. He would have stayed in the mill only he developed an allergy to the flour dust, so he became an electrician. He would have stayed an electrician except he had a fight with a boss and got blacklisted. He left Buffalo because of his father; he kept coming back because of his mother. When the Depression hit he tried to get a job in Detroit at the auto factories, but that was plain stupid in the face of the universal collapse, and he ended up working up in the peninsula as a farmhand, then as a logger. It was seasonal work, and when the season was over he was out of a job. In the winter of 1933, rather than freeze his ass off in northern Michigan, he joined the CCC. Now he sends twenty-five of his thirty dollars a month back to his mother and sister in Buffalo. And imagines the future.

When he thinks about it, there are two futures. The first is the one from the magazines and books. Bright, slick, easy. We, looking back on it, can see it to be the fifteen-cent utopianism of Hugo Gernsback's *Science and Mechanics*, which flourished in the midst of the Depression. A degradation of the marvelous inventions that made Wells his early reputation, minus the social theorizing that drove Wells's technological speculations. The common man's boosterism. There's money to be made telling people like Jack Kessel about the wonderful world of the future.

The second future is Kessel's own. That one's a lot harder to see. It contains work. A good job, doing something he likes, using his skills. Not working for another man, but making something that would be useful for others. Building something for the future. And a woman, a gentle woman, for his wife. Not some cheap dance-hall queen.

So when Kessel saw H. G. Wells in person, that meant something to him. He's had his doubts. He's twenty-nine years old, not a kid anymore. If he's ever going to get anywhere, it's going to have to start happening soon. He has the feeling that something significant is going to happen to him. Wells is a man who sees the future. He moves in that bright world where things make sense. He represents something that Kessel wants.

But the last thing Kessel wants is to end up back in Buffalo.

He pulls the sketchbook, the sketchbook he was to show me twenty years later, from under his pillow. He turns past drawings of movie stars: Jean Harlow, Mae West, Carole Lombard—the beautiful, unreachable faces of his longing—and of natural scenes: rivers, forests, birds—to a blank page. The page is as empty as the future, waiting for him to write upon it. He lets his imagination soar. He envisions an eagle, gliding high above the mountains of the West that he has never seen, but that he knows he will visit someday. The eagle is America; it is his own dreams. He begins to draw.

∞ ∞ ∞

Kessel does not know that Wells's life has not worked out as well as he planned. At that moment Wells is pining after the Russian émigrée Moura Budberg, once Maxim Gorky's secretary, with whom Wells has been carrying on an off-and-on affair since 1920. His wife of thirty years, Amy Catherine "Jane" Wells, died in 1927. Since that time Wells has been adrift, alternating spells of furious pamphleteering with listless periods of suicidal depression. Meanwhile, all London is gossiping about the recent attack published in *Time and Tide* by his vengeful ex-lover Odette Keun. Have his mistakes followed him across the Atlantic to undermine his purpose? Does Darrow think him a jumped-up cockney? A moment of doubt overwhelms him. In the end, the future depends as much on the open-mindedness of men like Darrow as it does on a reorganization of society. What good is a guild of samurai if no one arises to take the job?

Wells doesn't like the trend of these thoughts. If human nature lets him down, then his whole life has been a waste.

But he's seen the president. He's seen those workers on the road. Those men climbing the trees risk their lives without complaining, for minimal pay. It's easy to think of them as stupid or desperate or simply young, but it's also possible to give them credit for dedication to their work. They don't seem to be ridden by the desire to grub and clutch that capitalism rewards; if you look at it properly that may be the explanation for their ending up wards of the state. And is Wells any better? If he hadn't got an education he would have ended up a miserable draper's assistant.

Wells is due to leave for New York Sunday. Saturday night finds him sitting in his room, trying to write, after a solitary dinner in the New Willard. Another bottle of wine, or his age, has stirred something in Wells, and despite his rationalizations he finds himself near despair. Moura has rejected him. He needs the soft, supportive embrace of a lover, but instead he has this stuffy hotel room in a heat wave.

He remembers writing *The Time Machine*, he and Jane living in rented rooms in Sevenoaks with her ailing mother, worried about money, about whether the landlady would put them out. In the drawer of the dresser was a writ from the court that refused to grant him a divorce from his wife Isabel. He remembers a warm night, late in August—much like this one—sitting up after Jane and her mother went to bed, writing at the round table before the open window, under the light of a paraffin lamp. One part of his mind was caught up in the rush of creation, burning, following the Time Traveler back to the Sphinx, pursued by the Morlocks, only to discover that his machine is gone and he is trapped without escape from his desperate circumstance. At the same moment he could hear the landlady, out in the garden, fully aware that he could hear her, complaining to the neighbor about his and Jane's scandalous habits. On the one side, the petty conventions of a crabbed world; on the other, in his mind—the future, their peril and hope. Moths fluttering through the window beat themselves against the lamp-shade and fell onto the manuscript; he brushed them away unconsciously and continued, furiously, in a white heat. The Time Traveler, battered and hungry, returning from the future with a warning, and a flower.

He opens the hotel windows all the way, but the curtains aren't stirred by a breath of air. Below, in the street, he hears the sound of traffic, and music. He decides to send a telegram to Moura, but after several false starts he finds he has nothing to say. Why has she refused to marry him? Maybe he is finally too old, and the magnetism of sex or power or intellect that has drawn women to him for forty years has finally all been squandered. The prospect of spending the last years remaining to him alone fills him with dread.

He turns on the radio, gets successive band shows: Morton Downey, Fats Waller. Jazz. Paging through the newspaper, he comes across an advertisement for the Ellington orchestra Darrow mentioned: it's at the ballroom just down the block. But the thought of a smoky room doesn't appeal to him. He considers the cinema. He has never been much for the "movies." Though he thinks them an unrivaled opportunity to educate, that promise has never been properly seized—something he hopes to do in *Things to Come*. The newspaper reveals an uninspiring selection: *Twenty Million Sweethearts*, a musical at the Earle, *The Black Cat*, with Boris Karloff and Bela Lugosi at the Rialto, and *Tarzan and His Mate* at the Palace. To these Americans he is the equivalent of this hack, Edgar Rice Burroughs. The books I read as a child, that fired my father's imagination and my own, Wells considers his frivolous apprentice work. His serious work is discounted. His ideas mean nothing.

Wells decides to try the Tarzan movie. He dresses for the sultry weather—Washington in spring is like high summer in London— and goes down to the lobby. He checks his street guide and takes the streetcar to the Palace Theater, where he buys an orchestra seat, for twenty-five cents, to see *Tarzan and His Mate*.

It is a perfectly wretched movie, comprised wholly of romantic fantasy, melodrama, and sexual innuendo. The dramatic leads perform with wooden idiocy surpassed only by the idiocy of the screenplay. Wells is attracted by the undeniable charms of the young heroine, Maureen O'Sullivan, but the film is devoid of intellectual content. Thinking of the audience at which such a farrago must be aimed depresses him. This is art as fodder. Yet the theater is filled, and the people are held in rapt attention. This only depresses Wells more. If these citizens are the future of America, then the future of America is dim.

An hour into the film the antics of an anthropomorphized chimpanzee, a scene of transcendent stupidity that nevertheless sends the audience into gales of laughter, drives Wells from the theater. It is still midevening. He wanders down the avenue of theaters, res-

taurants, and clubs. On the sidewalk are beggars, ignored by the
passersby. In an alley behind a hotel Wells spots a woman and child
picking through the ashcans beside the restaurant kitchen.

Unexpectedly, he comes upon the marquee announcing DUKE
ELLINGTON AND HIS ORCHESTRA. From within the open doors of the
ballroom wafts the sound of jazz. Impulsively, Wells buys a ticket
and goes in.

∞   ∞   ∞

Kessel and his cronies have spent the day walking around the mall,
which the WPA is relandscaping. They've seen the Lincoln Memorial, the Capitol, the Washington Monument, the Smithsonian, the
White House. Kessel has his picture taken in front of a statue of a
soldier—a photo I have sitting on my desk. I've studied it many
times. He looks forthrightly into the camera, faintly smiling. His
face is confident, unlined.

When night comes they hit the bars. Prohibition was lifted only
last year, and the novelty has not yet worn off. The younger men
get plastered, but Kessel finds himself uninterested in getting
drunk. A couple of them set their minds on women and head for
the Gayety Burlesque; Cole, Kessel, and Turkel end up in the Paradise Ballroom listening to Duke Ellington.

They have a couple of drinks, ask some girls to dance. Kessel
dances with a short girl with a southern accent who refuses to look
him in the eyes. After thanking her he returns to the others at the
bar. He sips his beer. "Not so lucky, Jack?" Cole says.

"She doesn't like a tall man," Turkel says.

Kessel wonders why Turkel came along. Turkel is always complaining about "niggers," and his only comment on the Ellington
band so far has been to complain about how a bunch of jigs can
make a living playing jungle music while white men sleep in barracks and eat grits three times a day. Kessel's got nothing against
the colored, and he likes the music, though it's not exactly the kind
of jazz he's used to. It doesn't sound much like Dixieland. It's
darker, bigger, more dangerous. Ellington, resplendent in tie and
tails, looks like he's enjoying himself up there at his piano, knocking out minimal solos while the orchestra plays cool and low.

Turning from them to look across the tables, Kessel sees a little
man sitting alone beside the dance floor, watching the young
couples sway in the music. To his astonishment he recognizes

Wells. He's been given another chance. Hesitating only a moment, Kessel abandons his friends, goes over to the table and introduces himself.

"Excuse me, Mr. Wells. You might not remember me, but I was one of the men you saw yesterday in Virginia working along the road. The CCC?"

Wells looks up at a gangling young man wearing a khaki uniform, his olive tie neatly knotted and tucked between the second and third buttons of his shirt. His hair is slicked down, parted in the middle. Wells doesn't remember anything of him. "Yes?"

"I—I been reading your stories and books a lot of years. I admire your work."

Something in the man's earnestness affects Wells. "Please sit down," he says.

Kessel takes a seat. "Thank you." He pronounces "th" as "t" so that "thank" comes out "tank." He sits tentatively, as if the chair is mortgaged, and seems at a loss for words.

"What's your name?"

"John Kessel. My friends call me Jack."

The orchestra finishes a song and the dancers stop in their places, applauding. Up on the bandstand, Ellington leans into the microphone. "Mood Indigo," he says, and instantly they swing into it: the clarinet moans in low register, in unison with the muted trumpet and trombone, paced by the steady rhythm guitar, the brushed drums. The song's melancholy suits Wells's mood.

"Are you from Virginia?"

"My family lives in Buffalo. That's in New York."

"Ah—yes. Many years ago I visited Niagara Falls, and took the train through Buffalo." Wells remembers riding along a lakefront of factories spewing waste water into the lake, past heaps of coal, clouds of orange and black smoke from blast furnaces. In front of dingy row houses, ragged hedges struggled through the smoky air. The landscape of laissez-faire. "I imagine the Depression has hit Buffalo severely."

"Yes sir."

"What work did you do there?"

Kessel feels nervous, but he opens up a little. "A lot of things. I used to be an electrician until I got blacklisted."

"Blacklisted?"

"I was working on this job where the super told me to set the wiring wrong. I argued with him, but he just told me to do it his way. So I waited until he went away, then I sneaked into the construction shack and checked the blueprints. He didn't think I could read blueprints, but I could. I found out I was right and he was wrong. So I went back and did it right. The next day when he found out, he fired me. Then the so-and-so went and got me blacklisted."

Though he doesn't know how much credence to put in this story, Wells finds that his sympathies are aroused. It's the kind of thing that must happen all the time. He recognizes in Kessel the immigrant stock that, when Wells visited the U.S. in 1906, made him skeptical about the future of America. He'd theorized that these Italians and Slavs, coming from lands with no democratic tradition, unable to speak English, would degrade the already corrupt political process. They could not be made into good citizens; they would not work well when they could work poorly, and given the way the economic deal was stacked against them would seldom rise high enough to do better.

But Kessel is clean, well-spoken despite his accent, and deferential. Wells realizes that this is one of the men who was topping trees along the river road.

Meanwhile, Kessel detects a sadness in Wells's manner. He had not imagined that Wells might be sad, and he feels sympathy for him. It occurs to him, to his own surprise, that he might be able to make *Wells* feel better. "So—what do you think of our country?" he asks.

"Good things seem to be happening here. I'm impressed with your President Roosevelt."

"Roosevelt's the best friend the workingman ever had." Kessel pronounces the name "Roozvelt." "He's a man that . . ." he struggles for the words, ". . . that's not for the past. He's for the future."

It begins to dawn on Wells that Kessel is not an example of a class, or a sociological study, but a man like himself with an intellect, opinions, dreams. He thinks of his own youth, struggling to rise in a class-bound society. He leans forward across the table. "You believe in the future? You think things can be different?"

"I think they have to be, Mr. Wells."

Wells sits back. "Good. So do I."

Kessel is stunned by this intimacy. It is more than he had hoped for, yet it leaves him with little to say. He wants to tell Wells about his dreams, and at the same time ask him a thousand questions. He wants to tell Wells everything he has seen in the world, and to hear Wells tell him the same. He casts about for something to say.

"I always liked your writing. I like to read scientifiction."

"Scientifiction?"

Kessel shifts his long legs. "You know—stories about the future. Monsters from outer space. The Martians. *The Time Machine.* You're the best scientifiction writer I ever read, next to Edgar Rice Burroughs." Kessel pronounces "Edgar" as "Eedgar."

"Edgar Rice Burroughs?"

"Yes."

"You *like* Burroughs?"

Kessel hears the disapproval in Wells's voice. "Well—maybe not as much as, as *The Time Machine,*" he stutters. "Burroughs never wrote about monsters as good as your Morlocks."

Wells is nonplussed. "Monsters."

"Yes." Kessel feels something's going wrong, but he sees no way out. "But he does put more romance in his stories. That princess— Dejah Thoris?"

All Wells can think of is Tarzan in his loincloth on the movie screen, and the moronic audience. After a lifetime of struggling, a hundred books written to change the world, in the service of men like this, is this all his work has come to? To be compared to the writer of pulp trash? To "Eedgar" Rice Burroughs? He laughs aloud.

At Wells's laugh, Kessel stops. He knows he's done something wrong, but he doesn't know what.

Wells's weariness has dropped down onto his shoulders again like an iron cloak. "Young man—go away," he says. "You don't know what you're saying. Go back to Buffalo."

Kessel's face burns. He stumbles from the table. The room is full of noise and laughter. He's run up against that wall again. He's just an ignorant Polack after all; it's his stupid accent, his clothes. He should have talked about something else—*The Outline of History,* politics. But what made him think he could talk like an equal with a man like Wells in the first place? Wells lives in a different world. The future is for men like him. Kessel feels himself the prey of fantasies. It's a bitter joke.

He clutches the bar, orders another beer. His reflection in the mirror behind the ranked bottles is small and ugly.

"Whatsa matter, Jack?" Turkel asks him. "Didn't he want to dance neither?"

∞   ∞   ∞

And that's the story, essentially, that never happened.

Not long after this, Kessel did go back to Buffalo. During the Second World War he worked as a crane operator in the forty-inch rolling mill of Bethlehem Steel. He met his wife, Angela Giorlandino, during the war, and they married in June 1945. After the war he quit the plant and became a carpenter. Their first child, a girl, died in infancy. Their second, a boy, was born in 1950. At that time Kessel began building the house that, like so many things in his life, he was never entirely to complete. He worked hard, had two more children. There were good years and bad ones. He held a lot of jobs. The recession of 1958 just about flattened him; our family had to go on welfare. Things got better, but they never got good. After the 1950s, the economy of Buffalo, like that of all U.S. industrial cities caught in the transition to a postindustrial age, declined steadily. Kessel never did work for himself, and as an old man was little more prosperous than he had been as a young one.

In the years preceding his death in 1945 Wells was to go on to further disillusionment. His efforts to create a sane world met with increasing frustration. He became bitter, enraged. Moura Budberg never agreed to marry him, and he lived alone. The war came, and it was, in some ways, even worse than he had predicted. He continued to propagandize for the socialist world state throughout, but with increasing irrelevance. The new leftists like Orwell considered him a dinosaur, fatally out of touch with the realities of world politics, a simpleminded technocrat with no understanding of the darkness of the human heart. Wells's last book, *Mind at the End of Its Tether*, proposed that the human race faced an evolutionary crisis that would lead to its extinction unless humanity leapt to a higher state of consciousness; a leap about which Wells speculated with little hope or conviction.

Sitting there in the Washington ballroom in 1934, Wells might well have understood that for all his thinking and preaching about the future, the future had irrevocably passed him by.

∞   ∞   ∞

But the story isn't quite over yet. Back in the Washington ballroom Wells sits humiliated, a little guilty for sending Kessel away so harshly. Kessel, his back to the dance floor, stares humiliated into his glass of beer. Gradually, both of them are pulled back from dark thoughts of their own inadequacies by the sound of Ellington's orchestra.

Ellington stands in front of the big grand piano, behind him the band: three saxes, two clarinets, two trumpets, trombones, a drummer, guitarist, bass. "Creole Love Call," Ellington whispers into the microphone, then sits again at the piano. He waves his hand once, twice, and the clarinets slide into a low wavering theme. The trumpet, muted, echoes it. The bass player and guitarist strum ahead at a deliberate pace, rhythmic, erotic, bluesy. Kessel and Wells, separate across the room, each unaware of the other, are alike drawn in. The trumpet growls eight bars of raucous solo. The clarinet follows, wailing. The music is full of pain and longing—but pain controlled, ordered, mastered. Longing unfulfilled, but not overpowering.

As I write this, it plays on my stereo. If anyone has a right to bitterness at thwarted dreams, a black man in 1934 has that right. That such men can, in such conditions, make this music opens a world of possibilities.

Through the music speaks a truth about art that Wells does not understand, but that I hope to: that art doesn't have to deliver a message in order to say something important. That art isn't always a means to an end but sometimes an end in itself. That art may not be able to change the world, but it can still change the moment.

Through the music speaks a truth about life that Kessel, sixteen years before my birth, doesn't understand, but that I hope to: that life constrained is not life wasted. That despite unfulfilled dreams, peace is possible.

Listening, Wells feels that peace steal over his soul. Kessel feels it too.

And so they wait, poised, calm, before they move on into their respective futures, into our own present. Into the world of limitation and loss. Into Buffalo.

∞   ∞   ∞

for my father